daddy p.i. 3.0

E. J. FROST

Created with Vellum

For all the readers who have taken my Daddy P.I. and his little into their hearts, my profound thanks.

author's note

Daddy P.I. 3.0 is not a standalone.

Although there are books in the *Daddy P.I. Casefiles* which can be enjoyed without reading the others, this is not one of them. Readers are strongly encouraged to read at least *Daddy P.I. 0.5, 1.0, 2.0* and *The Case of the Missing Collar* before this book. These stories have been collected here.

If you want to read the entire series before reading this book, the reading order is:

Daddy P.I. 0.5
Daddy P.I. 1.0
Daddy P.I. 2.0
Max's Bumble
The Case of the Missing Collar
Missing Ink
A Little Summer Sizzle
Seismic Daddy
Something Little This Way Comes
Blunts Tales I
Blunts Tales II

This is the last planned book in the series focusing on Logan and Emily, although they will certainly appear in future investigations. I promise.

This series contains subject matter that some readers may find triggering, including strong elements of power exchange. For a full listing of content warnings, please see my website, https://emmafrostuk.wordpress.com/warning-here-be-monsters/, BEFORE reading this book.

In line with other books in this series, I've included a glossary at the end to help explain both terms used in the context of power exchange relationships and some of the Britishisms used by Logan and other characters. There is, unfortunately, no Oxford English Dictionary of Kink, and terms like "master" are debated within the community. I've provided definitions which are in line with a number of different sources including the *Submissive Guide*, which I warmly recommend to people interested in the lifestyle, and my own experiences. I appreciate that the lifestyle varies not just regionally but also generationally and that all readers may not agree with my definitions. They are in no way intended to denigrate anyone's individual experiences, but to give readers a guide as to how these terms are used within this series.

one

LOGAN

I CROUCH low at the corner of a wooden wall and wipe sweat out of my eyes.

The sun's set but the November day has been unseasonably warm. The heat, combined with the coveralls I'm wearing and the need for stealth as I move through a maze of hedges and walls, have me dripping.

I wipe my hands on my pants, adjust my weapon, and raise my free hand. My teammates, Mac, Sean, Taylor, and Cole, shuffle from their hiding spots and tuck in tight to the corner. They adjust their own weapons. Together, we wait.

I listen, straining to differentiate sounds through the muffling effect of the maze. There are eight teams out tonight. Too many. I told Ry it was too many. Too much potential for confusion. Too much possibility of being caught in friendly fire. But Ry's not a military man, so he gave it the thumbs up anyway.

There. Over the city's night noises, the slough of the breeze, the shuffling of feet, a high, soft giggle. That's the sound I've been listening for.

"Attack!" I yell, willing to lose the element of surprise in favor of the panic my shout will induce in those listening.

I lead my team barreling around the wooden corner, my gun up and firing. A blob of bright pink paint catches a blonde head before it ducks behind an overturned trestle table. The rest of my ammo spatters across the wooden surface uselessly.

Three grinning faces pop up over the edge of the table, guns pointed at me like a firing squad.

"Ambush!" I shout at my team, hoping that at least one of them will make it to safety, even as splats of orange paint pepper the front of my coveralls.

"You're dead, Daddy!" Emily whoops, as she continues to fire.

I sit down in disgust. Mac plops into the grass next to me, scooping fluorescent orange paint out of his ear.

"I'm still going to beat her ass tonight," he tells me, tipping his head at his blue-haired submissive, who is still firing over our heads.

"Definitely. Rampant insubordination."

Mac chuckles and lies back in the grass, probably smearing paint all up his back. Since I'm going to need a shower anyway, I join him in staring up at the night sky. A few stars pierce the city's light pollution and I smile up at them, happy despite my team's route.

"This doesn't suck, son," he says to me.

"I led us straight into an ambush," I answer. "Kinda sucks."

Mac laughs. "Faster the game's over, faster I get to fuck my girl's cute little ass. Win-win."

"Now that is the honest truth." I lift my head to see what my girl's doing but she's ducked back behind the trestle to avoid a volley of glowing green paint coming from my left. "Give 'em hell, Emmy," I shout, to encourage her.

"I got this, Daddy!"

I lie back, chuckling.

"You staying the night?" Mac asks me. He shifts, getting more comfortable on the grass, steepling his fingers over his chest. The dim light from electric lanterns and fairy lights strung up around the maze illuminates his craggy profile. I know Mac's face almost as well as I know my own. This man I served under, sweated under, bled under. Now he lives under my roof. Eats at my table. Plays at my club. I can never repay Mac for what he's given me but it's a start.

"Yeah. Committee meeting in the morning."

"Ah," he says, like he's forgotten. I know he hasn't. His membership application is in front of the committee tomorrow.

"You'll pass," I reassure him.

Mac's profile shifts, white teeth gleaming in the low light, as he grins. "You've made sure of that, haven't you?"

"I have."

There are things I leave to chance. Not many, I admit. I'm a controlling bastard. But the happiness of the people who mean the most to me? No. I make sure of that. Mac wants to be a part of the club that's so central to my life. He's got the experience, and the money. He'd have been a shoo-in if we'd both been smarter and done things a little differently over the last few months. If I hadn't levied a financial penalty while punishing one of the house submissives for bullying my little girl. If Mac hadn't claimed and collared Brenna, who I can hear laughing her head off with Emily, for his own. More than one member is salty that he plucked her out of the pool of house subs. I've had to make a bad bargain and call in several favors. But I have enough votes.

I've made sure of it.

Mac grunts. "What time'll you be done?"

"Zero nine hundred." By which time he'll be a full member. "Meet us in the buffet at zero nine thirty?"

I need a half-hour to dress my little girl. And maybe give her an orgasm if she's a needy baby.

"Roger that."

"Speaking of which, you'll need to set up your own account for club expenses. Time to stop sponging off me."

Mac chuckles. "Guess I'll have to make the most of it tonight. Room's got a mini-bar."

"If you charge fucking fifteen-dollar bottles of water to my account, I'm tacking it on to your rent."

Not that I've let him pay rent, nor will I.

"Language, Daddy!" Emily shouts over another wet volley.

Mac joins me in laughing.

By dint of my team-mate, Sean, being a far sneakier bastard than I'd given him credit for, our team actually wins. Emily's band of submissives is the second-to-last knocked out. Once her cute, pink coveralls are spattered with paint, Emily trots over and flops on top of me for a cuddle. Mac's girl and the three other members of their team, Fleur, Lucy, and Austin, join us. A happy, wiggly pile of submissives is a fine blanket against the rapidly cooling evening.

When Sean finally takes out the last opponent, he and his submissive join our pile. Sean gives his subbie a couple of token swats with the game's prize: a golden leather paddle. He passes the paddle to me, and I line up Emily, Fleur, Lucy, and Austin to give them each a celebratory smack. When I hand the paddle off to him, Mac stretches Brenna over his knee and gives her a much longer paddling, while she writhes and stuffs her knuckles in her mouth to keep from making so much noise the club's neighbors complain. While the club building is heavily soundproofed, we're playing in the courtyard which is open to the sky.

Once Brenna's howled through a knuckle-muffled orgasm, Mac tosses the paddle back to Sean, throws Brenna over his shoulder, and heads inside. I pull Emily into my lap and tickle her under the chin.

"Ready to call it a night, my baby?"

She looks up at me, her big eyes luminous in her pale face. "Austin and Hunter have challenged my title, Daddy."

Ah, the ongoing Hearts War between my little girl and the house subs who taught her the card game and have been losing to her ever since.

"Mmm, I think they're going to have to wait for another night. Unless you want to miss out on a good-girl spanking."

"A champion has to defend her crown." Her plush, lower lip

trembles. "But I really don't want to miss out on a good-girl spanking."

I chuckle and kiss the tip of her nose.

"How about this? Invite Austin and Hunter over on Saturday for a Hearts Battle Royale. You three can play all afternoon. Daddy will cook tea."

The big eyes get even bigger. "Daddy will cook?"

"Daddy somehow managed before you came along, little girl."

Austin, who is lying on the grass with Fleur under one arm and Lucy under another, snorts. "On microwave dinners."

I kick him playfully. "Quiet, you."

"I'll bring Aunt Pearl's Banoffee Pie," he offers. "Hunt and I both have Saturday off."

"Is that a deal, little girl? Can you wait to defend your title until Saturday?"

She immediately lifts her pinkie finger. "Deal."

I shake her pinkie with mine before I draw her in for a deep kiss.

I barely take my mouth off hers as we wind our way through the club to the room I've reserved for the night. The Blue Harem room is my favorite dungeon in the club, although the Nursery we're building is likely to replace that. The only downside to the Blue Harem room is that it doesn't have an attached bathroom. Few of the dungeons do except the medical suite, which is semi-perpetually booked out.

Because I knew our play today would be messy, I reserved a room on the third floor. It's the "pink boudoir" room and has all the elements of a terribly cheesy Vegas honeymoon hotel, right down to the heart-shaped bed. Most importantly, though, there's a two-person hot tub in the attached bath.

Emily clings to me like the cutest baby koala as I carry her to the bathroom, dropping our overnight bags by the door. I'll unpack later. I strip off our paint-covered overalls and the street clothes we've worn beneath. Some of the paint is still wet, so I make sure to use it to daub hearts on my baby doll's butt-cheeks while I'm taking off her white knickers. That gets me a cute squeal that I muffle with my mouth as I pick her up and climb into the hot tub with her.

Kissing my little girl is an addiction I don't want to break.

Once we're in the hot water, I turn Emily around in my lap and braid her hair, taking my time to rub my fingertips over her scalp. She dissolves into a floppy koala, still clinging to me with her foot adorably hooked behind my calf. I love the points of connection she always creates between us.

I nibble her neck and the soft shell of her ear as I rub my hands over her. Sure, it gets the paint off but I'm really sensitizing her skin, warming her up for our lovemaking. Emily reciprocates sweetly, rubbing her foot up and down my calf, wriggling when I find a particularly sensitive spot on her neck so her soft bottom grinds over my lap.

"Who is this clean little girl?" I ask when I'm ready to move from the bath to the bed.

"You, Daddy," my clean, floppy koala answers, lazily trailing her toes up and down my calf.

"Confident I'm not a clean little girl. I might be a wolfy Daddy who's about to get down and dirty."

A soft giggle out of my floppy koala. "My bottom should be safe from you."

"Why is that, silly baby?"

"Cause I shot you dead at paintball. Only winners are allowed to get down and dirty with other people's bottoms."

I poke her in the ribs, eliciting a squeal and a squirm across my semi.

"I'll remind you that my team won."

"*After* you were dead," Emmy points out.

"You are a menace. Was it your idea to set up that ambush?"

A wilder giggle.

"You're in so much trouble. Right, little insurrectionist. I know how to deal with you." I slide out from under her and make sure she's steady on the rim of the tub before I climb out and gather towels. Blunts' towels are thick, soft, and smell like watermelon. I help Emmy out and wrap her in the towel, taking my time rubbing her pink skin. Every time a curve emerges from the cloth, I lean in to kiss and nip. Emmy gets increasingly weak-kneed. I sit on the edge of the tub with her straddling my thigh as I dry her. When I cup her breasts in the terry-cloth and take my time nibbling and kissing her nipples to tight peaks, the part of her spread over my thigh gets wetter instead of drier.

I pretend to dab at her wet patch while really getting my fingers into her. Bending her back over my arm, I worship her breasts. I encourage her to grind down on my thigh until she catches a rhythm, then help her along by rubbing her clit until she clamps her thighs around mine and comes in a long series of sweet jerks and soft moans.

I gather my baby doll and our bags and drag them into the bedroom. As I pass the mirrored alcove over the sink, I catch my reflection. My grin is feral. Doesn't matter. Emily's not scared of her Daddy, no matter how crazy our play gets. She's always been happy to follow me down the most twisted path.

Her trust and faith in me lights up my chest brighter than Times Square at Christmas.

I deposit my floppy koala on the heart-shaped bed, plant my hands on either side of her, and loom over her.

"Hi, little girl."

She blinks up at me. Such big baby eyes. "Hi, Daddy. You're looking very wolfy."

"I'm feeling very wolfy, my baby. Can you take some pain for me?"

"Always."

I kiss the tip of her nose.

Our play bag yields a juice box that I get Emily sipping while I unpack our toiletries, night clothes, lube, and a surprise for my little masochist.

"Um, Daddy? What is that?"

I work hard to keep my face straight as I hold out the paddle I commissioned for Emily from Fleur, who makes incredibly wicked toys. This one is clear silicone, swirled through with pink and black glitter. One side is flat. The other side has rows of short humps rising from the surface. It's going to give my baby *so* much thump.

"This?" I turn the paddle around in my hand so she can see both sides. "Just something I saw and thought was pretty for my beautiful baby."

She gulps loudly. "It, um, is very pretty. Ta, Daddy."

"You're welcome, little girl."

"It, uh, looks like that nubbly side will hurt quite a bit."

I smack the flat side against my palm. "Not very flexible. I wouldn't discount the sting you're going to get from this side."

The big eyes get even bigger. I let myself drown in those eyes with a smile.

"Definitely not discounting the sting from that side, Daddy.

"Shall we test it out?"

"Sure?" she squeaks.

I can't help but laugh. In a few minutes, she'll be moaning and begging for more sting, more thud, more-more-more. But the moments of trepidation leading up to that are delicious; they feed the wickedness in my soul.

I survey the ridiculous bed. It's on a raised platform. Looks like the right height. I reach over Emily and grab a pair of pink pillows.

"Over the edge of the bed, on your knees, little girl. Pillow under your hips and one for your head if you want one."

She finishes the juice box with a gurgle and hands it to me before arranging herself over the edge of the bed with her knees on the platform.

I tuck the empty box into our bag to recycle since Emily has doubts about the efficacy of Blunts' recycling efforts. Returning to the bed, sitting beside her, I take a moment to admire my fiancée's sweet curves, first with my eyes and then with my hands, tucking the paddle under my arm while I squeeze and knead her round cheeks, pink from the hot tub and still wearing faint marks from a flogging scene. I rub at the fading bruises, aggravating them gently, and make note of where they are for a little extra sting.

"Stretch your arms over your head, sweetheart. Let me see that long spine." When she does, I shape the dips of her waist with my palms and let my fingertips creep up her ribs like piano keys. I get the trill of her giggle in response: sweet, subbie music.

While her giggle is trailing off, I slap the paddle sharply across both firm cheeks.

Emmy shrieks. Her hands dig into the pink coverlet. Her toes curl and she crosses her ankles one over the other but she holds position, my good girl.

"Beautiful, Emmy," I praise her. "Such a good baby. Does it sting?"

"Sooo stingy," she groans.

I smack her bottom with the paddle again, enjoying the way her skin flattens like a spill of cream against the clear silicone. Redness rushes to the surface of her skin in the long rectangle shape of the paddle. I'm going to ask Fleur to make the next one with a heart cut-out at the top so I can leave a line of hearts down each cheek. Sadistic art for my little masochist to admire the next day.

When her ass is glowing and hot to the touch, I flip the paddle over. I run my palm up the paddle's face, feeling the nubs that will bite into my girl's soft flesh. With a smile that would draw a whimper out of Emily if she wasn't grinding her face into the pillow while wiggling her red bottom at me, I whack the bumpy side of the paddle straight across both cheeks.

Emily howls into the pillow. "Daddeee!"

"Owie, my baby?" I ask evilly.

She scrunches the bedding in her little fists, working through the burn. "Owie. Super owie."

"Mmm, it looks very owie." I rub my thumb over some of the spots blooming crimson in a waffle-iron texture across her bottom. "Four more for Daddy? Count them down."

She blows out a long breath, wiggles, and settles herself. Her back muscle soften. She clenches her ass-cheeks, then relaxes. "Ready-ready."

"That's my good girl. I love seeing you do that, my baby. Getting ready to take pain for me. Relaxed and accepting of whatever I'm going to give you. Such a good girl."

She rubs her cheek against the pillow. "Love you, Daddy."

"I love you, my little wonder." I give her ass a sharp rap with the paddle and take a deep breath, sucking her high moan into my lungs, into my soul. "I love the sounds you make for me. I love seeing your soft bottom go hot and red as you take what I want to give you. I love your acceptance of every part of me. I'm so grateful for you, Emmy."

"Daddy." Her breath breaks but I know it's just emotion. Emmy can take a flogging with my heaviest flogger. The paddle's giving her some good sensation but she's nowhere close to her limit. "I'm grateful for you, too. Oh, and that was one. And ta, ta very much for my good paddling."

"Good girl for remembering." I tap her softly with the paddle for the second hit, so I can build the last two.

"Two, ta, Daddy."

"Very good girl."

I tuck the paddle under my arm while I rub in the sting. The hot satin of her skin under my palms is heaven. She wiggles under my touch and the sweet tang of her arousal spices the air.

"Does my baby want to be fucked?" I ask rhetorically.

"Yes, please, Daddy!"

I chuckle at her enthusiasm. "Okay, two more."

I deliver them in quick succession, one after the other, with barely a breath in between for her to count. She shrieks on the second one, her whole body going tense. Her back jerks, her legs squeeze together. A deep red flush spreads down the back of her neck.

Her body goes limp, then she flips over onto her back, looking up at me with wide eyes. Tears spill.

"Baby?"

"Daddy, I'm so sorry!"

Chuckling, I lean over her. "Surprise paingasm, little girl?"

She nods tearfully.

"So, I'd say you like the paddle a little?"

She shakes her head. "It's an evil, evil paddle. Waaay worse than Belphegor."

"Way worse, huh?"

"So much worse. I'm really sorry, Daddy. The pain took me by surprise."

I give her a slow, licking kiss. "I'm not angry, baby. I love watching you come. I know it was involuntary. You haven't broken any rules. Lift your legs now, Daddy wants to fuck."

She blinks back her tears, still looking a little uncertain. My sweet baby who tries so hard to follow my rules. I'll reinforce that she's still my good girl while I'm fucking her.

She slides her legs up my hips and sides, silky skin on silky skin. Her hands slip around the backs of her knees, the way she knows I like her to hold her legs while I fuck her. I push us both up the bed so I can get my knees on the mattress before I sink down onto her.

I kiss my way down her, starting with her forehead, then each wet eyelid, then her rosebud mouth. I nudge her chin with mine until she tips her head back and lavish kisses and teasing nips down the line of her throat. She smells sweet here, in the folds of neck and shoulder. I rub my lips, the tip of my nose, and my cheeks over her delicately scented skin while I push her legs wide, cup her breasts in my hands, and roll her nipples with my thumbs.

"Are your little nips still sore, my baby?" I ask as I pluck at them. I got a new set of nipple clamps yesterday and she spent the day in them, to much protest. Compressive pain is never my baby's favorite thing.

"Don't feel anything but good, Daddy," she murmurs, her eyes hazy and unfocused.

I drop my face into the valley between her breasts and smile up at her rapturous expression as I lick and kiss my way down to her captured nipples. Rosy-red skin peeks between my fingers and I give each nipple a kiss before rolling them firmly. Emily squeaks and shivers. That suggests that even though she's swamped with feel-good chemicals now, her nipples are sore. I still suck and nip at them but I don't dig my teeth in the way I might if she hadn't suffered those clamps yesterday. Lighter pressure still has her moaning and wriggling, seeking the satisfaction of penetration. I'm eager for that, too.

Releasing one sweet peak, I slide my hand under her and lift her hips onto a pillow. Emily's body is wholly familiar to me after several months together but the moment of crowning her, of feeling myself sink into her hot, wet welcome, is always new. The sensation catches in my chest. Tugs on that deepest part of me that opens to her. My soul baby. My life-love. I suck on the side of her breast as I take her hips in both hands and pull her to me, sinking to the balls. Gasping, she squeezes down on me.

"Fuck, baby. So fucking good."

"Daddy," she mewls.

I reach out and capture one of her hands, twining our fingers together and holding her down as I circle my hips, applying pressure to every nerve in her divinely-responsive pussy. She keens with pleasure so I do it again and again, adding a snap of my hips with each rotation to give her the deep thump against her cervix that she loves. She throws her head back and howls.

"Oh, my little girl. Are you close?"

"Yes, Daddy. So close. I know I don't deserve an orgasm but please, please, a thousand pleases may I have one?"

I lift up so I can look right down into her eyes. Hers shoot wide, her black pupils so blown there's barely a green ring around them.

"You deserve all the orgasms, my baby. Come for me." Her little brow beetles as she succumbs to the sensations. Her face twists in what would look like pain if I didn't know how intensely she comes a second time.

I let her release, the delicious spasms around my plunging cock, the snap and wrap of her legs around me as she shudders out each wave of pleasure, pull me over the edge. A half-dozen hammering thrusts and I'm there-I'm there-I'm *there*, pouring everything that's in me into her. All the light and dark in my soul. It dives into the well of hers, ignites, and burns like a star.

With my release still firing behind my eyes, I roll us over so Emily's not trying to take my weight and hold my little love to me so tightly she knows her Daddy will never, ever let her go.

two

LOGAN

IN THE END, I have enough votes for Mac's membership but it's a near thing.

I sit at the oval committee table, tapping my pen on my notepad, while I listen to Ten rant. It's the first time I've seen the usually stoic, secretive Master of Rope lose his shit. By the silence and slack jaws of the other people sitting around the table, I gather it's a first for them, too.

"And then there's the issue of you working over in Jersey," Ten growls at me, crossing his burly arms over his even burlier chest.

Despite the fact that it's early November, and much cooler than yesterday, Ten's shirtless, wearing just low-slung leather pants and scuffed boots. The numerous X tattoos over his neck, chest, and arms that give rise to his club name stand out starkly against his fading tan. During their blanket-fort gossip sessions, Emily's learned from Brenna that there's a running bet among the house subs as to what the X tattoos mean.

I've thrown a tenner on "X marks the spot" just for the heck of it.

"How is Logan working at our sister club relevant to Mr. MacNally's application?" Maude asks from where she's sitting to my left. Her voice is cool and neutral. If she's surprised, or annoyed, by Ten's rant, she doesn't let it show.

"They live together," Ten says with a glower at me.

"And?" Maude asks.

While everyone's eyes go back to Ten, Maude curls her French-manicure over my pen. Guess I'm tapping a little too loudly. Maude pats my hand when I set the pen down on my notebook.

"Not sure either of them got Blunts' best interests at heart if Logan's working there," Ten grumbles.

I start to answer that piece of bullshittery but Maude's fingers tighten over mine.

I shut my mouth.

Javier, who doesn't hold a title but has been sitting on the management committee since some point in the sixteenth century, if the rumors are true, shoots the cuffs of his Huntsman suit. I've seen him do that often enough before he goes into battle that I almost feel sorry for Ten.

"Is there a problem between Blunts and Sacrum?" Javier asks. "Something of which I'm unaware?"

Ten grunts. "He's got one foot here and one foot there. Divided loyalties."

"I fail to see the issue," Javier says. "Sacrum's our sister club. Other than this security matter that Logan's helping them with, Mistress Jaimie and Master Olaf haven't informed us of any problem at the club. Certainly nothing that would create a conflict of interest."

All eyes swing back to Ten. He grunts but says nothing more.

"Excellent," Javier says drily. "Shall we vote? The morning's wasting and asses are going unsmacked."

That draws a chortle out of my friend, Bull, who is sitting on Maude's far side. His hand is one of the first to shoot into the air when the chairman calls the vote. His hand is followed by nine more.

Enough for Mac's membership. The hard knot my gut squeezed into during Ten's tantrum relaxes a fraction.

I half-expect Ten to kick off again when my roster for the month's Monday theme nights goes up for a vote. For the first time, I've included an age-play night. Other than glowering at me, Ten doesn't comment and my roster passes, with Ten and the Three Cs abstaining.

My pen begins a staccato tapping again before Maude reaches over and silences it.

"Do you need a Xanax, dear?" Maude asks under her breath as Chess moves to the next point on the agenda.

"Bandages," I grunt. "And an alibi."

Maude chuckles but leaves her fingers resting on my wrist. I give up any attempt at taking notes, laying the pen down and biding my time until the end of the meeting.

As soon as the Chairman taps his gavel to close the meeting, I'm up and out of my chair. Across the table, Ten rises and crosses his arms over his chest, clearly expecting a confrontation. Instead, I head to the top of the table, where the Three Cs sit. Chess and our Master of Coin, Cris, have already vacated their seats, leaving the woman I want to talk to sitting in her leather wing-chair, watching me approach with eyes that swallow the light.

"Did you have a change of heart?" I ask as I approach. I don't loom over her chair. That's a dick move whether the person I'm looming over is a top or a bottom but doing it to another top is just a blatant challenge. As annoyed as I might be at the waifish woman in the chair, I'm not to the point of challenging her.

Caddy shakes her thick falls of brown hair back over her shoulders and looks up at me through her fringe. Barefoot, in ripped jeans and an oversized sweater, she barely looks old enough to vote. But her eyes are ancient, and winter's-night cold.

"You didn't need my vote," she responds.

"You were the one who encouraged me to put an age-play night on the roster in the first place. Why do that if you're just going to cut my knees off when it comes to a vote?"

"I'll repeat, you didn't need my vote. If you had, I'd have cast it."

"But since I didn't," I grit. "You abstained with Chess and Cris so you can continue to pin me under your fucking thumb—"

I cut myself off when cool fingers wrap around my wrist.

"I think you're hangry, dear," Maude says in my ear. "Time for breakfast."

I grind my teeth in irritation.

"Save me a seat," Caddy says, holding my eyes.

"You don't get to—"

I'm cut off by Maude clamping down on my wrist again. Fuck, she has a grip.

"Of course we will, Catriona," Maude says. "Will darling Finn be joining us?"

Caddy purses her lips, then smiles. Although she has a pretty mouth, it's like watching a shark smile. "That would be nice, wouldn't it? I don't think Finn's been formally introduced to Emily. I'll call him."

She pulls a phone out of the breast pocket of her sweater. Maude pulls me away as Caddy begins typing.

Maude waits until we're out of the conference room and in the corridor before she gives me an earful.

"She's right: you had more than enough votes. I know you're still angry at her for maneuvering you back into Master of Training but antagonizing her serves no purpose, Logan."

It serves a major purpose. The purpose of letting me vent before I fucking explode.

"They got what they wanted. I apologized to Pence for threatening to dock his pay. I ousted my friend as Master of Training. I'm doing the theme nights, including the age-play night Caddy fucking recommended. Then we get into committee and the three of them cut me off at the fucking knees? Now, if anyone bitches, it's all on me."

Maude takes my arm and begins walking me upstairs, toward the private room where Emily's waiting for me.

"That's right, it is all on you. And when the age-play night and the Nursery are a grand success, as I'm confident they will be, then you will be our shining star. When we have a full roster of happy, healthy house submissives, then you're the man who fixed the mess. Then Javier and I can deal with the problem of our charming Master of Rope with total impunity and the Three Cs can't be accused of favoritism. Focus on the bigger picture, Logan."

Bigger picture, my arse. I know when I'm being hung out to dry.

"I'm inviting our entire fucking playgroup," I growl. "I'll fill the Nursery so full of littles that Caddy and her cabal won't be able to squeeze a toe through the damn door. I'll run them through the fucking corridors like a herd of cats and let them crayon all over the wood paneling—"

"Temper, dearest," Maude says soothingly, like she can't swear like a sailor when her own feathers are ruffled. "I know this feels like an attack, particularly coming after Ten's vitriol but I see it as an opportunity."

"Opportunity." I snort. "It's a lynching opportunity. That's what it is. And I don't appreciate it."

Maude squeezes my arm. "No one is getting lynched, particularly not our golden boy. I know you're frustrated—"

"You bet I am."

"You're not alone, Logan. I've been frustrated for longer than you have, both at the state of our house submissives and at how long it has taken our leadership to recognize it. But I believe in winning the war, not the battle. You're focusing on the battle."

"If Ten had cost me the vote on Mac's membership, that would have been more than a lost battle, Maude."

"But he didn't," she says as we reach the top of the stairs. "He didn't stop you from creating the Nursery. Nor from expanding the Stables. Your age-play night passed by fourteen votes. That would not have happened six months ago. We have real attractions for age-players here at Blunts for the first time in the club's history. And it's passed largely under the radar of some very hardline sadists, mostly because of the example you and Emily have provided. The balance of power on the membership committee is shifting. That is the war, Logan. Not one application that could have been raised again in six months when the membership committee has a different composition. I'm asking you to lift your head above the trees and look at the forest."

The rebuke stings and I swallow the remnants of my anger.

"Ten is angry and regretful," Maude continues. "I don't think he had any idea how much Brenna meant to him until she was gone. Emotions don't sit well on the man and I'm concerned about his mental state. I know you've never been close to him but I've known him for over a decade and consider him a friend. Punishing him will only make him mulish. Membership here and his status among the house submissives are what keep Ten level."

"He is *not* level. You saw the CCTV footage of his confrontation with Brenna."

"I did. I make no apologies for his behavior. It was repulsive. But it needs to be dealt with the right way. Ten clearly feels he has enough power to act with impunity. And he's not wrong. If he challenged Chess for the chairmanship today, I have deep concerns about who would win that vote, particularly after Chess has been so withdrawn since his wife's death. Seeking to remove him from the management committee, or even put him on probation for his actions towards DirtyGurl, will only cause his support to harden. That's not the way to proceed. You need to maneuver the man into getting the help he needs without making him lose face. I assumed that was your plan."

I blow out a breath. "I don't have a plan beyond making sure the house submissives are safe and happy," I admit.

"Then perhaps you'll listen to mine," Maude says. "Ten needs to talk with someone about many things, not the least of which is DirtyGurl. The new submissive that's started, the bartender, Krissy, is a qualified therapist. If I can persuade Ten to talk with her one-on-one, even if I have to involve Chess to coerce him, that's better than humiliating him in front of the committee. Do you agree?"

I nod. I'm open to that.

"In the meanwhile, we should be alert to situations which allow Ten to cast doubt on your loyalty and integrity. How are things going at Sacrum?"

"Fine." I shrug. "The system will go live in a couple of days and then we'll see who has been evading my temporary cameras."

"How much has been stolen?"

"In total, less than three hundred in cash but it's making everyone feel unsafe. It's not the amount. It's the breach of trust among the club members."

Maude nods her stylishly-bobbed silver head. "Of course it is. Jaimie and Olaf must be very anxious."

They are. Worse, I think it's an inside job. I'm not just looking for someone they've played with, or a guest. I'm looking for someone who is, or was, employed by the club to create a safe environment. Someone Jaimie or Olaf hired, and probably think of as part of their kink-family, is stealing from them.

Maude pats my arm. "I'm sure you'll resolve it quickly. Now, shall we talk about what wonderful scenes you're planning for the age-play night?"

She's changing the subject unsubtly but I let her, in part because I respect the woman so damn much, and in part because we're a minute away from the room and I don't want to argue with Maude in front of Emily.

"Emily loves fairy tales—" I begin.

"Oh, I know, dear. She read me some of those fabulous stories by Baroness d'Aulnoy. I hadn't heard any of those before. I'm afraid my education was limited to the Brothers Grimm."

"Emily likes those, too. One of the scenes we're planning is based on the Pied Piper—"

"I get to play the witch," Maude says.

"Uh, I don't think there is a witch in that one."

"There is now, dear."

three

EMILY

DADDY THINKS he's being sly. Like I don't know him so well by now that I can read his mood as soon as he walks into the room.

Today, as he returns from the management committee meeting, he's super-tense. His muscles are so rigid I could bounce a quarter off his biceps. He's wearing a full frowny. But he jokes as he dresses me for the day like everything's fine.

I can dress myself, of course but I always wait for him. Dressing me relaxes him. It's not only that he needs the control of picking my clothes—and often a kinky accessory or two, today it's the evil, wire nipple clamps—but also focusing on me clears his mind. My friend Cynnie calls it "doing the daddy."

He relaxes as he "does the daddy." By the time he's pulled on my purple and black thigh-highs, a hot pink corset with the half-cups so he can torture my poor nips, and a flounced vintage smock over a pleated, black leather skirt, he's smiling. Hearing me whimper as he fixes the clamps in place brings the light back to his eyes. After he laces me up, he helps me into a cropped cardi and kisses me on the forehead.

"You look gorgeous, baby doll. I know I tell you all the time how much I love seeing you in these clothes . . . what do you call them again?"

"Goth fairy, Daddy."

"I feel like I'm looking at your soul, my baby." He twirls his finger in the air and I spin for him. "Mmm."

He strokes the inch of thigh that shows between the bottom of my skirt and the top of my thigh-highs.

"Can I put on some cat ears? They complete the outfit."

"Of course."

I take out black furry ears on a headband and pop them on top of my curls. I don't know what it is about wearing the cat ears—or puppy ears, they make me feel the same—but I love them. I feel cute in the goth fairy clothes Cynnie's helped me assemble but I *know* I'm cute when I'm wearing ears.

I take Daddy's hand and dance at his side down the stairs to the room where the breakfast buffet is served.

Daddy has a ridiculous number of friends at Blunts, even though he was worried about whether he had enough to win the vote for Master Mac's membership, so it's never just us when we eat at the club. This morning, we're at a big, round table with a dozen subs and Dom(mes).

I smile at everyone. There are some tense faces, and a few that are too impassive, probably masking their tension. One of the impassive faces is Mistress Caddy, with whom Daddy has a complicated relationship. In part because she's a complicated lady. Master Javier mentioned to Daddy a while ago that she was molested as an adolescent by her own uncle, David, while he was the chairman of Blunts. That started me down a rabbit-hole and although Blunts' own records have been heavily redacted, I am a Research Goddess™. Master Javier doesn't know the half of it, or he didn't tell Daddy if he does.

Master David was a monster. His modus operandi was to give his underaged victims intoxicants. He then staged gladiatorial-type

23

scenes where he provided them with weapons. He fought them, beat them, and raped them. Mistress Caddy's whole family suffered under David's regime, especially her brother, Bram, who is still on suicide watch over a decade later at an in-patient facility upstate. Mistress Caddy was instrumental in bringing David down, even though she was only twenty-one when she did it. David sponsored her when she became the youngest-ever member of Blunts. She got him removed as chairman and then helped prosecute him. He's serving seven consecutive 25-year sentences at Five Points in permanent solitary confinement due to threats on his life from other prisoners.

I wondered more than once when I was doing my research if Mistress Caddy hadn't funded some of those threats.

I give her an extra-bright smile. There's a man sitting next to her who came to our Day-Before-Halloween-Halloween-Party but I didn't get to talk to him. I claim a chair next to him once Daddy and I are through the buffet line.

His name is Finn and he's Caddy's submissive, which I could have guessed by how he glances at her, seeking approval, every few minutes. His accent is noticeable and when I ask him a question in French, he eagerly responds in the same language.

We chat all through breakfast. He tells me about how he and Caddy met, through a modern art museum where he had an exhibit and where Caddy's a major benefactor. He tells me about some of the wonderful scenes they've done. Her sadistic streak is no surprise but she also has a playful side I wouldn't have guessed. I tell Finn about the fairytale scenes Daddy and I are planning. The longing I see in his eyes makes me wonder if Finn has a bit of *little* in him.

While I'm talking with Finn, Master Ten pulls up a chair and squeezes in on Caddy's far side. He grunts at Master Mac, sitting a few seats away, glances at Daddy, and starts in on his breakfast.

Those are some weighty looks. Daddy didn't tell me who he thought might oppose Master Mac's application for membership but it's clear Master Ten did. That's probably not a surprise since Mac's fiancée used to be one of Master Ten's unofficial harem when she was a house submissive. There were hard feelings when Brenna resigned from the club, and although Master Ten partied with us at Halloween, it's looking like not everyone's feathers have been unruffled.

Daddy grumbles to Mistress Maude, who is sitting on his far side. Then he takes a sip of tea.

I've been waiting for him to try his tea, since I switched his usual Earl Grey for turmeric while he was getting an extra helping of scrambled eggs.

"Emily," he growls.

I lean against his firm shoulder and blink up at him innocently. See, this is the super-power of the cat ears. No one could think me guilty of anything while I'm wearing cat ears.

"This is not the tea I got," he complains. "Would you know anything about that, trouble?"

"Turmeric tea is better for you." I squirm in my chair. "But I don't want to be in trouble."

A tolerant smile teases the edges of Daddy's lips.

"Just a little bit of trouble," he grumbles, then softens it with a wink.

"Tickling-level trouble?" I ask with a wiggle.

Daddy stretches his arm around the back of my chair and leans in to rub noses.

"Could be," he says.

"Tickling with orgasms?"

"I'll consider tickling with orgasms if you ask Master Ten to play the Pied Piper."

There was a time when I'd have done anything to get out of asking one of the Blunts masters to participate in a scene. My intro-duction to them after Daddy was injured was overwhelming and people aren't always my best thing. But most of them have gone out of their way since then to make me feel at home. Although he was really mean to Brenna and is at odds with Daddy and Mac now, I'm not afraid of Master Ten anymore.

I grin up at him. "I can do that."

"Good girl." He kisses my forehead, sits back in his chair, and takes a sip of tea before he remembers. "About this tea."

I blink at him. Look at me, all innocent in my cat ears.

"If you drink that whole cup, I'll get you a cup of Earl Grey," I wheedle.

"If I tell you to get me a cup of Earl Grey, little girl, you'll get me a cup of Earl Grey."

"Of course, Daddy. But it would be *better* for you to drink the turmeric tea first."

He shakes his head at me, because we both know he's going to drink the turmeric tea. I try hard to take care of him and, even though he stages a token resistance, he appreciates my efforts.

"Does Daddy get a kiss for every sip?"

I grin. "Absolutely."

He holds his nose and gulps down half of the cup, then points to his mouth. "Kiss."

I beam at him, lean in, and press my lips to his. He lets me get away with a gentle peck for a second, before he bites down on my lip until I shiver and squeak. He laves away the little hurt with his tongue before he masters my mouth with his. When he pulls back, I'm panting. He runs his knuckles down my cheek until I can focus again.

"Don't you want another sip, Daddy?"

He taps the tip of my nose. "Not really but I definitely want another kiss."

My answering giggle makes his eyes light up.

Daddy tucks me under his arm as we walk from the subway to his townhouse. Every step we get closer to our house, he relaxes further.

Daddy treats the club as his second home but sometimes it's more like a visit with prickly in-laws. Particularly now that Mac and Brenna have moved in with us and we're starting to realize Daddy's desire for an extended family home, he's happiest at the townhouse.

It doesn't hurt that we have Cappa and Austin with us. Daddy acts like it's an imposition for our friends to stay with us but I know he actually loves it. After Daddy's daughter arrives, we'll have even less space but I doubt Daddy will discourage any of our friends from staying over.

Inside, my kitty greets us at the door with purrs and a lashing tail. I give him the petting he demands before turning him over to Brenna and then to Cappa, who carries Sable through to the kitchen after we all take off our shoes and line them up by the door.

I prepped dinner before we left for the club yesterday, so all I have to do is take everything out of the fridge and pop it in the oven. I pull out a tray of snacks as well since the men always get the munchies while they're watching sports. They've already settled on the couches in the living room to watch some team take on another team. I don't want to offend Daddy but I can't keep the teams straight and have to Google who is playing every time.

I make up a tray with the beer I know Daddy, Mac, and Austin like and take it through to them, dancing a little to the hip-hop Brenna has playing in the kitchen as she mashes potatoes. Daddy pulls me down for a kiss and the promise of a reward later that sends me back into the kitchen floating on a happy cloud.

Once everything's cooking, I plate up the snacks and take them through to the living room along with my laptop. I have a couple of deadlines coming up for my publisher. Daddy's been keeping me on track with my word count so I don't have to pull a week of all-nighters the way I used to with big deadlines. If he had to relax my bedtime so I could meet my deadlines, he would. But he'd be disappointed in me, and I never want that.

So, while Daddy, Mac, and Austin watch the game, and Brenna settles on a cushion at Master Mac's feet with her sketch pad and pencils and starts sketching Cappa, who is handsome enough to be an underwear model, I open my laptop and start writing.

Daddy watches me type for a minute, then takes out his phone. He taps up the app for the house's heating system and dials up the heat. Setting my laptop aside, I start stripping off my clothes, since I know where this is going.

Daddy waits until I'm down to my stripey, cotton thigh-highs. He taps the back of my hand, which is his signal for me to stop what I'm doing. I leave the thigh-highs on, fold my clothes into a neat pile, and smile at him before I pull my laptop back across my legs.

"Such a good girl, Emmy. That gets you a bubble-bath with Daddy tonight as well as your reward."

I wiggle happily on the couch cushion.

"Austin, leave your clothes on. Cappa, clothes off. Bren, Mac's choice," Daddy tells the other subbies.

Master Mac grunts. "Clothes off, snuggleslut. And go get your clamps. The pretty ones with the hearts on them."

Brenna grumbles at her Dom but climbs to her feet and trots off to fetch the nipple clamps.

Daddy wraps his arm around my shoulders and twirls a curl of my hair between his fingers. "If you get chilly, baby doll, tell me."

"Okay, Daddy."

"What are you writing?"

"Naughty words for that erotica anthology," I admit, staring at my fingers on the keyboard and feeling the heat rise into my cheeks. It's silly for me to feel even a twinge of embarrassment about what I'm writing, given all the things Daddy and I have done. A lot of them in front of the people in this room. But that doesn't stop the rush of blood to my face.

"Mmm, you can read it aloud to me tonight. I want to hear it."

"We all want to hear it," Master Mac says.

My cheeks are so hot I could fry eggs on them. "It's not any good yet."

"Then Daddy will help you make it better," Daddy promises.

Could I have a better Daddy? I tap with renewed zeal. "Ta very much."

I work all through the game the men are watching, in my zone despite the grumbling and hissing and occasional cheer from Austin, whose team is winning. Between the golden November sunshine pouring through the French doors, the roast in the oven, and the central heating, I'm not cold, even mostly nakey. Daddy checks my fingers several times over the course of the game and I'm happy to wiggle my pink digits at him.

Master Mac finds another way to keep Brenna warm. Her feet get cold easily and she doesn't have my toasty thigh-highs. Master Mac gives her a long foot massage that has her squirming all over the floor cushions. As he's digging his thumb into a spot on her instep that makes her writhe, he says to Daddy, "Now the vote's behind us, son, we have some work to do with the house subs."

My ears perk up. Although I'm not a house submissive, I'm more than a little interested in what's happening with them.

Cappa, who was lolling half-asleep on the other section of the couch, rolls over to look at Daddy and Master Mac.

"Something to say, boy?" Daddy asks.

"Just that—if you wanted to talk with some of the subs who are struggling—I could suggest where to start."

"Someone other than Mally?" Daddy asks.

"Yes, sir," Cappa says.

We had a dinner with Cappa and Mally back in September. I thought Mally was going to tell Daddy about the problems the house subs were having. But the timing was all wrong. Mally was totally preoccupied with Mistress Dana hooking up with Austin. All Daddy took away from the dinner was that the Blunts Doms had to do a better job of setting expectations about exclusivity with the house subs. Daddy got Mistress Dana to talk with Mally and that was the end of it.

It definitely wasn't the end of the problems, though. A lot of house submissives are going outside the club to find Doms. Lucy

29

asked Daddy to top her. And just a few weeks ago, Cappa picked up a Dom who ignored his safe word and beat him so badly that he needed sixteen stitches.

Daddy's been working with Cappa ever since, and although I wouldn't exactly call Daddy Cappa's Dom, Daddy provides Cappa with a lot of structure. Daddy gives Cappa a daily schedule and punishes him if he deviates from it. Cappa has more rules and conse-quences about self-care than even I do. Daddy's been vetting all of Cappa's scenes to make sure he's topped in a safe way and that his tops are clear on Cappa's signals and safe words.

Cappa's already so much better than he was. I can't resent the time and attention Daddy's given him when it's clearly what he needed. Daddy's good about making sure we still have a lot of one-on-one time, even when Cappa stays over, although he hasn't been doing that this week. It also makes a difference that Master Mac and Bren live with us now. Any pique I might have felt during the time Daddy's focused on Cappa is offset by having Master Mac, my confi-dante and co-conspirator in all things relating to Logan's daughter, and Brenna, my Big Sub Bestie, around all the time.

I wish I was a big enough person to feel the same way about Daddy topping Lucy. But that's a different story.

Unfortunately, all of Daddy's efforts so far haven't improved things for the house subs. Annabelle, a newer sub and one Daddy didn't train, quit over the weekend after a scene with Master Emmett. Brenna said that she, Austin, Fleur, and Master Javier tried to talk with Annabelle to understand what went so wrong and if it could be fixed. Annabelle wouldn't talk to them but she told Master Chess when she resigned that nothing could bring her back to the club.

Maybe Cappa's gotten through to her and wants her to talk to Daddy?

"Let's start with them," Master Mac says, rubbing between Bren-na's toes so she's a floppy puddle on the floor. Daddy chuckles against my temple as we watch her melt. "Something low-key. I don't want anyone feeling like we're interrogating them."

"Movie night," I suggest.

"Movie night," Daddy echoes. "Something neutral like Titanic."

I hide my grin as everyone around the room groans.

"No, Daddy," I say gently, patting his knee. Daddy doesn't cry at movies, so he wouldn't understand why watching Rose's goodbye to Jack would reduce someone who might already be emotionally fragile to rivers of tears.

"Maybe something a little less loaded," Master Mac says.

"Die Hard," Daddy grumbles, which makes everyone laugh.

Brenna and I have breakfast down to a fine art.

With all of us having very different schedules, breakfast could be chaotic. Daddy doesn't like chaos and I hate displeasing Daddy. Bren and I have worked out a schedule that suits everyone. On the island between the kitchen area and dining area, we set out a cold buffet with cereal, homemade Bircher, and a bowl of different kinds of energy bars. When Cappa stays over, he usually sticks to the buffet but he took off after dinner last night.

Once the buffet's set up, Brenna starts the coffee and puts links on the grill. She also puts on some music that we both dance to as we grill tomatoes from the little greenhouse Daddy's built me in the backyard, scramble eggs, and pop bread into the toaster. How much do I love starting my day dancing with my Big Sub Bestie? By the time Master Mac and Daddy come up from the basement, still sweaty from their workout, we're plating up the hot food to take to the table.

Daddy smiles and kisses my forehead as he takes his seat. I sit beside him, while Master Mac and Brenna sit across the table from us. We often have High Protocol dinners where Brenna and I kneel to our masters but so far, Daddy and Mac have kept breakfasts informal.

"What are you doing with your free time this morning, little love?" Daddy asks as he plows into his eggs and links. I notice he's pushed the whole wheat toast I made for him to the side. I nudge it closer to his eggs with the handle of my fork.

"Bren and I are going to work on the fairy book this morning. My editor wants the galleys approved by the end of the week."

"Bet you didn't think you'd end up a published author," Master Mac says to Brenna.

She shakes her head. "Emily's the author. I'm just the illustrator."

"That's not true," I protest, because Bren tends to hide her light under a bushel, as my aunt used to say. "You were the one who came up with the whole idea of the Bunny Queen rescuing Olivia from the troll. You wrote those scenes as much as I did. I already told Maxine that you need to be listed as co-author, as well as illustrator, so it's too late."

Brenna glowers at me but she's blushing. I think she's secretly happy about being listed as an author.

Daddy lays his big hand over mine and squeezes my fingers. "Have I mentioned how proud I am of you, baby doll? Not just writing a whole book for Olivia but for going outside your comfort zone."

"A good-girl flogging level of proud?" I ask, wishing I was wearing my cat ears this morning. Daddy would immediately agree to a good-girl flogging if I was wearing cat ears.

"Is that what you want?" he asks. "Because I was thinking that we might do that breeding scene I mentioned."

"Breeding scene level of proud," I whisper, delighted from my nonexistent cat ears down to my toes. "That's really proud."

"It is," he agrees.

I toy with a crust of my whole wheat toast. "You, um, also

mentioned, maybe, giving me the second brand while we were doing a breeding scene."

"I did," he says.

My breath catches as joy fills up every cell. Daddy's going to brand me again. It's Christmas and every birthday rolled up together. I know even some of my fellow submissives don't understand why I'd want to be branded, or why Logan would want to give me such excruciating pain.

It's hard to explain but nothing Daddy and I have done together except my collaring felt more intimate, more *spiritual*. I had an out-of-body experience when Daddy gave me the two-moon brand. My soul was subsumed in Daddy's: consumed, uplifted, floating somewhere up among the stars. I've never felt so submissive, so completely in Logan's control, as that moment when the red-hot metal touched my skin. It was overwhelming, agonizing, sublime.

I've seen art that captures a moment of spiritual fractioning, like Bernini's "Ecstasy of Saint Teresa." But even in subspace, I've never felt it.

Until Daddy branded me.

After Daddy and Master Mac leave, I head up to the third floor with Bren. We've got everything for the book spread out in what we've all started calling "the studio." It's next to the area Daddy walled off for storage and too small to be another bedroom. We've squeezed a desk with a drawing board and lots of shelves into the space and Bren's taken it over as her workspace in the house.

Currently, it's covered with sketches and proofs for our book. I stop and take a minute to admire one of the finished plates. It's the moment Olivia meets the Bunny Queen, with the crowned rabbit peeking out from behind a tree as Olivia sits under a rainbow toadstool. The colors of Bren's art are so vibrant, and she's perfectly captured the mutual delight of the rabbit and little girl on meeting each other. The piece brings a happy tear to my eye.

I run my fingertips down the framed edge of the plate before I turn to where Bren's standing beside the messy desk.

If I didn't know Brenna better, I'd say she looks . . . embarrassed. She stares at her wool-socked toes, twisting the hem of Mac's dress shirt between her fingers. Her cheeks are so pink it looks like she has a fever.

"Everything okay?" I ask.

"Look, you don't have to wear it, okay? I don't even know why I had it made. You'll probably think it's stupid."

I sidle over to her and slide my arm around her waist. "You had something made for me?"

She rolls her eyes. "You and the baby."

"You had something made for me and the baby? Like matching outfits?"

She clears her throat. "I heard you talking with Logan, about how you wanted to take Livvy to baby swim class. That it's good for babies to learn to swim really young so they never develop any fear of the water. I, um, wish someone had taught me when I was a baby, because swimming's still hard for me and I just thought, well, whatever."

"Whatever?"

"Ugh, I hate you."

Bren moves to one side, revealing a long box sitting on top of the pile of galleys.

I drift over to the box, admiring it. The paper wrapping is blue and purple and silver, patterned to look like scales. I carefully untie the blue-green metallic ribbon. I'll save it and add it to a scrapbook I've started making. Logan has me writing a journal for him once a week, and I've kept my own journal for years but my scrapbook is more for impressions, little keepsakes, things I want to remember forever. This ribbon is definitely going in it.

I open the box and peel apart the tissue paper inside. Shimmering, silvery fabric fills the box. I lift out the first piece, admiring the way the warm, morning light sparks highlights of pink and blue in the fabric. There's a bikini top, a bottom with a long skirt and trailing, filmy, blue fins. Underneath is a baby's one-piece swimsuit in the same fabric with a detachable skirt of the same filmy fabric but in purple.

I hold the swimsuits up, my eyes filling so they merge into a silver blur. "Bren, these are so perfect. Livvy and I can be mermaids together."

Bren blinks. "You really like them? You don't have to wear them if you don't."

"I love them! Did you get yourself one, too?"

She shakes her head. "No. But I, uh, well, I'll show you."

She pushes around some of the sketches on her drafting board and holds one out.

It's a delicately rendered silhouette of a mermaid, her hair and tail flowing behind her as she surfs a rolling wave. In her arms, she holds a baby mermaid, its tail curling into the foam of another wave. The figures are black, with color on their tails and in the waves, blue, green, purple, and bright points of orange like the sunset over the ocean.

"Bren, it's gorgeous."

"Yeah? I thought I could get it on my back, kind of where Mac's mermaid is, although this piece would be smaller than his."

"That's so perfect. But don't you want to be in it, too?"

"Naw, I'll never be a mermaid. That's for you and Livvy."

"Bren, you'll always be a mermaid," I tell her.

She rolls her eyes. "Let's look at these galleys."

I hug her again before I replace the swimsuits carefully in the box and set it aside.

I can't wait to show it to Logan. Daddy's mermaids. He'll love that so much.

four

LOGAN

MY MIND'S all over the place today.

It's with my baby doll, who is happily heading off to the 6BC Botanical Garden with Mac, Bren, Warrin, Aggie, Jack, and Sammi for a picnic.

It's with Max, who is packing to fly to England tomorrow in De Leon's tiny, private plane.

It's in London, where my daughter's getting discharged from the ICU where she's been since her complicated birth.

It's at Blunts, where the problems with the house submissives seem to be spinning further out of control with Annabelle's resignation.

It's in New Jersey, where I'm headed to finish wiring in the CCTV system that I hope will finally catch a thief.

My business partner, Manny, drops me off before heading down the Turnpike to a job in Elizabeth. I'd like to say that Manny and I coordinated our jobs so he's not shlepping over half of Jersey but it's all Max. He's made our lives so much better in the few weeks he's been onboard. I always know where I'm going, how much time I have on a job, and where I'm going next. I wish he'd joined us a year ago.

Max has also entered the wrangle between my insurance company and Pink Pearl's insurance company over my medical bills with both guns and his keyboard blazing. I have no idea where he gets his information—and I probably don't want to know—but he's already gotten Pink Pearl's insurer to cough up half of the costs. He's now going after my insurer for the other half plus the selling costs on Emmy's house and emotional distress. I would feel sorry for them if they hadn't been such utter asshats, hiding behind subrogation clauses for so long that I thought I was going to lose my house to the debt collectors.

Given that so many of the things that were weighing on me over the summer have been settled, and settled in my favor, I should be relaxed.

I'm not.

I sigh and roll my shoulders as I use an electronic fob to disarm the security I've recently installed on the employee entrance of Sacrum, Blunts' sister club, and enter its cool, dark confines. I collect my kit out of the club office, grab the note taped to the office door with my name on it, and get to work, wiring in the last cameras in the new CCTV net I've created for the club.

These are cameras I didn't think I'd need. This project didn't initially call for coverage of the administrative areas of the club. I was hired to bring the club into the 21st century and make sure there was coverage in the play spaces and the kitchen, where the club might have liability. I expected the cameras I installed for the initial spec would also catch whoever's been dipping their fingers in the club's petty cash.

I didn't anticipate I'd be going up against a master thief.

Whoever has been getting into the club at night—something I've been able to document at last—is substantially wilier than I antici-pated. They've evaded all my cameras like they know exactly where I've installed each one. They have a bloody Ph.D. in lock-picking and it's taken the fob access, which is *substantially* out of the spec for this job, to finally keep them out of the office. No such luck with the kitchen. According to a text I got as I set off from Manhattan, a tray of sandwiches intended for today's social committee meeting disappeared overnight, along with a new jar of instant coffee. The thief never steals much; nothing worth involving the police over. But the thefts have freaked out the club's owners and rumors are spreading among the members.

I'd probably be freaked, too, if the thief hadn't started leaving me notes.

Today's reads:

Sorry, Master Logan. I couldn't keep my bratty paws off the "sarnies." That's what British people call sandwiches, right? I think you need to punish me. Love, The Joker's B

I fold it and tuck it into my back pocket to add to my collection.

The other notes have all been in the same vein. I've noodled them around with Mac and Max. We agree the thief isn't malicious. We also agree this is an inside job, although I'm certain it's not the club's founders or the members of the management committee. Pinning the blame on one of the club's subs doesn't feel like a perfect fit, either. I have pretty good instincts and something about labeling "The Joker's B" as an experienced submissive feels off.

Brenna and Emily have spent a lot of time whispering over the notes, too. Other than telling me she thinks "The Joker's B" is a girl, my little font of theories has dried up. I'm willing to wait, though. While I never want to exclude my baby doll from my investigations, I don't want to involve her more than she wants to be, either. When she's ready, she'll tell me what she thinks.

And she'll probably be close to the mark. Her natural empathy has been honed—and possibly twisted—by her novel-writing. She knows what makes characters tick, and when she applies that to the people around her, she's terrifyingly astute.

I reach into what Emily laughingly calls my Batman utility belt, pull out my small caulk gun, and caulk around the plate I've screwed in. While the caulk dries, I pop into the kitchen, grab the hand vac, and tidy up. I got read the riot act about "Doms who can't clean up after themselves" by Miss Vizzi, who runs the club's cleaning committee, the first day I was here. I've made sure she doesn't have anything to blister my ears about again.

The lady herself arrives as I'm returning the hand vac to its place on the wall. She gives me the side-eye. "You emptied it, right?"

I open the vac to show her the empty canister before sliding it into its holder. She loves having something to be irritated about, and I take a sadist's glee in thwarting her. Smiling to myself, I move around her to the counter and make myself a cup of tea.

"Tea or coffee?" I offer.

She tosses her glossy, black hair back over her shoulders. "Tea, thanks. I hear a tray of sandwiches went missing."

I nod.

"And there was another note."

It's a statement, not a question but I nod again.

"Are you actually trying to catch this Joker person, or just flirting with them?" she demands.

I'll admit I've been more amused by the Joker's B's notes than anything else but I am taking the job seriously.

"I'm trying to catch them," I say. "The lack of routine in the club isn't helping. There were eleven people in and out of here after the club closed last night."

"Clean up. Coffee and tea for stragglers. Getting things ready for today's meeting and tonight's event. I'm honestly surprised it wasn't more," Vizzi responds tartly.

I sigh and push a teacup toward her. To be fair, there are probably more people in and out of the staff spaces in Blunts after closing on any given night. But Blunts has a rigorous security system. There are two layers of security at every entrance. We change the entry codes weekly. After hours, anyone passing through a doorway needs a key card. With the new chips in them, the key cards are hard to duplicate. Members and house submissives know that loss of a key card means suspension from the club, and most of them are conscientious about club security anyway. We haven't had a key card lost or stolen yet.

Until I got here last month, Sacrum barely had a lock on any door other than the office and bathrooms. More than upgrading the physical security, getting the staff to adopt a security-first mindset has been a challenge. They all understand the need for it but I think they've liked being the more relaxed, casual, and friendly sister club. Me coming from Blunts and telling them they need to trim their jib has been greeted with resentment.

Which makes the animosity Ten expressed over me working here a particularly bitter pill to swallow.

"I'm wiring in the last of the cameras today," I tell her. "Hopefully that will solve the problem."

"And if it doesn't?" she asks.

I don't have an answer to that. I don't have a Plan B. The club doesn't have enough money for a physical security guard. I know Jaimie and Olaf are trying to keep membership dues low, particularly in the face of rising living costs but it leaves the club with very little float. They've blown their budget, and then some, with the CCTV system. And I gave them a hefty discount. If it doesn't work, it might be me and Mac camping out in the club for a few nights *gratis*, because I don't really know how else to catch their thief.

"We'll cross that bridge when we come to it," I say.

She gives me a glower that would absolutely have me shaking in my boots if I had an ounce of submission in my blood. Instead, I just raise an eyebrow at her and pass the milk when she waves a hand at it.

"You've never offered me any theory about who you think it is," I note.

Jaimie and Olaf both had views but I've found nothing to substantiate their theories.

Vizzi shrugs. "I just hope it's not one of us."

"I hope that, too. Sacrum's as much of a family as Blunts, from what I've seen. Nothing hurts worse than betrayal by a member of your family. I sincerely hope that's not what this is."

"But you think it's an inside job," Vizzi says. "You told Jaimie that."

"I think it would be hard for someone who isn't very familiar with the club to evade the cameras I initially installed. That doesn't mean it's a current member of Sacrum. It could be someone who used to be a member and has a bit of an axe to grind. It could be someone involved in the renovation two years ago. There are plenty of possibilities that don't involve a current club member."

Vizzi's shoulders drop an inch. "I hope that's the case."

"Me, too." I finish the last of my tea and salute her with the cup before I wash it and leave it in the draining rack to dry. "Back to work."

Vizzi grunts softly then says, "I'm making a run to the store to replace the sandwiches. If you're a good boy, I'll bring you one. Ham and cheese or tuna?"

I chuckle. I will never be a good boy. And Emily packed me a three-course lunch. "I'm all set, thanks but I appreciate the offer."

She shakes her head at me as I back out of the kitchen.

Once I have all of the cameras wired in, including the two panning cameras, I spend the early afternoon calibrating and testing the system. When I'm happy with everything, I pull up Max's instructions on my laptop and connect the system to the cloud account he's set up. I'll admit I'm not sure exactly how it works but Max and his back-up guy in Singapore will be able to monitor the system in real-time, including overriding the cameras' programming and redirecting them.

I assume Max will be too preoccupied with his trip to pay attention to this job today but, as always, he's on top of it. He pings me almost as soon as the system connects to the cloud account.

Max: Squid and I are going to run some fire drills. We'll set the system to go live at midnight. If you want to take off for the day, I'll send Manny your way.

I smile at his message. People underestimate Max because he's better with machines than humans. Their mistake. He's twice as smart as I am and almost as perceptive as my baby doll. I'd give a lot for a few free hours.

That would be great.

I begin packing up my kit. I leave the tools I need to tweak the system if there are physical adjustments to be made but box up my heavy drill and other power equipment. I collect the drop cloths from the hallway where I was working and pack all but one of them away, then return the ladder to the office closet.

Max texts as I'm debating over my caulk gun.

Max: Manny's on the way. ETA 5 min.

I toss the caulk gun into the satchel I'm leaving, pick up my box, and head out to meet Manny. We might not have the precision we had in the Navy but with Max coordinating things now, we're not far off.

Manny's not sorry to beat the worst of rush hour traffic as we head back into the City. He tells me about the job he's been on and I listen with half an ear as I consider how to spend the hours I've been gifted.

First, I flip my phone over to the app Max created for me, which is a modified version of the app he uses with his little. The app tracks what I've come to think of as "subbie wellness." It covers the physical aspects of a submissive's health: eating properly, drinking enough water, getting enough exercise and sleep. But it also tracks their moods with blood pressure and heart rate monitoring as well as asking them questions at random intervals to establish their mental state.

Emily's not a fan of the app, so I've only asked her to log her water consumption. I'm constantly in touch with Emily and can evaluate her without mechanical assistance.

I didn't give Lucy or Cappa the choice. I only see Lucy once a week for scheduled scenes. I still see Cappa most days but it's less than immediately after his injury. He's back at work and the club full time. He was evicted from his apartment at the beginning of the month, even though I offered to help him with the rent. He's moved in with Fleur; as far as I can tell, that's working out well. The app lets me keep tabs on both of them from a distance, and alerts me when I need to step in.

Both of them have had good days. Cappa's blood pressure is way down from where it was after his eviction, which was stressful for him despite the offers of assistance and having a place to land. Lucy's been having a little trouble at work, some kind of conflict with a co-worker but her signs are all good today. I tap in rewards for both of them, then flip over to the message string with my baby doll.

She's been on a high since Halloween. Her "Halloween Eve-Eve" party was a huge success. This book that she and Bren are working on is coming together and although she won't let me see it, Mac says the artwork he's seen Bren working on brought a tear to his jaded eye. Despite her ongoing tussle with Mac for control of the kitchen, Emmy's loving living with "the Mac Grandaddy" and her "Big Sub Bestie." Every night's a sleepover.

But the changes turning my world on its ear are going to impact Emmy. It's inevitable. The biggest is Olivia's arrival in a few days. Although Emily says she wants to be the "best little babysitter in the world" to Livvy, the truth is that we're suddenly going to be parents of an infant. Emily's preparing for it like she's prepping for the apocalypse but neither of us has any idea what it's going to be like.

I need to make it as easy for Emily as possible. And put some mechanisms in place so that if she's not okay, I know before she spirals.

"Man," I say to my business partner, "how do you know when Jen's struggling with the kids?"

He flexes his hands on the steering wheel. "Easy. It's the five o'clock check in. If I call at five and ask her how things are goin' and she says, 'fine,' I head straight home and take the kids for the night so she can chill. If she tells me that Tabby broke a toy and Mickey colored all over the walls, I don't have to worry, she's got it under control."

I chuckle. "Fine is code red, huh?"

"When a woman tells you somethin's fine, put your emergency recovery plan into action, hermano. Nothin' is fucking fine."

Thinking of the times the women in my life told me things were fine, when they absolutely were not, I smile.

"I'm worried about how Emmy's going to take having a baby dumped on her. *Someone else's* baby."

"She's gonna take it like everyone else does when they become a parent, whether it's expected or unexpected. She's gonna do her damn best. There'll be things she's absolutely unprepared for and there'll be things she thinks she's prepared for and ain't. Just take it one day at a time. Things went bad yesterday? Baby cried all night or puked all over the place? You forgot to pack their lunch or didn't buy them the right pair of school shoes? Take it easy on yourself. Most shit is fixable and I can guarantee someone's made the same mistake before. New parents think they're all alone, doin' everything for the first time. They're not."

I pat him on his very solid shoulder. "Very true. Thanks, Man."

"You and Em are going to be fine. I know this has been a big fucking shock but you're doing the right thing. And as soon as you said Emmy'd started writing a book about Olivia, I knew it was gonna be okay. She's already involving the baby in her inner world."

That's astute. Manny isn't always the most perceptive guy but he's on the mark with that observation.

"I hadn't thought of it that way but you're right," I tell him.

"And you got one big advantage. Em didn't give birth. The gates of hell are still open, buddy."

I shake my head at him. "Idiot. I'm amazed Jen hasn't kicked you to the curb yet."

He sticks out his tongue and waggles it like he's licking the windshield. "Never. She knows I got the goods."

He keeps me laughing all the way back to Manhattan.

five

LOGAN

AN EMPTY HOUSE is a rarity now.

Which is good because after being home alone for less than fifteen minutes, I hate it. I'm so used to the house being full that I find myself wandering from room to room as I talk with Emmy on the phone.

"I made extra and put it in the fridge, Daddy. I didn't want you to miss out on the picnic food," she tells me.

"Thank you, baby doll. Should Daddy be naughty and spoil his dinner?"

A sweet giggle. "Just a snack, Daddy."

"I'm cooking dinner," Mac grumbles in the background over the noise of the train they're on coming back from the botanical gardens.

"But I got that fish yesterday and marinated it overnight," Emily objects, her voice muffled like she's turned her face away from the phone. "I'm going to steam it Thai style."

I grin into the phone at this latest skirmish in the ongoing Battle of the Pans. Emily may be submissive but she's all Domme when it comes to the kitchen. Mac has his work cut out for him to wrestle a dinner or two out of her a week.

"Bebe J's blackened beans would go well with that," Brenna says. "Want me to show you how to make them while Emmy's doing the fish, Sir?"

Bren's started playing peace-maker between them, which I don't think is a role that comes naturally to her.

Emily and Mac both concede with huffs. A détente that I'm sure will break into warfare again tomorrow.

"I don't have to be back in Jersey first thing, baby doll, so I was thinking we could go to Blunts tonight. Make sure the Nursery is ready. Give the cradle a test drive."

Emily gives a soft squee. "Yes, please, Daddy."

"I'll call over and reserve some rooms. Ask Mac if he wants to come and maybe I should invite Sean and Moon, too? What do you think?"

"Yes, Daddy. If you think the Nursery is ready, could I send out the Grand Opening invites?"

I chew my lip. I've been hesitating on the opening. The Nursery is ready. There are finishing details, like the sterilizer for pacifiers and bottles, which is on back order. But everything essential is in place. I kept justifying it to myself that the management committee hadn't signed off on an age-play night. They have now; there's no reason to delay.

And I'm still hesitating.

"Let's talk about it tonight, baby doll."

"Okay, Daddy. Mac says he and Bren are due for a flogging scene, so could you please reserve the Stocks for them?"

"I see how this is going to go. I'm just going to be Mac's social secretary now that he's a club member, aren't I?"

Emily giggles, which draws a smile out of me. There's nothing as enchanting as my baby girl's giggle.

"Sorry, Daddy."

"Uh-huh. I hear so much regret in your voice, little girl. What's your ETA?"

"About a half hour. Can I make a request?"

"Of course."

"Can we have a shower together before dinner? If we're going to test drive the cradle tonight, I'm afraid I'll fall asleep and I won't get a bath and I feel yughie after the Botanical Gardens today. The greenhouses were hot and I got sweaty."

I chuckle. I love the words she invents.

"Your shower request is approved. There might even be time for a play with the bath crayons."

Another small squee.

"I'll see you in a half-hour, sweetheart. Come straight upstairs. Daddy and the bath crayons will be waiting for you."

I hear the happiness in her voice when she says goodbye. I flip my phone over, fire off a message to Sean, and call Niall.

He answers on the first ring. "Gobshite?"

"Wanker."

"Need me to get on a plane?"

Niall's offered to go to England to retrieve Olivia about a dozen times. I didn't see Niall talking to Max while Niall's trio was here for Emily's Halloween party but they must have put their heads together at some point. Niall cuffed me hard and hugged me tight and told me that all I had to do was call and he'd get on a plane.

"No, everything's set for Max to go tomorrow. I need help thinking something through."

"Fire away."

"Nursery at Blunts is ready. Management committee's agreed to the age-play night. And I'm dithering over sending out the Grand Opening invites. Why? I want this. I've been working toward this for weeks. What's wrong with me?"

Niall sighs heavily. "Club's still divided over age-play, right?"

"Somewhat."

"Anyone you give a fig about?"

I grunt. I shouldn't care what Ten thinks. He and Karl and their clique of "hard sadists" have always turned up their noses at me. I've never given their disdain any mental space.

His opposition to Mac hits at a different level. Mac's a man I've looked up to for as long as I've known him. I think more of Mac than I thought of my own father. Having anyone think badly of him, speak badly of him, strikes hard against my heart. And his judgment of Emily's littleness? That's not something I can think too closely about or I'll end up going for him.

"One of 'em fought me hard on Mac's membership. Stood up and made a big speech about my divided loyalties. And the support I thought I had from the Chairman and his inner circle melted away like butter in a hot pan." I grumble as I open myself to what's been percolating in my heart since the meeting. "I've known them for coming up on a decade. Fucking stings."

"You're dithering 'cause you're afraid this will prove them right. 'Cause it'll bring more judgment down on you and Emily."

Niall cuts to the heart of things. The way he always does.

"Yes," I admit.

"How many you figure'll come to the open house?"

"Thirty plus. Everyone in our playgroup plus some age-players other members know who are excited about the prospect of having a dedicated nursery."

"I know it's not all about numbers, Lo but that's thirty people who will get to express what's in their souls, if only for one night. Anyone who opposes you can feck right off. Not every day you get to feed thirty souls."

That thought soothes the sting. I smile into the phone, even though I know he can't see me since I haven't video-called. "Lanced a boil, mate. Thank you."

"I could tell this was festering when we saw you at Halloween. Shoulda stuck around to knock some heads together. You know as soon as we find a place there, I'm applying for membership. Between you, me, and Mac, we'll be running that place in no time. Kick some heads outta some arses."

I chuckle at the visual. "I've never cared about their approval before. Why's it bothering me now?"

"Cause you were never invested before. Your other subbies? They were playmates. Emmy's your world. Mac's the only man who's approval you care about. Completely different. Someone gave me the hairy eyeball over the way I play with Shaan or Vashi? I'd be more than resentful. I'd be on the fecking warpath."

He's right. Ten's attack on me and my loyalties smarts a little but what's really got my back up is the suggestion that Mac's unworthy of membership or that Emily's littleness and the way we live are wrong.

"I've never questioned it. It feels right. It's what Emmy needs. I just—"

"You just want the people you respect to accept it."

"Yes."

"Give 'em time. Let them get to know Mac. Show 'em how you play with Emmy when she's little; they might come 'round. If they don't? They weren't worth your time to begin with."

"You're right."

"Course I am, tosspot."

"Wanker."

"See you in Vegas."

"Not if I see you first, Irish Elvis."

Laughing, Niall hangs up.

Lighter, I put out some wet food for Emily's stinky cat and head upstairs to get the bath ready for when my little girl gets home.

six

LOGAN

I'VE NEVER SEEN Emily's eyes go as round as they do when I open the door and flick on the lights, revealing Blunts' newest dungeon.

"Daddy," she breathes.

She's seen it in several stages of construction but she hasn't seen it since the painters left and Brenna got started.

I haven't always been Bren's biggest fan, and I'm still against Emily getting a tattoo but I have to admit what Bren's done with the Nursery is enough to fulfill any little's dreams and bring a happy tear to any daddy's eye.

"Is everything dry?" Emily asks. "Some of it is still shiny like it's wet."

"Bren told me it was ready to go. I think the shine is just whatever she sealed the paint with."

Emily slowly gravitates to the central, and most eye-catching, feature of the Nursery. It's a huge tree, growing out of the middle of the floor, the twisting, gnarled trunk spiraling up and *through* the ceiling. I had to get the architect who did Max's loft in to help with the structural supports and permitting; she created a thing of wonder.

The ceiling has a fifteen-foot, clear plexiglass circle in it, so you can see up into the upper floor of the Nursery, where the tree branches create a canopy for the Tree House that forms the upper floor. Brenna's painted the tree trunk. Lines of mushrooms with caps in sunset colors march up the wood. A smiling face with black button eyes peeks out from under each mushroom cup. Winding between the mushrooms are swirls of dancing fairies, their diaphanous wings glittering. A clutch of baby, fairy dragons peep out of a hollowed bole.

Emily drifts to the dragons and strokes their noses. When she turns to me, her eyes are glittering brighter than any of the fairy wings. "Are they emerald dragons . . .?"

"For Laurel? Of course they are. I didn't forget, baby doll."

She rushes to me and I fold her into my chest. "You like it?" I ask.

"I *love* it. So much, Daddy. Everything's so beautiful. It's like my dreams."

I kiss her on the forehead as I look around. I don't usually bother patting myself on the back. If I've done something right, I allow myself a moment to bask and then move on to the next thing.

But with the Nursery, I can pat myself on the back. I listened carefully not just to Emily's fantasies but to what many of our little friends wanted. I incorporated as much as I could. More than was practical, according to the architect. She had to design a retrospective structural support for the kitchen and cellar below the wet play side of the room, where the tree, fish tank, water table, and sand box add so much weight to the room that the design exceeded the building's load-bearing capacities.

But she did a damn fine job, and so did I.

Once Emily finishes her happy cry, I walk around the room with her. Brenna's murals pull the three separate play areas together. The waves framing the jutting corner structure—which can be made into a pirate ship or castle just by spinning the center-mounted "planks"—lead to the clouds butterflies, and steampunk dirigible of the reading and napping corner, with its adult cradle. The clouds roll away from the corner toward the wet play area, turning into a rainbow bridge that unicorns and pegasi dance across, framing the two tables for coloring and artwork. The last unicorn has a fish tail, leading to the underwater mural with curious tropical fish, laughing dolphins, and mermaids that peek around the actual coral reef tank and tactile discovery wall, wet play corner, and sand box.

I show her some of the hidden features of the room: the bins of dress-up clothes concealed as wooden casks on the pirate ship; the "cannon" that converts into a spanking bench; the huge cupboard between the pirate ship and napping corner that opens into a changing table and curtained-off cage beneath; the built-in book-cases that Twitch has stocked with everything from Beatrix Potter to Cynnie's bumblebee books; the rolling carts of art supplies. Emily touches everything with light fingers, her eyes shining.

"Daddy, can we go upstairs?" she asks, peering up through the cut-out into the second floor of the Nursery.

"That's a space for bigger girls. Wouldn't you like to be very little tonight?"

She glances at the cradle and I see the longing in her eyes. Oh, baby doll, try it. Show me that very little soul that keeps trying to break free. I sidle in that direction and pull out something I've been keeping in reserve for this occasion.

A pacifier with her name on it, edged in pink rhinestones.

She swallows and edges toward me. "Daddy? Is that for me?"

"It is. Would you like a spanking on the table here?" I open the diapering cabinet. "And then I could rock you with a hot bottom?"

Her breath catches. "I could see upstairs tomorrow."

"You could," I agree.

She nods.

I undress her reverently. If there was a time when I thought Emily was anything less than the most beautiful woman I've ever seen, it's long past. Every curve, freckle, dimple, and fold of her body has become the table at which I feast, the altar at which I worship.

"I adore you, baby doll," I tell her, as I kneel to unlace her boots.

Would my friend Sean, who pokes his head into the Nursery as I'm easing off the first boot, think I'm submitting to Emily, given our relative positions? Maybe. If he does, Sean's too distracted by the wonder of the Nursery, as he leads his submissive in, to comment. Moon trots straight to the pirate ship.

Emily places a soft hand on my shoulder to steady herself as I take off the second boot. "I adore you, too, Daddy," she whispers.

"Look around," I say to her. "This is for you. This is because of you. Look at all the magic you've brought to my life, little wonder."

She glances around, then back at me, and smiles tremulously. I flick my fingers across her cheek to catch a tear that spills.

"Good tears?"

She nods. "The best tears."

I unzip and slip off the dress she's worn and the black lace thigh-highs underneath. When she's standing in just a black lace bralette and tiny knickers that make her skin glow like marble, I say, "Put your hands on my shoulders. I'm going to pick you up. That's the last time you stand on your feet until we leave. My baby girl crawls for Daddy tonight."

Her eyes are so huge and round, they encompass my world. "Yes, Daddy."

I lift her onto the changing table. It has a thick pad, much thicker than on a child's changing table. More like a mattress. It's sized for an adult and Emmy can stretch out on it. It's at the perfect fucking height. There are several shallow drawers built into the walls on either side, where the supplies are kept. I open one and take out a cloth diaper and a pair of diaper pins.

I've read about diapering in every parenting book and online guide I could find since finding out about Olivia. Reading doesn't prepare me for the reality of it. The warmth of Emily's soft curves as I draw her knickers off and run my fingertips reverently over her hips.

The weight of her legs as I lift them over my shoulders. The sweet musk that rises to me as her thighs part naturally.

"I'm going to put a diaper on you, my angel baby." A spark kindles in her eyes. She's known this was coming. We've talked about it. She's seen the cloth diaper and pins I've set next to her. But the reality of it just hit her. And filled her with heat. "You don't have to use the diaper. But if you do, Daddy will clean it up. Just like Daddy cleans up all his little girl's messes."

She nods, her shining eyes never leaving mine.

"Daddy's going to give you a warm bottom to start but I can think of another use for these." I pick up one of the diaper pins. "If I wanted to see a ladder of pins up your sides, would that be too much pain for tonight?"

"No, Daddy, it wouldn't be too much pain," she breathes.

"That's my wonderful girl. I want you to feel free to be as little as you'd like during this scene. If that means you can't talk, that's good with me. If you feel like baby talking, that's good with me. This Nursery is a safe space for you, Emmy. You can be whatever you want here."

Her lower lip trembles. "As little as I'd like?"

I stroke my hands up and down her legs. "Yes, little love. As little as feels right to you."

She nods. "You'll be my daddy no matter what?"

"Emmy, baby, *nothing* could stop me from being your daddy now. Nothing you could do. Nothing you don't do. If you told me tomorrow you don't want to be my little girl anymore, I would *still* always be your daddy in my heart. That will never change for me."

A crystal tear wells, spills, and runs down her temple before I catch it on my thumb and tip it to her lips to lick off.

"My forever-Daddy?"

"Yes, baby. Your forever-Daddy."

"My forever-Daddy who gives me a hot bottom?"

I flick her curved lips with my thumb. "Little mischief. Grab your ankles."

She does. I adjust her position until her bottom's right at the edge of the pad and I have clear access to every part of her sweet, curved ass.

As I'm rubbing to warm up her skin, I hear a sharp *smack* from my right. While continuing to circle my hands over Emily's deliciously soft curves, I look over my shoulder at the source of the sound. Sean's flipped over the ship/castle's barrel and has Moon bent over the padded bench. He's ahead of me. His handprint is already blooming on Moon's golden cheek.

I wink at him before I apply my hand to my own subbie's bottom.

Emily's eyes go from glittering to glazed as I heat her ass. She whimpers when I focus on her sit-spots, making sure they're a glowing red before I move to her upper thighs. She's flushed with endorphins now, her face as red as her bottom, the flush spreading up to her delicate ears and down her throat. She whimpers when I concentrate on the crease between her thighs and buttocks but that's not because of the increased sensitivity but rather because my hand is so close to her pussy lips, compressed between her trembling thighs.

"I know what my little girl wants," I murmur to her.

"You, Daddy," she whispers.

"Yes, me. What else do you want, baby? I think it's a pussy spanking you're whimpering and wriggling for. Aren't I right?"

She nods fervently. "Please, Daddy. And please may I come?"

"Are you that close, little girl?"

"Yes, Daddy. I don't want to come without permission."

I stroke her soft, slippery slit with my thumb. Parting her gently, I tease her clit until the pearl of it peeks out of its hood. Leaning in, I blow on it and grin at her shudder.

"Please, Daddy?"

"Mmm, not yet. Hold it for me, Emmy."

Her legs shake and she shifts restlessly, getting a better grip behind her knees.

I bend down and run the tip of my tongue up her slit, then push inside until I find her opening. Emily keens softly. I fuck her with my tongue for several strokes, then lick up her bready sweetness while she writhes.

"Daddy, Daddy, I'm close. Please, Daddy?"

I lick up her thigh and look at my little girl. Her body's bowed off the pad as she strains, trying to hold back her orgasm without losing position. Her flush has spread down to the tops of her breasts, throwing her adorable freckles into sharp relief. I reach up and run my hands down her body, appreciating each tremble of restraint.

"I'm so pleased with you, Emmy. Do you want Daddy's cock for long enough to come?"

"Please, please, Daddy."

"Good girl. Hold back long enough for me to get all the way inside you so I can feel you come on my cock. Then you have permission to come."

"Yes, Daddy."

She's so good, my baby girl. Even though I can feel her gripping at me as soon as I push the head of my cock in, she holds back, her neck straining, body taut. I tease her, slipping in and drawing back, knowing each moment she holds back will make the release stronger when I finally let her have it. She pants, each breath harsh in the changing table's alcove. Her fingers flex on the back of her calf, reaching for me. I twine my fingers with hers as I sink all the way in, making sure she feels the bump of my balls.

She howls softly on a long exhale, all the tension in her body unraveling. Her pussy rolls over and over my shaft, deep draws that have my own muscles shaking. I'm close from our play but I hold myself back. Our months together have strengthened my control. Knowing I can have Emily anytime I want has made taking her like this, glorying in her release while staving off my own, strangely satisfying. The longer I wait for my orgasm, the more often I can fuck her during one scene. It's not selfless, because I derive a huge amount of pleasure from the fucking but Emily's pleasure has definitely become more important than my own.

When her body goes completely limp around mine, I withdraw and tuck myself back into the soft pants I wear for scenes. I stroke Emily's legs until her eyes focus on mine.

"Daddy?"

"Hi, my baby. Good one?"

She grins. "Love you most today, Daddy."

"I don't think that's possible." I pull out a pack of baby wipes and clean her up, then tip her hips up further and slide the diaper under her. I loosen her hands—she's held position for me so perfectly—and let her knees fall open naturally as I bring the front flap of the diaper up.

She lifts her eyes to the alcove ceiling, painted with clouds and a herd of little elephants dancing around the light fixture, huffing out a soft breath.

"No, baby. Eyes on me. I know this is a hard moment for you. Daddy's right here for you. Stay focused on me."

Her eyes immediately snap down to mine. They're hazy with afterglow, gleaming with emotion as she lets go of all the fears that have held her back from expressing her deepest little self.

"That's my good girl. I'm so proud of you, Emily. My wonderful angel baby. Look at you, taking this big step. Being brave and vulnerable for Daddy. There's so much strength in you, baby doll. You awe me."

"Daddy," she breathes.

"That's right, little girl. Daddy's in awe of you." I pull up the diaper's sides and secure them to the front flap with the diaper pins. "Diaper's on, my good girl. How does it feel?"

"Soft. Strange. You won't-you won't be mad at me if I can't use it?"

"Never, baby. You've taken such a big step in letting me diaper you. It doesn't matter to me if you never use it."

Her stomach collapses as she lets out a big breath. "Thank you. Ta, Daddy."

I wipe down the soft curves on either side of her tummy, above the diaper's edge. The sharpness of the alcohol wipe cuts through the musk of her pleasure. "Deep breath in."

She sucks in a breath and holds it. I pinch a bit of skin an inch above the diaper and push a diaper pin through it. The diaper pin's not as sharp as an acupuncture needle and a bead of blood rolls over her pale skin. I wipe it away as she lets the breath out shakily.

"Good girl. How does that feel?"

"Sharp pinch and then dull ache," she mumbles, processing the pain.

I watch her closely, feeling that dark bloom in my heart. The gratification is almost as strong as an orgasm. It's the peak of control, demanding another suffer for you. It's undistilled love. Complete devotion. I stroke my palm up and down her breastbone, caressing her throat. "Good girl. Ready for another?"

She nods. I pinch another bit of skin an inch above the first piercing and push the pin through. I've done better with this piercing and only a dot of blood wells around the metal. Emily trembles but doesn't even whimper as I dab both piercings with alcohol wipes to make sure they're clean, then match up her other side with two pins.

I stop there, even though there's a cruel impulse to continue the ladder up to her bra-line. But Emily's cheeks have lost color and I don't want to ruin what's been an amazing scene by pushing her too far. As always, Emily's love has filled that void inside me, that dark craving only my submissive's pain can sate. I run my fingertips down each set of pins to hear her breath catch, then wipe them again with an alcohol wipe, before giving her the praise she's so richly earned.

"My wonderful girl, I wish you could see yourself through my eyes. Lying there wearing the diaper Daddy's put on you. Bearing Daddy's piercings. You fill my eyes. I can't see anything but you, baby. You fill my heart and soul. I feel nothing but peace and love in this moment, Emmy. You've given me that. As long as I have you, I'm the richest man on Earth. Your trust and love is worth more than anything else in the world."

She smiles even as tears spill down her temples. "You're everything to me, Daddy."

I wipe her tears away with the backs of my hands to avoid getting any of the disinfectant on my fingers in her eyes. "You're everything to me, baby doll. I never imagined how much happiness you'd bring into my life. I'm so grateful for you, Emmy."

"Daddy. Same, Daddy."

I chuckle. "Same, huh?"

She nods and I wonder if she's getting overwhelmed. Emily's so articulate; when she gets less verbal, it's a sign her emotions are swamping her linguistic cortex. But this could also be what she's like in very littlespace. I'll have to watch how it goes.

But for now, I want to give my little girl something she's wanted for a long time.

I lift her off the changing table, wrapping her around me so she straddles my hips, which puts no pressure on the piercings. Grateful I've finally recovered enough that I can carry her without strain or risk of dropping her, I walk over to the long cradle near the reading and napping corner.

It's shaped like a dingy, narrowing to a point at one end. The other end is flattened. With the prow, it would be an uncomfortable squeeze for a tall man or woman but for my tiny baby doll, it's an easy fit. I lower her into it and check on the piercings to make sure they haven't started bleeding again. Once I'm reassured, I cover her with a light blanket and slip the pacifier into her mouth. Her eyes shutter, reddened lids coming together and parting slowly.

"That's right, my baby girl. You relax and let Daddy rock you. If you feel sleepy, let yourself drift off. Daddy will wake you when it's time to go."

She nods sleepily.

I pull a stool over from the reading nook and park myself next to the cradle.

I rock her for less than five minutes before the pacifier drops out of her slack mouth. She gives a tiny, adorable snore.

Even after she's asleep, I rock her for a long time, looking down at my little wonder. Feeling the swell of impossible emotion in my chest. Her hand's clutching the blanket between her breasts. The pink diamond glinting on her ring finger reminds me that as hard as that diamond is, there's a harder, more unbreakable core of trust and faith between us. We've had to fight to get to this place. We've battled through injury and adversity and insecurity to get here. And it's been worth every scar.

seven

EMILY

KNEE TIME.

Those two words strike fear into the hearts of submissives everywhere. Well, the heart of *this* submissive. Kneeling to your Dom and baring your soul? That's daunting.

But today? Today, I'm undaunted.

I position the ladderback chair Daddy likes to sit in during Knee Time and leave a cushion on the chair's seat. I used to put it on the floor so everything was ready when Daddy came in but now I leave the pillow on the chair so Daddy can put it on the floor to invite me over. He likes the way that sets the scene better.

I take off the cute corduroy overall dress and cotton sweater with its ruffled sleeves Daddy put me in this morning, fold them, and leave them on the bed. I brush out my hair, resettle my cat ears on the top of my head, check that my white thigh highs with their cute pink ribbons around the top are even, then kneel by the door to wait for Daddy.

While I wait, I go over the things Daddy will want from me. He can ask anything but he always starts with a good thought and a worry. I have two good thoughts and one little worry. Daddy wants me to be scrupulously honest with him, so I'm not going to invent a big worry. Then I just have to weather whatever questions he's thought up. I love my Daddy but he is a demon with probing questions, as well as with his evil, knobbly paddle.

I might love that paddle a little bit. Wow, did it get me into subspace fast.

But Daddy definitely doesn't need to know that. It's evil. Even more evil than Belphegor. I'm going to have to find a suitably evil name for the knobbly paddle. Belial? Hmm.

As I'm pondering, Daddy walks through the door. His stride is even, his footsteps firm. It makes something bright and smiley blossom in my chest to hear him walking so steadily. For the longest time after his injury, he had a hitch in his step. It wasn't a big one but I registered it on some level. I was always aware that my Daddy was hurt.

He's not anymore.

He puts his phone in the speaker dock and taps up a playlist. It's not one of his spank-tracks, which is slightly disappointing but he did give me a super-spanking last night before the fucking and the diapering and the rocking.

Which was one of the more transcendent experiences of my life.

The music he puts on isn't immediately familiar but the longer I listen, the more familiar it sounds. Behind the melody I almost know, there's a pounding beat. It's classical but classical played by a house DJ.

"Daddy, what is this?" I ask.

"Myles turned me on to it. It's by a group called Pink Elephant Music. According to them, they sexy-up classical."

I didn't realize Daddy was on playlist-buddy terms with Mr. De Leon. I guess planning for the Great Baby Caper changed things between them.

"I like it."

"Me, too." He turns to me and winks. "Guess this old dog can learn a new trick or two."

I shake my head at him. Daddy's hardly old.

He strips off the white dress shirt he wore today and unbuckles his belt, coiling it on the dresser. He lets his pants slide down to hang on his hips, showing off his strong core and hip dips. I duck my head before he catches me drooling. I'll never get tired of looking at my Daddy.

He places the pillow on the floor before he sits in the chair. "Come, baby doll. Knee Time."

"Yes, Daddy."

I rise, focusing on moving gracefully, then sink to my knees beside Daddy's chair. He strokes my hair and I let myself drift into that calm, meditative place I seek during Knee Time.

After several minutes, Daddy murmurs, "One good thing, baby doll?"

"I have a good thing, and a thing I want to say about it but I don't want you to take it the wrong way. It is a *good* thing, Daddy."

"Okay," Logan says slowly. "Tell me, baby."

"The good thing was how amazing it felt for you to take complete care of me during our scene in the Nursery. Which is super-awesome, by the way. I'm blown away and can't wait for it to open and all the littles to play together. We're going to have so much fun."

I can hear the smile in Logan's voice when he says, "I'm so pleased, sweetheart. That's everything I wanted out of the Nursery."

"The thing I have to say about it is that I don't want to be diapered again. I liked doing it once. I felt very safe and comfortable. I loved the rocking and I want to do lots of that. I loved the piercing and I want to do lots of that, too. But I don't want to be diapered again."

Daddy strokes my hair in silence for a moment. "Can you tell me a little more about how you felt about the diapering and why you don't want to do it again?"

"I felt good and safe," I tell him honestly. "I liked it. I loved our scene. It was awesome."

"Then why wouldn't you want to do it again, baby?"

"Because I woke up feeling icky. The diaper was sticking to me with, um, stuff and it was super-gross. I want sex when I'm little, and I know that makes me weird—"

"No," Daddy growls. "It does not make you weird."

"Okay, different," I correct. "It makes me different. I know lots of littles don't want sex when they're little. But it's a continuum for me. Feeling loved and safe and free the way I do when I'm little, it also makes me feel hot and needy. I want to make love with my Daddy when I'm little but I don't ever want to feel gooey in the diaper again. It was icky and took me straight out of littlespace."

"Is it because of the taboo of wetness in the diaper and losing control or something else?"

I mull that over for a moment. "I don't think so. I was prepared for the diaper to be wet when I woke up. I wasn't prepared for it to be gooey and sticking to me. It was nasty."

"Do you think this is part of your worries about mess? Did you think Daddy would be disgusted when I cleaned you up?"

I shake my head before laying it on his thigh. "I didn't think about that. It was just the feeling of it. It was yuck. I would have liked you putting a towel down and rocking me instead."

"Ah, okay," Daddy says. "I can do that. What about the towel feels different than the diaper?"

I compare the sensations in my mind. One is okay. I often put a towel in the bed before we do a scene so neither of us have to sleep in a huge wet spot. Even pulling the towel up between my legs is fine in my head. Nothing icky about that. Waking up with that diaper all gooey and stuck to me was disgusting and not something I want to feel again.

"The towel's really absorbent and it doesn't stick to me. The diaper did. I didn't feel little. I actually started thinking about Maman and her having to wear a diaper now and I felt sick."

"I can see where that association would bother you, baby. I liked diapering you but you know I'm flexible. I'm happy to just put a towel under you instead."

"I liked the diaper-pin piercing, Daddy. I don't want to lose that."

"I took note of that, sweetheart. I'm very proud of you for telling me all of this. This is exactly what Knee Time is for. Do you want to tell me a worry and then we'll talk about mine?"

"Mmm-hmm. My worry is about you."

"About me? Sorry, sweetheart, I keep interrupting. Keep going. Tell me what you're worried about."

"I'm worried there's all this pressure on you. You have lots of worries, too. Much more than just one. I know I'm very little but I want you to share them with me. I know you talk to Niall some and Mac some and Max some and Warrin some—I know you have domly support—but I also worry that you censor yourself so they'll think you're okay. It's okay not to be okay, Daddy."

Logan's breath hitches. He curls over me, resting his head on mine, his hand sliding down my back. "Baby, my baby, you're so wonderful."

"Love you, Daddy."

"I love you, too, sweetheart. I haven't been okay. Finding out about Livvy flattened me. It was the worst feeling, knowing Miranda had done that. I don't think I've ever been that angry. It felt like I'd never get away from her. I'd always have this reminder of how she broke my trust and used me. I felt victimized. That's not a feeling I've ever had before, Emmy. I had no idea how much it hurt."

Daddy, my poor Daddy. I reach up and wrap my arms around his shoulders even though it's a weird stretch. Daddy realizes it in a second, straightens up, and pulls me up into his lap. I curl around him, hugging him hard.

"I've never hated anyone the way I hate her. It's a terrible emotion, hatred. I've been angry at people before. The pirates who killed my crewmate. The drunk driver who caused my parents' deaths. I've felt rage but nothing like this. I wasn't even sure I could be your Daddy while I felt so much hatred toward her. I know I pulled away from you and drank my emotions for a day. Thank you for giving me that space, sweetheart. Thank you for rescuing me that night. I needed both so much."

"I'll always rescue you, Daddy," I promise.

He rocks me, his arms so tight around me it's hard to breathe but I don't need oxygen when I'm a fierce, white baby-dragon, protecting my big Daddy-dragon against the Mir-witch.

"And on top of it was the wonder of being a father. I didn't really want that until I met you. Now I want a great, big family with you but not with *her*. She took that away from me: the amazing feeling of finding out I'm going to be a father, which I should have shared with you. Instead, she has those moments, and I hated her all the more for that. I've been ruthless in taking Livvy away from her. I know I have. I've been brutal and uncompromising. And I've been worried you would think less of me for that. But I needed an outlet for all that hatred or I was going to explode."

Oh, poor Daddy. I didn't realize he was concerned about what I'd think of the custody case. Honestly, I was just so worried he wouldn't win that I didn't think of much else.

"I understand, Daddy," I say soothingly. "I actually think you've channeled it constructively. I don't know everything about Miranda the way you do but I know you'll be a much better parent than she would be. She's a narcissist, just like my ex-husband. Narcissists aren't good for anyone, much less a little kid."

"Thank you, baby doll. I'm going to try very hard to give Livvy the father she deserves. I worry that I'll look at her and see that woman. That I won't be able to separate them in my heart. Do you think that could happen?"

I rub my cheek against his while I think it over. No, I don't think Logan is like that. I think once Livvy gets here he'll be so head-over-heels in love with her that he'll have a hard time remembering Miranda's name. Particularly since he's working through so many emotions before she even arrives. But I don't want to shut the door on any of his concerns.

"I think the further away we get from everything that's happened with Miranda and the more memories you make with Livvy, the less you'll connect them," I suggest. "But if you start feeling that way, please talk to me about it. I won't blame you, Daddy. I'll help."

He squeezes me. "I know you will, my baby. I do have a lot of worries about this situation but the thing I'm not worried about at all? Talking to you about it. You've been so supportive about everything. Thank you, sweetheart. I can't thank you enough."

I huggle him for a long time before wriggling back down to the floor and resting my head on his thigh. "Did you want to tell me a good thing?"

He chuckles. "Yes, I got sidetracked in my worries, there, didn't I? The good thing, other than you because you're my little wonder, is Mac becoming a member at Blunts. I didn't realize how alone I'd started to feel there until his membership came down to the vote. I know I've got Bull and Maude and Javier in my corner but it's not the same. I began feeling like it was me against them with all this age-play business. Having Mac in my corner makes all the difference. He's a ringer. They really have no idea what's coming for them."

I rub my cheek against his thigh. "Is age-play still really divisive, Daddy?"

I hate that it is but I've come to accept it. Some of the Masters and house submissives won't ever feel comfortable around me. As Daddy says, that's on them. I'm living my truth. If they don't like it, they can stay away from me.

"It is but I think it's more about change than age-play. I've come back to the club and made all of these changes. I got rid of Rachel and shifted the balance of power among the house-submissives. Brenna fell for Mac and resigned. She was a big favorite among the hard sadists, particularly Ten, and he's struggling to get over her. I've reinstated the

Monday play nights and organized activities and group scenes that emphasize play rather than punishment. I've demanded that age-play be accepted and created the Nursery. I've taken back the title of Master of Training. It's a lot of change in a short time and I've been feeling the backlash. But with Mac at my back, it's just the beginning."

"Wow, Daddy." I wrap my arm around his shin and hug his leg. "That is a lot when you put it all together. I'm glad you have Master Mac to support you now. I know you have to keep management committee stuff secret but you can talk to me about your worries, even if you just make it super-vague."

Daddy chuckles and strokes my head. "I don't want you to feel left out, sweetie but I also don't want you to feel resentful toward the members who have opposed me. You doing things like inviting Ten to participate in the Halloween party helps heal the rifts my insistence on change is creating. I need your support just as much as I need Mac's."

"You have it, always-always-always, Daddy."

"Thank you, my baby girl. Should we have five minutes of subbie-Zen? Then I know a little girl who needs her sit-spots revisited with Belphegor, because Daddy neglected them last night."

He really didn't. I shift on said achy spots. "Could I just have Belphegor on my boobies instead?" I ask.

Daddy chuckles. No, I didn't think so.

eight

EMILY

IF KNEE TIME was unexpectedly easy, then journaling is unexpectedly hard.

Sometimes when I journal, I just sit down and the words flow out like water from the tap. Other days, not so much. I remember reading *Tarzan* in high school. When Tarzan's teaching himself to read—as unlikely as that actually is—he thinks the words are bugs on the page. That's how I feel about words today: they're bugs on the page, scrambling around with all their little legs going every which-way and not making any sense at all.

I tap my pen against the smooth paper and write a hasty line.

The more I love my daddy, the more I can love him.

Ugh, wriggling bugs. That doesn't make sense and it's not what I'm trying to say.

I scratch through the line. I don't erase it or scratch it out so thoroughly Logan can't read it, because Daddy likes to see the evolution of my thoughts. But it's not right. Rubbing the sore spots in my side where the diaper pin punctures are healing and shifting on the very sore spots I'm sitting on, I try again.

The more I love my daddy, the more capacity I have for love.

That's closer but it's not about capacity. My chest is already much too small to contain all my adoration.

It's about depth.

The more I love my daddy, the deeper my love gets.

That's right. It's not my most elegant turn of phrase but maybe that's good. My feelings transcend words. Their expression should be raw.

I put my pen aside and pull out my sticker box. I go through my collection one by one, trying several combinations on the page before settling on a combination of hearts, a skull with a rose, a black cat, and the Batman logo.

Daddy likes puzzling out what the stickers in my journal mean. He usually figures them out. When he doesn't, I don't enlighten him. Daddy likes little mysteries.

I wiggle in my chair. My butt's so-so-so sore. Belphegor is an evil, evil, evil paddle that must be destroyed. Sable, who is lying on the table, trying to worm his way onto the journal so I pay attention to him instead of writing in it, looks up at me and purrs.

I put my face down to his and kiss between his ears. "You're awesome, boy but Daddy's a little bit awesomer. Not much. You're the most awesome kitty in the world. But Daddy's Daddy. He's hard to top."

"That's good to hear, baby doll," Daddy says, strolling into the kitchen through the open door to his office. Master Mac's a step behind him, looking extremely bleary after a scene last night that went late. He mumbles something about dinner I pretend not to hear before he stumbles upstairs.

If I'm speedy, I might have dinner prepared before he wakes up. Mwahaha.

Daddy makes tea and brings two cups over to where I'm sitting. He puts both cups down in front of him as he sits at the breakfast table across from me. He blows into one cup several times before testing it with his pinkie and passing it to me.

"Ta, Daddy."

"You're welcome, sweetheart. It looks like Mac and I are going to have to stake-out Sacrum to see if we can catch this thief."

"Really? What about all the cameras you installed?"

He seemed so sure the cameras would work. I know he even gave the club extra cameras on his own dime, because he asked me what I thought before he did it and I encouraged him if it would give everyone at Sacrum peace of mind.

"One caught an image of someone in a black hoodie. All the rest were disabled with electrician's tape. Out of my own damn bag. Joker's B didn't do any damage to them, just stood under each one and put a piece of tape over the lens, without getting caught in any of the overlapping fields of view. I swear, baby doll, it's like she watched me install them. She knew exactly where each camera was."

"Could she have watched you install them?"

"I have no idea how. I was alone in the hallways most of the time."

"Spooky, Daddy."

He nods but the frowny doesn't leave his face.

"I know you and Bren think Joker's B is harmless but I'm not comfortable with you coming on the stakeout, baby. This isn't a sexist thing, even though I know you and Brenna think I'm a caveman. I just can't take any risks with your safety. Can you understand that, sweetheart?"

I bite back my smile. Bren and I discussed our respective Dom's caveman tendencies a great deal after a business rival and two of his Neo-Nazi friends attacked her before Halloween. Brenna's a kickboxer and they got the surprise of their lives when she turned the tables on them. That wasn't enough for our Doms. Daddy and Mac and some of Mac's biker friends tracked down the bad guys and made sure they would never bother Brenna again. Daddy won't tell me what happened but Bren found out that bones were broken. *More* bones were broken.

I slip out of my chair, kneel next to Daddy's, and put my arms around his waist. "I know you'll keep me safe. I'll be sad that you're away overnight but I'll be fine. Brenna's here. And I could have a Littles' Army sleepover."

Daddy groans. "We need to talk about this Littles' Army thing, Emmy. I don't approve of militarizing your playgroup."

"*Militarizing* is a strong word, Daddy. And you said I should make friends. Sammi, Yummy, Aggie, Cynnie, and Amy are becoming really good friends. Littles' Army is just what we call our friend circle. Like a boy band, only for littles."

Logan rubs the bridge of his nose. "Baby—"

"Master Mac is having T-shirts made, Daddy. Think of how disappointed he'd be if we didn't wear them?"

"Okay but promise me no more glitter bombs. I'm still picking glitter out of places it has *no* business being."

It's hard to keep a straight face because I'm particularly proud of that prank. Daddy tried to give Max a lesson in spanking technique. Cynnie and I—very coincidentally and *purely* in celebration of National Glitter Day—had glitter packets in our back pockets.

Glitter really does get into strange places when ejected from pockets at high speed.

I unwind my arm from Daddy's waist so I can hold out my pinkie. "Promise."

He shakes my pinkie and pecks a kiss on the tip of my nose. "You can have a sleepover as long as Brenna agrees to supervise and Max can monitor you. I'm not sure what his schedule will be like after he's landed."

"Could it be someone other than Max? Sammi's still very angry at him."

"Because Max scuttled your butts on the fainting mini-goat escapade, yes, I know. Don't think the caregivers haven't been talking about that a great deal, little girl."

I have to duck my head to hide my grin. "You said you weren't angry about Harry-the-Mini-Goat, Daddy. The bad scientists were *experimenting* on him."

Daddy wraps his arm around my shoulders and gives me a squeeze. I burrow my face into the curve of his shoulder. "I'm not angry about rescuing Harry. I'm *concerned* you didn't bring the situation to me. This is the sort of thing that Daddy helps his little girl with."

"I *would* have if Max had refused to drive. We were still in the *planning* stage of the rescue, Daddy."

"I accept that, sweetheart but I want it to be very clear that if you ever get to the *execution* stage of another of the Littles' Army's crackpot schemes without involving me, there will be punishment. You could have been arrested for trespassing on private property and stealing a goat, baby. That's not okay."

"I promise it wouldn't have gotten that far without me telling you. Promise-promise."

Logan gives a long-suffering sigh. Poor Daddy.

"As long as we're clear. I know Sammi is planning some sort of revenge on Max. Jack's monitoring Sammi's messages. I'm telling you right now, baby girl, that's not a ball you want to start rolling."

I tip my head back so Logan can see my face. "I've been staying out of that. I know Sammi is angry at Max. I'm not. I understand why he told the daddies. I really was about to bring it to you once Cynnie said Max wouldn't drive. I'm not part of any revenge plan. Cross my heart."

Daddy kisses my forehead. "That's a good girl. I want you to have friends and do fun things with them."

"You just want me to be smart about our shenanigans. I understand, Daddy. I can have fun in a safe way. Promise."

He cuddles me against his side. "That's right, sweetheart. I trust you, you know I do. I just have to know you're safe. Getting arrested upstate for trespassing and goat-napping is *not* safe."

I give him a squeeze before slipping back into my own seat, because my knees are getting ouchy. There's no rug under the breakfast table the way there is under our big dinner table and kneeling on the hardwood floor is double-tough.

As soon as I'm back in my seat, I stretch my hand across the table. Daddy folds his big, warm paw around it.

"I promise to be safe, Daddy. You promise to be safe, too. No more hits to the head."

Logan nods. "That's why I'm taking Mac with me. No ops without backup. That's the new rule."

It's a good rule, given Logan's injuries over the last six months. He's recovered really well. He says he feels stronger and healthier than he did before the evil massage man broke his skull. Or after Rick-the-Dick aggravated his injury by punching him in the face. He can carry and toss me around the way he did before he was hurt, and, crazily, I think his stamina is even better than it was. But repeated head injuries are a bad idea by anyone's estimation. Max and Mac have promised me they'll never let Daddy be hurt like that again. I trust them but I'm glad to hear they're putting rules in place.

"And don't be too harsh on Joker's B if you catch her?" I ask.

"Baby, I know you think she's not malicious but she's creating chaos at Sacrum. It has to stop."

I nod. I'm not sure why I'm convinced Joker's B isn't a bad person. I just am. Her notes to Daddy, the way she only takes small things that are easily replaced, the way she never damages anything. I know it's not okay; theft is wrong. I just feel like there might be some justification for what she's doing, like our plans for liberating Harry-the-Goat. Sometimes you have to do the wrong thing for the right reasons. Even Daddy, who adheres as rigidly to rules as anyone I've ever met, agrees with that.

"Are you going tonight?" I ask.

Daddy rubs his hand over the back of his neck. "If Mac's up for it, I think so. If not tonight, tomorrow. Club's too busy over the weekend and Joker's B almost never steals anything over the weekend anyway."

"I'll wait until Master Mac wakes up before I post the sleepover in the playgroup chat."

Daddy nods. He checks his phone then puts it face down on the table. We've already had breakfast so it's not against the rules for him to check his phone but I know what he's waiting for. Max and Mr. De Leon are flying to England today. Their take-off was delayed by a fault with the plane. Max's text said it wasn't hard to repair but they needed to wait for a part to be delivered. Daddy's waiting for the text that says they've taken off.

"It will be okay, Daddy." I squeeze his fingers.

"I know, baby. I'm just . . . excited? Anxious? Impatient? Nervous? I'm feeling a lot of things. I want Livvy to be here with us. I know it's not long now. I just have that sense that things could go wrong at the last minute."

I know he's all those things. Logan has a good poker face but I've learned his tells over the last few months. The way color pinkens his cheekbones even after he's been sitting for several minutes; the way two fingers on his right hand keep tapping the table, his thigh, his teacup; they're all signs of agitation. And I know he's precariously balanced right now. That's why I put the Batman sticker in my journal. He's my Batman Daddy as much as he's my dragon-Daddy. He feels driven to protect everyone around him. I love that about him but it's also a huge weight on his shoulders that he needs help managing.

"Do you want to call the hospital again?" I ask.

He shakes his head. "Doctor Amadi has my number if anything changes. I don't want to harass her. She's been great about providing updates. She confirmed that Miranda's visitation privileges were revoked yesterday. Miranda won't have access to Livvy again before Max arrives. I just—"

"You're just worried. It's totally understandable, Daddy."

"Thank you, baby. I don't want you to worry. Max has dealt with Miranda before. He can handle her if she pulls anything at the eleventh hour."

"If you don't have to go to Jersey today, could we do something to get your mind off things until Master Mac wakes up?"

Daddy's handsome face creases into a smile. "Yes, we certainly could. Is it a good day to visit the Rexes?"

"Really?" I bounce in my seat. "Or-or-or, could we visit the big ships instead because I'm saving the Rexes to visit with Livvy?"

Daddy took me to the Intrepid Sea, Air and Space Museum on a rainy day after Halloween. I loved all the naval history but better than that was seeing Daddy's fondness for the big ships. He talked more about his time in the military while we were there than he ever has before. Having him remember those times today might be a good pressure valve for his anxiety.

"You liked those big ships, huh? We could definitely do that."

"And maybe Cappa could come with us? It's near where he's living now, isn't it?"

Daddy hums. "We're going to have a lot of people-ing once Livvy arrives, baby doll. Sure you wouldn't like a day with just the two of us?"

I nod eagerly because I always want a day just with Daddy. I feel selfish when I've kept him all to myself for too long, though. So many people love Daddy and want to spend time with him. I don't want to deprive them, or isolate Daddy from his friends. But I really do love spending time just with my Daddy.

Once we agree on the plan for the day, we move fast. I make sure Sable has food and water. Sticking pork chops in marinade only takes a few minutes. I leave a note for Mac and Bren telling them about the picnic leftovers in the fridge in case they're hungry and reassuring Mac that I have dinner covered. Then I run upstairs to let Daddy dress me and help him pack my backpack.

Now that the cooler weather's settled in, Daddy loves seeing me in tights, a short skirt, and oversized sweaters. There has to be a little pink, of course, because it's Daddy. But he's gotten into my pastel Goth aesthetic more than I ever could have hoped. Today, it's stripey black and teal tights under a black cobweb-edged mini with a hot pink crinoline and an off-the-shoulder black sweater that says "Daddy's Little Ghoul" in pink rhinestones, which Bren and I made after enduring days of Daddy's terrible Halloween jokes. The sweater has thumb holes in the sleeves so the cuffs make half-gloves, something I've *always* wanted, and corset-style lacing from my wrists to my elbows with dangly ribbon laces.

While Daddy laces up one sleeve, I sneak my black cat ears off the dresser and slide them into my curls. When Daddy looks up, I grin.

He chuckles. "That's how it's going to be today, huh, little girl?"

I nod. "It's a cat ears kind of day, Daddy."

"Then I think you need to wear something for Daddy."

Uh-oh. Wearing something for Daddy is inevitably owie.

I try it on, as Daddy would say.

"But, Daddy, everything I'm wearing is for you."

"Nice try, little girl. Go to the cupboard and get me the flat pink clamps."

Grimacing, I shuffle to the big armoire where Logan keeps all of the instruments of nipple and bottom torture. Tragically, I know where everything is by heart now. I fish out the horrible clamps, which not only bite in but close over the tip and squish my poor nips flatter than pancakes. The only good thing about them is the pretty pink enamel on the clamp's face but even that quickly pales with how sore I'll be from the nasty little teeth and squashy-squash-squash in a few hours.

Daddy fastens them on, left then right, his eyes holding mine and drinking in each flinch as the teeth pinch in and the top squashes. He plants a kiss between my breasts before he smooths my sweater back down over my breasts. I look down, hoping that the clamps will be visible under the sweater, since Daddy didn't give me a bra to wear today. He doesn't like other people to be able to see my nipples, so maybe he'll take the awful clamps off if they're too visible.

But no, any outline that might show against the cloth is covered by the "Daddy's Little Ghoul" lettering. I sigh, resigned to a day of nipple torture.

"I'll check them every hour, baby doll. Yellow if you need a check-in sooner."

"Ta, Daddy. Thank you for taking care of me even if your nasty nipple clamps are more bitey than a Rottweiler."

Logan laughs. "What are you like, little girl?"

"I'm like a baby with chewed-up nips."

"I'll make sure they're not too chewed-up in an hour. If you can keep them on through lunch, I'll make time to fuck my baby good and hard before I go to Jersey. How's that for a good deal?"

"Deal, Daddy!"

"That's better. There's my enthusiastic girl. Let's go have fun."

Despite the horrible clamps, we do.

New York's changeable fall weather cooperates, spitting rain while we're on the train but clearing to blue skies and scudding gray clouds as we walk down to Pier 86. Daddy's quiet as we clamber over the huge aircraft carrier. I make him pose with me since he looks extra rugged and Daddyish today. He hasn't shaved in a few days and his beard has come in dark and soft. Daddy's eyes are always wolfy and magnetic but never more so than when he wraps me in his arms and poses for selfies. His white teeth flash when he sneaks a hand up my sweater to tug on one of the clamps, which gets me squealing and batting at him. He captures a shot of that on his own phone and sends it to the playgroup chat, which causes my phone to light up with suggestions from the Littles' Army on how to deal with nipple-clamping daddies.

He gets more serious when we get on the submarine. He tells me about the men in his unit, including Manny and Max, and what it was like to live and work in such confined quarters. That Max is an unbeatable chess player doesn't surprise me; that Manny is good enough at Uno to play at the competitive level does.

"I didn't even know there was such a thing, Daddy," I say as I peer into one of the bunk rooms.

"Mmm-hmm. First world championship was held not too long

ago. Manny was invited to play in the qualifying rounds but he turned them down. Too busy with our business, Jen, and the kids."

"Wow."

"Don't ever get drawn into playing Manny for anything but pennies. He's phenomenal at Uno but he's also damn good with other card games. He used to clean me out regularly at blackjack and poker, too, the bastard."

I giggle, imagining Logan's chagrin losing to his business partner. Daddy's very good at games. Card games, board games, sports games, Daddy loves them. Except Hearts. There, I reign supreme.

"Does he play Hearts, Daddy?" I ask.

"I've never seen him play Hearts." Logan rubs his hand over his mouth. "You are extremely good at Hearts."

"Blunts' Hearts Crowned Champion," I say, pretending to buff my nails against my sweater but not actually doing it because I don't want my sweater to press against the nipple clamps. They are owie enough.

Logan claps his hands together. "I know what we're doing after dinner the next time Manny and Jen come over."

Grinning, happy to have diverted Daddy both from his worries about the Great Baby Caper and somber memories of his time in the Navy, I link my arm through Daddy's as we tour the rest of the sub.

nine

EMILY

MAX VIDEO-CALLS RIGHT after Daddy's gone to bed.

Daddy's stake-out of Sacrum with Master Mac was a bust. There wasn't a single sign of Joker's B all night. Daddy and Mac took turns keeping watch and neither got more than a few hours' sleep. Master Mac declared that after two sleepless nights his "tank was empty" and crashed. Daddy tried to stay awake in the hopes that Max would call but even two cups of coffee couldn't keep him from nodding off. After hearing him snore and finding him with his head back in his office chair at an angle sure to give him a very stiff neck, I woke him and he admitted defeat.

Worrying my lip with my teeth, I take Max's call. "Daddy's napping. I think I should wake him."

Max grins such a huge grin it almost reaches his ears. "Let him sleep. I'll call again before we leave. I just wanted you to meet Livvy."

He flips the camera over. Mr. De Leon scowls into the camera and then the view pans down his chest to what he's got cradled in his arms.

My first impression is of bountiful dark brown curls, touched with red highlights in the hospital's overhead lights. Then an adorable, round-cheeked face with big, cloudy gray eyes. Livvy smiles, showing an expanse of pink gums, before she stuffs her fist in her mouth and coos around it.

"Hello, Livvy," I breathe. "I'm so happy to meet you."

Max holds the phone camera on Livvy as she wriggles in Mr. De Leon's arms. She's dressed in one of the long-sleeved onesies that I sent over with Max: yellow with purple flying elephants all over it. Her chubby legs are bare and she kicks them, showing off the knitted booties that match the onesie. She has the cutest dimples on her knees. Max's hand enters the picture, his pinkie wiggling at Livvy. She coos. Max chuckles.

"She's a really happy baby, Em. The ICU nurse spent an hour with us going over her feeding and sleeping schedule and kept saying what a happy baby she is. She started smiling last week and has been grinning non-stop ever since, the nurse says."

"Probably gas," Mr. De Leon grunts.

"Ass," Max says.

"Yup, gas from her baby arse," Mr. De Leon retorts.

"Ignore him, Em. He's just sour because the nurse corrected him on how to hold the baby."

"I told you, I haven't held a baby since my niece and she's a teenager now," Mr. De Leon grumbles.

"Try not to break Daddy's baby, Mr. De Leon," I tease gently. "And thank you again for doing this."

"You're welcome," Mr. De Leon says. "Tell Logan we're still on schedule. We should touch down by eight p.m. if you want to meet the plane."

"Daddy definitely does. He'd also love to see her if you can call again, Max."

We've seen pictures of Livvy but she was asleep or drinking from a bottle in all of them. Daddy's going to purely die when he sees Livvy's smile.

"I will. Ah, here's the nurse with her bottle. I'm going to feed her and then we're going to head to the hotel to get some sleep before tomorrow's flight home. If De Leon doesn't drop my phone the way he tried to drop Livvy, I'll have him take a video to send to Logan when he wakes up."

"I didn't *drop* her, you twat. I just wasn't supporting her head right. Emily, don't listen to a word this arse says. I'm an excellent babysitter."

I chew on my lip, not sure what to say. Daddy has strong views about who should be spending time around Livvy and for all that Daddy let Mr. De Leon come to playgroup with us, I'm not sure he fits the bill.

My soft response is drowned by Max's guffaw.

"Here, trade," Max says, his voice still full of laughter. There's a spinning view of Mr. De Leon's beard and nostrils, the unicorn baby blanket I sent over with Max, and the ceiling. The view steadies on Max, now seated in a modular chair with Livvy tucked against one elbow while he holds a bottle with the other. She suckles eagerly, her pink lips working, her eyes fixed on Max's face.

"Hey baby," Max says, his deep voice gentle. "Does that taste good?"

In an unrecognizable falsetto, Mr. De Leon says, "So good, Daddy Maxie."

"Creep," Max says. "You better have that recording."

"How'd you do that again?" Mr. De Leon asks. "I'm used to handling million-dollar, prototype field equipment. I don't know what to do with all these buttons on your older model smartphone. It's con-*fus*-in'."

Max chuckles. "You're even more of a dick on five hours of sleep."

I've only seen Max and Mr. De Leon together a few times but from their banter it's clear they're good friends. Daddy banters with Master Niall the same way.

Livvy begins fussing: kicking her feet and spitting out the bottle's nipple. A woman's soft voice from out of the camera's frame says,

"Just elevate her head a bit more. She's probably getting a bit of trapped wind."

Mr. De Leon laughs. "Who broke the baby, Maxie?"

Max adjusts Livvy, who immediately begins feeding again. He curls his fingers around the bottle to give Mr. De Leon the bird.

Masculine chuckles join the chorus of the baby's sucking.

Daddy looks less exhausted after his nap but he's almost tentative when he joins me in the office where I'm writing. He brings me a cup of tea and leaves it on the edge of my standing desk. He kisses the top of my head without interrupting my dictation, and seats himself quietly behind his desk.

Definitely not a wolfy daddy entrance.

I work until I've hit my word count for the day. I don't dare the wrath of the Avengers. Then I hang up my headset and join Daddy at his desk. I kneel next to his chair and wait for him to acknowledge me. He immediately swivels his chair and holds out his arms. I climb into his lap.

His eyes are red-rimmed, which could just be the broken night's sleep. I cup his face in my hands and kiss his cheeks before snuggling in. "What's wrong?"

"Nothing's *wrong*. Other than the fact I can't seem to catch the Joker's B. That's majorly annoying. That aside, I'm just wondering how you're feeling after seeing Max's video of Livvy?"

He's worried about me? Of course he is. Because my wonderful daddy puts me first. I wrap my arms around his neck.

"I'm feeling infatuated."

"Infatuated?" Logan barks a small laugh. "That's actually a good word for it. I feel lightheaded and excited and terrified. What if I make the same mistakes Myles and Max made but there's no nurse there to correct me?"

"Master Mac and I are here and we're both really good with

babies, Daddy. I took care of my friend Gracie's baby for months when he had colic. I won't let you hold Livvy wrong."

He rubs his warm hand up and down my back. "You're turning the tables on me, aren't you, baby doll? I keep expecting you to have doubts about this. I gear up to reassure you but you're the one reassuring me."

"I've been around babies plenty, Daddy. They don't scare me."

"This terrifies me, little love."

"Promise I'll be here for you every step of the way, Daddy. You're not doing it alone. We'll make the best daddy-little babysitting team there's ever been. You'll see."

"You really don't have any worries about her coming?"

I shake my head against his shoulder. I have little worries. Do I have enough booties? Will she like the sensory toys I've gotten for her or should I have bought different ones? Will she get along with Sable or will I have to keep him out of her nursery?

But big worries? No, I don't have any of those. I'm confident in my ability to take care of a baby and I'm confident that Daddy will douse Livvy in all the love that's in his big heart.

I might have had a niggle or two wondering how Daddy would balance our dynamic with taking care of Livvy. But having seen the fearsome schedule he and Master Mac have worked out, I think it's going to be more a case of trying to snatch some baby-time back from all her enthusiastic carers than it is getting Daddy-little time.

"I really, really don't. I'm so excited to have her here. I can't wait to show her the Rexes and take her to baby swim and read to her and give her all the cuddles. But if you have worries about anything, you can tell me. I want to be the best little babysitter in the world and the best little babysitter helps her Daddy."

"Emmy." He chuckles softly and cuddles me even closer. "I just don't want to overload you."

"Promise I'll tell you if I'm feeling overloaded. Do you promise to tell me? Because I can help. Something I learned from helping Gracie with her son, if it's just you and the baby, you're outnumbered.

Always better to be two-on-one. Whenever I can help you, just tell me."

"I will, baby doll." He strokes my head and we sit in silence for several minutes while I enjoy being held by my daddy. Finally, he says quietly, "Emmy, I know you want to be the world's best little babysitter for Livvy. I'm very happy with that. I was just wondering if you might want to be more?"

"More like what?" I ask.

"I never want you to feel that you have less rights than her biological mother. Not in any way. You asked me for permission to create the book about Livvy and I was very happy to give it but I don't want you feeling like you need my permission to make decisions about Livvy's care. I trust you completely, baby doll. I know you'll always do the right thing for our daughter. I just wonder if—maybe—you might want her to be your daughter legally?"

I tip my head back until I can look into Logan's dark eyes. I've noticed he's stopped using Miranda's name. Miranda can't have anticipated how thoroughly dead to Daddy she'd become. It's her own fault but I can't help feeling a smidge of sympathy. She's lost everything: her marriage, her home, her baby. And now her name.

"Is that something we could talk about after the wedding?" I ask.

"Of course."

"If I wanted to adopt her, would it give Miranda another chance to get custody of Livvy?"

Logan shakes his head. "That's something I've had both the solicitor in England and Franco at the club look at. You adopting Livvy is a formality once we're married. Franco doesn't even think there will be a hearing."

"Okay, Daddy, I'll think about it."

"Something else I'd like you to think about, sweetheart. You don't need to give me an answer right now. I want you to start thinking about it and then we can talk about it again during Knee Time. Maybe it's because Lizbeth and I are close in age but I'd like Livvy to have close siblings, too. You said you wanted to have a couple of children. What do you think about coming off birth control next year and getting started?"

I don't even need to think about that one. Where the idea of usurping whatever last connection Miranda has to her daughter—even though I totally understand that Daddy doesn't want her to have any connection at all—makes me feel a little funny, I'm already on board with getting pregnant. So much so that I already made an appointment with my gynecologist for January.

"Yes, Daddy."

"You'll think about it?"

I shake my head. "I'll come off birth control. I've already made an appointment for January to get my implant removed."

His reddened eyes light up. "You have?"

"Yup. I know you and Master Mac are working really hard so that Livvy joining us doesn't upset our dynamic but it's inevitable that there will be adjustments. Small kids are like that; they need a lot of attention. I'm not saying I want to get it over with but—"

Daddy chuckles. "You want to get it over with. I understand, Emmy. I remember what the twins were like as babies and toddlers. It's not the easiest time."

"It's not and I don't know how long it will take me to get pregnant. We know your swimmers are up to the job but I've been trying *not* to get pregnant for nearly twenty years. My body may take a little time to get with the new program."

Logan kisses my forehead. "We're not on a schedule."

I nudge him gently. "Well, *that* would be a change."

He laughs. "You like my schedules."

I do. And I like snuggles with Daddy. I cuddle in and enjoy.

ten

LOGAN

NOTHING IS HARDER than focusing on the thief I can't seem to catch when all I want to do is watch that video of Livvy over and over.

I had no idea what a visceral reaction I'd have to seeing my daughter. The pictures I've seen made me feel warm and fuzzy inside. The video provoked a completely different reaction. Suddenly, I feel like that baby's father. I'm nervous about failing her and anxious for her safety but I can't wait to hold her and I'm so fucking proud. How did I have a hand in making that adorable little human?

But mooning over my daughter is not going to solve the situation at Sacrum, and its owners are getting desperate.

Now that we've both gotten some much-needed sleep, Mac joins me on a video call with Jaimie, Olaf, Vizzi, and two other members of Sacrum's management committee to report on the stake-out. Everyone at the other end of the call is frowning by the time we finish.

"This Joker's B had some way of knowing what you were doing,

Logan," Olaf says, chewing on the tuft of beard under his lower lip. "It had to be someone who was here that day, who saw you arrive."

"That's just the people in this room," Vizzi responds. "I cleared out the club fifteen minutes before Logan and Mac arrived."

"I hate to say this but I think the Joker's B has a way of monitoring the club," I say. "They knew exactly where I'd placed the cameras and where the blind spots were. It's entirely possible they have their own camera or cameras in the club."

This is something I've told Jaimie and Olaf before but we've been keeping it quiet to avoid panicking the larger membership. When my stakeout netted nothing, Jaimie and Olaf agreed it was time to let the management committee know.

A burly, black-bearded Dom throws up his hands. "How do we find them? Cameras today can be just a small, black dot."

"I'm working on that," I reassure them, remembering how Max found a hidden camera planted at Brenna's shop by tracing its signal. "There are some scanning tools I can use."

"How much is that going to cost?" Jaimie, who is the club's money person, asks.

"Nothing. I'll do that for free. I'm invested in resolving this. I'm not going to abandon you. I'm in this until the Joker's B is caught."

Beside me, Mac clears his throat. I know what he's thinking. I've done what I was hired to do. I've installed a much better CCTV system than they could pay for. I've secured the office. They can't afford much else. I should be calling it "job done."

But I haven't solved their problem. And that's what I do.

"Thank you, Logan," Jaimie says. "What are the next steps?"

"I haven't given up on the stakeout idea. I think that's how we catch the Joker's B. We just have to be sneakier about it. After I scan the club to make sure the Joker's B hasn't tucked cameras in every corner, we're going to set a trap. I'll need some manpower. I'd love volunteers from the management committee, since I don't believe any of you are involved."

There are nods all around the table.

"I'll round up a posse," Vizzi says, smirking. "We'll catch this filly."

"Let me guess, it's Western theme night," I say to her.

"Yippee-kay-ay, motherfucker," she responds, absolutely straight-faced.

"Okay, let's plan that for after the weekend. It's too busy at the club on weekends to try anything and the Joker's B is a weekday thief. You should have a few days reprieve now."

More nods.

"I'll remind everyone to use the lockers," Vizzi says. "We can do phone and key collections for anyone who's worried."

There's agreement, and a few more suggestions, before we say goodbye. Once I close out the call, I turn to Mac.

"What am I missing?"

He ruffles his graying crew cut. "Nothing that I can see, son. Slippery little minx."

"You agree with Bren and Emmy's theory that it's a woman?"

He shrugs. "I'm willing to entertain any theory at the moment." He cracks a huge yawn. "Particularly after I get another hour or two of sleep. Were you thinkin' of that newfangled tech Maxie used to find the bug at Bren's shop?"

I nod. "We'll have to wait until Max is back but I think that's the next step. I don't see any other way Joker's B could have known where all the cameras were."

"Uh-huh. You gonna show me this video of the baby?"

The subbie network. It's terrifying.

I key up the video on my phone and offer it to Mac. He watches it, a slow smile creeping across his face. When the video finishes, he thumbs my phone and watches it again.

"Not sure what's cuter, your little 'un or this bromance Maxie and Myles got going."

I chuckle. "I think they're good for each other, don't you? Myles challenges Max and Max softens Myles."

"They bring out the best in each other, like any good marriage."

That gets me laughing. "Don't let them hear you say that."

"Myles needs a girl," Mac observes.

"I'm not a hundred percent sure but I think he swings both ways."

"Then Myles needs a boy." Mac shrugs. "Whatever gender, he needs someone other than Maxie to fixate on. They're cute together but Maxie goes home to Cynnie when he's done having their Hardy Boys adventures. Myles goes back to an empty house. He's been alone too long. I know the signs."

I know the signs, too. But I still worry about inflicting Myles on a little, although he was extremely well behaved at playgroup. He interacted with all the littles but didn't seem to have any instant connection with any of them the way Max did with Cynnie. He played board games with them and let Brenna paint the Union Jack on his cheek, since face-painting was our activity for the day. Still, I can't help but wonder if his internal darkness would be too much for a little.

"Cappa mentioned that he and Myles spent time together after Emmy's Halloween party. From everything Cappa said, it went well. Evidently, they're going on a date when Myles gets back from England."

Mac scrubs a hand through his hair again. "That boy's awfully fragile."

I nod. "I'm concerned about that, too. He's had a rough time of it lately. I plan to keep topping him. Keep an eye on things."

"Seems wise. This phone thing of Max's work well for that?"

"It actually does. I can keep tabs on Lucy and Cappa all day without them feeling like I'm breathing down their necks." I take my phone from Mac, flip it over to Max's app, and show Mac the charts I have for Lucy and Cappa. "These are wellness graphs. The app tracks hydration, eating patterns, and hours of sleep. When they remember to wear their cuffs, which isn't as often as I'd like, it also tracks heart rate and blood pressure. It asks them questions through the day to track mood. That's this line here."

"All these are trending upward," Mac points out, tracing Cappa's sleep line with his finger.

"They're both doing better. Lucy's had a setback or two. The first time I gave her a warning. The second time, I had Karl and Rob punish her. That seemed to really help. She's been much better about self-care since then. You can see here and here she's earned small rewards and she's working toward a big one. Cappa's not responding as well to incentives. He's stable but I'm worried he's going to spiral, particularly as we get toward the holidays."

"Holidays a trigger for either of them?"

I nod. "Cappa's estranged from his family. Holidays are a tough time."

"And you've got just a little going on through the holidays. Want back up?"

"Yeah, I'll take you up on that. If things continue to go well between him and Myles, I'll let Myles have access to the app, too. He can use it to set rewards for Cappa. That might keep Cappa going in the right direction."

"You don't think Myles will want to take over? He's a man who needs control."

I tap my fingers on the phone. "I don't mind giving him some control but I'm not giving the reins to a baby Dom."

"I wouldn't use that term in his earshot, if I were you." Mac snorts.

Remembering Max's reaction to me calling him a baby Dom, I shrug. It might be mildly insulting but it's a good reminder that they're in the learning stages of being Daddies.

"I'm not afraid of gatekeeping his ass. Bravo seems to think he'll mind his Ps and Qs because he wants into our lifestyle. I'm not sure I share his confidence; Myles strikes me as a wild card."

"Agreed." Mac puts his heavy hand on my shoulder. "Watch yourself. We've all had to make hard calls. Myles has made too many. Nothing against the fella but it's scarred his soul. He's also scary smart and has way too many resources. I had a frank conversation with a guy who knows the guy he reported to in the SAS. Did you know he's the oldest son of British nobility? He's a fucking baronet, or he will be when his father dies. Old man's absolutely loaded. I'm not sure how much Myles has access to now but figure on him having the kind of money that he can throw at problems and make them disappear."

I nod. I did my own due diligence on Myles before I let him come to playgroup. I know about his family money, and that his father's been making noises since Myles left the armed services about retiring and turning the management of the family estates over to the "younger generation." Myles was listed as the keynote speaker for the family at a conference on land management and conservation of the Forest of Clitheroe last year. His father had to step in after "urgent business" called Myles away—all the way to east Africa.

Having done my own time in west Africa, I know the kind of urgent business that calls a former SAS sniper into that part of the world. It's the kind of urgent business that won me a friendly call from a deep-voiced gentleman on a D.C. number in the investigation lottery. After being told in the interests of national security to bugger off or I'd find myself audited by the Internal Revenue *and* the British tax authority every year for the rest of my life, I stopped poking around.

But I didn't need to poke any deeper, because my team has a secret weapon named Max. I didn't ask Max to investigate Myles because I didn't want to damage their friendship. I should have known better. With that weird preternatural sense Max has—probably arising from monitoring my search history and phone calls—he sent me a huge file on Myles, covering everything from where the man went to primary school to his kill count.

"He doesn't need family money to make problems disappear," I tell Mac. "He's connected in Washington. And then there's his K-count. It's a number that makes me deeply uncomfortable. What his buddies in Washington can't make disappear, he can accomplish with his own L119A2. I understand the need to handle Myles like a feral cat but there's no fucking way I'm letting him hurt Cappa. Or any other submissive."

Mac pats my shoulder. "Bravo thinks that highly of the fella, let's bring him in. More eyes on Myles the better. You shouldn't have to beard that particular lion on your own, son. You've got enough going on."

I nod. Myles will probably object to mentorship by committee but he's going to have to suck it up if he wants into our lifestyle. Our submissives are too precious to risk.

eleven

LOGAN

I STARE AT THE SQUIDGY, plastic envelope Emily puts in my hand. The yellowish liquid inside sloshes slightly.

It looks . . . rheumy. It should not be that color. Has it gone off? My stomach rolls along with the package's contents. "Milk's white," I point out.

Emily smiles tolerantly at me. "Breast milk ranges, Daddy. There's nothing wrong with it. When Gracie was pumping for Connor, her hindmilk was always yellow. She ate a bunch of roasted beets one time and her milk turned pink! A little variation in color's nothing to worry about."

I tip the package back into her hands. I completely support her decision to feed Olivia with donor breast milk. Emily's educated me about the benefits of breast milk for babies and I want Olivia to have every advantage. I'll admit I didn't think through the logistics of it. I was surprised as hell when a forty-something woman named Alice showed up with a toddler on one hip and a cooler on the other. Ridiculously, I envisioned glass bottles left on our doorstep by some erstwhile milkman driving a horse-drawn cart.

There's nothing old-fashioned about this operation. The packets Emily takes out of the cooler and loads into my beer fridge, where we can set the temperature precisely, look like they belong on the space shuttle. Emmy goes through the delivery schedule with Alice over a cup of tea while I entertain Alice's son with a tub of chunky Lego. Emily and Alice part with hugs and a promise to coordinate baby swim classes.

After we wave off Alice into the City's golden winter afternoon, I draw Emily into my arms. Stroking my finger down the bridge of her nose, I say, "Have I told you today how proud of you I am?"

Her beautiful, hazel eyes go owl-wide. "You are?"

"I am. Any idea why that might be?"

She nibbles her bottom lip. "Because I made my word count without the Avengers shouting at me?"

"Yes, I'm proud of you for that. Anything else?"

"Because I drank all my water?"

"Yes, that, too."

"Because I didn't whinge when you paddled me with Belphegor after breakfast even though your paddle is very, very evil and my thighs are super stingy?"

"Also that, although Belphegor objects to being called evil and will correct that misconception tomorrow morning with double the number of strokes. Anything else?"

That gets me an angry koala face and a little hand that steals down her backside as though trying to protect her already-red bottom from the paddle's coming bite. "I can't think of anything else, Daddy."

"I'm proud of you for being a little wonder. For making such an effort to give Olivia every advantage as she starts her life with us. For loving her already even though we haven't met her yet."

Emily's eyes gloss. "Is it bad that I love her already? Maybe it's too soon, Daddy?"

I kiss the tip of her nose. "It's not too soon. I love her already, too. It's not about biology, baby doll. It's about us getting ready to be her parents. It's about our hearts making room for her, welcoming her into our family."

Emily blinks as rapidly as she nods. "I do feel that. I feel like she's part of our family."

"I can tell. Thank you, baby. This means a huge amount to me."

Her smile breaks through. "That video of her with Max and Mr. De Leon got you in the feels, didn't it?"

"So much. So, so much. I'll warn you in advance that I might get a little emotional tonight."

Her smile widens into a grin. "It's manly to cry, Daddy."

"Hmm, I must have missed that day in Masculinity 101."

"Well, *I* think it's manly to cry. Anyone who says different is a poopy-head and you shouldn't listen to them."

"Good to know, sweetie. Good to know. I still might try to control myself in front of Manny, Max, and Myles. I think they might have missed that class as well. But just know that even if I'm quiet, I'm feeling a lot."

"We can share feels when we get home."

"That's a deal. Manny should be here in twenty minutes. Can I help pull things together to take in the car?"

"Just the baby seat. It's in the closet under the stairs on the high shelf if you could get it down. I have everything else packed. I'm going to make a bottle to take with us now that the milk's arrived but otherwise, I'm ready."

I kiss her forehead. "You really are a little wonder."

She beams and, when I release her, skips off through the great room toward the kitchen. We may not have as much Daddy-little time after tonight but I plan to make the most of it. My little wonder deserves a big reward.

I find the car seat and leave it by the door. Then I head upstairs to tell Mac and Brenna we're setting off before I stop in our bedroom to pick up the book I've been reading to Emily. We've got a drive ahead of us to the private airstrip where De Leon's landing. Manny volunteered to take us in his limo, so I'll have time to read Emmy a story or two. We recently finished Grimm's Fairy Tales. I only learned the whitewashed versions when I was a kid, so the bloodthirsty originals were a surprise. Then we moved on to Angela Carter's *Book of Fairy Tales*. They're no less bloody than the Brothers' Grimm stories but they're funnier and dirtier. I'll admit I'm more engaged by Carter's tales.

I pack the book and pull on a sweater. It'll be dark by the time we get to the air strip and the nights are cold now. I consider Emmy's side of the closet for a moment. These adorable but slightly macabre, pieces have been sneaking into her wardrobe. I noticed a new one recently: a black sweatshirt with a cartoon kitty embroidered on the front in hot pink. The kitty was missing one ear and its eyes were Xs, like they'd been buttons but the buttons fell off. Underneath, pink glitter letters spelled out: "Perfectly Imperfect."

Which is my baby doll to a T.

I find the sweatshirt, fold it over my arm, and pad downstairs to meet my perfectly imperfect little girl.

She's set a duffel bag by the door. It's bulging with baby supplies: soft blankets, spare diapers, a fresh onesie, a funny, armless sleeping bag that Emily's friend Gracie swears by. I pop the book and sweatshirt into the top of the bag and wait for my little girl. She's only a minute or two, rushing in soft-footed, dark curls bouncing, eyes bright. She's wearing what I dressed her in today: black tights, a pink plaid, pleated mini-skirt, black top with corset lacing on the bodice and sleeves. She's adorable in everything, anything but her school-girl look kills me. I've been half-hard all day. By the time we pick-up Olivia and return home, it'll be close to Emily's bedtime but she's getting such a fucking before we sleep.

I let her tuck the insulated bag with the bottles in it into the duffel before I open my arms. She throws herself into them the way she always does. I lift her onto my chest and hold her there so we're nose to nose, her feet dangling.

"Wolfy-Daddy will be making an appearance at bedtime."

Her eyes round, pupils expanding. "He will?"

"Indeed. He's going to bite all these laces off you." I shift her in my arms so I'm holding her with one arm, fumble for her hand, lift it to my face and snap my teeth at the ribbons dangling from her wrist. "And then he's going to bend you over and spank your pussy for being such a mighty temptation."

Emily shivers and stares.

"And then he's going to eat his Little Red Riding Hood all up."

"Including her bottom?"

Ah, is someone asking for a rimming? Emily's slowly getting past her fears about anal sex but remains hung up about it being messy. After talking about it with both Niall and Warrin, I got some dental dams and have been using them to rim her without the kind of extensive clean-out we did the weekend of the collaring ceremony. But she hasn't *asked* for it.

I rub my nose against hers. "Yes, including her little rose."

Another, harder shiver.

"Is this because you're proud of me?"

"It is, and because I love you and can't get enough of you."

She squirms against me. "I love you, too, Daddy."

At a ping from my phone, I lower her to the ground. I slip on my shoes, help Emily into her little boots, and hustle us out to Manny's waiting limo. We sit in the back so I can use a reading light without distracting Manny. He lowers the divider and I bump knuckles with him.

"De Leon's right on time," Manny says. "He might be *loco* but the man knows how to keep to a schedule."

I chuckle. "Everything good?"

"All good, hermano. Jen wants to come over to meet your little one this weekend."

"Yeah, we're going to do an open house on Saturday afternoon. I'll text you the time."

"Sounds good. You got everything you need?"

Emily giggles. "In duplicate."

Manny chuckles. "I know how that is. Buckle in. We'll be there in about an hour."

I put on Emily's seat belt, take out the reading materials and a juice box for Emily, and stow our bag in the footwell, before I strap in myself. Manny pulls out into the street and rolls away through the evening traffic.

De Leon's plane is as unassuming as the man himself. It's white and gray on the outside, white and blue on the inside. No pictures or logos anywhere, just black numbers on the tail to identify the plane. Knowing what Myles is worth, the plane could be furnished with mama llama leather and burled walnut without making a dent in his wallet. But he always keeps a low profile and his plane is no exception.

The stairs lower and the man himself walks down them. At the bottom of the stairs, he turns and holds his hands out.

Max comes to the plane's doorway with a car seat. He hands the car seat to Myles and disappears back into the plane's interior. Myles cradles the car seat in one arm and wiggles his forefinger at the seat's occupant. The hangar is noisy from a plane taxiing down the runway just beyond the hangar doors, so I can't hear what Myles says or how the seat's occupant responds. But I can see the tiny fist that rises out of the pile of blankets and waves around.

My chest clenches.

I put my arm around Emily and lead her forward. Myles strolls toward us, his head down so his hair curtains his face. It doesn't look like he's watching where he's going but I've never seen him misstep. If anything, I'd say Myles is hyper-aware of his environment, the way I was when I first got back from Somalia and after Jason-the-murderous-bastard hit me twice in the head with a fire extinguisher. My hair trigger has calmed down considerably in the months since then.

I'm not sure Myles' hair trigger will ever relax.

He stops at arm's length without lifting his head. I lean over the car seat and see my daughter face-to-face for the first time.

I've heard that all babies look the same. That you can't tell anything about what the adult will look like from a baby's face. But I'd have known Livvy's mine just by looking at her, without any need for the paternity test. She looks exactly like my sister Lizbeth when she was a baby, except for the eyes. I don't know if her eyes will darken to my brown or remain their current, cloudy gray but they don't detract from the resemblance.

"Hey, baby." I swallow hard to clear the thickness from my voice. "Nice to meet you."

"Can I pick her up?" Emily asks.

"Of course, baby doll. You don't need permission."

Emily smiles at me and reaches into the car seat. She deftly unclips the safety straps and lifts the baby out of the seat. Somehow she bundles the baby's blankets around Livvy's body without the blankets ending up on the ground. Emmy smiles and the baby immediately returns her smile, then sticks her fist into her mouth and gums it.

"Happy baby," Max says, joining us with two bags slung over his shoulders. Myles sets the car seat at my feet and takes one of the bags from Max.

"Thank you both so much for bringing her home," I say.

Max claps me on the shoulder. "Always glad for an excuse to visit moldy old England. I've got some not-great news, though. Miranda made a scene at the hospital yesterday, demanding to see the baby. The hospital staff were firm with her but she said she's taking a flight today and will be in New York by nighttime."

I tip my head from side to side to crack my neck. "She can do whatever she wants. I can't stop her from coming to New York."

Emily turns worried eyes up to me. "Daddy?"

I stroke her soft head before I lean over to smile at Livvy.

"Nothing to be worried about, my little love. My little *loves*. Neither of you ever have to deal with her again."

Emily straightens her shoulders and pulls her face back into a smile. I kiss her forehead so she knows I appreciate her effort. We've spent a lot of time talking about Miranda since her last visit. Emily's worked hard on overcoming the insecurities that allowed Miranda to bait and wound her. I'm very proud of my little wonder's efforts. I hope that Miranda showing up in New York won't set her back. But I meant what I said. There's nothing I can do to keep Miranda from coming to New York. But neither Emily nor Olivia ever have to deal with her again.

Miranda's my problem. And if she makes herself a problem, I'll deal with her my way.

We say our goodbyes and I spend much too long figuring out how to strap the car seat securely into Manny's limo, despite studying the damn schematics for what felt like hours before we sent the car seat off with Max and Myles. Emmy hands me Olivia and I hold my daughter in my arms for the first time. It should feel smooth and natural, right?

Instead, I'm nearly paralyzed with fear that I'm not supporting her head enough. She begins fussing, probably because I'm holding her wrong, so I tuck her into her car seat quickly and then spend five minutes trying to figure out the straps.

Emily takes pity on me. She straightens the blankets around Olivia and pops in a pacifier, then clips her in the seat with three easy movements. Grunting my chagrin, I climb in beside my baby doll and cuddle her into my side while I fasten her seat belt.

"This all comes totally naturally to you, doesn't it, little girl?"

"No, Daddy. I've taken Gracie's son lots of places in his car seat. I bought a similar model for Livvy so I'd know how to use it. I spent about an hour trying to get the seat out of the car the first time."

I chuckle. "That makes me feel better."

She curls her small hand around mine and squeezes. "No reason to feel bad, Daddy. You'll pick it up and I'm here to help with everything."

"I know you are, sweetheart. I appreciate it."

"Can I ask . . . what are you going to do about Miranda?"

"I'm going to give her no reason to stay. She's blocked from our phones. She's not allowed at the house. She has no right to see Livvy. If she wants to spend the holidays in New York, that's up to her but she's not interacting with us."

"If she hangs around the house, what do I do?"

"Report her to the police for stalking. I know a certain detective who will be happy to take your call."

Emmy tips her head onto my shoulder. "Okay, Daddy, I get it. Zero contact."

"Zero contact," I confirm. "She has no right to your time, Emmy."

"I just feel a little bad for her."

My sweet girl and her endless empathy.

"You can feel sorry for how she's fucked up her life without allowing her any access to your physical, mental, or emotional space, my baby."

"Right. You're right, Daddy."

"I know I am. I trust you to follow my rules and respect the boundaries I've set up. If you do, Miranda will have no place in our lives. But if she does anything to harass you, Emmy, I want to know about it straight away. Daddy will deal with it."

"Okay, Daddy."

"I want you free to focus on your daddy and your writing and your kitty and bonding with Livvy. You would have been free to focus on those things if I'd done a better job creating a safe space for you. I've told you I'm sorry for letting her into your safe space before and I'll say it again. I'm sorry, baby doll. I'm not making the same mistake a second time. She doesn't have any contact with you."

She nods and cuddles in. "ILY, Daddy."

"ILY too, sweetheart."

twelve

EMILY

BABY'S first night in a new place. It could be filled with screaming.

Instead, Livvy falls asleep in the car, sleeps the entire ride home, wakes up when we take her out of the car just long enough for a feed and for Brenna and Mac to coo over her, then falls asleep in Logan's arms. He manages to settle her in her crib without waking her, which shows he has parenting-superpowers already. Whenever I tried to put Gracie's son into his crib after he'd fallen asleep, he'd wake howling.

Following Gracie's sleep regime, I wake Livvy at ten. I introduce her to Sable, who sniffs her and then runs away to hide. It may take a little while for them to be best friends. I play with her, introducing two of the sensory toys I got her, then prepare the baby bath. Daddy's so good at giving me baths that I encourage him to give Livvy her bath while I get everything ready for what Gracie calls "the big bedtime" in her schedule.

When I hear him singing the Rubber Duckie song to Livvy and her magical giggle, I know I've made the right call. Daddy's uncertain about his ability to care for Livvy but the things that make him a great Dom will make him a great parent. He just needs to relax and not worry about making mistakes.

Wailing from the bathroom tells me Daddy's tried to end Livvy's bath without giving her something to divert her. I don't blame her for crying. Who wants bath time to be over?

When I enter the bathroom, Daddy's trying to wrangle a wiggling, wailing baby into a onesie while not dropping her back into the bath. I dump out the baby tub, then line it with a dry towel so Daddy can put her down. All the things I've prepared for Livvy are in baskets above the toilet, so I grab the "after bath" basket and put it beside the sink.

"Before we dress her for bed, let's give her a massage, Daddy. That always helped calm Gracie's son after his bath."

"Oh, that's a good idea," Daddy says, looking relieved. He lays Livvy on the towel and tugs off the onesie he was trying to get over her kicking legs. He managed to get a diaper on her but I bet she's still chilly. I fold up a baby blanket and lay it over her tummy. Then I tip a little baby oil onto my fingers and start at her shoulders. Daddy follows my lead, starting at her feet. The vein that was throbbing in his forehead goes down with each stroke. Livvy quiets, looking up at us and hiccupping.

"You needed some transition, didn't you, Livvy?" I ask. "It's double-tough to be made to stop something warm and fun to do something cold and not-fun. But this is nice and then we'll get you fed before night-night."

She blinks up at me with big, wet eyes and coos hesitantly.

"So many changes but you're a trooper, Livvy-bit," I croon to her. "And your very own bunny, Little Peter, is waiting for you in your crib. You're going to love cuddling up with him."

I finish with her hands. Babies hold their hands in fists but when I rub the baby oil in circles on the back of her hands, she uncurls her hands and flexes her tiny fingers.

"There you go," I say encouragingly. "That feels good, doesn't it?

Daddy, do you want to pull the onesie up her legs now and I'll pull it up the rest of the way while you put her legs in the sleeping sack?"

Daddy grunts. "I can do that."

Livvy's quiet and unresisting as we dress her in a long-sleeved onesie and the sleeveless, sleeping-bag-like contraption that Gracie swears by. I encourage Daddy to pick her up so he gets more comfortable carrying her. He scoops her up and begins singing "Scarborough Fair" to her, which makes my eyes prickle. Daddy has a lovely, deep voice. He should sing more often.

Daddy's sitting in the rocking chair in Livvy's room when I follow them in. I put the bottle warmer at his elbow for when he's ready to give her a feed, toss a pillow by his feet, and curl up on it.

"Do you want to feed her, baby doll?" Daddy asks once he's finished the song.

I shake my head and prop my chin on his knee. "Should we dial in to Storytime while you give her the big bottle?"

"Sure."

I take out my phone and join the voice channel Max set up for us. It's Daddy Jack's turn and we're a little late joining. He's already well into the story. Tonight, he's reading *The Little Mermaid.*

I smile happily and wrap my hands around Daddy's firm thigh, listening to Daddy Jack's deep voice, the baby's quiet sucking, and Daddy's slow breathing. Hearing that Miranda's coming to New York was a nasty surprise and cast a pall over the day. But sitting at Daddy's feet, in the peace of the house, filled with love for my Daddy and his daughter, everything settles.

I'm exactly where I should be.

I don't feel quite as serene the next day. Livvy's finally balked at all the changes and fusses from the moment she wakes up, although she does sleep until almost eight a.m., only waking once around two a.m. and going back to sleep after a little cry but without even needing a feed. Gracie's awesome schedule at work.

Breakfast doesn't go too badly. Everyone passes the baby around and she's quiet for a while in the rocking swing I've set up in the corner of the dining room while we eat and clean up. But by the time I've showered and dressed and take her from Daddy so he can wash up, she's in full melt-down. She spits out her pacifier every time I offer it to her. Walking her around the house doesn't help. Knowing Daddy will try to take her off my hands if he feels she's giving me trouble, I decide it's time for our first outing.

After clipping the last of the asters from the garden and making a small bouquet, I wrap Livvy up warmly, pop her in the chest carrier, and sling her baby bag on top of her stroller. One great thing about having a baby is that no one will question me about carrying around piles of stuffies. I load up with Peter Aloha Bunny, Little Peter, and a horde of Little Larrys. Then I head out into the November sunshine.

The chilly air makes Livvy sniffle and fuss, so I tuck another blanket around her and pop a soft, crocheted cap that Mistress Maude made over her dark curls as I walk the fifteen minutes to Maman's nursing home. Livvy quiets and gurgles around her fist, looking around. Even though I know she can't see very far, I can't help pointing out the community garden and my favorite café, Konk, as we pass.

When we reach the covered porch of my mother's nursing home, I pause and take a deep breath to steel myself. Maman doesn't recognize me anymore. She hasn't for some time but the move to New York from Syracuse made her worse. Something Frances keeps blaming me for, even though Maman's carers all tell me her decline is inevitable. I hope seeing Livvy will engage her, since not much else seems to. The fluffle of therapy bunnies now housed at Blunts were a big hit with the other residents when we brought them but Maman didn't even pick one up.

Straightening my shoulders, I push the stroller through the front doors and into the reception area.

My phone goes off. Daddy knows where I am but I check it anyway, stepping out of the way of the doors.

Daddy: Your heart rate is high, BD. All okay?

Instead of responding by text, I tap a video call.

Daddy picks up, looking surprised as he holds his phone up so I can see his face. He's sitting in his office. "I keep forgetting you can do that."

"Twenty-first century," I sing-song. "Are you catching the thief?"

He pulls a face. "I'm distracted."

"Everything okay?"

"Yeah, everything's fine. How about I meet you on the way back? It's a sunny day. We could have some time in the park."

Poor Daddy. He's clearly desperate to play hooky.

"We like that plan," I tell him.

"Good. Anything you need me to bring?"

I shake my head. I'm equipped for anything short of an asteroid crashing into Manhattan.

"Your heart rate's come down while we've been talking," he says. "If seeing your mum's too stressful, make it a short visit, okay?"

I nod. Visits with my mother are never anything other than stressful now. But connecting with Daddy makes everything better. "Meet you at the park in forty minutes?"

He blows me a kiss and then blows another. "See you in forty minutes, my little loves."

Smiling, I end the call and sign in at reception. They direct me to where Maman is in the orangery. There's no outdoor garden at this home the way there was at the home in Syracuse but they have a lovely greenhouse. Maman's always loved flowers.

My mother's sitting in a wheelchair between two palms. She can walk but the lesions on her brain give her vertigo, so she's prone to falling. She's always been small like me but sitting in the chair she looks birdlike. So very fragile. Not at all the woman who dominated my childhood.

I park the stroller and pull a chair near to her. She looks at me incuriously. Her eyes are like the ones I see in the mirror, except there's no spark in them.

"*Bonjour*, Violette. I'm Emily. This is Livvy. *Nous sommes venus vous rendre visite.*"

She smiles pleasantly. "*Bonjour, merci d'etre venue.*"

It's funny how the mind works. She remembers how to speak two languages but can't read either anymore and doesn't remember her own children.

I fish out the bouquet of asters I've tucked among the stuffies and offer it to my mother. She takes it and turns it around in her hands.

"What are these flowers called?" she asks in French.

"Asters. Aren't they a lovely purple? I thought you might like them because your name is Violette."

I don't mention that her favorite color has always been purple. She doesn't remember and telling her things she doesn't remember anymore just confuses and upsets her.

"They're very pretty. Thank you for bringing them."

"I thought I might read to Livvy while we're here. Would you like me to read to you, too?" I ask in French.

Her brow wrinkles but I'm not sure if it's because she doesn't want me to read or because she doesn't remember who Livvy is. After a moment, she nods.

I pull *In the Night Kitchen* out of my bag and hold it in front of me so Livvy can see the pictures. I read slowly, turning the book around so Maman can see the pictures after I finish every double-page spread, and put it away with a sad smile when I'm finished, remembering when the tables were turned and Maman was the one reading to me. Both Livvy and Maman are quiet. I can't see Livvy's face with the carrier hitched up high on my chest as I sit but from the list of her head and soft sucking on the paci, I think she's fallen asleep. Maman's looking meditatively at the flowers.

"I had a little boy," she says.

She remembers my brother, not me. I swallow hard. "His name is Frances."

Her eyes lift to mine. "Not Max?"

"No, Max is the boy in the story."

She nods but I don't see any spark of understanding in her eyes. "My little boy liked to play airplane, too."

I don't remember that. Frances is older than I am and must have been out of his airplane stage by the time I came along.

"My little boy's dead," she says.

My throat seizes. "No, Maman. Frances is alive. He has a little boy of his own. They'll come visit after Thanksgiving."

"My little boy's dead," she repeats.

I don't know what to say. In my bag, my phone pings and I know it must be Daddy, worried about my heart rate, which I can feel thudding in my temples.

She thrusts the bouquet at me. "Would you put these flowers on my little boy's grave? They won't let me leave here to visit him."

"I'll buy a big bouquet for his grave," I promise, feeling a hot prickle in my eyes. Am I doing the right thing, going along with her delusion? Or should I argue with her? I don't know what to do. "You keep those. I brought them for you."

She nods. "Thank you."

"You're welcome."

"Will you go now and buy the bouquet? I don't like to think of his grave without flowers."

"Yes, I'll go now. Don't worry, I'll take care of it," I promise, dashing wetness from my eyes with my fingertips. I stand jerkily and Livvy wakes with a wail. I try to shush her but she won't be appeased and I hurry out of the building, just stopping to sign out.

Out on the street, I take a deep breath and try to pull myself together. I knew this was coming. Her doctors in Syracuse warned me. I just didn't know . . . I didn't realize how stupid and helpless I'd feel.

I blow out a long breath and say my mantra. It centers me and helps me block out Livvy's cries for a moment. I'm no good to the baby if I'm falling apart myself. I repeat my mantra a second time, reminding myself that Daddy loves me and holds me in his hands. I'll ask Daddy what I should have said to Maman, what I should have done. If he doesn't know, he'll help me find out. I'm not alone.

My Daddy has me.

Once my breathing's normal and my head no longer feels a second away from exploding, I check my phone. The ping was from Daddy, so I send him a text to reassure him that I'm okay and am setting off for the park now. I check the time. It's twenty minutes off when Livvy can have her next feed, according to Gracie's schedule, so I open up the insulated bag I've brought and crack the heat pack to warm the bottle. Then I bounce on my toes to see if that quiets Livvy. When she settles from a wail back to fussing, I set off for the park.

Daddy's waiting for us on the street. When he sees me coming, he strides to me and wraps his arms around us both.

"What happened?"

I tell him. He kisses my eyelids and wipes his thumbs under my eyes. "We'll call her doctors when we get home but I'm sure you did the right thing, baby doll. There's no point in arguing with her. It would have agitated her and the doctors have told you that's not good for her."

I nod sadly. "It just felt like everything I could say or do was wrong."

He strokes his hand down the fall of my curls over my shoulders. "I understand, sweetheart. I'm very proud of you. It's not easy, what you're doing."

After comforting me for another moment, he wraps his arm around my shoulders and leads me down the street and into the park. There are people playing ball on the basketball courts, mostly men but seeing a woman among one group, her pigtails flying as she chases the ball down the court, makes me smile. We stop to listen to a busker singing Simon and Garfunkel. "Bridge over Troubled Waters" seems apropos for the moment and I smile up at Daddy.

"Are you relaxing, baby?" he asks, although I'm sure he can see that I am.

"Much better now. Can we find a bench and feed Livvy?"

"Sure."

We walk until we find a bench in the sun, facing a copse of trees that have lost their leaves. I unclip the chest harness and pass Livvy to Daddy, who cradles her in his arms with the same tender expression as last night. I hope he never stops looking at his daughter that way. I check the temperature of the milk on my inner wrist before passing it to Daddy. Livvy stops fussing as soon as Logan offers the bottle to her and for a moment I doubt Gracie's schedule. Maybe I should have fed her as soon as I woke her?

Trust the process, I remind myself. There's a big-time difference between London and New York. Livvy's system will be all out of whack. It's a minor miracle she slept as long as she did last night.

When Livvy starts spitting the bottle's nipple out, I put a cloth over Daddy's shoulder and show him how to burp her. His deep laugh bursts out when she rips off an amazingly froggy burp close to his ear.

I check her diaper before I put her back in the chest carrier. It's dry which probably means she's dehydrated from the plane flight. It's also warmer here than she's used to. I make a mental note to give her an extra few ounces with her feeds. That could be why she's fussy: she might just be thirsty.

Daddy encourages me to put her in the stroller after she's fed and burped so that he can push her. I dig out the many stuffies that are occupying the seat and put them in the mesh carrier bag hanging off the back of the stroller, keeping a Little Larry to carry myself.

My chest feels cold and empty without Livvy's weight on it.

I shake that thought off. Babysitter. I'm Daddy's little babysitter. If he wants to push his daughter in the stroller, he should.

She falls asleep as soon as we start walking. Daddy suggests taking a longer route home and we walk around the East Village in the bright winter sunlight. Daddy tucks me against his side and steers the stroller with one hand, which he can do because he has huge daddy hands.

I slip my arm around his waist and turn my face into his jacket collar to get a hit of his warm, spicy scent. He kisses my temple.

"Baby, I know it's easy to focus on other things to avoid facing how you're feeling about your mum. Should we have another Knee Time tonight?"

"Another Knee Time!" I exclaim. "What is this fresh hot place you speak of?"

Daddy chuckles. "It's not that bad."

It's not bad at all.

"Could we have a milk and cookies date tonight instead? I promise to tell you how I'm feeling."

"Yes, my baby. We can definitely have a milk and cookies date instead. I'm thinking, sugar cookies."

"I'm thinking oatmeal, Daddy."

"Can we compromise and have oatmeal cookies with frosting?"

"Oookay," I say, like it's a hardship. Which it's not. I'll make half the cookies with frosting for Daddy—and probably for Brenna and Mac—and the other half without. Maybe I'll double the recipe and drop off a box at Maman's home tomorrow. That would be a good reason for a walk with Livvy. The home prefers visits on visiting days, three times a week but they don't mind deliveries any day.

"That's a date then, little girl. Our kitchen. Nine p.m. In your jammies."

"Yes, Daddy." I nuzzle into his jacket and enjoy walking under my Daddy's arm.

thirteen

LOGAN

I LOOK around the great room with satisfaction. My family, close and extended, all in one place. Under my roof. Mac, Brenna, Max, Cynnie, Austin, Dana, Hunter, Myles, and a surprisingly fresh-faced and smiley Cappa are clustered around the baby in Mac's arms. Maude and Javier are in the kitchen with Manny, Jen, and Emmy. Everyone's safe and accounted for.

I put my feet up on the long sectional, sip my beer, and watch the game out of the corner of my eye while keeping Livvy in view.

Manny plonks down on the couch next to me. "You cooked up a good one, Daddy Logan."

"She's cute, isn't she?"

"Sure. They're all little red aliens until they're about six months. Then they become interesting."

I punch his shoulder without any force. "Wait until I tell Jen that."

He grins and takes a pull on his beer. "She's pregnant again. Just finishing her first trimester."

"Congratulations!" I slap him on the back. "A boy this time?"

Manny shrugs. "I've stopped caring. 'Long as they're healthy, I'm happy."

Good attitude. I nod.

"Maxie mentioned something about Miranda coming to New York," Manny says, his tone cautious.

"I haven't heard anything from her but I've blocked her on every electronic avenue, so she'd have to knock on the door to contact me." I look around for wood and rap my knuckles on the coffee table. "Touch wood, she'll give up and accept defeat before it comes to that."

Manny grunts. "You ready to get a restraining order if she don't?"

My jaw knots. "I'm ready to do whatever it takes. She's not welcome in this house."

Myles sits down on the L of the couch, his profile to us. He snaps his fingers and after a moment, Cappa folds himself down on the floor between Myles' feet. Myles rests his hand in Cappa's glossy, black hair.

Manny eyes this display but doesn't comment. "You comin' to Mass with us?" he asks.

Myles shakes his head. "I'm out of town. Logan, do you want me to review your physical security before I go?"

"You met Miranda in England?" At his nod, I ask, "Do you think it's necessary?"

"I think she's determined," he responds. "Happy to do it before I go."

"Yeah, if it's no bother."

"It's no bother." He clears his throat. "I was hoping to come to the group again but I'll be traveling. You'll give my regrets to Ginger and the others?"

"I will." I put away whatever concerns I have about Myles being around littles. "We'll miss you."

He nods but doesn't lift his eyes beyond Cappa's head. "You'll keep an eye on this boy while I'm gone? Make sure he stays out of trouble?"

Cappa huffs. "I'm never *in* trouble."

I snort. "I will. Cappa, there's an outing after playgroup—"

"Emily already invited me. Fleur's coming, too."

My baby doll. Her efficiency is terrifying. "Great. We'll check your schedule and make any adjustments then. Myles, do you know when you'll be back?"

He shakes his head. "It takes as long as it takes."

I know those kinds of missions. "No worries."

"Thank you." He's quiet for a moment, then says, "I want you to try what we talked about for a week."

Cappa turns crimson. He draws his knees to his chest. "Four days."

"Five. If I'm not back by then, I'll text to release you."

Abstinence? Orgasm denial? Cock cage? I'm betting it's one of those. Blood rushes to my groin at the thought. Emily hates orgasm denial but it's a big turn-on for me. If Cappa's going to be suffering this week, maybe my baby girl needs to suffer alongside him for a day or two.

"Five and I'm done at midnight no matter what."

"Agreed," Myles says. In the shadow of his hair, his smile flashes. "Logan, I'll text you the extra rules Cappa's agreed to."

I give Cappa a slow, evil grin. "I'll be rigorous in enforcing them while you're gone."

Cappa groans.

After dinner, and yet another Hearts Battle Royale, which Emily wins, people filter away, leaving Mac and me watching a match while Emily and Brenna lay on cushions at our feet. Bren's got her tablet and digital pen and is working on a sketch. Emmy's reading something on her phone while she rocks Livvy's bassinet. I don't quite understand the schedule Emily's following but her friend Gracie swears that it'll have Livvy sleeping through the night from seven to seven. Livvy's down for the "little sleep" now. We'll wake her at ten for a feed, a play, and a bath before her "big sleep." Emily's told me to block off an hour around ten p.m. every night for the next few weeks until Livvy settles into the seven-to-seven routine.

Since I was utterly gobsmacked at how well Livvy slept last night after hearing horror stories about newborns waking every hour, I'm not arguing.

The doorbell rings and I tap my phone to bring up the door camera. A heaviness settles in my gut when I see the face I least want to see.

I lift my eyes from the phone screen to meet Emily's hazel eyes. "Miranda's at the door. You do not need to talk with her, interact with her, or even look at her."

She frowns briefly but her face smooths. Her lips move and I can see her subvocalizing her mantra before she says, "Yes, Daddy."

Bren sets her tablet aside and rolls to her feet. She pulls on Mac's shirt that's been lying over the end of the couch. "I have something to say to the Mir-bitch."

While I can only see the possibility of violence in Brenna confronting Miranda, I nod.

I climb off the couch, look down into my daughter's peaceful face, and drop a kiss on the top of Emily's head before I go to the door.

Brenna follows me. With her blue dreadlocks up in a wild topknot, she looks like Medusa but her attitude is one hundred percent Valkyrie. I'm a little surprised she hasn't slung a flaming sword over her shoulder.

I close the door into the great room behind Brenna. If Emily wants to come out into the hallway, she can but Miranda's not getting a view into my home, with my two girls nestled in its heart.

I open the front door but neither invite Miranda in nor make way for her to enter. I block the doorway with my body and put my foot behind the door so she can't push it open.

"Miranda," I say without any welcome.

Her eyes flick from me to Brenna, standing just off my shoulder, and back to my face. She looks bad. Her face is puffy but there are hollows under her eyes and cheekbones deep and dark enough to be bruises. She's wearing a wool coat with the collar turned up around her throat, unbuttoned over a cranberry-colored knit sweater and dark trousers that hang on her; they might have been maternity wear. Her breasts and belly are visibly swollen under her clothes but her fingers and wrist, as she brushes a hank of hair back from her face, look thin.

"Logan, may I see Olivia?" she asks.

"No."

She waits, like I'm going to elaborate. I'm not. When she realizes I'm not going to say anything she can turn back against me, she presses her lips together. "I'm still nursing her."

"No, you *were* nursing her. You're not anymore."

Tears well in her big, blue eyes. "Please, Lo. She needs her mother's milk. And I'm in agony without her. I've been pumping while I've traveled but it's not the same. Please, I need my daughter."

Knowing I'm going to sound like a monster not just to the woman in front of me but also to the one standing behind me and the one in the other room who I'm sure is just on the other side of the door, listening to every word, I say, "No."

Miranda crosses her shaking hands over her breasts and rubs gently. "Please. Please, Lo. If you ever cared about me, please let me see my baby."

Jesus Christ. "No."

"Um," Brenna says behind me. "Not to get into the middle of this but if you're pumping, we could put the milk into Livvy's rotation. Did you keep it cold?"

Miranda nods. "I have a cooler in my hotel room. I'll bring it."

"No, you won't. I'll come get it." Mac's voice sounds from behind me. Fuck, he's a ghost when he wants to be. I never heard either of the doors to the hallway open. "There's no reason for you to step foot in this house again."

Miranda shrinks back. "Mac."

They've met a few times over the years. Mac was never Mir's biggest fan but he wasn't openly disdainful. He is now.

He moves up to stand behind Brenna, looping his arm around her chest. "Since what Logan's saying doesn't seem to be sinking in, I'll repeat it," he tells Miranda. "You're not welcome here. This is our home. Logan's. Mine. Emily's. Brenna's. Olivia's. You don't belong here. Am I understood?"

Miranda flinches. "Mac—"

"Am I *clearly* understood?" Mac repeats.

"Yes," Miranda says. "Please, Mac, I just want to see Olivia."

"Logan already told you no. I'll come back to your hotel with you and pick up the milk." Mac pulls his jacket off the rack next to the door and shrugs into it.

Tears roll down Miranda's face. She blots them genteelly with the backs of her hands.

Mac steps past me and steers Miranda around with a hand on her shoulder.

"Hey," Brenna says. "I don't want to kick someone when they're down but I want you to know something, Miranda."

Miranda and Mac pause on the top step. Miranda looks back over her shoulder, her eyes and nose red.

"You ever come near Emily again, and I'll kick your ass. I'm not threatening you. I'm just telling you how it's going to be."

Miranda's face works but she doesn't reply before Mac drops his hand to her elbow and ushers her down the steps.

I close the door and rest my forehead against it.

Brenna's hand lands light and quick on my shoulder. "Good job, Daddy Lo."

I roll my head until my neck pops, releasing some of my tension. "I hoped she'd stay away."

"Maybe she will now. Maybe she won't. What matters is that you're a brick wall. You don't react. You don't lash out at her. You just block her from any aspect of your life, or Emmy's life, or Olivia's life. You stand. No matter what she throws at you." Brenna sighs. "I know

118

that sounds melodramatic. You'll be surprised at what crazy people come up with and Miranda is certifiably crazy. But all you have to do is stand tall and let her break herself throwing herself at the brick wall."

"You've seen this before?" I ask, turning to look at her, because she's speaking with the ring of experience.

"Oh, yeah," she says. "Guess I never told you how I got the scars on my back? I went into foster care when I was a kid. Bounced around a couple of homes. I'll admit, I wasn't an easy kid. I had some serious fucking anger issues. One of the group homes was run by a lady called Mother Kay. Other than Emmy, she's the best person I've ever met. She got me under control really fast. But after I'd been with her for a couple of months, my social worker took me out of the group home and placed me with a couple who said they were looking to adopt. The lady of the house was a ticking time-bomb. Crazier than Miranda." She shivers and wraps her arms around herself. "She caught me sneaking out. She had this clothesline she'd knotted up. She beat me with it until I passed out. She tried to hide what she'd done, telling my social worker I was sick. The social worker yanked me out of there and put me back with Mother Kay. Mother Kay never let me be moved again. My social worker tried a dozen times to put me in single foster placements. Mother Kay was my brick wall."

I push myself away from the door and hold my arms out. "I know you don't need a hug but I do."

She smiles wryly before letting me pull her close. "Having Mother Kay be my brick wall made it okay. Having you be their brick wall will make this okay for Emmy and Livvy. Just stand firm, Daddy Lo."

I pat her back before letting her go. "I'll do my best. If you see any chinks in my wall, tell me so I can break out the mortar and trowel."

"I will. I meant what I said about kicking her ass. Just so you know. Emmy's gotten over what happened the last time Miranda was here, I think but the Mir-bitch doesn't get another shot at her. Not while I'm here."

"I'm not arguing with you. If you catch her sniffing around Emily, kick her ass."

Brenna chuckles. "You got it."

Emmy's not waiting right on the other side of the door, as I'd anticipated. She's all the way across the great room, standing by the back doors, looking out into the night. Livvy's bassinette is at her feet. Emmy's got her cat in her arms and has her face pressed to the top of Sable's head, kissing him between his ears. Sable's pretty cuddly but he's not crazy about being picked up and held off the ground, so I'd expect him to be squirming. He's not. He's curled against Emily and purring like a motorboat.

I walk up behind her and wrap my arms around her. I rest my chin on the top of her head. "She doesn't come in the house. You don't have to talk to her. You don't have to look at her. You don't even have to think about her."

"It's hard not to think about her a little, Daddy," Emmy says, her words muffled in kitty fur.

I kiss the top of her head. "Tell me what you're thinking."

She sighs. "I've promised to always tell you the truth. But this isn't a truth you're going to want to hear." She heaves a deeper sigh. "I think we're being cruel, not letting her nurse her baby."

I let her words sink into me. Roll around in my heart. I always take my baby doll's feelings into account.

But I don't always let them rule my decisions. Sometimes, I have to make the hard call. That's what being a Daddy is.

"I understand why you would feel that way, my little wonder. I value your feelings and I appreciate you telling me. I always want you to tell me the truth."

"You're not going to let her nurse Livvy, are you?" Emily shifts in my arms so she can look up into my face.

"No, sweetheart. I'm not."

She nods and sinks back against me. Although the thought of

being cruel to Miranda is probably bothering her a little, she's also much more relaxed than she was when I first hugged her. Keeping Miranda away is the right call, even if it seems cruel.

Mac returns in record time. He probably ran back. Emily puts Sable down and moves to help Mac label and store the packets of milk. They have a system I don't pretend to understand. I just know to use the packets at the front of my beer fridge first.

When she's finished, she comes back to me with her arms wrapped around herself. I know my baby doll. That's *please hold me, Daddy*.

So I do. I wrap her in my arms and carry her over to the couch. I keep her on my lap, cuddled up against me, while I watch the end of the match. Then I take her upstairs and give her a bath. Livvy wakes while Emmy's playing with the bath crayons, so I bring Livvy into our bath. She probably doesn't get very clean but we don't either. Bath time is about play. It's about relaxing and being together, slippery skin to slippery skin. It's about Daddy showing his girls how much he loves them.

Livvy's fussing, yawning, and rubbing her eyes by the time we get her ready for her last feed and the "big sleep." Emily rocks her in the rocking chair for barely five minutes before she's out, her rosebud mouth open, lower lip puffing in and out with each breath.

I watch Emily as she rises from the rocking chair and carries the baby over to the crib. Emily's face is shining with tenderness, her eyes misty as she goes up on her tiptoes to lay Livvy down. If I ever needed proof that motherhood isn't only biological, it's right in front of me. Emily's already fallen for my daughter.

I hold out my hand and when Emily comes to me, I check her over carefully in the nursery's dim light. There are faint purple shadows under her eyes and she's working her engagement ring on her finger, which is one of Emmy's tells. She's tired. It's been a long day. This is not a night for a milk and cookies date.

"Bedtime," I tell her.

She gives me big eyes. "It's only a little after ten."

"And my little is tired."

"I'm not *that* tired—" A yawn interrupts her protest.

"I'm not negotiating with you, baby. But I am in an indulgent mood. If you agree to go to sleep whenever we're finished, I can see a good girl spanking while we listen to Storytime in your future."

"And Wolfy Daddy after," she says, immediately bargaining, the way she does, my imp.

"We'll see if you stay awake," I agree. "Also, De Leon's asking something from Cappa this week while he's gone. I'm not sure if it's abstinence or orgasm denial or what yet but I think a day or two of edging and orgasm denial would help keep your mind off both your mother and Miranda."

Her sweet face screws up ferociously. "Yuck."

"That's not a no."

"It's a yuck. I hate orgasm denial."

"I know you do, my baby. Think hard about why Daddy would ask you to do something you hate at a stressful time."

The face she makes is hilarious, adorable, and not at all contemplative. "Because Daddy likes yucky things."

"Yes, that's definitely the reason."

"There are other ways to distract me," she points out. "Lots of other ways. Like visiting the Rexes. Or the evil nubbly paddle. Or tying me up in a new way. Or drilling my teeth. All of those are substantially better than No O for a week."

I chuckle. "I didn't say a week. Can we agree to two days?"

"How about one?"

"How about two and a session with the new paddle at the end?"

"Thirty-six hours."

"Forty-eight."

Emily sighs and hangs her head. "Oookay."

I kiss the top of those cute, droopy dark curls. "That's my girl. I'll give you a day's warning before you become a No O Zone, so you can stock up."

She giggles softly. "I want a dozen in the No O prep day."

"Mmm, we'll see if you earn them. Come on, my sweet baby. Let's get you ready for bed and your spanking."

She takes my hand and tucks herself into my side as I lead her down the hall to our bedroom.

Bravo has Storytime tonight and he's reading from Shel Silverstein's poems when we join, which Emmy loves. She recites them while I brush her hair and dress her in a soft cotton nightgown. I think this one is vintage. There are tiny pleats all across her chest and pink ribbons threaded around the neckline, sleeves, and hem. When she's dressed, I stand her at the edge of the bed and kneel in front of her.

"Daddy?" She looks down at me wonderingly.

I cup her ankles. "This is my baby," I say softly. "My darling girl." I run my hands up her calves and tickle behind her knees until she giggles. "My sweetheart." I continue up the backs of her thighs, squeezing gently. "The woman I adore." I cup her round bottom, bare under the nightgown. "My little wife."

"Daddy," she breathes. "I love you too."

"Every day, you delight me, Emmy. Every day, I love you more. You make even the hardest times easy."

"Daddy." A tear slips down her cheek. I push up to lick it away.

"You're allowed to have rough days, baby girl. You're allowed to be sad. You're allowed to struggle with your feelings. But you're not allowed to ever, for one minute, forget how much Daddy adores you."

"I don't," she promises, her hands fluttering to my shoulders. "I won't."

"Good girl." I draw her forward with my hands cupping her sweet, soft cheeks, and lift her as I stand, smiling at my ability to carry her again. I climb up on the bed and lie down on my back with Emily plastered to my front. She wraps her arms around my neck and rubs her cheek against my collar, settling onto me with a happy sigh. I usually like to see my target, and the effects of my spanking but tonight I want to feel my baby doll over every inch of me.

I ruck up her nightdress, tugging the fabric so the ruffle tickles the backs of her legs. To her magical giggle, I bare her bottom and rub my palms over her warm skin.

"How's this little bottom?" I ask. When I dressed her this morning, she had a few fading bruises that I treated with arnica cream but sustained impact play like we engage in can leave deeper bruising, so I always check.

"Happy to have your hands on it," she purrs, nuzzling and cuddling.

"Really? Did your bottom tell you that?"

"It did," she says. I can hear the huge grin in her voice. "Do you know what else my bottom tells me?"

"Bottom-wisdom? I have to hear this."

"My bottom tells me it would like wolfy loving even though we're sharing all the feels tonight."

A laugh ripples up through me. My adorable little love. "I see. Bottom dictates, hmm?"

"Yep."

"Well, let me see what I can do about that," I say, before I give my baby girl everything she's asked for.

fourteen

EMILY

I TAKE a deep breath in and let it out slowly. "Ten!" I shout.

I pull off the blindfold—a makeshift one instead of the pink satin one Daddy uses when we play—and look around the circle in the corn field. A cold breeze rustles across the tassels of the towering corn surrounding me. I'm glad Daddy bundled me up in a knee-length coat, wooly scarf, beret, and mittens for our outing.

A giggle drifts through the corn stalks from my left. There are three entrances to the corn maze from where I'm standing. Daddy showed me an aerial picture of the maze before we set off this morning so I wouldn't feel lost. There are lots of twists and turns in the maze, which make a cool sunflower and bee pattern from the air but all paths lead to a single exit on the far side of the maze with no dead ends, so as long as I keep walking forward, I can always get out.

Sneakily, tip-toeing in my soft boots, I creep toward the entrance to my left. Another giggle and a voice that's clearly Sammi's saying "shhh."

I love my little friends but they're not very good at hiding.

I run down the path and turn a sharp right with the maze. Practically on the other side of the corner, Yummy and Sammi are standing a foot back in the corn with their arms around each other. Yummy's batting at a fat, sleepy bumblebee circling the horns of her green dragon onesie.

"Tag," I say.

Sammi pushes Yummy, not very hard, and she steps out of the corn.

"I told you she could hear you," Sammi says. "You're it."

"You're both it," I tell them, taking Yummy's hand. She swings mine as we skip through the maze, finding littles around practically every corner.

Not very good at hiding.

When we've found all eighteen littles and submissives who came with us to this farm in Yorktown Heights, we troop to the exit to find our caregivers. Daddy's standing with Max near a long, trestle table where a lot of the caregivers are sitting, eating cheese and apples that the farm sells and drinking the homemade cider. Livvy's strapped to Daddy's chest in her carrier, kicking her bootied feet and gumming Daddy's little finger.

As soon as we emerge from among the corn rows, Faolan, the new daddy that Master Javier introduced, comes toward us. I'm holding his copper-haired little's hand. Matty's a geoarcheologist and the discoverer of a huge horde of Nazi gold, which is the coolest thing I've ever heard. She also came to playgroup wearing kitty ears and a huge, floppy, blue bow, which made us twinsies. She's only just back from a trip to Russia; she's looking for her father who disappeared while looking for the Nazi loot she found. She missed Halloween, so we're planning a costume party for her birthday in December. I've been telling her about Laurel and being dragon friends.

"We're going to be a flight!" Matty announces, rushing to her daddy and hugging him. He's a tall, rawboned man with thick, wavy brown hair and a full beard dusted with gray. He reminds me of a hungry bear except that his eyes are pale, pale blue and they follow Matty wherever she goes.

"A flight? Like a tasting flight?" He catches her up against his barrel chest and twirls her around. Matty's corkscrew curls catch the sunlight in a blaze of red as she spins. "Beer? Vodka? Either sounds good to me."

"Like a flight of *dragons*," Matty says.

Faolan lets Matty drop to her own feet and stoops to rub his nose against hers. "Dragons, you say?"

She nods. "I'm an amethyst dragon."

"You're my little amethyst, that's for sure," Faolan says, kissing her cheek. Matty beams.

Daddy waves me over and tucks me under his arm. I take the opportunity to wriggle out of my coat, since skipping through the maze made me roasty-toasty. Once I'm coatless, Daddy offers me a cup of cider, which I drink down too fast because my throat is dry.

And then I get hiccups.

Livvy goggles at the noise, then grins around Logan's finger. I tickle her bootied tootsies. "Are my hiccups funny, Livvy-bit?"

"Could just be gas," Max observes.

I shake my head at him. "Babies aren't really that gassy, if they're being burped properly after they feed."

Max shifts his eyes right and left. "Yeah. We had some issues with that."

"Stop trying to break Daddy's baby, Max," I tell him.

He chuckles, then he grunts and bends at the waist. A pair of furry black arms come around his neck and Cynnie's face, surrounded by the bobbing antennae and black fuzz of her bumblebee hoodie, pops over his shoulder. Max straightens, looping his arms around his little's calves, and bounces her once to get her into a good position on his back.

"Hi, Oppa." She cranes her head around his to smack a kiss on his cheek.

"Hey, bumble baby. Did you win hide and seek?"

"I was the third from last to be found, so almost," she responds.

"You had an unfair advantage," I say. "That outfit blends too well."

Cynnie holds out one arm, examining her yellow-and-black-striped hoodie. "Corn is green."

She has a point but I'm not going to concede it. "But you're a bee and there are a lot of bees in the corn."

Okay, there was one bee in the corn that I saw but still.

"Sure," Cynnie says, evidently too high on hide and seek, apple-picking, and cider to argue. "Matty's birthday is next month, Oppa. We're going to be a flight of dragons for her party. I'm going to be a queen bee dragon."

"Uh, is that a thing?" Max asks.

"It is now. We need at least fifty sleepovers at Emmy and Logan's to make costumes."

Max laughs. "I know what you're angling for. You can play with the baby any time."

"Now?"

"Sure." Max squats to set her down. Cynnie wriggles off his back and approaches Logan, who slowly unstraps Livvy and passes her to Cynnie.

As soon as people see that Cynnie's holding the baby, a cluster of littles and caregivers gather around. Daddy sighs, not very loudly but I feel it and look up at him.

"All okay, Daddy?"

He nods. "I liked having her on my chest."

I know that feeling. I band my arms around his chest and squeeze. "It's just the novelty, Daddy. It'll wear off and then people won't be as eager to hold her. We'll have lots of time with her."

He tips his head down and brushes a kiss across the tip of my nose. "You're right, sweetheart. Are you okay with your friends descending for sleepovers?"

I nod. "As long as it doesn't mess up your schedule."

"I'll work a few in. I know you want to be the best little babysitter ever to Livvy but I don't want caring for her to crimp your social life."

I wriggle around until I can stand in the circle of his arms and look up at him. "Do you remember when we met?"

"Of course, baby doll. It wasn't that long ago and Daddy didn't lose that many brain cells to being whacked over the head."

I reach up, run my fingertips tenderly over the scar on his forehead, and swallow against the lump that swells in my throat. "In less than six months, you've changed everything for me. I had friends in Syracuse. Good friends. But nothing like now. Gracie tried to understand my littleness but I didn't feel safe enough to tell any of my other friends about it. I was always hiding. Now I can live my truth every day. I can have blanket-fort sleepovers. I can have dragon-costume-making parties. I *have* a real social life because of you. A social life where I can finally be myself."

Logan blinks rapidly, then scoops me up against his chest and kisses me breathless.

When Daddy finally lets me breathe, I turn my head to check on Livvy. She's made her way around the group to Max, who is blowing raspberries on her knuckles to elicit her gummy grin.

"I think Max will make a good daddy to more than Cynnie," I whisper to my daddy.

Logan nods. "I should have realized it when he took that kid who lives in his building under his wing. Maxie's a natural."

I squeeze him tightly. "You're a natural, too. Listening to you sing to Livvy when you were giving her a bath made me tear up."

Logan grins. "Was my voice really that bad?"

I squeeze him harder. "You know that's not why."

"I used to sing to Lizbeth when she had nightmares. I'd forgotten all about that until I was bathing Livvy." His Adam's apple works as he swallows hard. "It brought back some memories. Good and bad."

I know Daddy still feels conflicted about the feelings he had for his sister when he was an adolescent. I'm fine with them. They were the feelings that led him to being an amazing Dom. He focused on his sister because she was naturally submissive to her big brother but he hasn't carried the sexual feelings he had for her over into adulthood. Only the shame, poor Daddy.

Having talked about adolescent kink experiences with other Doms and littles in playgroup, I'm glad it was his sister. He loved her so much he never would have hurt her, no matter how strong his feelings became. If anything, having those feelings taught Logan how to control his worst impulses and to compartmentalize. A lot of other people weren't as lucky and their initial DD/lg experiences were bad enough to give *me* nightmares.

"When we're alone, if you'd like to tell me about those memories, I'd like to listen," I offer.

"Thank you, sweetie. I will."

A whimper from Livvy has Max trotting her back to Daddy double-time, which makes me giggle. Everyone wants to hold the baby until she starts crying. I check the time. It's thirty minutes until her scheduled feed but she's probably thirsty.

After she's had half of the bottle, I sit and rock her car seat on the table. She dozes while I talk with Aggie, Matty, Yummy, Amy, and a very excited Sammi, who has lots of questions about the gold Matty found. Mostly about where it is now and whether she got to keep any of it. He looks utterly crestfallen when Matty tells him it all got turned over to the British and Norwegian governments with the finder's fee going to the company who financed her dig.

"You didn't even keep one piece?" Sammi moans.

"They're historical artifacts, Sammi," Matty explains. "They need to be studied and taken care of in museums."

"One leeetle piece?" Sammi asks.

Matty shakes her head, grinning.

Faolan puts his hands on Matty's shoulders and kisses the top of her curly head. "She got to keep the clue her father left, which is the most important thing, isn't it, imp?"

Matty tips her head back and smiles at her daddy. "Well, the box of gold bars would have been nice."

Sammi's jaw nearly hits the picnic table. "The *box* of gold bars?"

Matty nods. "Uh-huh. Big box."

"The *big* box of gold bars," Sammi whimpers.

"Tell us more about the Ark," I say.

"The Ark." Sammi's eyes go round. "The Ark of the Covenant?"

Matty laughs. "It wasn't the Ark. It was a gold altar. Well, a gold-*plated* altar. The Nazi scientists and occultists who used Miller's Island were conducting some very strange pseudo-scientific rituals designed to create an ultimate weapon. Fortunately, they were *not* successful."

"Just like Indiana Jones," Sammi breathes.

"Nothing like Indiana Jones," Matty responds, grinning.

Faolan squeezes her shoulders. "Except your pup stuffie named Indy."

Matty swats him. "Daddy. You *gave* me Indy. And you named him."

"Did I? Oh, right, I did."

The daddies and mommies chuckle. Daddy humor. I trade sneaky eye rolls with Aggie.

Daddy leans over and whispers in my ear. "Saw that, little girl. You're busted."

I grind my teeth. I literally can't get away with a single thing with Daddy around. "I claim an exemption."

Daddy crouches by the picnic table, his eyebrows up. "An exemption?"

"I can't be in trouble for reacting to bad dad jokes told by other daddies. I only get in trouble for eye-rolls to your bad jokes."

"I don't make bad jokes and I don't think that's the rule."

"It's an *exemption* to the rule."

"That would be an *exception* to the rule and I didn't agree to it beforehand, so you're still busted. I'll discuss your chastisement with Warrin."

Because Warrin has daddy-hearing, too, he pops up behind Aggie. "Did someone say punishment?"

"Not us!" Aggie and I chorus.

"Do we have two little girls who have strayed off the path of righteousness?" Warrin asks Daddy.

"We do," Daddy says. "Gross disrespect for fine, daddy humor."

Warrin chuckles. "I'm aware this is a fault my little girl suffers from. Egregious. What example can we make of these miscreants?"

Daddy rubs his chin. Oh, no, I know that evil glint. "I decree a round robin of knock-knock jokes from all the mommies and daddies. Failure to laugh appropriately to any joke results in one minute of tickling."

"Nooo!" Aggie and I squeal.

"This is an excellent idea," Matty's daddy says as he rubs her shoulders. Great, another sadist. "I'll begin. Knock-knock?"

"Who's there?" The littles around the table groan together.

"Major," Faolan says.

"Major who?" We chorus.

"Made-jer day with this joke, didn't I?"

I can't even muster a chuckle that one's so bad, although I control an eye-roll. Only Sammi manages a half-hearted laugh.

Warrin and Daddy each hold up a finger. Bravo joins them.

Aggie, Yummy, and I groan.

fifteen

EMILY

"WHY DOES she keep staring at me?" Cappa asks me.

I glance over at Livvy, who is sitting in a rocking seat on the counter as Cappa and I cook. She's well back from the potential splash-zone in the semi-reclined seat, probably two feet from Cappa. She is staring at him with those cloudy-blue eyes very fixedly.

"You're just so handsome she can't take her eyes off you," I tease.

That's probably not the reason. He's standing just on the edge of her range of vision as he slices carrots for crudités and she's trying to bring him into focus. He also keeps swaying from foot to foot. That could be because of the music Daddy's got on, which is pretty good Eighties dance music, I'll admit. Or it could be because of the butt-plug Daddy put in him, evidently on Mr. De Leon's order, before we started cooking, which I swear was bigger than my fist. *My* eyes started watering when Daddy produced that thing and ordered Cappa into the bathroom.

To my surprise, Cappa's cheeks flush pink from that little bit of teasing.

"Shut up," he mutters.

"Pretty, pretty boy," Bren teases, walking past us to get beers for everyone. Daddy, Mac, Warrin, Javier, Faolan, Jack, and Bravo are all in the great room, watching college football, while Max supervises the extremely competitive Chutes and Ladders game that's being played at the dining room table.

Cappa turns bright red. I don't understand why. He *is* a pretty boy. Handsome. Almost beautiful with his deep-set, sexy-sleepy eyes. Maybe it's a masculinity thing. Or maybe it's because he switches, although I can't see him trying to top Mr. De Leon. That man screams dominant from a distance.

"Bitchy, bitchy girl," he mocks her back.

Bren tosses her dreadlocks. "That's Queen Bitch to you, pretty boy."

Cappa snarls at her back as she walks back into the great room with her double-handful of beers.

"There's nothing wrong with being pretty," I say softly to Cappa.

He sighs. "I know. I just don't want it to be *all* I am. Playing with De Leon's made me realize that some of the Blunts Doms think I'm shallow."

I put down my knife and turn to look him in the eye. "No one who has spent more than five minutes with you would think you're shallow. And if anyone who has known you as long as they have thinks that, that's on them, not on you."

Cappa lowers his beautiful eyes to the carrots on the chopping board. "It's on me if that's all I've let them see."

"Why would you hide what you are?"

He chews on his lower lip. "Because what I am is pathetic."

I take his knife and put it down on the counter before I hug him. "If what you are is pathetic then everyone in this room is pathetic. We all need to give up control. We all want punishment to enforce arbitrary boundaries. We'll be the Pathos Crew together."

Cappa chuckles weakly. "You're not pathetic. You're great. Logan's crazy about you."

"You're great, too." I hold him at arm's length. "Daddy's taught me I'm the only one who gets to decide my own worth."

"That's right," Daddy says, walking around the counter and putting his arms around Cappa from behind. OMG, Batman Daddy hearing. "Your partner's investment doesn't determine who you are inside. You are the only person who determines your own value, Cap."

Usually when Daddy touches Cappa, Cappa melts. Not today. He holds himself apart. Not rigidly. Not rejecting Daddy's touch. But not seeking it, either. That's new.

"Have you seen me as weak?" Cappa asks Daddy.

"Submissives are the strongest people I know," Master Mac says, leaning into the conversation from the other side of the counter. I hope he followed Daddy into the kitchen and doesn't share Daddy's ridiculous radar, otherwise Bren is screwed. "And I've known some hard-cases."

Cappa nods but he doesn't look at either Dom.

Daddy releases Cappa with a squeeze of his shoulder. He tips his head at Mac and they meander back toward the couches in front of the television.

Once the Doms are gone, I pick up my knife and get going on my peppers again. "What about playing with Mr. De Leon makes you feel pathetic?" I ask.

"No, it's the other way around," Cappa says. "I feel *seen* with him. Like he's trying to worm inside my brain and pick it apart. Really break me down so he understands how deep my submission goes. I don't think . . . well, I *know* I haven't been tested like that, not in a long time. Maybe the Blunts Doms are just too comfortable with me? What's the saying, familiarity breeds contempt?"

That is the saying. Not a very nice one.

Since Cappa seems to be giving me his truths, I give him one of mine. "When Daddy's ex was here over the summer, she warned me that Daddy would get bored with me. That he needs constant stimulation—*newness*—to keep him engaged. Because my ex-husband cheated on me, that's something I've feared. I wasn't enough to keep Ash faithful, so why would I think I could hold the attention of someone as awesome as Daddy?" I swallow. Admitting this stuff is hard. "But after she left and I thought about it more, I realized that I can't control what my partners do. Ash straying was *his* decision. If he'd been honest with me and talked about the reasons he felt tempted and if my behavior was feeding into that, maybe we could have fixed things. But he didn't. That's on him. I am worth more than a partner who isn't honest, who doesn't talk to me about their feelings. Daddy's always honest with me and I'm always honest with him. That's why we'll go the distance and she's wrong about us."

"Wow," Cappa says quietly.

"Wow, I'm naive? Daddy's ex thinks so."

"No, wow, I never thought of it that way. Just . . . give me a minute."

He pulls his phone out of his pocket and slips away, pecking a kiss on my cheek before he disappears into Daddy's office.

I finish slicing up the carrots and arrange the sliced vegetables on two trays with homemade hummus and baba ghanoush. I carry one tray to the dining table and the other to the living room table. Daddy snags my hand as I head back into the kitchen.

"That was a very serious talk you were having with Cappa," he says, rubbing my hand between his huge paws.

I nod. "I think he's going through some stuff."

Daddy dips his head to give me butterfly kisses. "Very proud of you, my little wonder."

"Because I've been working on my insecurities?"

"Yes, and because you're generous with your friends. I'm proud of my kind, big-hearted girl."

"Even though I'm very little sometimes?"

"*Especially* because you're very little sometimes."

I stretch up to give him a kiss before returning to the kitchen.

To keep Master Mac out of my kitchen, I've made the easiest of party dinners. All finger foods. Nothing that requires more than defrosting and a trip through the oven. There aren't any complaints about the simplicity of the food, not even from Master Javier, since I've made the wild-rice-stuffed eggplant rolls with sriracha drizzle that he's crazy for. Because it's a mixed group of littles and non-littles around the table, there's no High Protocol tonight. I lean against Daddy and sigh wistfully.

"What's that noise for, sweetheart?" Daddy asks after swallowing a mouthful of pulled pork.

"Could we have another High Protocol dinner soon?"

Daddy grins a wolfy grin. "We could. Maybe after the Nursery's Grand Opening. Which, by the way, I think is a fine way to end your coming days of orgasm-abstinence."

I glare at him. "It would be a fine way of celebrating *not* having any orgasm-abstinence."

"Not going to happen, little girl."

"Boo," I say.

"Without doing anything so gauche as inviting myself to dinner," Master Javier says from across the table, "I could find a submissive or two to join in those activities."

He slides his eyes toward Shannie and Fleur, who are sitting to Daddy's right.

"Not it," Fleur murmurs.

"Too late," Master Javier tells her.

"Monday after the Opening suit you?" Daddy asks.

"To a T," Master Javier replies.

"But not to an O," I grump.

Too many of the Doms around the table chuckle. They're all giant meanies.

"If there's wide-spread enthusiasm for a High Protocol dinner, I'll book the Trattoria," Master Javier says.

"Oh, there is." Faolan leers at his little. Poor Matty, is her daddy a sadist, too?

"How many days of orgasm-abstinence are we discussing?" Bravo asks.

Beside him, Yummy freezes with her knife and fork in the air.

"Two for Emily but I believe that it's five for Cappa. Do I have that right?" Daddy asks.

Cappa hangs his head. "Yes, sir."

The Doms chuckle. They're an evil, evil bunch.

"Three is an excellent compromise," Bravo says.

"Compromise?" Yummy squeaks, the horns of her green dragon onesie shaking above her head. "Compromise? There hasn't been any compromise. I demand a negotiation."

"Yeah!" Sammi pipes up. "We have rights. Pooyah!"

Jack lifts his dark eyebrows at his boy. "No, little boy, you don't. Daddy owns your orgasms."

Sammi gulps. "Oh. I forgot."

"Too bad for you. So that's six days."

"Six? Wait! That's not a compromise!" Sammi protests.

"It's a compromise from twelve," Jack points out.

"Every day feels like a month when there are no orgasms!"

Everyone laughs at Sammi's consternation.

"Four," Sammi demands, his lower lip jutting.

"Six," Jack responds. "This is not a negotiation, little boy."

"Five?" Sammi asks, his lip trembling.

"Is six days of pleasing Daddy so terrible?" Jack counters.

"No?" Sammi responds but it's definitely a question.

Jack chuckles. "Five, little boy."

"We hates orgasm-denial, precious," Sammi mutters.

"It could be five in a cock cage," Jack says.

"No!" Sammi squeaks. "It's fine. Good, good even. Five days is good. All good."

Jack grins at his submissive. His grin is almost as wolfy as Daddy's.

"Feeling lucky, baby doll?" Daddy asks me.

"Yes," I whisper, not wanting to either antagonize Daddy into adding more days to my sentence or attract the jealousy of my fellow littles.

"I feel like five days is a good length of time," Daddy says.

I swallow. I'll die if I have to go through five days of Daddy's wolfy fucking with no Os. Seriously.

"I feel like five days is setting me up for failure," I say, looking up through my lashes at Daddy so he understands I'm being earnest. And pleading a little.

"You're breaking out the big eyes. Good lord, those are killer." Daddy chuckles. "I'm not ever setting you up for failure, my baby. We'll keep it at two days."

I sigh with relief. "Ta very much, Daddy."

He leans in and presses a kiss to my temple.

After the horror of mass orgasm-denial, everyone settles back into their conversations. Sammi keeps questioning Matty about the gold she "gave up," which makes her and Faolan trade knowing smiles. Faolan talks to Daddy and Max about the clues they found on their trip to Russia. Aggie regales our end of the table with the story of how Sammi cheated to win Chutes and Ladders, with Fleur providing imitations of Sammi that have even Sammi cracking up. The only person who doesn't seem to be participating in the conversation is Shannie, sitting on Daddy's other side.

I don't know Shannie very well. Unlike Skye and Zuki and some of the nightclub subs, it's not because she's standoffish. She's always been really nice to me. I know she's one of the last house submissives Daddy personally trained, which could make things between her and me weird but she hasn't ever acted like she and Daddy were lovers. She treats him like a high school teacher, with a kind of distant respect and affection.

She came with Master Javier and Fleur. I figured Master Javier inviting her was a ruse cooked up by Daddy and Master Mac so they could talk to her in a non-threatening way. Particularly after I scuttled Daddy's *Titanic* plans. Watching how she eats with her head down, silent and sad, I hope whatever they discuss helps turn things around for her.

Submission isn't a guarantee of happiness. I know that. But it hurts to see the Blunts house subs so lost and withdrawn. Brenna found her happiness with Master Mac. It looks like Cappa might be finding some with Mr. De Leon. Surely the other house submissives can find theirs with some help from Daddy?

Livvy wakes up and starts to fuss just before dessert, which is non-dairy ice cream cake and cookies for the littles, tiramisu from the Italian deli down the street for the Bigs. I take Livvy out of her rocking seat and change her, then pop her on her sensory mat and fasten the soft toy mobile over her head. She wriggles and coos at the bright, dangling shapes, so I figure that will keep her entertained through dessert.

Bren and Mac have cleared the table while I've been dealing with the baby. I help them bring out fresh plates while Daddy passes out spoons and serves the ice cream cake.

Once everyone is enjoying their processed sugar, I lean into Daddy. "Can I put on a movie and put up the tent once dessert is finished?"

Having endured some mighty blanket-fort-building efforts, Daddy bought me a pop tent. It's long and low so lots of my friends can sleep in it. The walls and ceiling are gossamer pink and Daddy fixed it up with tiny, winking lights so it's like being in a fairy cottage. The last time Vashi visited, we painted mandalas all over it with fabric paints. I love my tent.

"Of course," Daddy says. "And before you ask, yes, everyone can stay over but you're in our bed."

"Oookay." I make it sound like a hardship in case anyone's listening but I'll always prefer to sleep with Daddy.

"What's the movie tonight?" Daddy asks.

"*Encanto*, because everyone needs to find their own gift."

Daddy kisses my temple again and smiles. "And because you like to sing along to the crazy flower song."

I do like that song. Particularly with the alternative lyrics I've developed.

"I wish Laurel and Jiro were here so we could all be dragons together," I tell Daddy. "Matty's going to be an amethyst dragon but I want to be a flower dragon. Maybe a sundew dragon. They're carnivorous, you know."

"And a little sundew just won't do. Yes, you've told me several times. I'll be suitably wary around my meat-eating flower dragon."

I grin at him. He doesn't have anything to be wary about. Although we *could* role-play the sundew dragon gives Daddy-dragon morning head . . .

When everyone's finished their dessert, I leave Daddy, Bren, and Mac to tidy up and watch the baby while I drag Matty and Sammi off with me. Matty, because I want to show her my little room. Sammi, because I don't dare leave him to his own devices for more than a few minutes. Even with his daddy nearby, Sammi is a chaos gremlin and can cause an amazing amount of destruction in a very short amount of time.

Matty's suitably impressed by my little room. She looks through my puzzles and board games, reads my mantra poster, and examines the tools of my latest hobby, calligraphy, which are spread out all over my desk. When Matty says she'd like to practice calligraphy with me, we set up a playdate.

"I'd like to do calligraphy," Sammi says, just before he knocks three bottles of ink off my desk with an ill-timed, Tigger-type bounce.

Matty and I pick up the bottles, which were fortunately capped, with matching grins.

"We'll make it an Art Attack playdate," I offer to Sammi. "I'll set up a calligraphy station, a coloring station, and a Play-Doh station."

Sammi bounces again. "I like Play-Doh!"

I know. Play-Doh can distract Sammi from almost anything. "Run downstairs and ask everyone what the best day is for an Art Attack playdate?"

With a whoop, Sammi rushes out, waving his arms over his head.

"No calligraphy for Sammi?" Matty asks.

"No sharp objects or anything that can create a permanent stain," I say.

Matty grins. "Do you mind me asking what your little age is?"

"I'm mostly a middle. But, um, Daddy's been helping me go younger." I wring my hands together, not sure if I should tell my new friend so much but uncomfortable truths seem to be the order of the day. "He diapered me during a scene and rocked me to sleep. It was really good. And he pierced me with diaper pins." I rub the spot on my side where the scabs are a little itchy. "It was all amazing."

Matty's coppery eyebrows shoot up. "Wow. I haven't tried any of that."

"What's your little age? If you don't mind saying."

"I don't. I came into age-play backwards, so I'm still figuring it out. Maybe seven or eight? I know I like the discipline side, so at first I thought I was just into domestic discipline with a bit of a daddykink. But after my dad disappeared, I found I really loved the release and mental freedom of playing with dolls and sleeping with stuffies. I'm also a terrible hoarder. Not piles of newspapers or anything but I've always collected things. Dad made me get rid of my collection of bird skulls before I went to college but I still collect coins, odd carvings, and gemstones, most especially amethysts."

"And gold," I point out. "Like Smaug."

Matty beams. "Just like Smaug. I want to plate my whole belly with amethyst crystals." She rubs her belly under the corduroy romper she's wearing. "I love the idea of being an amethyst dragon. I love being part of a flight. Is this the kind of thing your playgroup does all the time? Hide and seek in the corn maze and costume parties? I haven't done anything like this before."

"This is new to me, too. Daddy loves group scenes. I'd only been to dungeon parties before. We went on a cruise together when we first started dating and he organized this scene where his knights stormed my castle and he took me captive and flogged me. I knew then that he was the best daddy I could ever find."

Matty nods enthusiastically, her curls bouncing.

"I like hard play like that, too. More than a spanking. I know a lot of littles don't but I do. Faolan's the first daddy to give it to me safely. He's very stern. I love it."

I catch her hand and give it a squeeze. Being a masochistic little can be isolating. Not that I feel Cynnie or Yummy or Amy ever judge me. Just that I can't really talk to them about things like the best cream to use for deep bruises. I've been very grateful to my Big Sub Bestie and the other masochistic house subs for giving me a tribe.

"I love how stern Logan is, too. He never lets me get away with anything. And he has Batman hearing, I swear."

Matty giggles. "Faolan has some hearing loss from when he was in the service but it would be wrong of me to try to slip stuff by him. But I'll admit to the occasional muttered minced oath."

"What's a minced oath?" I ask.

"Where you say 'good gosh' instead of 'good god' or 'sheesh' instead of the poop swear-word."

"Uht-oh, I say those."

"Faolan doesn't let me get away with minced oaths."

I giggle at the thought of not even being able to say omigosh.

"I hope your daddy doesn't talk to my Daddy."

"Right? It's like they only share the worst ideas! Faolan's been so much harsher since Mister Javier invited us to Blunts. Like throwing gasoline on a fire."

I giggle again. "How does your daddy know Master Javier?"

Matty wiggles her shoulders. "Daddy said they were old friends and discovered the lifestyle around the same time. But he was vague and warned me off spending too much time with Mister Javier. Which made me curious. So, I went digging."

"You *are* a geoarcheologist."

She grins. "I am!"

She pulls her phone out of her romper pocket, taps open the

photos, and scrolls to a picture. I have to clap my hand over my mouth to keep from squealing and summoning Daddy. I wouldn't have recognized Faolan. He's baby-faced in the picture, no beard, and hair cut close to his head. But I immediately recognize Master Javier. Has Master Javier always looked the same? Same dark sadist eyes, same aristocratic features. Not even a full head of deep brown hair makes him look any different. He and Faolan are wearing graduation caps and gowns, their arms thrown around each other.

"I'm amazed it's in color."

Matty giggles. "Right? I think they're wearing corduroy bell-bottoms under those gowns. They went to NYU together for two years and then they went to Aix-Marseille University. For *philosophy of art.*"

She crosses her eyes and sticks her tongue out of the side of her mouth which makes me crack up. She's so STEM.

"They were roommates in France for that year. Then Faolan went into the Army for three years. He got his Ph.D. at Oxford." She rolls her eyes. I would be so dead if Daddy caught me doing that. "He stayed in England to teach for five years and, get this, lived in a flat in Oxford owned by Mister Javier's family. Then he moved back to New York. Mister Javier was married by then—"

I'm sure my eyebrows disappear into my hair. I had no idea Master Javier was married.

"*Many* trips together to the south of France." Another eye roll. "Daddy stayed there a couple of summers when he did sabbaticals to write his books. So *old friends* is a bit of an understatement."

Certainly is.

"I didn't know Master Javier was married," I say. "Do you know if his wife was in the lifestyle?"

Matty shakes her head. "Not for sure but I don't think so. She's quite the society lady. Old New York money. She's remarried now. She runs his big masquerade ball thing at a fancy club on Park Avenue. Daddy got free tickets. Would you and your daddy like to come? It's in January."

A masquerade ball? I'm all over that.

"I'll ask Daddy. We should have a ball at Blunts. A *Littles Ball*."

Matty grins. "We should. A winter water ball. In the pool."

I love that idea even more. "With synchronized water dancing."

Matty giggles. "I can't water dance. But I figure no one will complain about their feet hurting if we're dancing in the water instead of on land."

"Excellent idea. We can do an 'Under the Sea' theme."

"*Back to the Future*?" Matty asks.

I nod eagerly and Matty giggles.

I think I've found a new recruit for the Littles' Army.

sixteen

LOGAN

WITH ONE QUESTION, my whole night goes downhill.

"Shannie, I trained you. Why didn't you come to me with this?"

Shannie's soft brown eyes go hard. "You left."

"I was never further than a phone call away," I protest.

She shrugs and sinks further into the guest chair in my office. Mac crosses behind her and gives me a hard look. I'm fucking this up.

I rise from behind my desk, hold my hand out to Shannie, and lead her over to the couch. I sit in my desk chair when I'm dealing with Emily. It reinforces our roles. But Shannie doesn't need a Dom right now. She needs a friend.

I sit next to her on the couch and hold her hand loosely. Mac circles around to lean against Emmy's standing desk.

"I'm sorry, Shannie," I say gently. "I didn't realize you felt abandoned. I thought I was leaving the house submissives in good hands. When I did my last check in with you, you said you were developing some real connections at the club and working toward your submission goals."

"I was," she says. A crystal tear trembles on her dark lashes, then slips down her cheek.

"Do you want to tell me what happened?" I ask. Cappa's been pushing me toward interviewing Shannie but she was reluctant to talk with me. Now I understand why. I'm glad Javier wore her down and got her to come today, then gave me an excuse to take her into my office and question her.

She shakes her head. "It won't help."

Mac moves suddenly, kneeling on the carpet in front of Shannie. "You don't know me, Shannie. I know you've only got Brenna's and Logan's say-so that I'm trustworthy. But I care about what happens to the house submissives. Whatever you tell us stays in this room. And we *will* help. No matter what you say."

Shannie glances at Mac, then at me. I nod.

She looks down at our joined hands. After a moment's silence, she squeezes my fingers. "Remember how one of my submission goals was to submit to two masters?"

"I do," I say encouragingly.

"Master Rob's been asking to do scenes with me more an' more. He said we should start talkin' about being exclusive. I wanted to reach that goal before things got serious with Rob. Now I wish I'd just let it be."

Mac reaches out and takes Shannie's other hand. "Did something bad happen with Rob?" Mac asks.

Shannie shakes her head, her black braids swishing over her shoulders. "I haven't been able to tell him about this, though. I think . . . he'd take it wrong."

"How would he take it wrong?" I ask.

"He'd be angry at Ty and Hart. It wasn't their fault. I didn't use my safe word. If I had, they'd have stopped."

Mac rubs the back of Shannie's hand with his thumb. "Did they take a scene too far?" he asks, his voice going rough.

She shakes her head. "They were doing what we'd agreed on."

Mac and I are both silent for a beat, waiting for Shannie to continue. When she sits sad and slumped, tears dripping off her chin, I prompt, "Did you stop wanting the scene? Shannie, you have to communicate with your Doms—"

A grunt from Mac shuts me up.

"Shannie, I can see you're scared," Mac says. "What's more, I can see you're shamed by whatever happened. If the scene went too far, that's on your Doms. You have nothing to be ashamed of."

"Can Doms get scared, too?" Shannie asks.

"Yes, we can," I say, trying to recover from my fumble. "I'm scared right now."

Her dark eyes flash to me. "You are?"

"I'm scared of failing you. I'm ashamed I have in the past," I admit. "I want to do better. I want to make sure you feel safe at Blunts."

She sniffles.

Mac spreads his impressive wingspan, snags a box of tissues off my desk, and offers the box to Shannie. She blows her nose and then takes our hands again. "I don't feel safe at Blunts anymore," she says, her voice so small and soft it makes my stomach roil.

"Why, Shannie?" I ask.

"The scene with Masters Ty and Hart, it was an open scene," she whispers. "When they started the scene, it was with a paddling. Master Javier and a couple other masters were watching. There were some men I didn't recognize, too. People came and went while I was bein' paddled. I wasn't paying much attention to them. I was in subspace for part of it."

She stops and picks up the tissue in her lap, wipes her eyes and blows her nose, before continuing, knotting the tissue between her fingers. "They moved me to the bed. Master Ty was behind me. Master Hart was in front of me. They was . . . both . . . you know."

Shannie's soft, Southern twang becomes more and more pronounced as she speaks. When she was in training, I loved hearing her twang because it meant she was relaxed in the scene. That's not what this is. She's pulling back, drawing into her roots, to protect herself.

"They took you at the same time?" I ask.

She nods. "I wasn't really paying attention to who else was in the room until I began hearing the voices. They weren't talking. It was more like . . . chanting. They were gathered around the bed, real close." She drops her head and stares at the tissue in her hands. "The things they was sayin'. So hateful. I doan mind dirty talk in the moment but that's not what this was. It was like they were tryin' to spur Ty an' Hart on. To be rougher. To be mean and hateful like them."

I take one of her hands again. "I'm sorry, Shannie."

She twitches her head to the side like she's shaking off my words. "They all began sayin' the same thing. Chantin' it. 'Split her, split her, split her.' I got real scared. Scareder than I'd been since I came to New York. Master Hart was bein' rough with my throat. Really poundin' at it. I'm okay with that usually. But it felt like he was movin' to their chant, like he was caught up in it, an' I didn't know if I could stop him."

"The most important part of being a Dom is being in control," I say. "Did you feel Ty and Hart were in control?"

Shannie shakes her head. "Not really. I felt like if they went along with it, it'd be okay but if they stopped or told 'em to stop chantin', it would turn ugly real fast. They felt . . . I don't know how to describe it right but it felt like they were bigger than us. Like they were a group an' we were just us, too small to stand against them."

"I'm sorry you ever felt that way, Shannie," I say, shame curdling *my* gut. No submissive should ever feel that unsafe. "Who were the people chanting?"

"I didn't know them. They were with Master Drew when they came in but he left."

"He *left* guests alone with you in a scene?" Mac growls.

"Ty and Hart were there," I offer, knowing there's no club rule about leaving guests with other members.

Mac shakes his head.

"I don't want Ty or Hart to get into trouble," Shannie says. "It weren't their fault."

It was if they lost control of the scene.

"Did you tell them afterwards that you felt unsafe?" I ask, keeping my tone gentle.

Shannie hangs her head, shaking it slowly. "They were so happy with the scene they high-fived each other afterwards. An' at first, I felt good about it too. I'd submitted to both of them. I'd made them both happy. But that chant kept comin' back to me. It made me feel like nothin'. Worse than nothin'." She sniffles. "I haven't felt that way since I joined Blunts."

I rub her back. "I'm so sorry you felt that way."

"Shannie, what can we do to make this right?" Mac asks. "What can we do to help you feel safe again?"

She shakes her head. "I don't know. That's why I didn't want to say anythin'. I don't know how anyone could fix this. It's just some-thin' I gotta get past—"

"No, no, Shannie, it's not. We can start with a rule about staying with guests at all times. You shouldn't ever have felt that you, Ty, and Hart were outnumbered or unable to control Drew's guests. Drew should have stayed with them. We'll start there. Is that a good start?"

Shannie nods. "I don't want to do any more scenes with Ty and Hart," she whispers. "I don't know how to tell them without makin' them feel real bad."

"We'll take care of that," Mac says, patting Shannie's hand. "You focus on you. Feeling safe. Feeling more grounded and confident."

"Oh-okay, I'll try."

"Is this something you feel comfortable talking to Master Rob about?" Mac asks. There's a little edge to his tone, like he's gritting his teeth.

"I don't want to make this his problem. He spends time with Ty and Hart, like hanging out. He goes to Master Hart's gym. They're friends. I don't want him to be mad at them."

"I know this is hard but nothing improves if we keep secrets. Give Rob the opportunity to help you and deal with his relationships with Ty and Hart in his own way."

Shannie looks dubious.

"What's wrong, Shannie?" I prompt.

"Master Rob's just mentioned exclusivity. That's what I want. What if this scares him off?"

I glance at Mac to see if he has any thoughts.

Mac rubs the back of his neck. "We don't want to do anything to scupper your relationship, sweetheart. But if Master Rob finds out about this through the club grapevine, it might hurt him more than if he hears it from you."

Shannie dabs at her eyes and blows her nose. "I need to think about it."

"Okay, Shannie," I say. "We don't want to push you. We just want to help. You tell us the best way to do that."

"A rule about guests would be good. Then it wouldn't have happened."

I don't know Drew well, and some of our members use the club more like a country club, shuttling guests in and out of the nightclub, spa, and restaurant, than a lifestyle club with vulnerable employees. Maybe we need a retraining for members as well as a new rule.

"Is there any other way Logan and I can help make this better for you?" Mac asks.

Shannie glances from Mac to me. "Are you really stayin' this time?"

I swallow the lump in my throat. "I am. And Mac's helping me this time. We're not doing this alone, Shannie. Not any of us."

She nods. "I know why Annabelle quit. It ain't my story to tell and she's not gonna speak to you about it. You're part of the membership committee. But if Master Mac called her, I bet she'd talk to him."

Mac's eyebrows shoot toward his hairline. "I can do that."

"It's bad," Shannie says. "You're not gonna like it."

"This isn't about our comfort," I say. "It's about making Blunts safe for you again. Please give us time, Shannie. Please don't quit the way Annabelle did."

Shannie nods. "I wasn't plannin' to. I need the money. But I was gonna refuse scenes with anyone who asked until Rob an' I go exclusive."

"Fair enough," Mac says. "And don't worry about Ty and Hart. We'll talk to them tomorrow."

"Thank you." Shannie gives Mac a small smile. "I can see why Bren picked you. You're a good man." She flushes and glances at me. "I mean, you both are."

I pat her back. "It's okay, Shannie. I know Mac's a much better man than I am. That's why I've looked up to him for so long."

Mac snorts. "Logan gets the job done, which is the important thing here. You know how to reach Logan but I want you to have my number, too. You need anything, you call me, Shannie."

"I will, sir." She pulls her phone out of the pocket of the little sweater-dress she's wearing, since I've made an exception to the no clothes for subs in the house rule with Javier's friends Faolan and Matty joining us tonight. Mac puts his number in. Shannie tucks it in her pocket and then asks for a hug from each of us, which we give her. I rock her in my arms for a minute and murmur to her.

"I'm so sorry I let you down, Shannie."

She pats my back. "I forgive you. Just please don't do it again. All of us, we really need you."

"I'm here. I won't let you down again."

Her smile as we leave my office and rejoin the party makes the discomfort worthwhile.

Emily notices my mood shift. She sticks to my side like glue for the rest of the dinner party. She lets Mac and Bren clean up with barely any supervision and when I sit down on the floor next to Livvy's sensory mat, Emily worms into my lap.

"Hi, baby doll."

"Hi, Daddy. I know everything's not okay because you have your frowny on. Can it wait until milk and cookies or do you want to talk now?"

I circle my arms around her and hug her tightly. "You are such a little wonder."

"ILY, Daddy."

"ILY too, baby. It can wait until milk and cookies because you've already made me feel better."

She rubs her thumb over my forehead until some of my tension eases. Then she scoots around in my lap so she's facing the baby. While I dangle the brightly colored shapes, Emily puts her palm under Livvy's feet and encourages her to kick. When I ask her what she's doing, she explains that she's helping Livvy strengthen her leg muscles.

"Next month, we can start holding her upright with her feet on the ground or on our legs and see if she'll push against us but for right now, it's better for her to be lying down with her head and back supported," Emmy says.

"You learned all of this helping your friend Gracie?"

"Mmm-hmm and reading baby books."

"You've been reading baby books?" I ask. She's been doing it when I've been out at work if she has, because she certainly didn't tell me about it.

"Master Mac recommended a couple and we read them together."

Mac really is the best man I've ever known.

"That's wonderful, baby doll. Tell me about this stage of development."

She explains the physical changes Livvy's going through this month while the party winds down around us.

Javier, Faolan, and Matty are the last to leave. I wish I could offer a way for them to stay the night but our guest room's gone and Javier's given me his opinion on the bondage bed in the basement several times. Emily and Matty talk about an "art attack" play date they're planning, as well as their dragon costumes, while Javier and Faolan thank me for the fun day.

"Logan, I hope I don't offend you if I say that Blunts is more our speed than the playgroup," Faolan says to me.

"Not at all." I glance at Javier. "You may find a little resistance to age-play and daddykink at Blunts. But we're working to change that."

Javier nods. "We've talked about this."

"I plan to apply for membership," Faolan says. "I hope you'll support my application. If you have any concerns about it, please talk to me."

"I'm happy to support it and I don't have any concerns. Matty seems happy and healthy. I think she had a great time today."

Faolan nods. "She did but we need heavier play and I'm not sure how receptive the playgroup will be to that."

"I hear you," I respond. "Emily's one of the few masochistic littles at the playgroup. But Jack and Sammi also go for heavier play, particularly on the punishment side, which you'll appreciate Sammi earns often."

Faolan chuckles. "I noticed. I'll have a word with Jack. I plan to keep coming to playgroup but I think it's important for Matty to connect with other masochists. Javi tells me many of the house submissives are masochists."

I blink. I've never, ever heard anyone call the fearsome Master Javier "Javi." Not even Maude would dare.

Javier's mouth twitches but he doesn't acknowledge it otherwise.

"Yes, they are," I agree. "As is Mac's fiancée, Brenna." I glance around for her but she must be upstairs, because I don't see her with Mac, who is rocking Livvy in front of the TV while she coos madly at him.

"Good. I'll put my application in this week." Faolan offers his hand, which I shake. "I'll look forward to seeing you on Tuesday. I gather we're doing arts and crafts."

I gather that, too. "Emily will cook, because not even Mac can keep her out of the kitchen but if you'd like to bring some snacks, that would be welcome. Emily's food is on the very healthy side."

Faolan glances at our littles, who are hugging goodbye in the hallway. "I noticed. Matty makes an amazing trail mix that I could, quite frankly, live on. I'll encourage her to bring that."

Javier rolls his eyes. "What is wrong with potato chips? Long live salt and fat."

We all chuckle.

seventeen

LOGAN

WHEN I WAS at my lowest after finding out about Livvy's paternity and doubting whether I could be the Daddy Emmy needs, Max told me about his feeling of *Daddyness*. He described it as a swell of joy and terror. A sense that everything was right with the world when he was with his little and that he had to protect her from the entire universe.

Daddyness swells my chest as Emmy comes skipping into the kitchen. She's wearing PJs, probably because she's been playing with Olivia. We're still figuring out how to incorporate the baby into our naked-time but for now it's just when we're all in the bath. Emmy's dark curls are topped with the black cat ears she's been wearing recently, which turn the swell of Daddyness into a tsunami. Her hair's caught back in a ponytail after Livvy grabbed a big curl and stuffed it in her mouth earlier. Emmy's expression as she washed milky-saliva out of her hair in the kitchen sink was priceless. I predict her lingering issues with mess will dissolve under the messiness that is caring for an infant.

I quickly swallow the cookie I sneaked while waiting for my baby doll and open my arms. She snuggles in but turns a very suspicious glare up at me. I nearly choke at the adorableness of her owl-eye.

"You have crumbs in your beard, Daddy," Emmy observes.

I wipe my chin. Damn beard. I should have shaved. "Did I not tidy up properly after dinner, baby?" I ask innocently.

Her eyes narrow. "Those look like oatmeal cookie crumbs."

They are, indeed. "More likely those delicious mini-quiches you served tonight. I couldn't get enough of those."

She's not confident enough to call me a liar but I'm getting an intense owl-eye. "Do I need to count the oatmeal cookies?"

Damn, I didn't think of that. "Sable might have gotten one or two."

She swivels in my arms to look at her cat, who is lying upside-down on the carpet near the dining table, his belly distended from all the scraps he got fed under the table at the dinner party. He stretches in true cat nonchalance under Emily's regard.

"Please tell me you didn't give him oatmeal cookies, Daddy? Human food really isn't good for him. It makes him stinky."

Oatmeal cookies are probably the least egregious of the human food Sable got fed tonight. I saw Sammi sneak him a whole mini-quiche.

"I thought Ryan said he was okay eating human food as long as it doesn't make up the main part of his diet?"

"Master Ryan did but he gets so stinky when he eats human food. It can't be good for his tummy. Did you give him a cookie?"

"No?"

"Did you eat the cookies yourself?" she asks, planting her fists on her hips. Exasperated baby doll is such a cute look.

"Possibly?"

"Daddy!"

I laugh, swing her up into my arms, and spin around with her. She grabs at my neck to hold on and giggles her enchanting giggle.

I set her down on one of the kitchen stools and slide the plate of cookies and a glass of warm milk in front of her. Then I immediately steal a cookie off her plate and chomp it down in two bites. I lick frosting off my fingers. "Delicious."

Emily shakes her head at me but takes a cookie and nibbles at it. "They are good," she admits after chewing ten times. "Bren's right about the ginger. Really adds flavor."

I rub my belly emphatically. "Yum-yum for Daddy's tum."

She giggles. I hand her a cookie and encourage her to feed it to me, which she does, grinning.

"I saw you getting buddy-buddy with Matty earlier. What do you think of Matty and Faolan?" I ask.

She takes a sip of milk to clear her mouth before saying, "Matty's great. Did you know she's a masochistic little like me?"

"Faolan mentioned they go for heavy play."

Emmy nods, her ponytail bouncing. "Could we do some scenes with them at the club?"

"We could," I agree. "I'll talk with Faolan about scheduling a scene or two. He might make a fine Viking-Daddy."

Emily's eyes go rounder than any owl's. "Viking-Daddy," she whispers. "I think I need to be raided and pillaged."

I laugh. "That can be arranged, little girl. Are you okay with this 'art attack' play date? I don't want you taking on too much right now."

"I'm okay with it. As long as I keep my mornings free for writing, I'm good." Her face creases. "Mac's going to take Livvy tomorrow morning for the first time. I'm not sure how I feel about that, Daddy."

"Why, baby?"

She chews on her lower lip. I pinch it between my fingers and give it a tug until she looks up at me.

"I'm just really enjoying getting to know Livvy and I want to take her to see the Rexes. We haven't done that yet."

"Could we do that together soon instead of you going alone tomorrow?"

She nods slowly.

"Baby, I know you're having fun with Livvy but it's important you keep on top of your deadlines. Let's see how tomorrow goes and if you feel like you want to adjust the schedule so you have more time with the baby after tomorrow, we'll revisit it."

That gets me a smile. "Okay, Daddy."

I kiss her forehead. "Good girl. We haven't had a chance to talk again about how you're feeling about your mum. I know the last visit was very hard for you."

Emmy sighs. "I knew it was coming. I just felt so stupid and help- less when she got lost in her belief that Frances was dead. I didn't know whether to argue with her or go along with it or what. I know what the doctors said but it felt so wrong."

I shift so I'm standing close to her stool and she can lean against my chest. "You did all the right things, sweetheart. It's important not to upset her."

"I know."

I kiss her forehead again. "You're my very brave girl, Emmy. I know a lot of people who would simply stop visiting her. You're a good daughter."

Emily blinks wet eyes up at me. "She'll never know who Livvy is. I think that's the thing that hurts the worst."

I think she's displacing. Violette doesn't know her own daughter anymore. *That's* the thing that hurts the worst.

"Baby, remember what we talked about? You can only control yourself. What's important is that you're showing up for your mum. You can't control her reactions. The disease is dictating those now. But you can show up for her and keep showing up for her."

Emmy nods sadly. "She won't ever get better, will she?"

"The doctors don't think so, sweetheart."

"And she could live a long time."

"She could. But she's not in any pain. She's comfortable. She's safe."

"Is it enough, Daddy? Is that the best I can do for her?"

"I think so. What do you think of this new home?"

"It's good. It's clean and her room is nice. She likes the greenhouse. It's warm in there which is better for her. I was worried about her going out into the garden in the winter in Syracuse. She's not good about coming inside when she gets chilled. I worried she'd get sick. They can't check on her all the time."

"Then it's good she's at this home where she won't get cold. You've given her a nice environment where she can enjoy the same things but she's safer. You're doing all the right things, Emmy."

"I just wish she knew Livvy," Emily says, her voice so sad my chest aches. I slip my arm around her.

"I wish she knew *you*. I wish she could see what a little wonder you are. How well you're taking care of Livvy. How much you love our family. But I can see all those things, baby. Is it enough that Daddy sees them?"

She tips her face up to me and a smile peeks through the tears. "Yes, Daddy."

I give her a gentle, oatmeal-flavored kiss.

"Daddy, can I ask what happened with Shannie tonight? You came out of your office with a huge frowny on."

I tip my head forward so our foreheads touch and look into a single, hazel eye that blinks back at me.

"Shannie had a bad experience at the club with some of Master Drew's guests. We're going to have to review safety protocols with the members, and maybe put a new rule or two in place to ensure the house submissives are safe around guests."

"Guests hurt Shannie? I thought guests weren't allowed to scene with house submissives without a member?"

"They surrounded her and two Doms and scared her. They didn't touch her but they made the scene environment so frightening that she didn't want to continue the scene."

"Did she use her safe word?" Emily asks.

I swallow hard. Emmy's not being hurtful; she's just asking the questions anyone will ask. But it's a question I find hard to answer. And the answer hits differently when Shannie's not sitting beside me, radiating fear and shame.

"No. She was scared that if she did, her Doms would lose control of the scene."

Emily nods. "I've seen that once, where the crowd kind of turned against the Dom. It was a flogging at a dungeon party and the Dom kept going when a lot of people watching called for him to stop. I guess it's not exactly the same thing but it felt ugly and angry and dangerous. I left right afterwards because the vibe got so weird."

My shoulders drop an inch and the tension tightening my back recedes. Emily saying she's felt something similar normalizes Shannie's reactions. Not that Shannie's feelings need validation. They're real and valid on their own. I've just never felt anything like what Shannie and Emily experienced. I've always felt buoyed by the crowd watching my scenes. Hearing that Emily's had a similar experience gives me another point of access into Shannie's fear.

"She also said that Annabelle would talk to Mac. We need to get to the bottom of why she quit."

Emmy rubs my shoulder. "You will, Daddy. And you'll help fix it."

I squeeze my eyes shut. "Thank you for your faith, baby doll. I felt terrible talking to Shannie. I let her down in such a big way. I've let all of the house subs down."

Her little hand wraps around my biceps and gives me a squeeze. "You weren't any good to them the way you were, Daddy. Burned out and grieving. Grief is a funny thing. It twists your head around. Makes you doubt everything about yourself. I know I felt that way after my divorce. It took me a long time to feel like myself again. I know it's not your nature but sometimes you have to put yourself first for a little while before you can give other people what they need."

"Thank you for understanding, Emmy. I know she wasn't trying to be hurtful and she said she forgives me but Shannie emphasized that the reason she didn't come to me in the first place was because I withdrew from the club. I just wonder if I'd stayed and limped along, given as much as I could—"

Emily shakes her head, rolling her forehead against mine. "This isn't something you can half-bottom, Daddy."

A laugh breaks out of me. "Half-bottom, huh?"

She grins, the skin around her merged eyes crinkling. "You have to be all in with the house submissives, Daddy. Bren would have skinned you alive if you'd tried to limp along."

"Very true," I admit. "I still feel like I've failed them."

"You haven't failed them because you're here now, fixing things. And I know my Daddy will help fix it. Because that's what my Daddy does. He makes things better. He's not Dumbledore. He can't wave a wand at it. He's my Batman Daddy. He's the one who fights the hard fight. The fight he's not sure of winning. He's the one who does the things that need doing. The hero we deserve."

My throat tightens again. "Is that what I am, baby doll?"

She puts down the cookie and loops both arms around my neck. "You are. You're proud of me? I'm double-proud of you. Triple-proud, even. You could have walked away, too. You could have just been a club member and ignored the problems with the house subbies. You could have left it to Master Ryan. It was his problem. You made it yours. You stepped up. I love you so much, Daddy, and I'm a zillion-times proud of you."

I pull her off the stool and into my arms. She wraps her legs around my hips. "A zillion-times, huh? That's lots of proud."

"It is." She presses kisses over my chin. "I know helping the house subbies has been hard. It's made you feel guilty. It's made you feel inadequate. But my Daddy doesn't shy away from hard things. My Daddy keeps his baby on the horse until all the stinky green stuff comes out. My Daddy asks the hard questions and keeps asking until he gets the real answers. My Daddy doesn't give up."

"Baby, your faith in me, it's everything."

162

She squeezes my neck and hums a tune I recognize, "If I ever lose my faith in you . . ."

"Won't happen, baby girl. Because I will never give you a reason to lose your faith in me."

She plasters kisses all over my face and giggles when I carry her upstairs to bed.

eighteen

EMILY

LIVVY IS A PSYCHIC BABY.

I didn't know babies could be psychic but Livvy's the most awesome baby in the world and she's psychic.

She's quiet and alert from the moment she wakes up at 7:05—Gracie's amazing schedule at work—staring at me the way she stared at Cappa. I lean in as we dress her so she can see my face clearly. She blinks and grins her gummy grin but doesn't coo or gurgle. When I blow kisses at her, she puckers her lips like she's blowing kisses back but doesn't even giggle.

"She's quiet this morning," Logan remarks as he carries her downstairs.

The house is as quiet as the baby. Bren and Mac ate an early breakfast and left for her shop. Master Mac wanted to get in a run and a shower before he opens his daycare, where Livvy's going for the first time today.

While we share whole wheat bagels and lox from the deli down the street for breakfast, Daddy watches the morning news and I curl up next to him on the couch with Livvy on my lap. She blows milky bubbles but still doesn't make a sound. Sable hops up next to me and extends a tentative white paw, batting gently at the fringe of tiny pompoms on the hem of Livvy's dress. I praise him until his rusty purr starts up and I get a whiff of his breath. It smells like a sewer bursting. Sweet baby Jesus.

"Daddy, you gave him an oatmeal cookie, didn't you?"

Daddy crosses his heart. "I swear I didn't. Although I also admit that I didn't put the plate in the fridge, either."

There were at least three oatmeal cookies on the plate when Daddy carried me upstairs last night. There weren't any left when I put it in the dishwasher while I was making breakfast. I glare at my cat. He freezes with his paw in mid-air.

Livvy suddenly rips out a fart. The first sound she's made today.

Daddy chuckles.

"Are you sympathetically stinky, baby?" I ask Livvy.

The smell hits us both and Daddy begins to guffaw. Men and bodily functions, I swear.

"Goodness gracious! We're doing a diaper check after that one, Livvy-bit," I tell the baby.

She grins.

"I see you inherit your sense of humor from Daddy."

Once she's in a fresh diaper, I bundle Livvy up and pop her in her stroller for the walk to Brenna's shop. I leave Daddy in his office, planning something nefarious with Max. Sable follows me to the front door, meowing.

"Do you want to take a walk, boy? Might help your tummy." I retrieve the walking harness that Daddy got for Sable. My kitty takes one look at it, hisses, and darts under the couch.

"I think that's a no," I tell Livvy, hanging the harness on the coat rack. I've tried putting it on Sable to wear around the house a few times. It's gotten me the same reaction. Bren says he has separation anxiety and doesn't like me leaving the house but he won't come with me. I just don't think he's a kitty who goes on walks.

Livvy waves her mittened fists at me noiselessly. I offer her a paci but she spits it out and watches me gravely.

"It's like that today, is it, baby-boo?" I ask, shrugging into my coat. "Should we have a quiet day or would you like me to sing to you? I have to warn you that my voice isn't nearly as good as Daddy's."

Big eyes from the silent baby.

I start humming the first song that comes to mind as I carry her stroller down the front steps and steer it onto the sidewalk. It's "The Bare Necessities." I don't know why my mind's picked that to be our theme song for today but I know all the words and sing softly as I wheel the stroller down East Second Street.

When I get to the corner and pause for the light, breaking into the chorus, I hear a little giggle from the stroller.

Grinning, I up the volume and ignore the strange looks I get from the pedestrians I pass. A gray-haired gentleman waiting for the light at the corner of Tompkins Square Park sings along with me for a moment. I smile and wave at him when I steer the stroller into the park and around the basketball court. I've noticed girls playing more and more recently and I want Livvy to see girls playing sports from an early age, so I stop for a minute and let her watch. I don't think she can see details at that distance but her eyes do follow the play down the court, so maybe she can see movement or color or something.

Before we leave the park, I check to make sure Livvy's fingers and toes are toasty and offer her a paci again, which she spits out.

"Is it the silent treatment today, Livvy?" I ask her. "Have I done so very wrong?"

She grins at me but still not a coo or a burble.

We head out again, into a wind that bites at my cheeks and carries the smell of snow over the city's exhaust and concrete odors.

"Wouldn't a white Christmas be cool for your first Christmas?" I ask the baby rhetorically, then break into "I'm Dreaming of a White

Christmas," which wins me a tiny coo. Happy that I've snared the baby with Bing, I segue into "The Little Drummer Boy" as I turn the corner and see Bren's sign in the distance. She had it repaired and repainted after it was smashed by the baddies who stole her design book and tried to shut her down. It proudly proclaims "Missing Ink" in neon to everyone who passes by.

There's a small group of people waiting at the shop's front door. It's mixed adults and children, including two babies, which makes me smile. Livvy will have company. Master Mac's daycare filled up shockingly quickly considering he didn't advertise. Brenna's tattooist enrolled her littlest and told her friends. Before Master Mac could blink, all eight places were filled and he had a double-digit waiting list.

When I join the group waiting at the door, Livvy lets out an ear-piercing wail.

I rush to soothe her. A woman pushes through the crowd and stands over the stroller. For a moment, I think she's going to help me.

Then I look up into her cornflower blue eyes.

I stand up quickly and pull the stroller back two steps. Livvy screams.

"Miranda."

Her eyes are fixed on the wailing baby. "She needs me."

I shake my head. "No, she doesn't. She's fine."

Miranda clutches her leather-gloved hands to her chest, rubbing. "She needs her mother to nurse her. Don't keep me from my baby."

Her words ripple through the crowd and a lot of eyes turn toward us. They're not friendly eyes.

I have five panic buttons within reach, because Daddy is who he is. And I'll be getting a text any second asking if I'm okay because of the heart rate monitor. If I summon him, he'd be here in ten minutes. Or less, knowing Daddy. Brenna's just on the other side of the shop door and Master Mac's upstairs. Help's in easy reach.

But I don't need their help. I take out Livvy's paci and give it to her. Thank goodness she accepts it this time and sucks on it tearfully. I straighten my spine, keeping my hand on the stroller handle, positioning my body between Miranda and the baby.

"Logan told you to stay away, Miranda," I say. "He has full custody and he doesn't want you near Livvy."

She blinks those big blue eyes and tears roll down her cheeks. "Emily, you're a woman. You know he's being a monster. I'm her mother. Please, let me hold her. Let me nurse her. I'm in so much pain without her."

I swallow hard, because it does feel a little cruel to block Miranda completely from Livvy's life. But that's the rule and I obey Daddy's rules.

"I'm sorry, Miranda. No. Daddy told you no. I'm telling you no. You're not allowed near Livvy or me. You should leave."

It's only after the words are out of my mouth that I realize I've called Logan "Daddy" in public. In front of a group of people entrusting their children to Daddy's friend. But I don't try to take it back. Logan is my Daddy. I won't let Miranda kink-shame me.

Miranda cries, big gasping sobs that seem fake to me but there's no way I'm going to accuse her of acting. Not in front of this crowd that could so easily swing against me. I totally understand how Shannie felt. This situation is teetering, dangerous. My breath is coming in small pants and I feel like crying, too. But I don't. I'm a fierce, white dragon standing tall, protecting my baby dragon. I'm not scared of the Mir-witch. She can't hurt me. Her tears are fake. Her words are lies.

"I think you should go, Miranda," I say.

With a rattle, the door on the other side of the crowd bursts open. Brenna rushes out onto the sidewalk in a flurry of bright blue dreadlocks and oxblood leather.

"Miranda, get the hell out of here," Bren growls.

Miranda blots at her wet cheeks with the backs of her gloves before holding them up in surrender. "I just want to see my baby."

"You saw her," Brenna says, her low voice going even lower. She almost sounds like Daddy. She herds people into her shop, even though all eyes remain riveted on our little drama. "Now go. And if I find you loitering near my place of business again, I'll call the cops."

"No, there's no need," Miranda says, blinking and talking in a low, sweet tone. Like she's the victim trying to soothe the crazy tattooed bully. "I'll go. I'm not trying to make trouble. I just wanted to see my baby."

She backs up a few steps but it doesn't look like she's actually going anywhere. Certainly not fast. Bren makes it to me, grabs me with one hand and the stroller handle with the other, and pulls us into the shop. She shuts the door firmly.

I sigh and let the colorful, familiar interior calm me. Brenna grabs me and hugs me hard. "You okay?"

I hug her back, then bend over to check on Livvy. She's sucking on her paci, looking around with interest. No tears. When she sees my face, she wriggles and waves her fists at me.

I unbuckle her from the stroller and hug her. She wasn't at risk and she isn't really my baby but I need to hug her, so I do.

"She's psychic," I tell Bren.

"Huh?"

"She's been quiet all morning. She knew this was coming."

Bren tilts her head to look at me. "Sure."

"Just go with it. Psychic Baby."

"Qu'est-ce que c'est. Fa-fa-fa-fa, fa-fa-fa-fa-fa-fa, better run-run-run-run-run-run-run away," Bren sing-songs.

I shake my head at her. "That's Psycho Killer."

"Same thing," Bren says, slinging her arm around my shoulder.

She snags the stroller and pulls it after us as she leads me through her shop and upstairs into what used to be her apartment. Master Mac's daughter is living in it now and what used to be a living room with big storage spaces has been opened up and transformed into Master Mac's daycare. Bren's painted bright murals on the walls. There are play mats on the floor, a row of swings for the babies, a quiet tent for naps and time-outs, and a big, central table piled with coloring supplies where the first activity of the day is set out, ready for the kids who are already circling the table like tiny vultures.

Mac and his daughter, Naomi, are smiling, talking to the parents as they sign in their kids on a big white-board mounted on the wall near the door. Naomi's already got a baby in her arms and the excited squealing filling the room makes up for Livvy's silence.

I stay for a while, making sure Livvy's settled, helping Naomi sort out bottles for the babies' mid-morning feeding. The other two babies are older than Livvy. One's already crawling a little. Mac organizes the kids like a military unit, which is no surprise, and gets the three who don't want to color playing a game of "Simon Says" that has everyone giggling.

I don't realize Bren's waiting for me until Naomi takes Livvy out of my arms and casts a pointed glance at the door. I startle and trot over to her. She wraps her arm around my shoulders.

"Come downstairs and have a cup of coffee with me."

"Tea."

She rolls her eyes. "Tea."

I wave to Naomi and Mac and let Bren escort me downstairs.

"Was I hovering?" I ask her.

"Like a stealth bomber."

"Sorry."

"You don't need to apologize to me." Bren nudges me toward her office chair. She casts a longing glance at the fancy coffee machine Mac bought her before she starts up the little electric kettle in the corner of her office. "I just want to make sure you're okay after that confrontation with Bitch-face."

I pinch my lips between my teeth to keep from giggling at her name for Miranda. Daddy would *not* approve.

"I'm okay," I say honestly. Would I be okay if Daddy and I hadn't worked so hard on my insecurities? If he hadn't made the rules so clear the other night? Maybe not. But I'm unshakable in Daddy's love.

"You looked like a goddamn Valkyrie standing between Miranda and that stroller. Everyone who saw you was scared of you."

I don't think Miranda was scared of me but I did feel fierce.

"Is it wrong for me to feel a little sorry for her?" I ask.

Bren hands me a steaming mug and perches on the edge of the desk. "Look, we all love your empathy, Em but I think it's wasted on the Mir-bitch. She absolutely would not have had any for you if things had gone the other way."

"I know." I blow on my tea to cool it before taking a sip. Ouch, still too hot. "I just can't imagine how she's feeling. She's lost everything."

"She deserves it."

"Right," I agree. "But I just worry a little about what losing everything might drive her to."

"It might drive her to taking a good look at where her bad decisions have led her and turning her shit around. Although personally, I don't see that happening. People like her won't ever see themselves as being in the wrong."

I wrinkle my nose, unable to imagine that level of certainty. Maybe that's how Daddy feels? I'll have to ask him but I don't think so. Daddy asks for input on too many of his decisions to have that level of certitude.

"You didn't look in need of rescuing," Bren says. "But I've got your back. If you need me to kick Miranda's ass, just say the word."

I giggle at the thought. "I don't think so. Daddy wouldn't approve."

"Actually, he was fine with it."

Daddy agreed to physical violence? The spot in my chest that's been warm since I looked up into Miranda's blue eyes and felt serene and confident in my Daddy's love warms a little more.

"Well, it's not necessary," I assure Bren. "I had it covered."

"I saw." She leans over and *tinks* her cup against mine. "You handled that bitch like a boss. Proud of you."

My eyes sting and I blink the sensation away. "You are?"

"Sure." Bren shrugs. "I've had my own run ins with exes from Hell. Mac's ex is in the running for world's biggest bitch. I've had more than one unfriendly conversation with her. But I wasn't constrained by the rules you live with. And I knew if Amy got really up in my face, one good right hook would knock her right off her Louboutins. Miranda's got five inches and probably twenty-five pounds on you. I'm not saying you couldn't take her but I'd need to get you working on a bag for a couple of weeks first."

I giggle at the thought. "Bruiser baby."

Bren snorts. "Anyway, you dealt with her well and I know it can't have been easy, so good job, and if you ever need backup, call me. I got you, babe."

"Thanks."

I stay until Bren has to get ready for her first client, chatting about the book we're doing together, my ongoing war with Master Mac for control of the kitchen, and a scene Bren's salivating about that Mac's promised her. It's a full-on abduction and cage scene. Mac's planning it for the weekend before Thanksgiving and Bren's vibrating with anticipation.

I walk briskly back through the East Village. It's gotten cold and even though I'm wrapped up well in a coat, gloves, and scarf, the wind stings my cheeks and makes the tip of my nose go numb.

While I walk, I think over the confrontation with Miranda. I always overthink things like this, turning them over in my mind for days, coming up with comebacks that didn't even occur to me in the moment.

But today, there's nothing that makes me prickle with embarrassment. There's nothing I would have done differently if I had a do-over.

When I walk into the house, I hear Daddy still on the phone with Max. I take off my clothes, fold them, and leave them on the rack by the door. Then I walk into Daddy's office and kneel by his chair.

"Uh, I think that's it for now, Max," Daddy says.

I smile to myself at the sudden gruffness of his voice. Daddy likes seeing me naked and kneeling.

"Emmy just come in and take her clothes off?" Max asks.

I giggle.

"Bye, mate," Daddy says. "Email me with anything else."

"Will do." Max chuckles as he hangs up.

Daddy swivels in his chair and puts his big, bare feet on either side of my knees. His warm hand settles on the top of my head.

"Hello, baby."

"Hi, Daddy."

"Something you want to tell me?"

"Um-hmm. Miranda was waiting for me outside Bren's shop. I told her to go away. She did. Livvy's a psychic baby."

"She, um, did you say Livvy's psychic?"

"I did. I mean, how else do you account for her being so quiet this morning? As soon as she saw Miranda, she began crying, which is probably because she still identifies Miranda with nursing and babies cry to get the attention of the person nursing them but still, totally psychic."

"Okay, we'll come back to that. Tell me how seeing Miranda made you feel, baby doll."

"Warm."

"Warm? Could you explain that a little more?"

"My chest felt warm. Little bit adrenaline. Lots knowing I was safe and loved and she couldn't hurt me or Livvy."

"Baby," Logan breathes. He pats his thighs. "Come up. Daddy needs to hold you."

I climb up into his lap and wrap myself around him.

"I hate that she confronted you," Daddy murmurs to me, tucking my face into his neck.

I snuggle into him, taking big sniffs of his clean clothes and

Wolfy Daddy aftershave. "I know but I wasn't scared. I thought about how you were just a button away. If I'd yelled, Bren would have come to help me. But I didn't need it. I was a strong white dragon protecting my . . . um, protecting my dragon-kin."

"Oh, baby girl, I love that so much." Daddy squeezes me tight. "That's a good visualization. You are a strong white dragon. You were safe. You are loved."

"She doesn't scare me anymore."

"I'm sorry she ever did. Did she say anything awful?"

I shake my head, nuzzling in. "Nope, just asked me to let her nurse her baby. She said Livvy needed her. But she doesn't. Livvy's safe and loved, too. She's getting every immunological advantage. I felt strong saying no."

"The only thing Miranda offers is instability and neglect, sweetheart. I hope you know that."

I rub my palm up and down the smooth cotton of his nice sweater. "I believe that, Daddy. You haven't told me what you had on her that got you custody and I'm okay with not knowing. I know you have good reasons for not telling me. But I also know it must have been awful and it must have had something to do with her fitness as a parent to convince the judge to give you full custody. I feel sorry for her but I also know you've done the right thing getting Livvy away from her."

"Emmy, your belief in me is everything," Daddy chokes. "It humbles me." He holds me in silence for a long moment. "If you want me to tell you what I used to get custody of Livvy I will but I honestly don't want those thoughts in your head, baby."

"Nope, I'm good."

He sighs. "I love you so much, baby. I'm so proud of you. I'm so grateful to have you in my life."

"Samesies, Daddy."

He chuckles. "What reward can I give my little wonder, hmm? Would you like a good girl pussy spanking now and a big scene tomorrow night at Blunts?"

I bounce in his lap. "Always up for those, Daddy."

"That's my enthusiastic little girl. Let me clear off the desk, then my amazing little love is going to bend over and get her ass up so Daddy has a good, clear target."

"Yes, Daddy!"

Laughing, soft and wicked, Daddy helps me off his lap and starts moving everything off his desk.

nineteen

LOGAN

THE SECOND STAKEOUT starts off the same as the first. Me and Mac in a darkened, empty club with our overnight bags under our arms.

I'm determined this stakeout won't end the same as the first one. I have better tools this time. In my bag, there's a care package from Max with fancy equipment nestled carefully in foam. I'm not even sure what all the little machines do but Max is already yapping away in my ear. He'll talk me through them all.

Mac and I set up in the kitchen: unfolding cots and unrolling our sleeping bags. I check the locks, which don't look tampered with. It's been a few days since anything's been stolen but even before that, the few locks at the club never looked forced. Joker's B is either getting in some other way or has a Master's degree in lock-picking.

"What the fuck is that?" Max asks in my ear.

I look up from the bags I'm unloading on my cot. Mac is standing in the middle of the room, panning his phone around so Max can see the room's details.

"What?" I ask.

"That huge fucking vent in the ceiling," Max says.

I look up at the white slat-covered vent. "Oh, yeah, Sacrum's HVAC system dates back to the Victorian era."

"Lo, do the HVAC vents run to every part of the club?" Max asks.

"Most of it. Definitely the dungeons, changing rooms, bathrooms, and hallways. Not sure about the office. I don't think there's a vent in there, actually, because it has a window-unit air conditioner."

"Take the wizard wand out of my toolkit and hold it up toward the vent," Max says. Keys clack in the background.

"Maxie, there's no way a person could get through those vents."

Mac rubs his chin. "Could if they were a child. Or a very small woman."

I eye the vent. He's crazy. The vent cover is maybe one foot square. You'd have to be part cat to get your shoulders through it.

I unpack Max's box o' tricks and find the wand. If it's a wizard wand, it's the world's shortest wizard wand. It's maybe five inches long and an inch around, tapering slightly at one end. It's matte black. I swear, Max must custom-order all his cool toys from the same supplier. I bet he and De Leon jerk off together over the catalogue.

I pick it up and a ring of blue light runs around the fat end of the wand.

"Hold it up to the vent," Max says.

When I do, beeping erupts in my ear.

"Fuck," Max says. "Get a ladder and get that vent cover off. There's something with a localized signal broadcasting from the vent."

I look at Mac. Mac looks back at me. We both grimace. If there's a camera up in that vent, no wonder Joker's B knew exactly what we've been doing. They were watching us the whole time.

I hand the wizard wand to Mac and trudge off to get my ladder.

When I remove the vent cover and a hundred years of dust lands in my face, I find a square white box taped to the vent cover with electrician's tape.

"Damn," Mac says.

"Mommy cam," Max says. "Cheap. Good range of vision. Bad news, I can't trace the signal back to a phone number because it runs through a cloud app. Potentially good news is that those things chew through batteries, so Joker's B would need access to it frequently to replace the batteries. That means they're moving around through the vents, Lo."

I eye the dark maw of the vent. "I don't think even Emily could squeeze through there. Not without dislocating her shoulders."

"Face it, Lo," Mac says. "Joker's B is a kid."

I shake my head, although whether that's unwillingness to admit I've been outwitted by a kid or just utter chagrin, I can't say.

"It makes sense," Max says. "Those notes. What they've stolen. Young teen or tween maybe."

"I'm honestly not sure if that's better or worse," I say.

"Plaster over your wounded pride and grab the box out of the kit with Verifsys on it. Also take out the thing that looks like a fabric pouch."

I locate the correct matte black box and gray fabric bag.

"Okay, listen to all of my directions before you do anything. We're going to fritz that camera. Turn off all your electronic devices. Phones, your laptops, smart watches, everything. Put them in the fabric bag and zip it shut. Take the mommy cam and the Verifsys box outside, away from any telephone poles or electric lines. Find the on button on the Verifsys box. Turn it on and let it warm up. Then hold the camera against the Verifsys box for a count of thirty. That will kill it. Turn off the Verifsys box. Then you're safe to go back inside. Power up your phones, put your earpieces in, and call me."

"Will do."

Mac and I follow Max's instructions to the letter and are back inside in less than five minutes. Max runs us through using the wizard wand to test the mommy cam and confirms its dead.

"If you find any other mommy cams, follow the same procedure to kill them."

"What's the range of the wizard wand?" I ask Max.

"Less than five feet. You have to be right on top of it. There's so much clutter in urban areas with radio signals, home broadband routers, smart appliances, and smart phones that it's increasingly hard to isolate signals."

"You did it remotely with Bren's shop," Mac recalls.

"Yeah, because I have that place wired down to the ground already."

Mac clears his throat. "We'll talk about that another time."

I raise my eyebrows at Mac. Does he object to Max's monitoring? It makes me feel safer. Mac shakes his head.

Guess it's between the two of them.

"So, walking around and sticking the wizard wand at all the vents in this place is . . ."

"Inefficient but not a waste of time," Max finishes my question.

"Well, we do have all night," I say.

Mac and I divide up the task. While he has an hour's kip, I walk around sticking the wizard wand at random vent covers. No pings. Max is silent in my ear.

Maybe this is stupid. Maybe there's another reason there's a mommy cam in the kitchen vent, although I can't believe Jaimie or Olaf didn't mention it.

I rejoin Mac and we eat a late dinner together. Emmy's gone all out, in my little girl's usual fashion. Curried chicken sandwiches, potato salad with crunchy capers, fluffy rolls fragrant with garlic and sprinkled with sesame seeds, mini-quiches, tiny pork pies with boiled quail eggs hidden in the middle, and for dessert, Bakewell squares. My baby doll knows me so well.

"Emmy can cook," Mac admits. "Although I sense my girl's hand with spices in that curried chicken."

I chuckle and nod. Emmy knows I like strong seasoning but she was nervous about over-spicing my food until she started cooking with Brenna. Brenna believes Scotch bonnet peppers are just pleasantly tingly.

I sit back on my cot and rub my full belly. "I've never eaten better, not even when my mum was alive. How do you do it? Owing your girl for taking such good care of you while still being tough with her?"

Mac's always been a harder sadist than I am. Until he came to Blunts with me, I'd forgotten how heavy the play he goes for is. He wrings tears of pain out of Bren, and she is a leather-ass if I've ever met one. He's also unexpectedly inflexible when it comes to his rules. I put a lot of rules in place to keep Emmy safe. Mac has very few rules for Bren but even a hint of an infraction gets Bren a punishment that would break quite a few masochists of my acquaintance.

"Ah." Mac stretches back on his own cot. "First, I don't look at it as owing her. She takes care of me because she loves me. I'm hard on her because I love her."

I nod. I feel that way, too but sometimes it gets lost in the overwhelming rush of gratitude I feel toward Emily.

"Second," Mac continues, "it's not just about love. It's about respect. We respect each other's strengths and weaknesses. Bren's great about feeding me, physical affection, being in my corner. Her communication skills suck balls. I have decent communication skills. I'm pretty good about recognizing her physical needs. I don't always show physical affection and I'm not great about giving her space. I work on her communication. She reminds me to show physical affection and pushes back when I crowd her. We're better as a team. Respect. That's our love language."

I like that. I make a mental note to mention respect as a love language to Emmy.

"You look better," Mac grunts. "Healthier. I know it's not about your cholesterol or recovering from that head injury. It's overall. You're in a good place now."

"I am," I agree. "I didn't expect to be. A week ago, my head was in a goddamn shed with everything. Olivia coming. Worrying about how Emmy would adapt. The Nursery opening at Blunts. What the fuck is going on with the house subs. And this bloody job. But it's coming together. Emmy's solid and that gives me a foundation for everything. It's nuts to base so much of my mental well-being on another person. I know that. But everything comes back to her, Mac. Everything revolves around her."

"You know, before seeing you and Em, I'd have lectured you on the dangers of basing your happiness on another person. You have to be happy in yourself, fulfilled in your job, yadda, yadda. But seeing you with her, understanding what a caregiver relationship is, I get it. Taking care of your little fulfills a need in you that's never been met before. That's why you weren't satisfied with Miranda or any of your previous subs, Lo. You need to be needed."

"Do you?" I ask.

"Not like you do. But I had a hole in my heart. Wasn't even an Amy-sized hole. I'd given up on being her Dom a long time ago. It was a failure-sized hole. Maxie mentioned somethin' he and Myles talked about. About topping our girls being a chance for a do-over, a chance for a clean win. That's definitely the hole I was toting around."

"Is your relationship with Bren a do-over?" I ask. Because that makes sense. I knew Mac felt he'd failed Amy.

"Better," Mac says. "It's a do-above. It's a fresh start with better tools, better skills. I can't regret my failure with Amy because it taught me to be the Dom Bren needs. I wouldn't be able to handle my DirtyGurl if I hadn't topped Amy for all those years."

"She is a challenge," I say, not envying Mac that challenge at all. She'd drive me crazy.

"Fucking Everest," Mac says.

I chuckle, remembering Theo saying something similar.

"You know she got that worked into one of her tattoos?" Mac asks. I shake my head. I don't make close inspection of Brenna's tattoos. "It's the one on her thigh, with the barbed wire. She worked a little outline of the Himalayas and my name into the tattoo. She said she wouldn't overwrite her history but she wanted to show how I'd conquered her."

"Damn."

I need to look at the tattoo. And not feel too envious. I have no reason to be. Emily's wearing one of my brands already. But it's not my name.

I got the "X" brand custom-made. I bet they could make a "Daddy" brand.

Thinking happy Daddy-brand thoughts, I stretch out on my cot and take my shift of power-napping while Mac cleans up our dinner and goes to poke around with the wizard wand.

When I wake up, Mac tells me he found and disposed of three more mommy cams, including one in the central hallway that leads from the dungeons to the changing rooms, office, and kitchen.

"You're fucking kidding me," I grumble. "Joker's B watched me install all the goddamn cameras?"

"Looks that way. The vent's in the middle of the hallway. Good view in all directions."

I rub the bridge of my nose. "I fucked up. I was so focused on Maxie going to England to collect Livvy that I didn't use him on this job the way I should have. I should have had him sweep the whole building first."

"That's neither cost-effective nor in the spec for this job, Lo. Sacrum hired you to install a CCTV system. That's what they could afford. You went above-and-beyond, the way you always do, to solve their problem. But let's be clear, you have not failed them. You have not fucked up. You're taking the world on your shoulders again, son."

I roll my shoulders to show that I'm not bearing anything on them other than my sweater. "Taking on too much is kind of the job description for a Daddy Dom."

Mac nods. "Sure is, when it comes to Emmy. But this job is not your little girl. Separate them in your mind."

He's right.

"I hate not fixing shit," I admit.

"I know. It's what makes you good at your job, good at managing the house subs, and good at being Emmy's daddy. But there's a difference between fixing shit and tilting at windmills. You cannot take on the whole world's problems. Emmy's your priority. Take on too much when it comes to her. Everything else? Do what you can to fix the shit but accept that you can't solve the world's ills."

I nod. "You're right."

"I know I am. I also know it's going to take more than one of these talks to convince you. Tap me when you're ready for the next one."

I chuckle. "Yes, sir."

Mac rubs his chin. "It's been a while since you called me that. I've been getting used to not hearing it from anyone but my girl."

"Sorry, Mac. That hadn't occurred to me."

"S'okay. It's just a change. A good one." He steeples his hands over his belly. "Don't know if I mentioned it but I called Annabelle."

"Did she speak to you?"

Mac shakes his head. "Not in depth yet. She asked me for some time. She says she's still processing. I asked if I could call her back day after tomorrow and she said yes. We'll see how it goes."

"Good," I say. "I emailed Chess and asked to add member retraining and guest security issues to the next management committee meeting agenda."

"He get back to you?" Mac asks.

"No but he doesn't usually the same day. Chess likes to sleep on things, as he's told me a million times."

"Fair enough," Mac says but it's a grumble. "'Long as he's not asleep at the switch. Can't say as I'm overly impressed with his handling of the things I've seen. He's supposed to be top dog. Buck stops with him. Sure, we can blame the situation with the house subs on your friend Ryan but Chess should have realized things were going south long before it got to this state."

"This isn't an excuse but his wife died not that long ago."

Mac shrugs. "We all got shit going on. I'm not trying to be

unsympathetic but if he's grieving and not up to managing the club then he needs to step back."

"From a financial perspective," I say, playing Devil's advocate, "the club's running well."

"Financial matters can stay in the same hands," Mac allows. "I'm talkin' about managing people, not money."

"Agreed."

"You wanna be chairman?" he asks.

"Fuck." I rub my hands over my face. "Really?"

Mac sits back on his cot, propped on his hands behind him. He hums something. It takes me a moment before I recognize Tracy Chapman's "Talkin' Bout a Revolution."

"I figure you've got the seniority," Mac says. "But if you don't want it, I'd understand. Maude'd be my second pick."

"Maude," I confirm. "Emmy's always got to be my first priority. Maude's well-liked by most of the members. She's steady and thoughtful. She'll lead the club well."

Mac nods. "That's settled then."

"Good. I'm flattered you thought of me, Mac."

Mac shakes his head. "Someday, Lo, you're gonna see yourself the way everyone else sees you." He chuckles. "Maybe it's better you don't. I like the little drop of humility you got left."

I snort at him.

twenty

LOGAN

BEING Emmy's Daddy has given me what my mum used to call "me old mam hearing." Small sounds, quiet breathing, light footsteps—before Emily, I'd have ignored them and gone back to sleep. Now, they put me on high alert.

I'm dozing on my cot when me-old-mam hearing jerks me awake. I lay still and listen.

As I do, Max's voice crackles in my ear. "Lo, Mac, I've got a new signal. Lots of distortion. Could be in the vents."

I roll out of bed. I take my taser out of my bag before grabbing the ladder and setting it up under the vent. I have no chance of chasing Joker's B through the vents. I doubt I could even get both arms into that small square. I don't like doing it, particularly if Joker's B really is a teen but I need to scare the beejeezus out of them and make them come out of the vents.

The tiniest pop of metal and the softest sliding sound gives me a few seconds of warning. I crouch at the top of the ladder, keeping my body to one side, so Joker's B won't see me until they look down into the room from the vent.

I glance down at Mac. He's lying still, one arm behind his head but his eyes are open and he's got his gun in its holster resting on his chest.

I don't have to tell him not to fire. Mac's judgment is sounder than my own.

I also really do not want to tase someone in an enclosed metal space. Here's hoping the threat is enough.

Another tiny pop and a head of dark, thick hair appears in the open vent. Brown eyes in a black mask widen as they meet mine.

"Move and I'll tase you," I warn.

"Eep," says the masked bandit in the vent.

It *is* a kid. Long, dark hair hangs around the kid's face. Hard to tell if it's a boy or a girl, given the length boys wear their hair these days but the compact face with rounded cheeks and unlined skin below the mask tells the tale.

I hold my free hand up into the vent. "Take my hand. I'm going to pull you out. Fight me and I'll break your wrist, *then* tase you."

"Muh-master Logan?" the kid squeaks.

"Don't call me master. Take my hand."

"Cuh-can we talk about this?"

"Yep, we can talk a fucking lot about this. Once you're out of the vent."

"You're scaring me," the kid whispers.

Fuck.

"Come out of the vent. Nothing bad will happen to you."

The kid's eyes narrow. "That's a lie."

"No, it's not. I'm not a liar."

"Promise," the kid insists. "Promise nothing bad will happen to me."

"Lo—" Mac says, his voice low and warning.

I know he's right. I'm overpromising. But this is a scared kid.

"I promise nothing bad will happen to you," I say. "Take my hand."

A small hand slips out of the vent and grasps mine.

With a lot of maneuvering that includes Mac standing under the vent and helping catch the kid as she decants herself—yes, *her*self: small curves under a sweatshirt that's a size or two too small for her —out of the HVAC system, we all end up standing, dusty and the worse for wear, in the middle of Sacrum's kitchen.

The kid wraps skinny arms around herself. Under the dust, she's tattered. Her hair's unevenly cut and frizzy. The thin sweatshirt shows too much skin at her wrists and above the waistband of her worn jeans. A faded red sock pokes through a hole in the toe of her sneakers.

"Take off the mask," Mac commands.

Meekly, she pulls it off. As she does, I realize it's one of the club's blindfolds with holes sawed out for the eyes.

She's . . . cute. And probably all of thirteen.

Mac curses quietly. "How old are you?"

"Almost sixteen."

Yeah, in like three years.

"Logan promised nothing bad would happen to you but I did not," Mac says, enunciating each word. "Don't lie to us."

She shivers and hugs herself tighter. "I'm not. My birthday's in May."

"Your sixteenth birthday's in May?" Mac presses.

The girl nods.

"What's your name?" I ask more gently. Guess I'm playing good cop.

"My club name's Truly. True to my . . . friends."

I think Mac growls "ironic" under his breath but I ignore him.

"You're too young to have a club name," I say. "What's your real name?"

The girl shakes her head. "Truly's the name I've picked for myself. It's the name inside me. If I tell you my outside name, you'll turn me over to child protection. I'm not going back there."

I glance at Mac. He looks back at me.

I sigh.

"You can't keep breaking into the club," I begin.

"Why not?" she flares suddenly. "I haven't taken anything anyone will really miss. Just what I needed to survive. I'm not hurting anyone. I haven't damaged anything. I won't. I'm not like that. I just want a safe place."

I start to say Sacrum isn't a safe place but of course, that's exactly what we want it to be. Every sign, every flyer posted around the club talks about safety, consent, risk-awareness. As soon as she stepped through the door, or climbed through the vent, she was surrounded by indications this place would keep her safe.

"The club could be closed down if anyone found out a minor was inside," I say instead. And then a really awful thought hits me. "You said your friends call you True. Do you have any friends here? In the club? Have you been meeting anyone here?"

If she says "yes" and I find out one of the club members has been grooming this kid, I'm going to puke, and then kill them.

She shakes her head. "I heard about it at school, from some seniors who came. They said they tried things and it was safe and there were monitors and everyone was cool. They said the sand-wiches were good afterward. I just wanted a safe place. And the sandwiches *are* good."

Thank goodness for small mercies.

"I'm sorry, you can't keep coming here. We'll . . . we'll find you another safe place."

"Lo," Mac grumbles, shaking his head.

"Come on, Mac. We can't leave her here."

"We can't take her with us. What are you going to do, let her sleep on our couch tonight? You can't. She's a minor and you're not a foster."

Damn.

I rub the back of my neck, praying for divine inspiration.

A spark ignites and I pull out my phone. Tapping up my Blunts contact list, I thumb a number that I've called more lately than I want to but less than I should have, given our last interaction, which was decidedly unfriendly.

"Someone better have died," Theo answers with a groan on the third ring.

"Sorry to call in the middle of the night, mate," I say. "I have a situation at Sacrum. The thief's a fifteen-year-old girl. She says she has no safe place to go. What do I do?"

"Call Jersey's Division of Child Protection and Permanency."

True bristles and opens her mouth. I hold up a hand. "What *else* do I do?"

"Lo, fucking motherfuck, it's three in the morning."

"I know what time it is. I also know I have a fifteen-year-old kid here with no safe place to go. You're the cop. Tell me what to do."

"I'll tell you what you don't do. You don't take her home, because I know that's what you're thinking. Don't do it. The kid cries rape or abuse and you're fucked."

"I wouldn't!" True protests.

I hold up my hand again and add a glare.

Theo grumbles. "You need someone who's an emergency foster or law enforcement to take her for the rest of the night. In Jersey. You can't bring her to New York tonight."

"Mac and I figured that already," I tell Theo.

Mac grunts and takes out his own phone. With both of us occupied, True's eyes flick toward the door.

I hold up my taser.

She scowls.

"Then you call Franco," Theo says. "Wake him up at your fucking peril. Tell him you need to file an emergency application for the protection of a minor. The kid will have to give a statement. There will be a hearing. If you haven't figured out somewhere for the kid to go, I'm warning you, child protection will put her in whatever placement they have. Jersey's child welfare department was one of the worst in the nation. It's improved but last I heard, they were still under oversight of a federal court monitor because the problems are so severe. Keep your expectations low."

"Okay. If I needed you to call in a favor over the state line, could you?"

Theo swears colorfully. "Are you serious? *You* owe *me* after that bullshit with Brenna and those bikers."

"Keep your mind off my sub," Mac grumbles, as he types into his phone.

True's eyes track away from the door and settle on Mac. Is that . . . hero worship in her big brown eyes?

Theo huffs.

"Theo," I say, to refocus him. "This is a *minor* who does not have a safe place to go. A kid who has been breaking into Sacrum because she felt it was safe. Are you hearing me?"

I leave Emmy and Brenna's belief that she's a submissive unspoken but strongly implied.

Theo swears some more. "You owe me a hundred goddamn dinners at the Trattoria for this, you emotionally-blackmailing asshole. I know someone in the Jersey DA's office. I'll call her when her office opens."

"Thank you, Theo."

"Don't get your hopes up."

I wink at True. "We won't."

She smiles shyly.

"Oh, and call Maude," Theo says.

I know Maude's a nurse, well, former nursing administrator but I don't see how calling her could help. "Okay. Why?"

"Because she's a member at large for the Communication Workers of America. That's the union for social workers in Jersey. You want to pull strings for this kid? No one can pull more strings than that woman."

I chuckle at the image of us all dancing like marionettes at the end of Maude's strings. On second thought, there might be more truth in that image than is comfortable. "Thanks. I will."

"Good night. What's left of it," Theo grumps. "I'll set my alarm and make that call first thing. Keep your phone on."

"Always do. Sincerely, Theo, thanks."

"You're welcome. Don't call me in the middle of the night again unless someone's dying. Preferably you."

I chuckle and say goodbye.

Mac continues to type into his phone without looking up. "I think I might have a solution for tonight."

I don't question him, because if Mac says he has a solution, he has a solution. But I didn't know he knew anyone in Jersey.

His phone pings; he smiles at it. "We're gonna owe everyone in two states dinner by the time tonight's over but I got a place for her to sleep. Qualified foster *and* former law enforcement. Can't ask for more than that."

He's right, we can't.

True looks up at me, her brown eyes huge. "For all of us, right? You're staying with me, Master Logan? Master Mac? Please?"

She swings the big guns on Mac. He glances up from his phone, swallows, and looks back down to type.

"Don't call either of us master," I say gruffly.

"But you are, right? You have a submissive? A *little*? I've heard you talk about her with Miss Vizzi. Miss Vizzi's really scary, isn't she? And Master Mac just said the cop should keep his mind off Master Mac's sub. You're both masters. You both have subs you protect, who submit to you, right?"

"You're too young to have that conversation," I grumble.

"I'm not." True plants her fists on her narrow hips. "I know what dominance and submission is. I've watched scenes. I've already had sex."

Mac sticks one finger in his ear. "La-la-la, I'm not hearing anything about the tween having sex."

"I'm not a tween!" True flares. "I'm almost sixteen. When did you start having sex?"

Mac grimaces at his phone but doesn't answer. I keep my mouth shut. I'm not sure when Mac started having sex but I know if I say a word about this topic it'll be massively hypocritical.

"Mac and I both have submissives," I admit. "And my submissive is a little. But just because we're masters to them, doesn't mean we're masters to you. There has to be consent. Do you understand that? That everyone in a scene, in the lifestyle, has to consent. We don't inflict dominance and submission on other people."

True tucks her hands behind her back and nods solemnly. "I've just started learning about consent around vanillas."

I rub my free hand over my face, trying to get my head around a fifteen-year-old knowing what people in the lifestyle call people who aren't.

"Okay, so let's be clear, Mac and I are masters but we're not *your* masters. We do not consent to you giving us your submission. Does that make sense?"

True nods. "Even though I'd consent to you being my masters?"

"Fucking hell," Mac mutters. "No."

"Even if you'd consent to us being your masters. Do you understand why?"

True shakes her head.

"This is not personal. The first reason is you're not old enough to give consent. The age of consent in New Jersey is sixteen. You can't legally give consent until after your birthday in May. Even if you want to give consent, you can't. It's unsafe for other people to play with you until you can give consent. It's statutory rape. They could be prosecuted and go to jail. Do you understand that you'd be creating an unsafe space for your master if you tried to give consent when you can't?"

Her face falls. "I didn't think of that."

"Something to think about. The second reason is that Mac and I already have submissives. We have existing relationships with those submissives. Whether or not those relationships are romantic, D/s relationships are just as important. You wouldn't try to break up a boyfriend and girlfriend, would you?"

She shakes her head. "I'd never."

"Inserting yourself into a power-exchange relationship unasked is the same thing."

"Okay," True says, looking chastened.

Mac grunts and puts his phone away. "Pack up, Lo. Uber'll be here in 5. We've got a twenty-minute drive. They'll be ready when we get there." He settles his glare on True. "With a bed for you. Before you ask again, Logan and I can't stay in the same house because we're not certified fosters. We're going to a hotel. We won't even be ten minutes away. We'll both give you our numbers. You'll be safe. We're reconvening for breakfast at eleven after we've all gotten some sleep and had time to make some calls. Do you have school tomorrow?"

True shakes her head. "They think I have mono. I'm on distance learning."

"Do you have mono?" I ask, suddenly worried about what I'm taking home to Emmy and Livvy.

True rolls her eyes. "Obviously not. Jenny Ennis has it. She told me how to fake."

Mac narrows his eyes at her but doesn't say anything before he turns and starts packing up his kit.

I hold my hand out to True.

She raises her eyebrows.

"Phone," I say. "I know you have at least one."

She wiggles her nose and mouth. Kid has a face made for comedy. So expressive.

Eventually, she fishes a cheap phone out of a hidden pocket in the waistband of her jeans, unlocks it, and hands it to me.

While I type my and Mac's numbers in, I nod to her. "Smart not to keep it in an outside pocket. Most adults wouldn't frisk you."

She crosses her arms over her chest. "Are you going to frisk me?"

I chuckle. "No. What would you like for breakfast? Pancakes?"

Her arms lower slowly. "Waffles?"

"Sold."

"And bacon?"

Mac's head lifts from his packing. "Definitely bacon."

A small smile creeps across the kid's face.

twenty-one

EMILY

I PACE across the kitchen floor again, bouncing Livvy in her chest harness.

She's been an angel since Daddy and Mac went to Jersey to stake out Sacrum again. Even without Logan to give her a bath and put her to bed last night, she went down at ten o'clock on the dot for her big sleep and slept through until half-past seven. Yes, she slept in our bed but Daddy doesn't need to know that. It's really hard for me to lower her into her crib without waking her. Daddy's so tall, he just bends at the waist but I have to go up on my tip-toes and then lower her off my chest and she startles like I'm dropping her and starts crying. Climbing into our bed with her last night was so much easier.

Livvy's not what's gotten me pacing.

I'm pacing in part because I'm excited to meet Joker's B. Daddy and Mac are bringing her to breakfast. Well, brunch. But still, how exciting is that? A real-life thief! I have all kinds of questions for her. How did she find Sacrum? How did she first get in? How did she evade the posse? Does she know how to pick locks? How did she avoid Daddy's cameras? Sooo many questions. I hope Daddy will let me ask some of them.

The second reason I'm pacing is because of the letter that arrived this morning. It was addressed to me, so I opened it but I wish I'd waited until Daddy was back.

It was from Miranda.

Dear Emily,

I implore you to let me see my baby. I feel like I'm dying without her. You must have held her. You know her baby smell, how soft she is in your arms. Please let me hold her just one more time. You know Logan's punishing me by keeping me away from Olivia. You know this is a monstrous thing to do. He's hurting Olivia as well as me. You heard the way she cried for me. I've come all this way. I'm staying at the First Park hotel. Bring my baby to me. Do the right thing, Emily.

Miranda

I don't know what to do. I do know that baby smell, and how soft Livvy feels in my arms. I can't imagine anyone taking her away from us now and she's not even mine. I don't want to feel any sympathy for Miranda but I do. I hate what we're putting her through.

But I trust my Daddy. He's cut off contact with her for good reasons. I don't want to know what horrible things she did that resulted in the judge taking away custody of her baby—I mean, even more horrible than tricking Daddy into getting her pregnant, which is horrible enough on its own—I absolutely trust Daddy's reasoning.

But it does feel cruel.

I'm glad I'm not a daddy. My heart is much too soft.

The doorbell rings and I abandon my pacing to answer it. Sable's there before me, weaving back and forth on the welcome mat and sniffing. I know it's not Daddy. Manny only picked up everyone in Jersey twenty minutes ago, so they'll be a while. But there are lots of other people coming to this meeting, so I'm not sure who will arrive first.

I check the door cam and disable the security when I see Mistress

Maude. She walks through; a young man a few inches taller than Maude follows her closely. He's wearing a gray hoodie pulled up around his face under a big overcoat and loose sweatpants. That tells me he's wearing his fursuit today.

I hold my hands out for his outer-wear. Georgie kisses me on the cheek and peels off his coat, hoodie, and sweatpants carefully. He's been really generous about letting me inspect his fursuit. I know other fursons are not cool with having their fursuits handled. Georgie's mouse-suit is the softest, finest synthetic fur. He says it's durable but I've noticed he's careful with it, particularly when he's putting clothes on over it or taking them off.

He straightens his hood, lining up the ears, takes his paws out of his coat pocket and puts them on. He leaves his mouse-face off.

"I don't want to scare the baby," he says.

Mistress Maude strokes his shoulder. "There's nothing scary about your mouse-face, darling. Livvy will be enchanted."

Georgie's eyes search mine. "Do you think so?"

I think babies are adaptable. "Put it on and let's see," I suggest.

Sable chooses that moment to start winding around Georgie's ankles and purring like a motorboat. Georgie shakes his head. "Not today. I'm going to eat anyway. Better not to eat with my mouse-face on."

Mistress Maude sighs softly and strokes Georgie's nape. She slips off her high-heeled boots and they follow me through to the kitchen.

I've set up a buffet with breakfasty foods, including bacon, sausage links, scrambled eggs, and waffles. The waffles were a special request in Daddy's text this morning telling me to expect about a dozen people for brunch, which is odd because he usually prefers crepes but it's no trouble to make waffles. Everything's covered to keep it warm, and the eggs and meat are on the small hot plate I brought from Syracuse. But I think I'll ask Daddy to add some of those big food warmers that are heated with paraffin burners to our budget. We're entertaining so often now that he's recovered, it makes sense to have bigger warmers.

I start to make tea for Mistress Maude but Georgie gently brushes me aside after I get out a cup and teabag. He takes a small bag of loose tea and one of those pretty silver tea balls out of Maude's bag. The resulting black tea smells *heavenly*.

"What is that?" I ask after I make cups of green tea for me and Georgie.

"It's called Panda Dung but I promise there's no poo in it," Georgie says.

I giggle at the name.

As we're carrying the tea to the table, the front door opens. Bren's voice follows the sound of the heavy door closing. "Hey-ho the house," she calls. "It's just me."

"We're in the kitchen, just me," Maude calls back.

Brenna's grinning as she rounds the corner from the hallway. She went to the shop this morning to do a tattoo but Master Mac asked her to come back to meet with Joker's B. The house is warm, although we're all keeping our clothes on with Joker's B coming, she's stripped down to a T-shirt and her oxblood leather pants, her dreadlocks unbound and flowing over her shoulders. For the first time since I've known her, Bren looks her age. She's only twenty-seven, five years younger than me but she's been so down while I've known her that people always assume she's older than me.

Today, she looks a carefree twenty-something. She walks lightly through the great room, holding open her arms. "Baby time!"

I unhook the harness and hand Livvy to Bren. Livvy kicks and coos as I pass her over, then grabs at the blue peonies tattooed on Bren's neck. Bren lifts her up and blows a huge raspberry against Livvy's cheek, which has the baby squealing.

"Where's Daddy Lo and Sir?" Bren asks me as she cradles Livvy against her chest.

"Still probably fifteen or twenty minutes away, depending on the traffic."

Bren nods. "Didn't seem too bad as I walked over but no idea what the tunnel's like." She smooches Livvy's soft head, then turns to Mistress Maude and dips her a little curtsey. "Mistress. Georgie. Good morning."

"Good morning, dear. Georgie would like to stop by and look at your designs. I think a set of chains around his ankles would be delicious. Shall I bring him by over the weekend?"

Brenna nods. "I'm in both mornings. Georgie, if I can get a sample of your fursuit, I'll find some ink so I can tattoo your fursuit as well as your skin, if that's something you'd like?"

Georgie's naturally-hooded eyes go wide. "Yes, please."

Bren smiles at him. "I'm used to tattooing scar tissue. I do a lot of mastectomy pieces. I think it will be similar. I can try doing both your fursuit and your skin at the same time but I think it would be better if we did them separately to avoid the ink bleeding through the layers."

"Whatever you think's best."

The doorbell rings again and since Bren's got the baby, I patter off to answer it. Master Theo leans against the door frame. His expression is sour and there are deep shadows under his eyes.

"Hi, Master Theo."

"Hi, Emmy. Everyone here?"

I shake my head. "Mistress Maude, Georgie, and DirtyGurl."

He grunts and pushes off the door, following me into the house. He's used to Daddy's rules so he takes off his shoes without being asked and hands me his coat.

This is the first time since things got ugly with Brenna and the thief who stole her designs that I've seen Master Theo. He doesn't seem angry or resentful at the way Daddy and Master Mac treated him, just very tired.

"Can I get you a cup of coffee, Master Theo?" I ask when we reach the kitchen.

"God, yes. Make it a double. This is going to be a long-ass day."

"Yes, sir." I start a pot perking, then answer the door for Mistress Dana and Austin and make them drinks, too.

Everyone's got drinks and seats when Daddy and Mac arrive. A skinny, brown-haired girl walks between them. Her head is up, jaw jutting but her eyes dart to every face and away.

I greet her before Daddy and Mac make her feel any *more* like she's walking to her own execution.

"Hi, I'm Emily. It's so nice to meet you." I hold both hands out.

She glances at my hands like she's not sure what to do. Then she bursts into tears.

I look to Brenna, who hands Olivia off to Mac and comes up on the girl's other side. We put our arms around her. Maude fishes a pack of tissues out of her bag and passes them over to us. I help the girl mop up her tears.

"It's okay," I reassure her. "You're in a safe place."

She blows her nose and looks around uncertainly. "I don't know."

"I promise it is. Would you like some breakfast? I made sausages and bacon and lots of waffles."

"You really made waffles?"

"Sure." I tug on her hand. "Come and see all the toppings. I've got strawberries and bananas and blueberries and peaches."

The girl follows me without much prompting. Brenna trails after us. We load up a plate and I get her settled at the table across from Master Theo and next to Daddy. Then I go and make plates for Daddy and myself.

Daddy rewards me with a forehead kiss when I serve him and seat myself. He has Livvy tucked into his right arm, her head cradled in the curve of his shoulder. She's looking up at him, her face shifting with his every expression. I know from reading baby books that she's listening, learning, the way babies do but she looks up at him so adoringly. I can't believe it's not love. When he notices, he hums a bar of "Gaston" from *Beauty and the Beast*. She breaks into giggles.

I blink back tears, seeing how much Daddy's relaxed with his daughter.

Everyone serves themselves and eats. I've topped up everyone's tea and coffee before Master Theo finally addresses the elephant in the room.

"Sorry to play the heavy but I'm the cop Logan spoke to last night while you were listening," he says to True, who has been introduced to everyone by name only. The girl goes rigid in her chair. "I'd like to say that I'm not going to involve your social worker but I have legal obligations if I determine you're unsafe, so I'm not going to make a promise I'd have to break. Can you tell me why you felt your placement was unsafe?"

True looks at Master Mac, then Daddy. She shakes her head.

Brenna leans forward in her chair. "True, I was in the foster system for years. I had bad placements, too, including some where the fosters hurt me. I promise no one here is going to judge you for protecting yourself by leaving and seeking a safe place."

True swallows hard, her eyes darting around the table. She tips her chin at Mistress Maude. "What about you?"

Maude smiles. It's a gentle smile but even that looks pretty scary, I'll admit. Mistress Maude can only tone down so much. "What about me, dear?"

"You and him have the power in this room," True says, lifting her chin at Theo. "He's a cop. What are you?"

I glance at Daddy. He's folded his lips together to control his expression. I think he's as surprised as I am by how quickly True's picked up on the hierarchy in the room.

"A retired nursing administrator," Mistress Maude says with an amazingly straight face.

Brenna snorts. "Okay, stop trying to bullshit the kid. You're right, True. Maude and Theo hold a lot of power in this room."

"Is she—" True's voice cracks. "Is she here to evaluate me? Like for lock-up?"

A chorus of *nos* circles the table.

Maude silences everyone with an upraised hand. "I'm not a psychiatrist, True. I'm a retired nurse. However, you're right that I have influence. I know many people, including social workers in New Jersey. That's why I'm here."

True nods but looks thoroughly cowed.

"This is intimidating to *me*, much less True," Bren says. "You can't bring all this weight down on her. Someone reassure her that she'll have a safe place to stay tonight at least."

Master Mac clears his throat. "I can do that. True, did you feel comfortable with Walter and Erma last night?"

True nods.

"They're happy to have you back. They've offered you a place for fourteen days while we get the emergency application pushed through. It doesn't have to be any more than a place to sleep if you don't want. But you do have a safe place with them."

True's small shoulders drop an inch or two. "Thanks."

"However, Walter's insisting that we contact your social worker today," Mac says. "If you won't tell us why you feel unsafe, we're going to have a much harder time arguing that you should stay with Walt and Erma."

True's eyes slide from Mac to Brenna. She straightens under Mac's arm.

"You know what? There's too much Dom energy in here. It's giving me indigestion," Bren says. "How about we build a blanket fort and watch a movie? Subbie time."

I nod vigorously. Bren and Austin help me clear the table. Georgie starts to rise as well but Maude keeps him at her side with a manicured hand on his arm. After a minute, True gets up from the table and brings us a double-handful of dirty plates.

I thank her with a warm smile and get a shy one in return.

"Was Brenna serious about a blanket fort? Because I'm too old for that," she says as she lingers next to me at the sink.

"She was," I confirm. "And I don't think anyone's ever too old for a blanket fort and a movie. I'm certainly not."

True eyes me. "You're a little, right? I heard Master Logan talking about it. But, um, I'm not really sure what it means. You're not that small."

I grin at her. "Little's not a size. It's a state of mind. It's enjoying being taken care of and being free to do things I like doing, regardless of my physical age."

"Oh." True scratches her chin. She's clean, doesn't smell but I get the feeling she hasn't been able to take care of herself. Her skin and hair look dry, really dry, like she's been using antibacterial soap to wash herself. "I guess a blanket fort and a movie would be okay."

"Would you like a shower or a bath first? You can use anything in the bathroom."

"Is there a lock on the door?" she asks.

My heart breaks for her.

"Yes, there is," I say. "No one will come in. You can use Brenna and Mac's bathroom if you feel safer in there. They have a really nice bathroom with a screen Brenna painted. It's very cool."

True's eyes shift to where Bren's returning from the table with another load of plates. "She's an artist?"

I nod. "Tattoo artist."

True's mouth drops open. "Did she do all those tattoos?" She shakes herself. "Sorry, that's a stupid question. She didn't do her own tattoos. She couldn't reach."

"She drew all of them," I say. "Another tattooist who works for her did most of the actual tattooing."

"That's cool," True says. "I'd love to get some tattoos."

"Talk to Brenna about what you'd like done. She does amazing designs and she'll hold them until you're old enough."

True screws up her face. "I'm old enough now. I'd just need a parent or guardian to sign off on it and there's no way *Blaire* would agree to it."

I keep my expression neutral at her slip but fear flickers through True's eyes.

"Would you like Brenna to show you up to the bathroom?" I ask.

True nods. "I don't understand. Master Logan said it was his house."

"It is. We all live with him."

True glances back at the dining table. "Everyone? How? Like, I get you live here because you're engaged." She nods at my ring. "But how does everyone fit? This place doesn't seem *that* big."

"Some days it does feel like this many people live here because we love having guests but right now, it's just four of us. Logan, me, Mac, and Brenna. Oh, five, because Livvy lives here, too."

"She's your daughter?" True asks.

I shake my head. "She's Logan's daughter."

True's eyes bounce from Logan to his lapful to me. "But not yours?"

"Nope, not yet. Maybe someday." I don't use the word *adoption* because Bren's told me how difficult that word can be for foster kids.

True looks like she's mulling our living situation over with great seriousness. I wave to Bren and ask her if it's okay if True uses her bathroom. Bren nods. She holds out her hand to True. "Should we scavenge Emily's wardrobe for something you'll be comfortable in? Emmy has the best clothes."

True glances at me warily. I nod. "You're welcome to borrow anything. Comfy clothes for a blanket fort and movie are mostly in the dresser. Bren knows where everything is."

"Okay, thanks," True says. "I have my own clothes but every-thing's back . . . um, in New Jersey."

"Borrow anything you like," I confirm.

Brenna leads True off through the great room while I return to Daddy's side.

twenty-two

EMILY

ONCE LIVVY and I are tucked up in Daddy's arms, I tip my head up and whisper in Daddy's ear, "True asked if there was a lock on the bathroom door. Do you think she's being abused?"

"I don't want to jump to conclusions until she tells us more, sweetheart," Daddy responds. "But feeling safe is very important to her, and people who have never felt unsafe aren't as single-mindedly focused on being safe, so I think it's a good bet *something* that makes her fear for her physical safety is going on."

"I didn't expect her to be so young, Daddy," I admit.

"She's told us she's nearly sixteen but she could be lying."

She's a small sixteen if that's how old she is but I was an extremely small sixteen, so I shouldn't question her.

"I hate that she's so young and so alone, Daddy."

Logan sighs. "Baby, I'm concerned for her, too but this isn't something we need to take on right now."

He's right. We've got a lot going on. Still.

"We could just be her friends. And take her to see the Rexes this afternoon with Livvy?"

Daddy chuckles. "Yes, we can do that, baby doll. Mac and I probably need naps first, though."

"You could nap while we watch a movie." After he nods, I add, "She said she knows I'm a little. She asked me about it. Was I right about her being a subbie?"

"Uh-huh. I had to explain that Mac and I are Doms but we're not her Doms. She's having some trouble getting her head around that. She thinks she's looking for a Dom but I think she's just searching for a sense of safety."

"Those things aren't mutually exclusive, Daddy."

He stretches the arm he's got around my shoulders until he can reach around and tap the tip of my nose. "Cheeky monkey. I know they're not. I think she's conflating them. But it's moot. She's too young to submit to anyone, no matter how much she wants to."

Being too young to do something legally and needing it with your whole heart are totally different things.

I shift around so I can stroke his chest. "Please don't take this the wrong way. I don't want to dredge up old hurts. But you had domly-feelings really young—"

"I *didn't* act on them," Daddy says, his lips thinning down to a white line.

"You didn't act on all parts of them," I say, drawing a distinction I've thought about a lot, particularly watching Daddy interact with his sister. "Not on the sexual parts. But I think the line between you as Lizbeth's big brother and you as a dominant is thin, Daddy. I'm not saying it's bad. I see caretaking as a spectrum. Lizbeth's told me you were even tougher on her with rules like doing her homework straight after school and her bedtime and her curfew when she got older than your mom and dad. She said your parents never had to punish her when she did silly things like eat too much Halloween candy or got caught texting her friends past her bedtime because you would give her the cold shoulder for days until she apologized and promised she'd never do it again. You were being a good big brother, enforcing healthy habits. But you were also topping her, Daddy."

Logan's jaw flexes and I know I'm getting close to his line. This is still a touchy subject for him since he feels so very guilty about the thoughts he had about his sister.

I take his free hand and squeeze his fingers between mine. "I know this is wrapped up in your feeling that dominance and submission is sexual. But for lots of people, it's not. It wasn't for me and Matthew and although that became problematic by the end, at the beginning it was good and healthy and helped me heal after my divorce. Please can you see it that way?"

"I'll think about it," he grunts.

With anyone else, I'd feel he was giving me the brush-off. But not my Daddy. He will think about it. He'll turn it over and over and in a week or two, he'll mention it during Knee Time or when we're having a postcoital cuddle. Daddy's a deep feeler. He'll suck my words into his heart. I hope they'll assuage some of his guilt. I also hope they'll help him see that True's submissive needs could be met, even at her age, without crossing any line.

"So, if she's okay with littleness and understands about dominance and submission, could we make the trip to see the Rexes an outing for the playgroup?" I ask, moving away from the touchy subject.

"Sure. Max has already asked to meet her but he and Cynnie are doing something with her stepmother and dad today."

Oh, goodie. Cynnie's been estranged from her family for months after she broke away from them to be with Max. The only family member who has supported Cynnie's independence is her stepmother. They've been having meals and outings frequently to help Cynnie's stepmother get to know Max. Cynnie mentioned during our trip to the corn maze that her stepmother was trying to get Cynnie's dad to join them for a meal. I'll call her later to find out how it went.

"I'll put it in the chat," I say.

Daddy grins suddenly. "What you're really asking is whether I think it's okay for True to meet Sammi."

"Pretty much, Daddy."

He chuckles. "Yeah, I'm actually more concerned about what Sammi might do to the museum than what he might say to True."

"There aren't any bunnies at the museum," I point out.

Sammi's been banned from zoos across the Tri-State area for his . . . exuberance. We've had to put a "look with your eyes, not with your hands" rule in place with him for the Blunts' therapy bunnies.

Daddy raises his eyebrows. "Bones. Big bones. Sharp, pointy bones."

"Fossilized bones, Daddy. Even Sammi would have a hard time—"

"No, don't finish that thought. You're tempting fate. I'm having visions of Sammi spinning around the museum clinging to a T-Rex vertebrae like that scene from *Jurassic Park*."

I burst into giggles. "He wouldn't."

Daddy tips his head. "Not convinced, little girl."

I don't *think* he would. But taking Sable's walking harness and strapping it to Sammi's wrist for the day wouldn't be the *worst* idea, either.

My faith in the power of blanket forts and Disney movies slips a little when True watches all of *Brave* in my tent with its twinkly lights and still doesn't give up the goods. It worked on Bren when she and Master Mac were going through it and I honestly thought there wasn't a tougher nut to crack in the whole world.

But True's even more guarded than Brenna. By the time we've finished the movie and fielded five hundred questions—mostly from Sammi—in the Littles' Army chat about what we're going to do at the museum, she still hasn't told us her real name or who her social worker is. Daddy's upstairs napping but I can foresee this ruining our afternoon.

Nothing should ruin visiting the Rexes.

As we pack up the tent, I put a gentle hand on True's shoulder.

She startles and turns around quickly. I expect her to relax when she sees it's me but she doesn't.

Something finally clicks together. "Is a woman hurting you?"

Her face freezes. "Wh-wha-why would you ask me that?"

"Because of the way you interact with Daddy and Master Mac and me. You don't have to tell me anything but please tell Daddy your name and who your social worker is so you can go back to where you stayed last night. Daddy's a fixer. It's what he does. But he can't fix things if you don't give him the tools he needs to do the job."

"Like a plumber?" True asks.

"Exactly like a plumber," I agree.

Daddy-the-plumber. I wonder if he'd be willing to role-play that? Daddy-the-plumber with his hard pipe . . .

True glances over at the dining table, where Master Theo and Mistress Maude are sitting and looking at something on Maude's phone. I thought Master Theo would either leave after breakfast when Mistress Dana and Austin did or take Daddy up on the offer of a nap in since Daddy evidently woke Theo up in the middle of the night to help with True. But he hasn't. Despite a lot of yawning and three cups of coffee, Master Theo's stayed up, keeping an eye on things.

"Do you trust him?" True asks me.

Do I? He was horrible with Brenna, questioning her like a criminal after *she* was attacked. And I didn't like the way he was with Daddy even before that. But would I call him if there was trouble and he was the only one who could help?

"Yes. He's a policeman, always. But he also understands what we feel deep inside if that makes sense."

True's eyes track across the kitchen to where Brenna's putting out some scraps for Sable. "Was he Brenna's Dom before Master Mac?"

Wow, I wish I had half this girl's intuition.

"Daddy said he talked to you about consent, and how he and

Master Mac are dominants but do not consent to being your dominant, right?"

True nods.

"This falls in the same category. It's not fair of me to talk about any relationship Theo and Brenna might have had without their consent."

"Oh." She works her mouth from side to side while she digests that. She has a super-mobile face. I envy the range of her expressions. If I could move my face like that, I'd have Livvy giggling all the time. "I think I get it. I only asked because if Brenna trusted him to be her Dom, then I could trust him, too."

"Without answering your question, you can trust him," I say.

She smiles. "Okay."

I could push her toward Theo but I don't. I get the sense this girl has been pushed around enough. Instead, I finish packing up the tent, turn off the TV, and go upstairs to check on Daddy.

He's awake when I peek into the bedroom. I steal in quietly and wait next to the bed for him to acknowledge me.

"Turn around, little girl," he says.

I don't question why. I do it immediately. Daddy's given me an order.

He sits up and takes my wrists and crosses them behind my back. Taking my wrists in one hand, he pulls me back between his knees.

"Bend over."

I do, slowly, keeping my legs and back straight the way he likes.

He pulls down my panties and rubs his thumb up and down my slit. I close my eyes and tremble with delight. I love it when Daddy's abrupt and demanding like this. Also, orgasm-ahoy!

He dips his thumb into me and circles it around, spreading the wetness that flows at his touch. He pushes back in and brushes over my G-spot. Sparks flicker behind my eyelids.

"I see you trembling, little girl. Do you like that? Is your little pussy squeezing? Is your belly butterflying?"

"Yes, Daddy," I whisper. It's not that I think anyone will overhear us. I just like the intimacy of this moment and whispering feels right.

"Do you have permission to come?"

"No, Daddy."

"No. Not until I tell you. If it pleases me to edge you, I will edge you. If it pleases me to give you an orgasm, I will give you permission. But you do not own your pleasure. I do."

I'd fall over if he wasn't holding my wrists. Wolfy-Daddy destroys me in every sense, including my balance. "Yes, Daddy. I love you, Daddy."

"I love you, too, little girl. Keep those legs straight."

I lock my knees.

He slides his thumb out of my pussy and pushes it into my ass. Two long, thick fingers replace his thumb. He pumps his hand aggressively, the noise sloppy and obscene. Pleasure ripples all the way down to my toes. I shake so hard he pulls on my wrists to keep me on my feet.

"What are you thinking about, little girl?"

"You, Daddy."

"That's right. Your mind is on me. Always."

"Always, Daddy."

"Good girl. Bend your knees. You have permission to come."

I don't have time to thank him before he adds a third finger and pistons his hand in and out of me. I bite down on my lip so hard I taste blood to keep from wailing as my orgasm breaks, thunderous and debilitating. He more than destroys me. He *annihilates* my senses. I twist against his hold on my wrists, trying to maintain my position even as I writhe with release. Daddy's grip never slips. He holds me through every gasp, every convulsion. When he wrings the last tremor out of me and slips his fingers out, I hang against his hold, my tears cooling on my cheeks, my lips forming the words "I love you" over and over.

"Ta, Daddy," I finally manage. "Ta very much."

"You're welcome, little girl. When you can, stand up. Take your time. I've got you."

I know he does. There's nothing as sure in this world as the certainty that Daddy has me.

I open my eyes and blink to stop my head from spinning. I focus on the curtains, closed against the midday sun so Daddy could nap. There's a bluish sliver of sunlight peeking through the left edge of the curtains. The winter sun in the City has a completely different quality than the summer sun. I love living here so much. I love watching the City change with the seasons. I love seeing the way Daddy's home responds.

"I love living here with you, Daddy," I tell him.

He runs the heel of his hand up my back. "Emmy, I've lived in this house most of my life but it wasn't home until you made it our home."

I stagger upright and turn around. "Really?"

He opens his arms and I rush in. He cuddles me tightly against his chest. "Really, baby."

I bury my face in his warm neck and sniff his Daddy scent while I wet his T-shirt with happy tears. "Super-emotional, Daddy," I tell him.

"Good tears, bad tears, or just surprise orgasm tears?"

"All of them. I'm feeling so much. I'm happy about everything. I'm sad for True. I'm overwhelmed by the surprise orgasm. Ta very much."

He kisses my forehead. "You're welcome, little wonder."

"Also, and I'm not sure where this falls on the tear spectrum, I got a letter from Miranda this morning." Daddy's chest muscles go rigid under my cheek. "I left it on your desk. She wants me to bring Livvy to her hotel. I'm not going to. I'm not going to write her back, either. You don't want me thinking about her and I'm trying hard not to—"

"She's not making it fucking easy, is she?"

"No, Daddy. And I still do feel sorry for her. But I won't break your rules."

He strokes his hands down my back. "If you were the daddy in this situation, sweetheart, how would you deal with Miranda?"

"Funny thing," I say. "I was thinking when I read her letter that it's a good thing I'm not a daddy because my heart is too soft. I couldn't make the hard decisions you're making. I'd cave. I admire you, Daddy. I'm a zillion times proud of you. I know it must be really difficult to be so strong."

Logan blows out a long breath, weighted with pain and frustration. "The more she pisses me off, the easier it gets. Understand that she's writing to you because she can't get at you any other way. Do you feel unsafe?"

"No, just sad."

He presses his warm lips to my forehead again. "You're allowed to feel sad, Emmy. You're allowed to feel sorry for her, pity her, wish her choices had led her to a different place. But you're also allowed to be angry at her for harassing you."

"I am a little."

"I always want you to tell me what you're feeling. Anger is a normal emotion. You get angry so rarely. I know it can be harder for women to express anger. It's not as socially acceptable as it is for men. But you're safe with me and if you're angry, this is a safe place to express it."

I rub my cheek against his collar and open up my heart to everything I'm feeling. "I am angry at her. She thinks I'm a weak link. She thinks she can turn me against you after she failed to run me off. I'm not weak. I hate that she thinks I am."

"Good girl," Daddy encourages me. "Let it out."

"I hate that I let her get to me. I hate that she knows my insecurities. I hate that she saw those moments of weakness."

I pant a little after I let that all out. I hate things about what's between me and Miranda but in this moment, I let go of my hate of the woman herself. She doesn't deserve that much emotion from me. She doesn't deserve that much of my time and energy. It's time for me to let the tangle of my feelings for Miranda fade. She only feeds off my attention like an emotional vampire. Daddy's told me to ignore her and he's right. All she deserves is indifference; that's what I'm going to give her from now on.

"They're not weaknesses anymore, though, are they?" Daddy asks.

They're really not. Everything we've been through, the good and the bad, has convinced even my skeptical little heart that I can trust my Daddy. He's not perfect. No one is. But he loves me. Really loves me. Unconditionally and without limits. I didn't understand what unconditional love was before I met Logan. I'd only had conditional love from my mother, my brother, my ex-husband, my other Doms. When I did things they didn't like, their love for me dimmed. Sometimes it died completely, like with Ash. They all tried to "fix" me, which really meant they were trying to get me to change the things they didn't like about me. Daddy accepts all of me. Daddy wants me to be the best, happiest version of myself. But he's left it up to me to discover and determine who that is. Because he loves me, and he always, always will.

"No, Daddy."

"I'm a zillion times proud of you, my little wonder."

"Love you, Daddy. Thank you for making me a bigger person, even though I'm very little."

Daddy tips his head down to rub noses with me. "You're very welcome. Ready to go see the Rexes?"

"Always!"

Daddy chuckles at my enthusiasm and lets me slide off his lap.

twenty-three

LOGAN

MY LITTLE GIRL IS A MIRACLE.

Somehow, in the two hours that I napped, not only did she mobilize the entire playgroup to join us at the Museum of Natural History but she also broke through to True.

When I come downstairs, True's sitting at the dining room table between Theo and Maude. They're on a video call with True's social worker and the biker Mac pulled out of his back pocket who is somehow law enforcement *and* a certified foster parent. I take in the expressions of the three people I can see—amused, defiant, and out-for-blood—and decide I don't need to be involved right now. Mother Maude is on the war-path. My work here is done.

Instead, I intercept my little miracle-worker as she's heading into the kitchen to make lunch for everyone. I send her off to pack a day-bag for Livvy, which takes her all of two seconds because she's so organized but at least it prevents her from preparing another seven-course meal.

I thumb over to the caregivers chat and post that we're going to the Deli at West 76th to pick up sandwiches before we head into the

215

museum. Everyone quickly agrees on the Deli as a meet-up point. Warrin organizes sandwich orders to call in so the Deli's not overwhelmed when we descend on them. Bravo says he'll bring chips and snack packs for the littles since he's got an industrial supply. Henry offers to bring drinks for everyone who is non-dairy or no-carbonation, which is the majority of the littles. Emmy, reading over my shoulder, volunteers a bag of oatmeal cookies, so I throw that into the chat.

I'm used to how things get done in large groups of people because of my years in the Navy and at Blunts but the playgroup is a different experience. Maybe it's because we're caregivers. Maybe it's because Blunts is something of a rich man's club and the members are used to being catered to instead of caring for their subbies. But it's a completely different mindset. The mommies and daddies of the playgroup just get shit done. There's no waiting for a committee vote. There's no delegating to an assistant. Someone gets an idea and they do it.

I haven't felt as confident in the competence of a group of people since my days serving under Mac.

Although I'd planned to take the train up to West 79th and then walk back to the Deli, somehow Manny and his limo have been conscripted. Probably Emily. True's eyes nearly swallow her face when the big, black limo pulls up and we all climb in. Theo death-glares the kid when she starts opening the cubbies across from her seat but I wave him off. If she wants a can of pop, she can have one. She should have the complete limo experience. Manny doesn't stock alcohol in the limo except when it's been pre-ordered, so there's nothing she can get into that will hurt her.

We stop in Hell's Kitchen to pick up Cappa and Fleur, who seem to have become honorary playgroup members. Brenna pulls Fleur into her conversation with True and, before we hit the edge of Central Park, I can see True's got another friend among the subbies.

Warrin's waiting for us outside the Deli with a sandwich for Manny. Once we all climb out of the limo, the group of caregivers and littles staying warm inside the shop emerge. There are hugs all around for Aggie, Amy, Robyn, Yummy, Sammi, Henry's little Leda, red-headed Matty, and a reserved, black-haired newcomer named Saoirse.

We're our own crowd as we start off down the street toward the museum. Sandwiches in crinkly butcher paper get passed around along with warm drinks. I steer Livvy's stroller so that Emmy can enjoy her sandwich. She reserves meat for dinner, usually, and rarely eats red meat but the hot roast beef from the Deli on West 76th is an exception. I've gotten it, too, souped up with horseradish gravy. The Deli's rare roast beef is so good it should be its own food group.

Emmy's eyes roll back in her head with her first bite and I wrap my free arm around her waist to keep her from bumping into anyone.

She chews ecstatically ten times and smiles up at me with her eyelids fluttering. "Omigosh, Daddy, sooo good."

"Orgasmic, baby doll?"

"Not Wolfy-Daddy big Os." She shakes her head, curls bouncing under the adorable blue beret she's popped on top of them. "But sooo good."

On Emmy's far side, safely sandwiched between Brenna and Fleur, True exclaims over her own hot roast beef sandwich. She's gotten hers with crispy onions and her cheeks bulge like a chipmunk's as she chews her mouthful of beef and onions. Nothing wrong with the kid's appetite. Either she's naturally small and skinny like Emmy or she just hasn't been getting enough food.

If it's the latter, I'm pretty sure this group is going to ensure that changes.

Our progression to and through the museum is slow with a group this large but it's marked by excited chatter and laughter. Such a contrast from Blunts, where most large scenes and gatherings are quiet except for moans, groans, and the slap of flesh. Although many things about kink are serious, I wonder if the club hasn't lost the sense of fun, of play, that's the heart of kink. Maybe the Nursery opening will bring laughter back to the club's halls and dungeons.

I'm not the only one enjoying the group's exuberance, I discover, as we linger in the Hall of Gems. Matty and Faolan, who are some combination of geologist and archeologist that I didn't quite understand when it was explained to me during our outing to the corn maze, are holding forth on why some of the sapphires on display have stars in them and some don't. "Oohs" and "ahhs" rise from the excited littles and teenager. Even Livvy is gummily cooing at the gems as Emmy holds her up to the glass.

A tall blond man stops near me, watching the group, his eyes lingering on the black-haired little, Saoirse. He looks vaguely familiar but I can't remember if he's been to playgroup or if we've met at an outing.

"It's good to see them enjoying themselves," he says.

I nod. "The laughter of littles is a balm to the soul."

His green eyes flick to mine.

"Well said." He holds out his hand. "Sutter James. I don't think we've been introduced yet. You're Logan, Emmy's Daddy, right?"

"Yes, good to meet you, Sutter. Your face is familiar. Have you been to playgroup?"

"Mmm-hmm. I think we missed you that week. But we have another connection. You voted me in at Blunts last week."

It takes me a minute and then I place his face: on a picture attached to an application I barely read. There were four applications voted on during the meeting but I gave them cursory attention, consumed by the vote on Mac. "I remember. You came to Blunts on a recommendation from a club in England, right? Winter's Sin?"

The man gives me a megawatt smile. It doesn't reach his eyes and for no reason I can name, it reminds me of De Leon, even though Sutter maintains eye-contact in a way Myles avoids.

"Winter's Sin is my family's line of clubs. My aunt runs it. She's friends with Chess."

"Ah," I say, noncommittally. I know, of course, that there's a lot

218

of "good old boy" networking at Blunts. It's a little surprising Chess would welcome someone who's basically playing for the other team, even if that team's across the Atlantic. There certainly wasn't any mention of it when Sutter's application was voted on. It was barely debated at all. "Did you put on your application that you're in a care-giver relationship?"

"No." A dangerous gleam lights his eyes. "Was I supposed to?"

I scratch the back of my neck. These are choppy waters. As a committee member, if I find out that someone's withheld informa-tion from the club, I'm supposed to bring it to the committee. But on the other hand, I'm happy to have another daddy at Blunts.

"Did you check age-play and DD/lg on the kink list?" I ask, refer-ring to part of the membership application.

He nods.

How the fuck could Ten and his cabal have missed that? Were they as wrapped up in Mac's application as I was?

"No issue, then," I say, pleased at getting one by Ten and his pack of assholes. "Are you coming to the Nursery's grand opening?"

"Wouldn't miss it. We've played in there the last two nights. I've already ordered an adult cradle for home, my little darlin' loves the one at Blunts so much. The Nursery's awesome. I've never seen anything like it anywhere. I heard you and your little designed it?"

"With a lot of help from Brenna," I nod at the blue-haired submissive, who has her arm draped over True's shoulders as they exclaim over gemstones bigger than their fists.

"Get ready for a stream of requests to design nurseries at other clubs. I predict word of Blunts' Nursery will spread through the kinky world like a shot."

That wouldn't be the worst thing. Emmy and Bren make a great team. I can see them designing a nursery here and there once they've finished the book they're collaborating on. Something to while away the short days and long nights as winter settles in.

I shrug. "We'd be open to that. Designing the Nursery was a lot of fun. I'm glad to welcome another caregiver to the club. We're a bit of a rare breed."

"I've heard," Sutter says. He nods at his submissive. "My baby girl used to work at Blunts. She never explored her little side there because the members condemned age-play. I put my application in expecting to have to knock some heads together but I see the revolution's already underway."

I chuckle. "Yes, it is."

Sutter's eyes wander away from mine, over the group of caregivers and littles. "Wouldn't be surprised if you have a few more applications after the Grand Opening, either."

Warrin's already mentioned it; he slipped it into conversation casually, idly wondering aloud what the application process was like. I explained it and said I'd be happy to find him a sponsor. It was while we were at playgroup and I'd have had to be blind not to notice how closely Bravo, Jack, and Henry were following our conversation.

"Good," I say. "The more caregivers there are among the membership, the easier it will be to sweep away any lingering prejudice."

Sutter grunts. "Is it the old pedophilia argument?"

"Mostly a lot of resistance to change."

"Well, I put on my application that I'm bringing youthful enthusiasm and energy to the club. Happy to weigh that against the old guard and see how the scales balance."

I look more closely at him. He's deeply tanned, with some white lines fanning from the corners of his intensely green eyes but I think those lines are from squinting into the sun rather than age. His skin's very smooth, no bags under his eyes, no five-o'clock shadow.

"I must have missed it on your application, how old are you?"

That wide, white, slightly vicious grin breaks across his face again. "Twenty-two."

Fuck's sake, can he even grow a beard?

"Youthful enthusiasm and energy, huh?"

"Mmm."

I've been fucking played. We all have. Chess used Mac's application as a distraction to push Sutter's through under everyone's radar.

"You're the youngest member of the club," I say. "By about a decade. Possibly the youngest member of the club ever."

Sutter nods. "I'd assumed so."

"What do you want with Blunts? To take it over for your family?"

Sutter shrugs. "My immediate interest is revenge. The club hurt my little. It made her afraid. It made her feel *less than*. No one hurts my baby. I'd thought about exposing the members, making the club's activities public. Maybe an exposé in the New Yorker."

I swallow hard.

"And longer term?" I ask.

"Dismantle it, brick by brick. No institution that hurt my darlin' girl stands."

I cough to clear the tightness in my chest. This kid's six years older than True. Over a decade younger than me. Yet I don't have any doubt he means every word. Could he take on Blunts? Maude's not the only heavy hitter there. There's serious wealth at the club and wealth can make a formidable obstacle.

But there are a lot of secrets within Blunts' walls, too. If Sutter makes those secrets public . . . the walls might crumble.

"If the club could make amends to you and your girl?" I ask cautiously.

"That'd be something worth considering."

I rub my hand over my face, the good taste of roast beef in my mouth souring. "Excuse me."

He tips his head to the side. "Hope our talk hasn't put a stone in your shoe."

I give him a hard look. "I understand being protective of your girl—"

"Fiancée," he corrects.

"Fiancée," I acknowledge. "I would feel as strongly about any group, any institution, which hurt my little."

"But?"

"But the club's my family. Some of my best friends are members. You're threatening my family."

Sutter nods slowly. "I considered it gentlemanly to give you fair warning. I've heard you're a power player on the membership committee. As one daddy to another, I thought giving you a head's up was only sporting."

He sounds like he's at the country club. But he doesn't look like part of the polo-playing crowd. He looks like he wrangles broncos for breakfast. He just needs a black cowboy hat and some spurs.

"And if I run back to the management committee and have you punted out of the club?" I ask.

Sutter tips his head from side to side. "It will be interesting to see who has the greater punching power. You and your *friends* or the Chairman and my family."

"This is a test," I say. "You want to see how much clout I have."

"And to see if you take care of your own problems or squeal to the committee like a little piggie."

Heat rises to my face. I feel my nostrils flare as my body gulps oxygen. I know he's baiting me but my body's rising to it.

"Are you making yourself my problem?" I ask.

"Not today," Sutter responds. "Today, I'm just enjoying a trip to the museum with my girl's new friends. Tomorrow." He shrugs. "Tomorrow's another day."

"So it is. I guess we'll see what comes tomorrow."

"I guess we will," Sutter says. "See you at the Grand Opening."

I nod. "Enjoy the rest of your day."

"You, too." Sutter rocks back on the heels of his boots, which look like they've seen their share of real work and hooks his thumbs in his belt loops as he watches our littles.

I cross the room to Emmy, tap her on the elbow, give her the hand-signal for "follow me" and lead her out of the Gem Hall to the nearest bathroom. I walk into the handicapped bathroom and close the door behind Emmy.

"May I kneel, Daddy?" she asks, her wide eyes on my face.

I shake my head. The floor looks dirty.

"How do you know what I'm feeling before I say a word?" I ask.

"Your frowny line." She blinks, a rim of crystal forming along her lashes.

I hold my arms out. She rushes to me. I catch my girls up in my arms, cradling Livvy between us.

"You met Saoirse and her daddy?" I ask, pressing my lips to her forehead.

"Yes, Daddy. You looked like you were having an intense conversation with Sutter."

"You could call it that. He wants to tear Blunts apart. I guess his little used to work at the club. I don't know who it was but they scared her and intimidated her about her littleness. He's back for revenge."

Emmy rests her head on my collar and turns so she can see Livvy. Livvy reaches up a fist; Emmy blows a raspberry against her fingers.

"I love you, baby," I say softly. "I don't want to hurt someone who could be your friend. But I'll fucking crush him like a cockroach if he tries to destroy the club."

"Cockroaches are uncrushable, Daddy. They'll survive a nuclear apocalypse along with Twinkies. Saoirse said her daddy was just voted in. Why would he join if he's going to destroy the club?"

"Easier to do it from within, I guess."

"I don't think that's the whole story, Daddy."

"I wish you'd heard the conversation. You could tell me what I missed. He certainly seems hell-bent on revenge."

"Can you hold Livvy for a moment?"

I nod and Emmy passes my daughter to me. I cradle her in my right arm and smile down at her.

Emily wraps her arms around me, sliding her hands under my sweater and rubbing her palms up and down my bare back.

"Thank you, baby doll."

"You're shaking, Daddy."

I am. I flushed with adrenaline talking to Sutter. When I

managed to control myself and refused to rise to his bait, the adrenaline had nowhere to go. That's why I needed Emmy. I need to bleed off the adrenaline or I'm going to crash.

"That feels good, sweetheart. Talk to me."

"Should I tell you about the exhibit? Or what I learned about Saoirse and Sutter? Or what Matty was telling us about the properties of corundum?"

"The first and last sound a little dull, baby. Gimme the tea."

She smiles up at me as she continues to rub, giving me the tactile comfort I need.

"I really like Saoirse. She's a swimmer; she was headed to the Olympics when she tore her rotator cuff. She had a reaction to anesthesia during surgery. She's much better now but she still has seizures under stress. She teaches swimming. That's how she met Sutter. She was working at a lifestyle club out west. He was cleaning the pool."

My eyebrows shoot skyward. "That bloke is not a pool cleaner."

Emily grins. "No, he's a billionaire. Or a multi-millionaire at least. His family business is wine and kink clubs. Isn't that cool?"

"Very cool, except if part of his motivation for joining Blunts and destroying it from within is eliminating the competition."

"Daddy, I'm not sure what's happening but Saoirse really didn't seem like that. She's friendly. She wants little friends. She's excited about coming to playgroup and she was describing the most wonderful scenes that they've been doing. I understand why her daddy might want revenge if the members at Blunts hurt her but I don't understand him bringing her back to the club for all those good scenes if he's going to destroy it. You wouldn't do that. I think . . . I think maybe Sutter's more like you than is comfortable. Maybe that's why he made threats and upset you, Daddy. Maybe he needs to start from a position of strength. I've seen you do that, too, sometimes. Like when you interact with Mr. De Leon?"

I sigh and relax even further into her touch. "No one starts in a position of strength when dealing with Myles. We all start at a severe disadvantage and just claw our way up the hill."

"What's the hill?" Emmy asks.

I shake my head.

She peers up at me, squinting one eye closed. The quizzical koala. The cuteness of it does as much to even me out as the gentle circles she's rubbing over my back.

"Is this like the Miranda thing that I don't need to know and don't want to know, or is this like the Lucy thing where I don't need to know but kind of want to know?"

My breath catches in my chest. What now? Emmy's seemed okay with me topping Lucy. I've been careful to include Emily in any scene where there's physical topping. The mental topping and caregiving has all been via Max's app. Emmy doesn't like the app and only uses it to log her water consumption. I thought what I've set up to help Lucy is sufficiently different from our relationship that it wouldn't bother my baby girl.

"The second. We're going to circle back to that in a minute, little girl. The hill with Myles is that he'll always be willing to do *more*. Myles doesn't operate within the social and legal limits the rest of us do. Everyone's at a disadvantage in dealing with Myles because there's a point at which all of us stop where Myles keeps going." I drop kisses on Emmy's forehead and then Livvy's, smiling at the soft giggles I get from each of them. "Now, let's circle back. What do you mean like the Lucy thing where you don't need to know but kind of want to know? What do you want to know about Lucy?"

"I don't really need to know why you're still topping her but I kind of want to know."

I shift Livvy until she's cradled in my right arm and I have a hand free to stroke Emmy's cheek. "Still? Did you think there was an expiration date on me topping her?"

"Not an expiration date but I thought once she was better, she'd go back to the club."

"Ah, I see. Yes, that's the goal. I don't have a twelve-point plan or anything but that's what I'm working toward. I specifically asked Rob and Karl to handle the punishment she earned last week in order to reintroduce her to Karl. I'm planning to do the same thing with Franco when she next earns a punishment. I think that's better than just throwing her at them when I feel she's up to their level of sadism."

Emmy smiles up at me. "You're right, Daddy."

It's good to be right about one thing today.

"I need to talk with a few people about Sutter. I can't let them be blindsided by this."

Emmy runs her warm hands up my back and squeezes my shoulder blades. "The way you were?"

I nod. "Chess set me up. He set us all up. He ran Sutter right through under our noses, while we were all fighting over Mac's application. I don't understand why. Even if he doesn't know about Sutter's revenge, he knows Sutter's working for the competition. Why let him in?"

"Keep your friends close and your enemies closer?" My little wonder suggests.

"Mmm, maybe." I press a final kiss to her forehead. "I love you, my sweetheart. Let's enjoy the rest of the day, huh? I'm sorry I let him get to me."

"I'm not." She smiles up at me. "Always happy for Daddy-time."

"I'm always happy for little girl time. You're amazing, Emmy."

She stretches up on her toes to press a kiss on my chin, then takes Livvy and bounces her until Livvy breaks into giggles. I take her hand and lead her back to join the group.

twenty-four

LOGAN

I NEED A FUCKING break from the intensity of today but I don't get one.

When we return to the house, Mac's waiting for us. As soon as I've shed my coat and shoes, he beckons me into my office.

A red-eyed former house submissive is sitting on my couch.

I cross the room and sit next to her. "Annabelle, thank you for coming to talk to us."

She sniffs and dabs at her eyes with a tissue. Mac has moved the box that I keep on my desk to the couch next to her. Bloodshot eyes and red nose aside, she looks rough. Her curls are snarled and ratty around her face. Upset or sleeplessness has carved shadows and lines in her rounded, motherly features.

"I'm sorry for being a coward," she says.

"May I touch you?" I ask and when she nods, I rub her back. "Why would you call yourself a coward?"

"I ran away. Instead of standing my ground and fighting, I ran away."

Mac sits down in one of the wingback chairs that he's pulled up across from the couch. "I know this is gonna sound strange from a man who used to fight for our country but there are times to fight and times to retreat. If you needed to retreat for your safety, that's not cowardice, Annabelle. That's survival."

She nods and mops at her eyes. "I feel terrible for leaving the other subbies in the lurch. I abandoned them. I let everyone down. Master Javier's been so wonderful with me and I disappeared without a word."

I continue rubbing gentle circles over her back, feeling her nervousness in the damp fabric. It gave me huge amounts of comfort when Emmy rubbed my back in the museum bathroom; I hope rubbing Annabelle's back gives her a fraction of that relief.

"D'you feel up to telling us why you left, Annabelle?"

She takes a deep breath and dabs at another tear. "They're going to ruin my son's career for this but yes, I'll tell you."

Mac sits forward, letting his hands dangle between his knees. "I swear to you, sweetheart, if it's in my power, I will stop any repercussions from touching you or your family. No one should fear speakin' up, speakin' the truth."

She sniffles. "I believe that, too but they have ammunition on almost all of the house subs. They're very careful about that before they start hunting."

The word hits me like a blow in the chest. "Hunting?"

She nods. "They call themselves the Wolfpack. They believe being Doms makes them predators."

"And the house submissives are their prey?" Mac asks.

"Any submissive. They hunt anywhere. Blunts. Other lifestyle clubs. Private parties."

"Who are *they*?" I ask, my voice cracking.

"I only know Emmett and Drew at Blunts but there are more."

Hearing Drew's name—again—in the context of our house subs being hurt, sends my blood racing. This is more than a rule about guests.

"I'm not doubting you, Annabelle, I just need to understand why you think that."

"Emmett likes to brag after he's come," she responds. "He says they're growing the Pack within the club and soon they'll have the numbers to take over."

I swallow hard, trying to control the flush of anger. I don't know Emmett much better than I know Drew. Emmett's mostly at the club on weekends. He's never held a role on the management committee. He hasn't come to any of the Monday Madness nights I've organized. If I've ever done a scene with him, it's been a group scene. I don't have any idea of what he's like as a Dom. The only thing I can remember about him, except that Bren jokes he has the second-best hair at Blunts after Rob, is that I've seen him around the pool and sauna a lot recently. But that could just be because I've been there frequently of late while Mac teaches Bren to swim.

"I will not let that happen, Annabelle," I say firmly.

She presses her lips together and flicks her eyes over my face. I'm not sure what she's looking for but I give her the same honesty I'd give Emmy. I will not let Blunts be destroyed. Not by that twenty-two-year-old saboteur, not by a group of predatory Doms who think they have some God-given right to terrify our subs, not by anyone.

"I wasn't here but the other house subs, they say you left. Master Logan, I'm not trying to insult you. I just . . . I'm afraid. I'm afraid they'll hurt me again. I'm afraid they'll hurt my family if I don't keep my mouth shut. I'm afraid."

"I'm back to stay," I promise. "I've taken back the role of Master of Training so I can help the house subs fix whatever the hell went wrong while I was gone. If that includes members getting the idea that they can hurt subs with impunity, that's the place I'll start. I'm your cannon, Annabelle. Give me ammunition and a target."

A smile peeks through her tears. "It'd be nice to have a cannon."

"You have two," Mac says. "Give us ammo."

"Emmett began asking me for scenes about a month after I started at Blunts." She wipes her eyes and sits up a little straighter. "I was flattered at first. I'm not young and beautiful like your subs." When Mac opens his mouth to object, Annabelle shakes her head. "I'm not putting myself down. I'm realistic. I love my body but I know I'm the oldest house sub by quite a few years. I know I'm not the ideal of beauty I see among the house subs. And I didn't have any expectations coming to the club. I was flattered to be hired. Even more flattered when I had so many requests for scenes. It's lovely to be wanted again. So I accepted any member who asked me for a scene. I didn't talk to the other house subs about them. I didn't negotiate my limits. I assumed a Blunts Dom asking to scene with me would know and respect them. Most did."

Her lower lip quivers and she takes a fortifying breath.

"Emmett began pushing my limits from our first scene. I know what you're thinking. That should have been a red flag and I should have refused future scenes but he has a way of saying things to make you feel like it's your fault. He said he'd always respect my safe words but that it was his job as my Dom to challenge me." She twists the damp tissue between her hands. "It was anal at first, which I'd done before but not like he wanted it. Big plugs and toys to stretch me. Very rough and with less and less lube. I won't lie, he made sure I had orgasms but the pain was like nothing I've put myself through before and I've given birth to two babies. Aside from the pain, he made all the right noises. He asked for regular scenes. Praised me to the moon and back when I overcame something I thought I couldn't. Plenty of aftercare, asking about me, my interests, my family. Now I realize he was just gathering information to use against me but at the time it was so flattering. I'm not complaining, please don't think I am but that *investment*—it can be lacking at the club. I've done the same number of scenes with Emmett as with Masters Javier and Theo and I don't know a single thing about their lives outside the club. Emmett made me feel like he cared about me as a *person*."

She rubs her lips together and dabs at another tear. "It was all a lie. He wasn't invested and he didn't give a shit about me as a person. Once he found out my son's in banking, he began using it to push me more and more. If I didn't agree to the scenes he wanted, he'd tell my son's employers and business associates about what I do with my days. Double-penetration was first. I had to take sick leave for three days to recover after he and Drew went at me. Then it was two in one hole. You'd think all those plugs and toys would've made it bearable but they didn't. He scheduled a four-in-two scene with three guests and I just couldn't. I resigned and went to stay with my son upstate. That's when the threats started. If I didn't return to the club, he'd make good on his threats against my boy. My other son stepped in when he saw what a mess I was. He took me to see a lawyer who told me sex clubs are illegal in New York and that Emmett and the other members have more to lose than I do. You could be prosecuted just for being members, much less hiring house submissives. Is that true?"

I glance at Mac. His jaw is set but he nods.

"Yes, that's true," I tell Annabelle.

Franco and the club's other lawyers have tried to protect the members as much as they can but the bottom line is that we're all investors in an illegal sex club.

Annabelle nods. "That made me feel a little stronger. I messaged Emmett back and told him what the lawyer said. I said nothing could make me come back. He changed his tune then and told me to stay away from the club, keep my mouth shut, not say a word to the two of you . . . but Shannie told me she trusts you, that you're trying to help, and I know keeping quiet won't stop them. I've seen abuse before; it doesn't stop. People like Emmett, they don't stop once they get a taste for it. They'll do it to someone else, if not at Blunts, then someone they hunt in the clubs. Just like that man did to Cappa."

Mac's jaw drops.

"I'm sorry, Annabelle, what did you say about Cappa?" I ask.

"Emmett told me that Drew gave Cappa to one of the pack as a reward. He didn't name names but Emmett said Drew knew what the wolf would do to Cappa. They've been trying to get that date rape drug, roh-something, so that subs wouldn't remember what was done to them. The wolf who hurt Cappa—he's their supplier."

"Rohypnol," Mac spits. He's flushed; his hands are clenched into fists between his knees. "I will fucking kill them."

I nod. "You've given us plenty of ammo, Annabelle. Give us targets. Emmett, Drew, anyone else?"

"Emmett mentioned two other names, Jared and Hans. I'm not sure about Jared but I know Hans was there during Shannie's hunting."

"Did Emmett call it that, sweetheart? Shannie's hunting?"

Annabelle nods. "She's refused scenes with anyone but Rob since but Drew was planning on asking her for a scene and then letting the pack go at her after he drugged her. Just like Cappa. That's what Emmett bragged about."

Mac flexes his hands and reaches out. Annabelle takes his hands. He rubs his thumbs over her knuckles. "We're locked and loaded, sweetheart. How do we protect your son?"

Annabelle bites her lip. "I don't want to be like them."

"You're *nothing* like them," I say.

"Maybe I am if I tell you what I know about Emmett."

"It's totally up to you, Annabelle."

She nods and squeezes his hands. "Emmett works in banking just like my boy. His father's high up in the bank and got him the job. Nepotism, right? Is that what it's called?"

Mac and I nod.

"His father's real conservative. Church-going, pillar of the community and all that. Emmett's afraid of him. He does everything his father tells him to, right down to the gal he's engaged to. Emmett keeps putting off the wedding but he knows it's inevitable. That's why he's a member at Blunts. He's sowing his wild oats 'cause he knows his future's a five-bed Colonial in Connecticut with three kids, two dogs, and matching beemers, working for his daddy for the rest of his life. He'll never do anything to rock that boat. If his father found out about what he gets up to at Blunts, Emmett would lose it all."

"He told you that?" Mac asks.

"Yeah, like I said, he likes to talk after he comes. He got real chatty after he found out my son works for another bank. I think he knew he had me locked down then."

"He does *not* have you locked down, Annabelle. I'm disgusted any Dom would do something like this but a Blunts member? No, this won't stand. I understand you have reasons to distrust us but will you let me pull some people in on this? Our business partner, Max. He's an IT whiz—"

"Cynnie's daddy." Annabella nods her head, curls brushing against her cheeks. "He's a good man. You can tell him everything. Masters Javier and Theo—I know he's a cop, all the house subs know —I trust them. I'll call Master Javier and apologize for shutting him out. I was upset and scared but he deserves better from me. He's been a wonderful Dom. Mistresses Maude and Dana, too. They always made me feel wanted and safe. Please pull in anyone you need. I want the Wolfpack stopped."

Mac squeezes Annabelle's hands. "Sweetheart, you don't have to answer this yet but have a think about it. If we can clear out the bad eggs, would you be willing to come back to Blunts? I know people miss you—"

Annabelle smiles tearily. "I want to come back. As much as what Emmett and Drew did hurt me, what's hurt more was losing the friends I found at Blunts."

"No one wants to lose you, Annabelle," I reassure her. "You'll be welcome back."

And if anyone has anything to say about that, I will fight that fight. No one should live in fear. No one should be penalized for the things they do to feel safe.

Annabelle declines to join the group that's come back from the museum with us. I could see how their company would give her comfort, so I ask twice but when she declines a second time, I suggest a subbie get-together in a few days. Mac nods and I don't need to ask him if he's going to get Bren to organize it. He and I are back in sync the way we were in the Navy. We don't need a lot of talk. We know each other's strengths and weaknesses. We know how to work as a team to get things done.

After Annabelle leaves, still teary but much more relaxed than when I arrived, I check on my girls. Emmy's opened her little room to the subbies who came back from the museum with us and they're "doing art." There's such a haze of glitter in the air when I poke my head in that I quickly retreat and leave them to their creations. I don't see Livvy in the sparkling miasma, so I check downstairs and find her in her bouncy seat on the table, sitting between Brenna, Fleur, and True while they have what looks like a very heartfelt and intense conversation. Livvy's rapt, her eyes moving from face to face, so I remove my unwanted Dom presence, tap on the shoulders of the five Doms sitting on my couch, and tip my chin at my office. At least two of them have military training and Theo's a cop but they're still an amazingly quiet group as they follow me out of the great room into my office.

Daddy-stealth. It's a skill.

When everyone's seated—Bravo, Warrin, and Jack on the couch, Theo in the other guest chair beside Mac, and Faolan leaning against my desk—I begin, "This is about Blunts. I know Warrin's interested in joining. Jack, Bravo, I'm guessing you're planning on applying, too. Am I off base?"

They shake their heads.

Faolan offers, "My application's just gone in."

Mac sits back in his chair and crosses his arms over his chest. "Hopefully it won't be as controversial as mine. We're getting a bit of push-back from the old guard."

Faolan glances at me.

"Javier has a lot of clout at the club," I reassure him. "He'll get you in."

I'm not worried about Faolan's application. Warrin, Jack, and

Bravo, on the other hand, may be a fight. But it's a fight for another day.

"I've mentioned to you before that there's some anti-age-play sentiment at the club," I say, nodding at Warrin. "That's come back to bite us. Sutter James approached me today at the museum. He gave me a . . . well, he called it a fair warning. His little, Saoirse, used to work at the club. Some of the Doms treated her badly and made her feel she had to hide her littleness. Sutter's joined the club to take revenge. He's told me he's going to tear it apart from within." I hold up a hand when Theo starts to sputter. "I'm not telling you this to turn you against the kid. I actually understand where he's coming from. If anyone hurt Emily like that, I'd go on the warpath. I want your help showing him revenge isn't necessary, because Blunts can change. It's already changing but there needs to be more. I need your help to show Sutter that Blunts is more than four walls and some floggers. It's a family. And like any family, we disagree about things but we love and support each other, too. I need your help showing him that."

"You have it, Logan," Warrin says. "Anything you need."

"I'll need you to be present at the club, as often as you all can be. Doing scenes. Involving other members and the house submissives. Showing them our way of playing. Showing them the joy our littles give us." I look at Mac. "That's the way we win this. By showing them the truth at the heart of age-play and daddykink."

Mac tips his head to the side. "Sounds good for this whipper-snapper."

The men around the room, all of us on the far side of thirty-five, trade grins.

"But this Sutter fella's not the only one making threats," Mac continues. "Lo and I have been investigating what's going on with the house submissives. Seemed like a bunch of isolated problems at first. But when we dug down, we found somethin' more sinister. Couple of the Doms and their friends have gotten it into their heads that they can *hunt* our submissives. Intimidate them during scenes.

Drug and injure them. They call themselves a 'wolfpack.' We *will* catch these fuckers and make sure they get what's coming to them. But in the meanwhile, we've got to be careful. Make sure our subbies aren't alone. Keep an eye out for the house submissives. Do scenes in foursomes at least. Group scenes are even better. Stay sharp."

Bravo grunts. "I'll run point on that. I'll coordinate scenes. Make sure no one's at the club alone. Okay if I pull Henry in? She's talking about applying for membership, too. She loves the courtyard and pool for primal play. She won't take any nonsense. Not from some kid and not from a fucking wolfpack."

I nod. "Thank you."

We talk it around for a few more minutes but there's no dissention. These men, these daddies and Doms, are on board. Just the suggestion that someone would intentionally target and hurt submissives has them all shifting gears into over-protective mode. I know, because that's where my clutch has been stuck for months.

I shake their hands as they file out of my office and back into the living room to watch the game they abandoned without question at my silent request. Theo's the last in line and instead of taking my hand, he shuts the door and stands facing me.

"Names," he says.

I don't argue with him. If I ever needed Theo as an ally, it's right now.

"Emmett and Drew at the club. Annabelle knew the names of two of their guests as well, Jared and Hans."

"Shit." Theo chews on his lower lip. "Not the first time I've heard those names. Chess mentioned something about Emmett and a guest named Hans scaring Tessa in the sauna. Chess had a talk with Emmett about it."

"It's gone way beyond a word between friends and brother Doms. Way, way beyond."

"How far beyond?"

"Emmett made threats. Surely those are actionable."

Theo grunts. "You know as well as I do that a threat, even of bodily harm, without any more isn't going anywhere."

"It gets him out of the club at the very least. Them. All of them."

Theo nods.

"I'm not trying to shift my shit onto you, Theo but—"

"Will I raise it with the committee? Yeah, I will. I heard the vote on Mac's membership was tense."

I grumble. The first rule of management committee is you do not talk about management committee. But I also know the Blunts grapevine produces more juice than Napa Valley. "It was," I admit.

"Ten, Karl, Shedo, Franco," Theo ticks off their names on his fingers. "Who else?"

"Three Cs shafted me when push came to shove."

Theo's brows shoot up. "Really? That's fucking cold."

"I thought so, too."

"I'll call Chess now," Theo says. He taps a finger against my chest. "You probably called in a few favors to get Mac in. You got enough left to get rid of this Wolfpack?"

"I'd hope I don't need to call in any favors to protect our house subs."

Theo nods. "Sure. But maybe you should make some calls, too."

I do.

twenty-five

EMILY

"KNEEL, LITTLE GIRL."

That's a command I'm always happy to hear. I don't expect it in the hallway outside the bathroom but when Daddy says kneel, I kneel.

I tuck my hands behind my back and look up at him expectantly.

"Why have I asked you to kneel, baby?" Daddy asks, looking down at me.

He's dressed up for the Nursery's Opening. Looking hot in his Mad Hatter costume from our collaring weekend in Niagara Falls. I should be dressed, too but I'm running a little behind. I glittered my outfit for tonight during the Littles' Army "art attack" playdate. But then Sammi got the idea that he needed to wear my tutu around his neck and recite Shakespeare—not very accurately—and in the ensuing tug-o-war over my tutu, some of the glitter fell off. I've been doing last-minute repairs. Can't have uneven amounts of glitter. It's a rule.

"You're checking in with me because I'm running late?" I suggest.

"Yes, that's one reason. How much longer until you're ready?"

I make some fast calculations about the drying speed of glitter. "Ten minutes."

"Good girl, that's fine. That's not the only reason. What else?"

I smile hopefully. "Because I'm getting orgasms again tonight?"

I've been on orgasm denial, along with Cappa and a bunch of other unfortunate subbies, for two days. Which *sucks*. But I have to admit it hasn't been too awful this time. Daddy's mostly used my throat and only edged me during the day. I haven't had to go to bed needy and angry. I've been on low simmer but I haven't been as hatefully desperate as I've been in the past.

"Yes, you're getting orgasms again. But tell me about guilt."

"Gilt as in gold glitter?"

Daddy chuckles. "No, my little glitter bomb. Guilt as in feeling bad about something that's not your fault."

"Oh, guilt with a 'u'."

"Yes, baby, guilt with a 'u'."

"Guilt with a 'u' isn't something I need to feel. My Daddy's told me that, and my Daddy tells me the truth. I can only control myself. If I've failed to control myself and something bad's happened, then I should feel remorseful, apologize, and try to fix the situation but I don't need to feel guilty."

Daddy strokes my head with his warm palm. "That's right. Tonight is a big night for us, isn't it? We've both worked hard to get the Nursery open. There's a lot going on. You may hear some of it tonight. But you do not need to feel guilty about it, or for enjoying yourself. If you have any worries about what's happening at Blunts, or with True, or with Livvy, I want you to put those aside and focus on enjoying yourself tonight."

"Yes, Daddy."

"Stand, baby."

I rise, focusing on moving smoothly. Daddy hugs me when I reach my feet; I go up on my tip-toes to kiss his chin.

"Daddy, you don't feel any guilt tonight, either, okay?"

"I've already given myself a pep talk, sweetheart. I think I can stay focused on the Opening."

Daddy has been super-distracted since he and Master Mac met with Annabelle. Daddy didn't tell me everything she said but I understand Master Emmett hurt her and not in a good way. I don't know Emmett beyond passing him in the hallway but I thought all the masters at Blunts were good Doms, safe Doms. It hurts my heart to know that some of them aren't.

Daddy's been so sucked into what's going on with the Blunts house subs that he left dealing with True almost entirely to Theo, Maude, and Brenna. Which isn't like Daddy at all. Not saying Daddy likes to micromanage but . . .

After our trip to the museum, Theo, Maude, and Brenna got True placed for ninety days with Mac's friend. True, whose real name is Ellen but we've all kept calling her True at her request, can finish the school year via distance learning. Her new foster mother works in the City, so she's been dropping True off at our house on her way in to work every day and picking her up on the way home. True studies in the mornings while I write. In the afternoons, there's been a parade of house subbies coming to spend time with her: Cappa, Fleur, Charlotte, Justine, Austin, Hunter, Allyn, Moon, Shannie, and Lucy. They've been talking with True about their own submissive journeys and how they wish they'd been able to explore submission safely in their teens. I've been moved to tears a few times listening to the subbies talk about their experiences. None of them had a really *safe* introduction into submission. No more than I did.

I haven't shared my own journey with True yet but I plan to when she's had more time to process. The way she looks at Daddy and Mac tells me she's still struggling to separate her desire for dominance from her crush on the two Doms who "saved" her.

Tonight, True's going to see a different kind of family. Daddy's partner Manny has offered to babysit Livvy overnight while we're at the club for the Nursery's Grand Opening. True and Livvy are coming with us in the limo to Blunts, then Manny's going to pick up his cousin who is a police officer and head home. They're going to feed True dinner and True's going to babysit until her curfew under their supervision. Once True has some experience, she's going to take a babysitting certification course, then she can start earning her own income.

That's only one of the subbie plans for True but I think it's a good one. True needs to be around healthy, loving families so she can see that her experiences with a neglectful family and abuse in foster care aren't the way families are supposed to be.

"How are you feeling about being apart from Livvy for the night, baby doll?" Daddy asks.

"Okay. Jen's a stickler for bedtimes so I'm sure she'll follow Gracie's schedule. I just hope Livvy's good for her and True."

Daddy leans in and kisses my forehead. "Livvy's behavior one way or another is not a reflection on you as a parent—"

"Babysitter," I say quickly.

"Uh-huh, babysitter. Best little babysitter in the world." He gives me another soft, warm kiss. Daddy's forehead kisses make me swoony. I clutch at the lapels of his purple and red-checked jacket. "Hurry up, my glitter bunny, and let's go have some fun."

"Okay, Daddy!"

He swats my bottom and I hop off to the bathroom like a good little glitter bunny.

I've already showered and done my hair so I'm just swiping on a little mascara because Daddy likes tear tracks and cleaning myself out in case Daddy wants my bottom tonight. I spend a moment looking in the mirror, admiring the nubby paddle marks on my ass from our session with Belial this morning. I know it's crazy but seeing Daddy's marks makes me crazy happy. I love being owned by him; I love wearing the proof on my body. Listening to the subbies talking to True, I realize I'm not in the minority, even though not all of the house submissives are masochists. Most of them like seeing marks after a scene. They're not just a reminder of a good scene but they help carry that submissive headspace into the rest of our lives.

Daddy lets me live my best little life but not all submissives can be submissive all the time. Not all of them want to, of course but even the ones who do like Bren and Fleur struggle to pull their submission into their jobs and lives outside their relationships with their Doms.

As I brush my teeth and do quick gag reflex training, I let gratitude for how Daddy's reshaped his world around me fill up my soul. It hasn't been easy for either of us. I didn't realize until my confrontation with Miranda that I would struggle with it, too. But as I look at myself in the mirror, seeing the healthy glow of my skin, the light in my eyes, that weren't there even six months ago when I was on my own, I see not the struggle but how far we've come. I look at the beautiful platinum collar glinting around my throat and, despite everything that's going on around us, I feel at peace.

Ablutions completed, I bounce out of the bathroom, pull on my glitter-edged tutu, white thigh-highs, black garters, and a criminally short, black-and-blue checked pinafore over a sheer black shirt with thumb holes that I adore. There's no point in a bra tonight and the shirt's mesh chafes my nipples deliciously with every breath. I'm going to be a puddle by the time we get to the club.

When Cynnie and I found what she calls my "pastel goth Alice" outfit, we thrifted a blue velvet top hat to go with it. I glittered a veil to go on it but I'm feeling too little for a hat tonight. Instead, I pull back my curls with a blue bow, slide my feet into black platform Mary Janes, and run downstairs to meet Daddy.

He blinks rapidly when he sees me, grins, and holds out his arms.

"Hello, Alice," he growls. "You're going to get a taste of my biggest hat tonight."

I giggle. "You're bad, Daddy."

"I am. You in those thigh highs gets my motor revving, always. I love this outfit." He slips a hand under the bib of my pinafore and tweaks a nipple. "Easy access. Brilliant."

I wriggle happily and hold my arms out so he can help me into my winter coat. Manny's ferrying us to Blunts, so I could go without but when I'm wearing a play costume, I feel safer either changing at the club or wearing a coat over top. I'm getting more and more comfortable wearing little clothes out, even when I'm not with Daddy but costumes are different. Even if they're not as revealing as what women wear to nightclubs, the littleness of them could attract very bad attention.

The world still isn't safe for my otherness. It won't ever be. That sense of safety, of Daddy creating a world that's as safe for me as possible, fills me up again. When he leads me out to Manny's limo, I look up at him with all the love and gratitude in my heart.

He buckles my seatbelt and cups my face in his hands. "What's that look for, naughty Alice?"

"You're the best daddy for me in the whole universe and I'm very grateful for you."

Logan clears his throat and snaps his own seatbelt as Bren, Cappa, and Fleur climb in and take their seats. True's the second-to-last in, carrying Olivia in her car seat, followed by Master Mac. There are a lot of hands to help True strap the car seat in; I stay hands-off to let True earn her babysitting stripes. Once everyone's got their seatbelts on, Daddy signals to Manny that we're ready. The limo pulls smoothly into the early evening traffic.

Daddy leans in, his breath warm against my ear. "You're making me emotional, little girl. What's this all about?"

I wiggle in my seat until I'm cuddled close to his side. "When I was getting dressed, I looked at myself in the mirror and saw how different I look from when I lived in Syracuse. I always had dark circles under my eyes because I didn't have a consistent sleep schedule. My skin was pale and dry because I didn't get enough sunlight or drink as much water as I should. I had happy moments. I had good friends and I've always loved to write. But I wasn't crazy happy. I wasn't so happy I thought I'd explode. Not the way I am now."

"You're always beautiful to me, sweetheart," Daddy says. "But you do look very healthy. And hearing that you're crazy happy makes me crazy happy, too."

"Even with everything going on?" I ask.

"*Especially* with everything going on. You're my whole world, Emmy. If you're crazy happy even with all the messiness of my life spilling into yours, then everything I've had to do to control that mess is worthwhile."

I tip my head onto his shoulder and smile dreamily out the window at the denim-blue twilight.

The outside of Blunts looks the same as always: staid and nondescript. But once we're through the security doors, everything changes.

The main hallway is full of people. There are house submissives posed in every display nook along the paneled walls, bare skin gleaming in the club's warm lights. Red banners hang from the hallway's high ceiling, proclaiming "Blunts' Nursery Grand Opening." Beneath the banners, wait staff from the Trattoria circulate with silver trays loaded with juice boxes and finger foods. I didn't have any hand in this—my decoration for the Grand Opening was confined to the Nursery itself—so the food on the trays isn't all healthy but it's a little's delight. Chicken nuggies in animal shapes. Veggie flowers. Skewers of watermelon, pineapple, and mango. Popcorn balls. Fancifully decorated mini-cupcakes. It makes me teary to see the thought someone's put into this.

Lots of our friends from playgroup and the Elephant's Playground are already present, mingling, admiring the displayed submissives, talking in excited tones. The theme for the Opening is nursery rhymes and people have really gotten into it. Sammi is wearing nothing but a blue coat with gold buttons, bunny ears, and a huge, cotton-ball butt plug. He's trailing so much gold and white glitter he looks like he's in the middle of a dust storm. There are several Dumbos, a three-person caterpillar trailing a butterfly whose huge wings light up, and a Humpty Dumpty in nothing but white latex. Mistress Dana, in bright blue leathers and wielding a terrifyingly spiked shepherd's crook, herds Austin, Mally, and Zuki, all wearing white, glittered wigs and matching G-strings. I see Maude leading Georgie in his full fursuit by a golden collar and leash. Master Chess is deep in conversation with Claudia, the chairwoman of the Playground, who is in her foxsuit. Tessa kneels at Chess's feet in her puppy leathers, yipping for attention until he ruffles her hair. Moon and Allyn prance by in their pony tack and boots.

I clap my hands, spinning around in delight. When I cuddle against my grinning Daddy, I find Bren and Fleur looking at me with huge smiles.

I gesture to the banners. "Did you do this?"

Bren and Fleur crowd in for hugs. Fleur kisses my cheek. "Welcome to the Blunts family," she whispers to me. "We're a noisy family with a lot of strong personalities who won't ever agree about everything but no one loves harder than the people in this club."

I squeeze her. "Thank you."

While I'm in mid-huggle, Chess walks over to Daddy. He hands Daddy an oversized pair of silver scissors. "Do the honors, Master Logan," Chess says.

Daddy claps Chess on the shoulder and takes the scissors. He catches my wrist and draws me after him as he walks down the hallway to the huge stairs leading to the upper floors of the club. There's another red banner stretched across the stairs.

Daddy stops next to the banner. He opens the scissors and offers one handle to me. Grinning, I take the handle. Daddy positions the scissor blades between the words "Nursery" and "Grand."

He looks over his shoulder at the crowd. "Welcome, everyone. It's my very great pleasure to open the Blunts Nursery."

To cheers from the crowd, Daddy nods at me. I push my handle toward his and the big blades slice through the banner. The two halves flutter down to the stairs like falling leaves.

Daddy draws me to one side as people begin trooping up the stairs. Cynnie, in her black and yellow striped onesie with a fully glittered crown between her antennae, stops for a hug before Max leads her upstairs. Matty and Yummy run up, trailing glitter from their dragon costumes, followed by their daddies and Master Javier. Queen Twitch winks at me as they stalk past on white platform heels that must put them close to seven feet, holding up the skirts of a fully-feathered white swan costume. Master Harold walks in Queen Twitch's wake, holding the hand of someone in a blow-up, orange T-Rex costume.

I give Daddy the owl eye. He chuckles. "Pence must have earned himself another punishment."

"How can you punish someone in a blow-up dinosaur costume, Daddy?"

"Oh, Harry managed last time. Hands and feet aren't covered by the costume; Harry made full use of them."

I wince sympathetically.

Daddy leers at me. "I haven't punished those tender little toes in some time."

"Because my feet haven't done anything wrong," I point out.

"Incorrect. Those little ice cubes find my warm, unsuspecting calves unerringly in the night."

I screw my face up at him. "I can't be punished for things I do in my sleep."

"That's where we disagree, little girl." Daddy laughs. "Jiro and Laurel should be here within the hour and I think, in honor of their visit, we could have a Tickle Tondo Two."

I squint at him. The first Tickle Tondo was ridiculously fun but I did almost pee myself from laughing so hard. "I thought we were dancing tonight after the hunt? I can't dance on tickled toes."

"Is that a challenge, little girl? I bet I can get you to dance." He tugs the brim of his top hat down rakishly. "No one can resist the Hatter."

It's true I can't resist Daddy, particularly when he's playful.

When most of the crowd has made its way upstairs, Daddy holds his hand out to me. "Ready, little girl?"

"Ready, Daddy."

We join the stragglers making their way upstairs. Ahead of us, Master Theo is helping a woman dressed up as a fairytale princess, with full hoop skirts that she's struggling to manage on the stairs. Once he helps her get the hoop under control, he continues holding her hand as they walk up together. Under the princess' gauzy pink veil and conical hat, I recognize the brown curls of Amy from playgroup.

I squeeze Daddy's hand and tip my chin at the pair when he glances at me. He follows my gesture; a sly smile lights his face.

"Is the Little Matchmaking Bureau about to spring into action, baby?" he asks.

"Could be, Daddy. I think there's some potential there."

"Me, too. I remember the first time Theo met you. Do you remember?"

I nod. I was recovering from the wooden-pony punishment. Master Theo read to me. He held Peter Aloha Bunny. He shared his dessert with me. I actually liked him until I found out how horrible he'd been to Daddy later that night.

"He was *entranced* by you," Daddy says quietly, so the couple a few steps ahead of us doesn't hear. "I was the tiniest bit jealous."

"You weren't, were you?" I ask, tugging on his hand. I don't want Daddy to be jealous. I want him always to be as secure in my love as he's made me in his.

He holds up his free hand with his thumb and first finger almost touching. "Tiniest bit. But I realized he was responding to your littleness. It *is* entrancing. I can't blame anyone for falling for it."

"But Amy's not a masochist," I point out. That's probably a bigger issue than her littleness.

"He's an experienced Dom. If there's chemistry and he wants to be a caregiver, he might find that satisfies his needs. As much as I get off when you suffer for me, baby doll, caring for you fills an even deeper set of needs. I'm glad you're a masochist; I wouldn't change a thing about the way we play. But if you weren't, I'd still have pursued a relationship with you. I need your joy in my life more than I need your pain."

I lean into him and he slides his arm around my shoulders. "I didn't know that, Daddy."

"Do you really think I wouldn't shape myself to be whatever you need?"

I nod, rubbing my cheek against his shoulder blissfully. "Yes, because you're the Dom I deserve. You're my Batman Daddy."

He lets out a bark of laughter. "You called me that before and I didn't realize what you were saying. Is that what the Batman stickers are in your journal? Are those me?"

"Uh-huh. You've always been my Dark Knight, right from the beginning."

"Doesn't Batman get defeated? He's not like Superman."

"He does. He gets knocked down a lot. He's flawed and compromised and he makes mistakes. And he's a bazillion times better than Superman. Superman's perfect; he can do anything. Batman can't. Batman works hard for every victory, small or large. Batman gets back up, no matter how hard he's knocked down. That's my Daddy."

Daddy pulls me to the side of the staircase again and drags me up into his arms so we're nose-to-nose, my feet dangling.

"You're making me emotional again, my little wonder."

"Sorry, Daddy."

He rubs noses with me. "Never, ever apologize for telling me your feelings. I love you so much, little girl, and I will strive every day to be your Batman Daddy."

I wrap one arm around his neck and cup his cheek with the other, blinking mistily as I look into his deep, dark eyes. "You already are."

My Batman Daddy carries me the rest of the way up the stairs.

twenty-six

EMILY

LIKE OUR COLLARING ceremony which swelled from just the two of us to a crazy number when Daddy said I could invite people, almost double the number of people I invited come to the Grand Opening. The only person I made a point of inviting that I don't see in the crowd is Master Ten.

I guess I should have expected he wouldn't come, given how ugly things got between him and Daddy over Master Mac's membership but friction was pretty high between Daddy and Mistress Caddy and she's here. When we make it into the Nursery, I see Caddy's subbie, Finn, alongside a bunch of littles on the pirate ship, holding off their Doms with foam swords. Fleur has already been captured and bent over a ship's cannon for a spanking by Master Javier. She waves cheerily when Daddy drags me away after a quick circuit of the Nursery to make sure everyone's enjoying themselves.

I get my first orgasm in the hallway on the way to Long Gallery. Daddy's loving these surprise orgasms at the moment. He pushes me against the wall without warning, drops to his knees, lifts my skirt and tutu over his head, and eats me out until I scream for him.

Daddy kisses me through the afterglow, pushing my own tang across my tongue. When my legs can hold me up again, he straightens my clothes, threads my arm through his, and walks on like nothing happened. I blink up at him, dazed and blissed.

"How many orgasms tonight, baby doll?" he asks conversationally.

"I think we agreed on four, Daddy."

"Did we? Hmm. That seems a small number for such a big night."

"Well, I'm a very little girl, Daddy."

He chuckles. I steel myself for an onslaught of orgasms. It's a severe hardship.

In the Long Gallery, we find most of the members of Elephant's Playground lined up for a Hunt. In addition to the Dumbos, caterpillar, and butterfly, there are three foxes, two puppies, a kitty, and something that might be a bejazzled cow. Apple and Skye, who work in the nightclub, walk by hand-in-hand wearing Tweedle Dee and Tweedle Dum costumes. Mistress Dana herds her flock into line. Tessa prances over, yipping and wagging her tail at Master Chess. Matty and Yummy wait while Daddy unbuckles my Mary Janes, then grab my hands and pull me into the growing crowd of subbies.

A trembling, gray figure, hunched over and trying to make himself as small as possible, shuffles into line behind us.

I tug Yummy and Matty into a ring around Georgie. Our flight won't let anything bad happen to our mousie.

"Don't tell anyone," I whisper to Georgie, my voice almost lost in the hubbub of so many voices. "But I'm secretly a dragon, too. And remember that mice are the only creatures that can defeat a dragon. So you're safe with us."

Georgie's wearing his mouse-face, so it's hard to read his expression but his eyes are full of gratitude.

Master Ryan, who I haven't seen at the club in weeks, appears in his top hat and hunting jacket. He slaps his crop against his black riding boot for silence and when the chatter settles down, he says,

"Subbies get a two-minute head start. The Hunt is confined to the Long Gallery. Anyone going into the Library is out of bounds and disqualified. If you haven't played in the Gallery before, there are several secret passageways. You *must* be with a house submissive to use the secret passageways. House submissives, raise your hands."

A dozen hands go up in the crowd.

"I mean it about the secret passageways," Ryan says. "It's possible to get lost in them. You may only go into a secret passageway if you're with one of the people holding up their hands. Anyone going into a secret passageway without a house submissive will be immediately asked to leave. This is a safety issue. I expect you all to follow this rule. Say 'aye'."

A chorus of "ayes" rise from the cluster of subbies.

"There endeth the rules of the Hunt," Master Ryan intones in a voice deeper than Daddy's, somehow. In his normal voice, he continues, "If you're hunting a subbie that's *not* your own, this is a tag hunt. Tap anywhere on their body above the waist and the prey is caught. If you're hunting your own subbie, I trust you've negotiated the level of resistance your prey mounts to being caught. Whether or not your subbie has a safe word, the safe word 'red' is in use for the Hunt. If I or any other scene monitor hears the word 'red' in any context, play stops until we can check in with the players. Prey, on your marks, get set, go!"

I was listening so closely to the rules that I'm taken aback by the start of the Hunt. I stand there staring until Yummy yanks on my hand. Then I run with my flight, keeping Georgie between us.

Once we get around the corner so the Doms can't see us, some of the subbies take off in a sprint. I'm sure they're headed for the hiding places at the far end of the Long Gallery. I drag my flight to the side and grab Austin's hand before he gets too far away.

His deep brown eyes find mine. He's wearing a ball gag, so we're going to have to communicate via signals.

"The Doms will head to the far end of the Gallery. We need a closer hiding place that will fit all of us but is deep so they won't be able to see us if they take a cursory look."

Austin nods. He pinches his nose with his free hand.

"Smells don't bother me." I glance around at the rest of my flight and Georgie. Everyone's nodding.

Austin tugs on my hand.

We follow him in a line, picking up Tessa. I feel slightly bad about sequestering another house submissive in our hiding space but if another group wanted her, they should have been faster.

Austin leads us to a huge landscape in a really ugly wooden frame about a third of the way down the Gallery. Daddy told me the secret passageways out of the Long Gallery are a house submissive secret. Members aren't told about them. If members find them during hunts, they're not supposed to tell each other. Daddy doesn't think he knows them all—they're passed down from house submissive to house submissive during their training period and even the Master of Training isn't let in on the secret. Which is why the rule about using the secret passageways only with a house submissive is so strict. They evidently thread all the way through the club, letting out in other dungeons, the nightclub, the Trattoria's kitchen, even the underground parking lot.

Austin and Tessa work together to unlatch the picture. It swings away from the wall, revealing a dark tunnel that starts about waist height.

Before I even consider how I'm going to get up into it, Austin catches me around the waist and swings me up into the tunnel. He tosses Tessa straight in behind me. She grabs my hand and leads me into darkness.

Quick breathing fills the passageway as the other subbies crowd in behind us. The passageway isn't very high. I have to bend over to avoid hitting my head. Austin and Georgie are bent almost double. Daddy will definitely not want to climb into this vent or whatever it is. I can hear the soft rush of air ahead of us, although the tunnel we're in is still.

Tessa pauses and whispers, "There's a grate in the floor ahead of us. It won't support full body weight. We have to walk on the edges. Follow me, put your feet where I put mine."

"Okay." I glance over my shoulder into the mouth of the tunnel. Whoever was last in must have pulled the picture closed behind us because there's only the faintest gray light in the passageway. Matty's right behind me, her eyes and teeth glinting with excitement. Georgie's pressed up against her hip, on his hands and knees, which is smart although I hope he doesn't rip his fursuit.

"Put your hands on my hips," I suggest to Matty. "We need to step where Tessa steps."

Matty nods and grips my hips. Wow, her hands are strong like Daddy's.

Straining in the dimness to see Tessa's feet, I follow as she starts to move. I feel the uneven rungs and spaces of the grate under my left foot almost immediately and tuck myself as close to the wall as I can to keep my weight off the grate.

Tessa leads me around a corner and I sigh with relief. Even if Daddy or other masters know about this passageway, once we're all around the corner, they won't be able to see us. I can't see many of them crawling down this tunnel after us. *Not* very domly.

As I shuffle down the passageway after Tessa, I notice a growing smell. It's not horrible but it's not nice, either. It's stale and moldy, like cheese that's gone off.

"What is that?" I whisper to Tessa.

"Vent from the Spa," she whispers back. "We think it might be the pool filters. We've told the cleaners and they say they've taken care of it but the smell never gets much better."

I don't think a pool filter should smell like that. I make a gagging noise.

"No joke," Tessa whispers. "This is the least-used secret passageway and now you know why."

"Pee-eww," Matty whispers behind me.

I nod and cup my hand over hers at my hip. Even though we're playing and I'm not *really* afraid of the stinky dark, it's nice to feel my flight with me, supporting me, in this strange space.

"Everyone around the corner?" Tessa whispers.

I relay her question down the line. The answer comes back quickly. "All good."

Tessa shuffles a little further and then sits down. "We can wait here. Austin, you got the count?"

"Yes," he stage-whispers back.

"What's the count?" I ask Tessa, sliding down the wall to sit cross-legged next to her. There's stone at my back and under my butt, so we must have moved out of the vent, even though the smell doesn't get any better.

"Hunts are timed. Thirty minutes. If the Hunters haven't found us by then, we win."

"What do you win if Master Chess doesn't find you?"

Her eyes and teeth glint. "Unrestricted orgasms."

There's a collective giggle and several "me, toos." Hmph. I should have bargained for unrestricted orgasms.

"How often do you negotiate those with Master Chess?" I ask.

"Every week if I can. Sometimes he's too tense when the time comes and controlling my pleasure is his biggest thing, so I let it go. But whenever he seems relaxed enough, I go for it."

Dang. My negotiation skills are clearly lacking here. I barely ever negotiate for unrestricted orgasms. More often than not, Daddy offers them to me as a reward for being his good little girl. I need to be more strategic, which is not my best thing when I'm in littlespace. Maybe that's why I haven't negotiated for them more often. I'm in littlespace so much of the time now.

Matty elbows me. "You haven't been negotiating for unrestricted orgasms, either, have you?"

"No," I admit. "Why haven't you?"

"Oh, orgasm denial is one of Faolan's kinks. I'm honestly so grateful when I'm not on it that I never think to ask for *unrestricted* orgasms. I'm just delighted whenever he gives me permission."

"Eep. How often are you on orgasm denial?" I ask, trying to keep the horror out of my voice.

"Most weekdays. The only time I'm sure I'll get orgasms is on the weekends. If I'm having a really bad week, he might give me release just to help keep me from spiraling. No guarantee, though. It's gotten worse since we've been back in New York and he's been talking with Master J. Ohemmgee, that man *loves* orgasm denial."

I choke back my horror and feel a rush of gratitude that Daddy doesn't keep me in a No O zone all week. "I would purely die."

"Before we moved to New York and I started teaching, it was awful. It made me so angry. Faolan and I had fights about it. It's the only thing we've really fought about. But I've settled into it. It actually helps keep me focused during the week and looking forward to the weekends. Like, each weekend is a total break. Something separate from my work week. All I have to do on weekends is focus on me and Daddy and pleasure. I don't know, it works. We'll see what happens next month when school breaks for the holidays."

I put my arm around her shoulders. "You're so courageous. I'd have killed Daddy by now if he had me on O restriction all week."

Matty giggles. "I thought about it a few times. I got paddled a lot for mouthing off at him when I was needy. But since I've settled into it, I've kind of come to enjoy it. He edges me progressively through the week so by Friday night, I'm thinking about nothing else. I put everything behind me and we have wonderful weekends together. It's worth it. But I did have a list of creative ways to kill him and not get caught going for a while."

"Top of the list?" someone whispers from down the corridor and I realize Matty and I haven't been as quiet as we should have been.

"The quaking bogs of Rannoch Moor in the Scottish highlands," Matty says with the certainty of giving something extensive thought. "Most peat bogs are shallow but the Rannoch Moor bogs are really deep. Deep peat bogs are worse than quicksand. They're hard to see as you're crossing the moors. Once you go down in the bog, it's very dark, so you can't orient yourself. The peat is heavy and compresses your body, making it hard to move or breathe. You drown really quickly. I mean, I didn't want Daddy to *suffer* or anything."

Lots of low laughs from the group, many of whom have sadistic Doms who *love* our suffering.

"Too bad Scotland's so far away," I point out.

"Mmm, it was more practical when we were on Miller's Island, which is just a hop, skip, and a boat-ride from the highlands," Matty admits. "I have yet to find a good substitute here in the States."

"Vermont has cranberry bogs," someone, I think it's Georgie, whispers.

"I don't think they're deep enough," Matty says. "But it's worth exploring. Do you have a list?"

"Oh, yeah," a deep whisper responds. I think that's Austin. "Mercuric chloride. I use it in my dark room so I have it on hand. Very poisonous. Central nervous system failure. Like you said, I don't want her to *suffer*. At least, not for very long."

Despite how macabre this topic is, everyone laughs. We've all entertained these thoughts. We've all been angry and resentful at our Doms. It's natural, even for masochists.

"But I love her," Austin says. "More than I've loved anyone. Crazy, huh?"

We all agree.

Our whispered conversation stops dead when the corridor suddenly brightens. Matty and Tessa grab my hands.

"Oh, little girl," Daddy's voice slithers down the corridor. "Little girl, is this where you're hiding?"

I almost break. I cram Matty and Tessa's hands against my mouth to keep from answering him.

"Little girl, I'm coming in."

I shake my head, then my whole body as adrenaline dumps into my veins. *It's just a game*, I remind myself. But there's something so primal about being hunted that I can't control my fight-or-flight response. Tessa suddenly wraps her arms around me and I realize

I've started scooting down the corridor away from Daddy's voice, nearly bowling her over.

"Little girl, I can hear you moving."

It's not me he can hear moving. It's Georgie, who climbs over me. I get flattened against Tessa as he scrambles away from Daddy's voice.

"Little girl, what do you imagine I'm going to do with you when I catch you?"

I smash the heel of my hand between my teeth to keep from squealing. I can't hear Daddy moving over the rustle of Georgie's fursuit, so I don't know if he's really climbed into the small passageway. I hope not. Or if he does, he takes off his top hat. I really like that hat. But if I squeak or squeal or eep, he'll definitely come in.

"I brought lots of toys to torture you with, little girl," Daddy continues. "I have a Y-clamp, and the biggest butt plug you've ever seen, and my metal-tipped flogger, and—" There's a roar from the back of our group. "Gotcha!"

"Fuck!" Austin howls. "Not it!"

"You're all caught," Daddy says. "Be careful coming out around that grate. It doesn't look strong enough to bear your weight."

"We know!" We chorus, high-pitched in our disappointment.

"Damn," Tessa says as we all start crawling back toward the entrance. "I didn't think Master Logan even knew about this one."

"Daddy's very devious," I say, commiserating. "He probably found all the secret passageways when we were building the Nursery. I know he spent a lot of time with the architect looking over the building's plans. Bad Daddy."

We're almost to the grate when I realize we're one short. "Where's Georgie?" I ask Tessa.

She looks over her shoulder. "I thought he was right behind me. Georgie?" she calls.

No answer.

"He couldn't have gotten lost," Tessa says. "That branch of the passageway leads to the Stocks eventually."

257

"Okay, you go out. I'll get him. He knows me. Tell Daddy I'm coming. I'm just taking care of Georgie."

Tessa chews on her lip. "Are you sure?"

I'm a fierce, white, baby dragon who isn't afraid of the dark. Dragons don't leave their friends behind.

I nod and crawl back into the darkness.

twenty-seven

LOGAN

MY BABY DOLL would be in the *last* place I looked.

The rule of the Hunt is that prey who don't get caught after thirty minutes win. I've got three watches on my left wrist plus a pocket watch in this costume and they were all telling me the same thing: I had four minutes left when I remembered the Spa vent behind that bloody awful Hudson River landscape. It may be worth a million but it's the most boring painting ever. Shade after shade of brown, green, and gray. In fact, I think the club had it appraised on the basis of being one of the most boring paintings ever.

When Tessa climbs out of the vent and Emily isn't behind her, my eyebrows shoot toward the brim of the hat I crushed climbing into the cramped passage.

"Where's Emmy?" I ask.

"She's gone back for Georgie. He panicked when he heard your voice. It's okay. We were in the branch of the passageway that leads to the Stocks. They can't get lost."

I look over at Maude, who is having an intense-looking conversation with Twitch. "Maude, Emily and Georgie haven't come out."

She immediately breaks off whatever she was saying to Twitch and comes to stand beside me at the mouth of the vent. "He may have been spooked. Blunts is still somewhat unfamiliar territory."

"The passageway they're in lets out into the Stocks," I say. "You stay here. I'll head to the Stocks." I take out my phone and waggle it at her. "Call me if they come out. If I don't hear from you, I'll get in at the Stocks entrance and herd them back this way after checking they're okay."

Maude nods. She looks doubtfully at the vent. She's wearing a black leather skirt suit and four-inch heels. Getting up into that vent, much less crawling down it, is going to be a challenge for her.

"If I speak to him from here, can he hear me?"

"Possibly. It's an air vent but it's not making that much noise."

"Right." She squares her shoulders. "I'll try to talk him out from here. Call me if there's trouble."

I nod and head off to the Stocks. It's a short walk but I pick up company. As soon as I start off, Dana and Austin follow me. As we walk down the hallway toward the Nursery, we bump into Max and Cynnie coming toward us. Max takes one look at my face, reverses course, and falls in beside me.

"What's happened?"

"Emmy and Georgie crawled into a damn duct during the Hunt and haven't come back out." As I say it, heat crawls up the back of my neck. My little girl is not safe. "My Daddyness is not happy."

Cynnie pushes between me and Max and links arms with us in a shower of glitter. "We'z can't have unhappy Daddyness," she says. "Lez find them."

She begins to skip, which forces Max and me into a jog to keep up with her. My Mad Hatter costume isn't built for jogging and the toys tucked into various pockets bang against me unpleasantly but I keep pace. A bruise or two is a small price to pay for getting to my baby faster.

As we open the door to the Stocks, I hear Emily shout, "Stop it!"

My blood freezes, then rushes through my veins, pounds through my ears.

I break away from Max and Cynnie, accelerating into a sprint, which gets me around the corner and pushing through a group of people standing on the far side of the room, near an open armoire. I assumed the armoires in the dungeon held play equipment, although I admit I haven't investigated this one. There are some sheets and towels lying on the floor near the armoire, and a group of maybe ten people.

"Emily, come to me," I growl.

She pushes between the bodies and all but leaps into my arms. Her eyes are full of tears. "Make them stop. They're scaring Georgie. He's too frightened to safe word."

I hug her tightly with one arm and shove two people out of my way. I barely take note of who is around me until I see Georgie. He's standing, trembling, his paws over his mouse-face. The bottoms of his fursuit are around his ankles, baring his pale legs and a loin-cloth with a cock-cage poking out of it.

I put my little girl down, keeping my body between her and the crowd, and kneel to pull up Georgie's fursuit. Emily helps me find the tiny snaps that fasten it to the top. When we have him covered, Emily wraps her arms around him. I turn to the group.

Bull's standing behind me with his arms crossed over his chest, a flogger dangling from his wrist. There are a few faces I don't recognize around him but too many that I do. Franco. Shedo. Emmett. Al. Naz. Drew.

"What the bloody hell's going on here?" I ask.

"Georgie and Emily came in the middle of my scene," Bull responds, nodding at the Stocks where Al's submissive, MacKenzie, is pilloried. "It's a closed scene. They have no right entering. You know the rule."

I do know the rule about submissives entering closed scenes. They're fair game. I grind my teeth. My brain scrambles for an exception and latches on to a thin one.

"In case of emergency, any submissive can enter any space in the club and seek help. Emily, did you make it clear you and Georgie were in trouble?"

Silence behind me.

I look over my shoulder and find Emily worrying her lower lip with her teeth. "Not exactly, Daddy."

"In her defense," Al says. "We didn't give her a chance. Their appearance was unexpected."

"Georgie is on loan to Maude," Bull says, his voice rough. "I had every right to demand proof that the terms of the loan were being observed."

I grind my teeth. There's clearly shit going on between Maude, Georgie, Bull and his trio that I don't know about. I haven't heard fuck all about a loan, although that's not an uncommon way to deal with submissives who are playing with more than one Dom. The club keeps a register of subbie loans but I admit I haven't checked it in over a year, not since I started dating Rachel.

I don't want to get into the middle of their drama. But I'm also concerned that I just scared a vulnerable submissive half-to-death by playing with my little girl without thinking about the impact it might have on him.

Swallowing my pride and my irritation, I bow to the group. "I apologize for the interruption to the scene. It was my fault that Emily and Georgie came through the passageway. I didn't consider the impact playing with Emily might have on Georgie—"

"So, would you say that's a consent violation, Master Logan?" Drew asks with a smirk.

Rob and Emmett may have the best hair in the club but Drew's not far behind. He's a good-looking bloke all around. Wavy, dark blond hair carefully styled. Lightly tanned despite the cold weather. Runner's physique. Ridiculously cut jaw. He's dressed formally: black tuxedo pants with a satin stripe, burnt-orange waistcoat over a white dress shirt, black bow-tie undone and hanging loose around his strong throat. It all looks good on him.

But I have to wonder what's behind those preppy good looks because this guy was on my shit list before he opened his mouth. I'm not sure if Emmett's running this bullshit Wolfpack and Drew's just along for the ride or what but I hate everything about what I've heard about them in the last few days.

I glance around the group and don't find any support. Bull's glaring at Georgie and won't meet my eyes. Is this how Shannie felt surrounded by Drew's guests? There's a gut-ruffling sense that I'm in the minority and it could all go very bad in an instant.

I bow again. "I'll submit myself to Maude and Georgie's judgment of whether I broke the rules of the Hunt or committed a consent violation. Again, gentlemen, my apologies for interrupting the scene. Emily, Georgie, come with me."

I reach a hand back. Emily's small fingers immediately wrap around mine. I lead them out, shouldering my way between Franco and a man I don't recognize. I glance at MacKenzie as we pass her pillory. She's wearing a ball-gag, a lot of red stripes, and nothing else. I know she and Al do gang-bangs but there are ten men in the room and she's the only submissive. Is she really going to let all ten of them fuck her? That's a lot by anyone's estimation.

Shaking my head, I push toward the door.

"Is that disapproval, Master Logan?" Drew calls after me. "Do you not like our scene?"

A mutter of male voices chases me out of the room as Dana, Max, Austin, and Cynnie fall in around me.

Once we're out in the hallway, I let myself relax. That was tense but I deescalated the situation. Emily looked outraged on Georgie's behalf but not upset. I don't know what rules Georgie has in place, so I don't know if he's traumatized or just humiliated by being exposed in front of the group. I'll get him back to Maude and let her evaluate him.

The door into the Stocks bangs open behind me. "Oh, Master Logan?"

Drew. Again. He's really getting on my wick.

I stop and turn to face him. Max stops at my right. "Get Emily and Georgie out of here," I mutter to him. "Take Georgie to Maude. She needs to evaluate him."

Max meets my eyes, then nods. He takes Emily's hand out of mine and leads her away.

Her uncertain, "Daddy?" pierces me straight through the heart.

"Go with Max, little girl," I say without taking my eyes off Drew. He leans in the doorway to the Stocks, smirk firmly affixed. I really want to smack that expression off his face. Emmett and Al come up the doorway and stand behind Drew.

I have a lot of time for Al. He's been at the club longer than I have. He was one of the very first members of Chinese descent, which he's told me made him feel isolated for years. He's the club's doctor and I've found him to be progressive and caring as a physician, which many doctors in today's managed health care system don't have the time or opportunity to be.

Seeing him standing literally at Drew's back is a cold slap to the face.

"Yes, Master Drew," I say.

"Nice costume." His smirk widens, showing the benefits of fluoride and orthodontics. "Your hat's looking a little worse for wear, though."

I nod, acknowledging him and encouraging him to get to the bloody point.

"You didn't answer my question, Master Logan," Drew continues. His voice is really beginning to grate. "Do you disapprove of our scene?"

"Gang-bangs aren't my thing," I say. "But I hope you enjoy yourselves."

Drew pushes off the door frame and takes two steps toward me. "So that head-shake *was* disapproval. Will you be banning gang-bangs along with other forms of play you don't approve of as you push the club toward caregiver play?"

He sneers as he says "caregiver."

"I'm not aware of any forms of play that are banned by the club," I respond. "So long as its role-play and everyone's consenting, we're open to extreme play such as simulated necrophilia and vore. I don't yuck on anyone else's yum, Master Drew."

He snorts. "But you're steering the club toward pet and age-play."

"The only direction I'm steering the club, with the assistance of the rest of the membership committee." I nod at Al. "Is toward embracing all types of consensual play."

"Ah, right. So you'll be exiling Bull and Sean soon, then, the same way you did Sante? Their submissives don't have safe words. Surely you think their scenes aren't consensual anymore."

I grind my teeth. This is a topic that's debated in the community frequently. Emily and I have skirted it, too, since she wants to give up her safe word in some situations and I was the one who wanted to take it slowly since I've never played without a safe word.

"I'm perfectly comfortable with submissives giving up their safe words inside of established relationships—"

"But not outside them?" He lifts his eyebrows. "That seems limiting. I thought you didn't yuck on other player's yum, Master Logan."

Another man comes to stand behind Al. I don't recognize him but he's a very tall, African-American man with precisely-trimmed hair, mustache, and beard. He must be someone's guest, and we cannot be giving him a good first impression of the club, between the scene interruption and this confrontation.

I bow again. "Master Drew, I think this conversation should be tabled until a time when we're not further disrupting an ongoing scene. I don't want to distract Al from monitoring his submissive, particularly when she's restrained. I'll apologize again to everyone for the interruption—"

"Do you think I'd leave my submissive restrained without anyone monitoring her, Logan?" Al asks, his tone sharp.

Goddamn, now I'm pissing off someone I consider a friend.

"Absolutely not," I say quickly. "My apologies if it sounded that way, Al. Gentlemen, good night."

I turn and walk away quickly, knowing that I've lost that round.

Behind me, the door to the Stocks slams.

twenty-eight

LOGAN

THE PARTY'S RUINED. At least for me.

The Long Gallery's nearly empty when I return. Knowing where Emily likes to retreat when she's stressed, I continue into the Library. There's a crowd around one of the leather couches, maybe even the one Emily and I had our very first scene at Blunts on. Maude and Twitch sit with Georgie curled between them. A group of Doms— Jiro, Mac, Javier, Bravo, and Faolan—cluster behind the couch, talking quietly. A line of submissives kneel on the floor in front of the couch. Everyone's rubbing Georgie gently while Maude holds his head to her breasts and speaks to him.

I whip out my phone, take a picture, thumb over to my text messages with Bull, and send it to him. He's been my friend for years but he's letting whatever's going on between him and Maude cloud his judgment. A submissive should not look like this, not even after a breach of protocol.

As I move toward the couch, Javier walks around and puts his hand on my shoulder. "Georgie is okay. He had a panic attack and went non-verbal. Emily brought him out of it. Maude's giving him aftercare. He's okay, Logan."

I take three deep breaths, trying to calm down.

"This was not your fault," Javier continues. "Emily told us you apologized to Bull and Al for interrupting their scene. That's the end of it."

"That's so very far from the end of it," I say, grinding my teeth. "This is a fiasco."

He squeezes my shoulder. "Take three more deep breaths. There's no harm done. Everyone's enjoying the Nursery. No one's been hurt—"

"You didn't see Georgie in there surrounded by—"

Javier's fingers on my shoulder turn crushing. "Deep breaths," he says. "Let Georgie define what happened and how he feels about it. I'm aware there's some tension between Bull and Maude at the moment but Twitch is here, helping Georgie relax and process his fear. This only becomes confrontational if we allow it to. It's . . . unwise for Maude and Bull to be at odds right now. Do you understand what I'm saying to you, mon frere?"

I draw deep breaths through my nose. I understand what he's saying. He's thinking politically and I'm having trouble thinking of anything beyond the need to protect our submissives.

"Yes," I grit.

Bright eyes and dark curls poke around Javier's shoulder. "Master Javier, may I talk to Daddy, please?"

Javier steps away, nodding.

I open my arms and Emily rushes into them. She hugs me tightly, then pushes up on her toes and climbs me. I grab the backs of her thighs, pull her up into position, and settle her against me. She tucks her face into my throat and hums soothingly.

"Baby, what are you doing?"

"Calming you down. You have a full frowny on and your angry vein is throbbing."

"I have an angry vein?"

Her hand worms under my coat, waistcoat, and shirt to palm a circle over my back. "Yup."

I drop my face into her sweetly-scented hair and continue taking deep breaths.

"Do you have an angry vein?"

"Not that I'm aware of but I have very veiny wings."

As always, everything about my little girl soothes me, distracts me from my storming emotions.

"Do you?" I ask, supporting her bottom with my forearm and plucking imaginary wings out from her shoulders. "Hmm, yes, very veiny."

"My veins were throbby too. But now that I've seen Georgie is okay and you're okay, my wings aren't throbbing anymore."

I nuzzle her soft crown. "You're such a treasure, baby doll. I can't do without you."

"You don't have to, Daddy, because I'm right here. And after you check in with Mistress Maude, will you please come upstairs with me?"

"I'll go anywhere with you, any time you ask, my baby."

I feel her smile against my collarbone.

Maybe it's distance from the party, up in the Library's relatively quiet mezzanine. Maybe it's having apologized to Georgie for panicking him and having been reassured by Maude that he'll be okay. Maybe it's having my baby doll in my arms.

Whatever the reason, the pall that the confrontation in the Stocks threw over my night slowly burns away.

Emily's dedication to making me feel better helps. She leads me to a new piece of furniture, a kind of chaise lounge with a higher chair part and a long, sloping foot. The chair part is more chair-like than the other chaises we have around the club. The whole thing is upholstered in deep burgundy leather.

"Are we taking a nap, baby?" I ask.

She grins as she gestures for me to sit in the chair part. Once I'm seated, she climbs onto the long part between my knees and lies on her stomach.

I smile down at her. "What's this all about, little girl?"

"It's a *meridienne*, Daddy. Queen Twitch and I found some pictures of meridiennes in the historical materials we've been restoring and Master Chess gave us the nod to commission one for the Library. They were also called *chaise de pipe*. Can you imagine why?" She wiggles her eyebrows suggestively.

Laughing, I relax back into the chair and put my arms on the padded armrests. "My imagination fails me."

"Can I show you?" she asks, adding the cutest leer to the eyebrow wiggling.

"Yes, little girl, you may. Just a sec."

Maybe it's the lingering endorphins from the Hunt. Maybe it's that I've gotten so used to being naked around Emily. Whatever it is, I've had enough of wearing pants.

I strip off my shoes, socks, striped trousers, and boxers and sit my bare ass down on the leather, smiling at the buttery texture of it. Emily's eyes, already bright, gleam as she sees blood thump through a different part of my anatomy.

"Yes, just having you look at me does that, baby girl."

She grins and scoots up the chaise, holding one hand above my knee, so close I can feel the warmth of her skin.

"May I touch you, Daddy?"

"Anywhere, my sweetheart. Remember what I told you? Daddy's Fuzzie, Wuzzie, and Winky are always yours to play with."

She giggles. I reach out and shape her soft, pouty mouth with my thumb. She opens and when I tip my thumb between her lips, sucks gently.

What was twitching between my legs rises to full attention.

"Oh, little girl, what you do to me. I want to finish in you, so pace your craziness with Daddy's cock accordingly."

"Yes, Daddy," she says around my thumb before continuing with the soft suckles. Her fingertip trails ever-so-lightly up my thigh. Goosebumps rise around her touch.

"Teasing Daddy will not go well for you, little girl," I warn.

She gives me big eyes. "It woan?" she slurs around my thumb as her fingertip reaches the apex of my thigh. Instead of cupping or squeezing me the way she knows I'm already hungering for, she switches hands and starts sweeping a small fingertip up my other thigh.

"What do you think Daddy will do to a little girl who teases him when he's hot and ready to go?"

"Doan know?"

"I think you do know."

She crosses her eyes. "Pwaddle me?"

I slip my hand in the pocket of my jacket and pull out one of the many toys I brought. "I was thinking we could revisit our first scene here."

Her pupils blow. "Twase."

"That's right. Remember this tawse?"

"I dooo."

I play it out between my hands. "I think it remembers you, too. Remember coming from just this leather on your sweet skin, baby?"

Holding my thumb between her teeth, she nods.

"Mmm, we'll see what happens when Daddy sits on you on his cock and smacks that naughty little bottom with this stingy leather. I want at least two orgasms out of you."

She nods more vehemently.

"Let's get to that."

"Swuck you first?"

How can any daddy say no to that?

"Oookay."

Her eyes narrow and I can't suppress a bark of laughter.

I slide my thumb out of her mouth, take myself in hand, and wave my cock at her. "Up here, little girl."

She slides up until my tip bumps against her chin. I rub my crown across her lower lip.

"What do you say?" I ask.

"Please may I suck you, Daddy?"

I feather the fingers of my free hand through her curls. "Yes, my good girl, you can suck me. No rules, just enjoy your little self."

She grins and keeps her eyes on mine as she lowers her head. She takes my tip between her lips and holds there, with just the plush wetness encompassing me. She flicks her tongue out and tickles my slit; my eyes roll back.

"Yes, my sweet baby. Such a good girl for Daddy. That feels so good. So nice and warm. Will you hold me in your mouth for a minute and just keep Daddy's cock warm?"

She blinks enthusiastically, laves me with her tongue, and sinks down until my crown nudges the back of her throat. I control a shout at the sudden constriction. My balls tighten. I fuck Emily's mouth frequently but sometimes I forget the glory of just being encompassed in that soft, hot heaven. No friction, no pendulum motion, just the pure, perfect sensation of being held in her mouth all the way to my root.

She swallows around me and I let loose the shout I was restraining. Fuck. Fuck so good.

Someday, I swear. Someday, I promise myself. Someday, I will manage more than thirty seconds of cock-warming. Someday I will let Emily hold me in her mouth or pussy for hours.

But not today. "Suck, baby. Suck me so good."

After a deep breath, she sucks, opening her throat, drawing me down. My hips rise to her suction, giving her that last fraction of an inch. Her small fingers inch up and find my balls, tugging the way she knows drives me out of my mind.

"Fuck! Emmy!"

The smile that can't curve her lips, stretched around my root, lights her eyes. She blinks and a tear rolls down, telling me she's fighting her gag reflex. But there's nothing but light, love, and happiness behind the welling tears.

Before she gags, I pull back, gripping her hair so she doesn't try to follow me down. I wait until I hear the whistle of her breath, then let her suck me down again. I roar with pleasure.

There's clapping from somewhere nearby. I release Emmy's curls to shoot whoever it is the finger without tearing my eyes away from Emmy's before I gather up her hair again. I don't need to guide her into a rhythm because my baby knows me well. She knows exactly what I like. She bobs her head, sucking hard when I hit the back of her throat, holding on a second longer than I can so I have to pull against that divine suction as my hips swing back.

"Enough, enough, enough," I chant. "Get up here. Ride Daddy."

She releases me with a sweet little kiss before she scrambles up. She doesn't even take off her knickers, just pulls them to the side as she impales herself on me.

"Who is an eager baby?" I ask before drawing her to me for a deep kiss. The minty sweetness of her mouth is spiced with the tang of my skin. I lap it off her tongue.

"Me, Daddy," she admits when I let her up for air.

"Little you, huh? This little girl, so eager to ride her Daddy's cock?"

"Me, me, Daddy. Please." She groans, her stomach caving as she sinks all the way down on me. The sensation is different from being held in her mouth, softer, slicker, infinitesimally better. I'm happy I don't have to choose between Emily's mouth and her pussy because I never could. I'll just enjoy both with utter, profound gratitude that I somehow found my soul-mate who takes everything I give her and gives back more than I ever could have hoped for.

Before I lose myself in the pleasure of her pussy, I push her skirt and the tutu that's shedding glitter all over the place up to bare her round little ass. I rub her cheeks to give her a little warm up, then draw her arms over my shoulders and hold her wrists together behind my head.

With a snap of my wrist, I flick the tawse against her ass cheeks.

The pop and subsequent squeal are magnificent.

She pants through the sting. I don't rub it in, glorying in the way she shifts and clenches around my cock.

"More, baby?"

"Please, Daddy!"

I pepper her ass with stripes. Three have her shuddering, squeezing on me like the wettest fist. Five and she's nearly boneless against my chest, her hips circling as she works to absorb the pain. Ten and she's coming, remembering to beg for permission just before her right leg shoots off the chaise and she convulses, jerking against me like she's being electrocuted. She wails in my ear and I can only laugh with dark triumph as she gushes all over my cock, wetness slicking my thighs.

I wrap my arms around her and hold her steady as I pound up into her, planting my feet on the floor and pushing up with the strength of my thighs and ass. All those fucking squats with weights better be good for something. Emily wails and clings to me as I hammer myself into her, making sure to drag her down against each thrust so I bump her cervix. After a moment of laxity as her muscles recover, she begins jolting, clenching, howling with each collision of our bodies. I cross my arms over her back, sink my fingers into her slim shoulders, and yank her down as I sink deep and come so hard everything goes still for an endless moment: my thoughts, my heart, my lungs. The world stops turning; the universe misses a breath.

Then Emily's gasp gusts across my chin. I dip my head to kiss her, to blow my breath into her lungs and fill my baby up again. She lolls, limp and warm and so-so-so sweet, against my chest. Wetness trickles down over my balls.

"I think we ruined the meridienne," I say, panting between each word.

"It's treated," Emily slurs.

I kiss the tip of her nose. "I love you beyond anything rational, beyond anything sane. You make me crazy happy, little love."

"Love you more, Daddy."

"Not today. Today Daddy loves you infinitely and that's the mostest."

"Moistest," she says, shifting on my lap with a squelch. "I made a mess."

She doesn't sound like she cares in the slightest.

"We did. Let's do it again."

She giggles drunkenly.

twenty-nine

EMILY

I KEEP FINDING new sore spots. They make me smile.

Is there anything hotter than a wolfy Daddy? I know the circumstances were bad. I don't like it that the Blunts Doms are fighting, although maybe it's necessary but it still makes my chest ache.

Whatever the circumstances, the tangible memory of wolfy Daddy keeps me smiling. Daddy's mood isn't as buoyant as mine. I thought we'd stay the night at Blunts after the party but Daddy wants to leave as soon as most of the littles and their caregivers do.

I'm not *too* disappointed. Despite the hiccups, I still think the Grand Opening was a success.

Before we leave, I get to see the second floor of the Nursery. It's even better than I imagined. The magical tree comes up through the hole in the floor and I can stand on the plexiglass and wave down at my friends on the lower floor. There's a corner with a dollhouse, a corner with puzzles and games just like my little room, and a red-carpet corner for dressing up with a brightly-mirrored vanity built into the wall and a catwalk that's going to have to host a fashion show sooner rather than later. I text Cynnie with fashion show ideas;

she drags Max upstairs to see the red-carpet area. We huddle for a few minutes, making plans, before Daddy and Max pull us away. There's a very small part of me that wants to protest leaving before my bedtime, when there's still fun to be had. But Daddy's had a rough night and needs TLC. A little takes care of her Daddy, too, and tonight he needs lots of snuggles and reassurance and a few of the red-velvet cupcakes he likes so much that I squirrel away for a rainy day like this.

As we take a taxi home with Mac and Brenna, the Littles Army chat blows up. Sammi demands a full day of play in the Nursery, unsupervised by Bigs. Imagining him swinging from the tree and then launching himself *into* the wet play area with its beautiful fish tank, I propose an outing to the Aquarium instead followed by a few hours at Blunts playing mermaids in the pool and then napping in the Nursery.

I know just what to wear and it's a plan that can accommodate Livvy, too. Although I know Manny and Jen will take good care of her tonight and I'll see her in the morning, I've missed her.

As I cuddle against Daddy in the taxi, I voice that thought.

Daddy kisses my temple. "We'll see her in the morning."

"I know but I've missed her. Have you?"

Daddy sighs. "I honestly haven't thought about her very much, baby. I'm not sure what that says about me as a parent."

"Nothing other than you have a lot on your mind, Daddy. Maman was a parent who always said she lived for her kids. Even when I *was* her kid, I could see that wasn't healthy. We'd call it a helicopter parent now, always hovering. She spoiled Frances rotten and gave me anxiety and body dysmorphia. I'm not going to repeat her mistakes. I want to fold Livvy into our lives instead of focusing our lives *on* her. If we do that, it's natural there will be times we don't think about her as much because we have other things going on. It doesn't mean we love her less. You're a wonderful daddy to me and you're a wonderful daddy to Livvy. Don't ever think otherwise."

Daddy squeezes my shoulders. "Thank you, baby doll. I'm sorry I'm distracted. You still enjoyed the party, didn't you?"

"I did. Everyone did but you, I think. I'm sorry, Daddy. It should have been fun for you, too."

He kisses my temple again but doesn't answer. The party wasn't fun for him after the Hunt. I love and respect my Daddy but sometimes he sees the world in black and white. It's not a terrible quality in a daddy. It makes him a stickler for rules and I need that. But it also means that when something goes wrong and Daddy's mood goes south, it can be hard to turn around.

While I'm mulling over ways to help that exceed the restorative power of red-velvet cupcakes, Mac starts talking quietly to Daddy. Brenna's got her head down on Master Mac's shoulder and seems asleep—they did a whipping scene in the Stables while we were in the Nursery that I gather was super-intense—but Mac is awake and looking as troubled as Daddy.

"Think we have to accelerate our timeline, son," Mac says.

"I'm thinking that, too. The committee's not scheduled to meet until the first week of December. There's a provision in the by-laws for emergency meetings, though. I think I should call one with a motion to remove Drew and Emmett as members. If Chess refuses to schedule an emergency meeting, then maybe the meeting we call is a vote of no confidence in his chairmanship. I thought I had enough votes for Maude to take his place but after tonight I'm not so sure. I sent Bull a picture of Maude and Twitch taking care of Georgie during the party and he's left me on fucking read. Even if he'd sent back a 'fuck you' or something, I'd feel better. Ignoring me? That's not like Bull. I'm worried I've fucked a friendship tonight."

I blink up at Daddy, trying not to let my shock show. I knew he was worried about Masters Drew and Emmett after talking to Shannie and Annabelle, although he hasn't told me everything they said but I didn't realize it was that bad. And removing Master Chess as the chairman? Master Chess is as much a Blunts institution as

Master Javier. What will be left of Blunts once Daddy's through cleaning house?

I quietly take out my phone and thumb over to my message string with Queen Twitch.

Serious poop going down. We need to talk and help fix this.

A response immediately pops up.

Girl, I was just going to message you! It is a shitSTORM. Lunch tomorrow without the boys?

I send back a string of thumbs-up.

When we get home, Master Mac carries Brenna upstairs, which I've never seen him do before. She doesn't even argue, just curls into him and loops her arms around his neck. It's getting close to my bedtime and I'd really like a bath because I'm still a little sticky, even though I did clean up after wolfy Daddy had his way with me. But taking care of my Daddy tonight is more important, so I head into the kitchen, take some frozen cupcakes out of my secret stash in the freezer, and give my kitty some overdue attention while they defrost in the microwave.

My phone buzzes non-stop with messages. I've been added to a new "dragon + princess chat" with Laurel, Aggie, Sammi, Matty, Yummy, Amy, and Cynnie. I barely got to see Laurel and her Dom tonight. They had a family obligation earlier today so they flew up late for the party but they're staying for three days, so I'll have a chance to catch up with them. Turning the guest bedroom into Livvy's room means we can't offer them a place to stay anymore but Jiro told Daddy he didn't mind and was happy to stay in a hotel.

It occurs to me that they're staying at the same hotel as Miranda, which makes my eye twitch a little as I think about it. It's the closest hotel, so there's nothing sinister about it. Well, nothing beyond the Mir-witch's base level of sinisterness. Still, ugh.

Daddy joins me in the kitchen as I'm reading through the dragon plus princess chat and smiling at the enthusiasm for the Nursery. Everyone really did have a great time tonight except Daddy.

"Master Theo asked Amy out," I tell Daddy as the microwave dings.

Daddy smiles but it's a strained smile. "Glad something good came out of tonight."

I plate up the cupcakes on a pretty, flowered, China plate that Cynnie helped me thrift and take it over to the breakfast table. Daddy follows like a blood-hound. I swear, he's sniffing the air.

"Are those cupcakes for me, little girl?"

"Two are," I say casually, like offering him cupcakes after eleven o'clock at night isn't a big deal for me. "One's for me."

Daddy rubs his hand over his mouth, eying the cupcakes. I think I better be quick to claim my cupcake before the Cupcake Monster nabs it.

I return to the kitchen counter for the tea service: an adorable tea-pot shaped like Dr. Who's telephone box and Dalek-shaped mugs that I found in the same second-hand store where I got our mismatched China plates. Sure enough, by the time I bring the tea service to the table, Daddy's scarfed down one of the cupcakes and has his huge wolf paws curled around the remaining two.

"Daddy!"

With obvious reluctance, he pushes the plate back into the middle of the table.

"I really like your cupcakes."

"I *know*."

He chuckles. "Thank you for making everything better, little wonder."

"You're welcome." I cut my cupcake in half, take my half, and leave the other half on the plate which I push toward him. He eyes it like it's going to run away before he pops it in his mouth. I don't even think he chews. "I think Daddy needs to chew his food ten times."

He smiles at me guiltily as he unwraps the last cupcake. "But they're so good."

"How would you know? You can't possibly have tasted the one you just inhaled."

"I'm just making sure I eat the cupcakes before your cat gets them."

I laugh, remembering Sable's red-velvet-cupcake-stealing ways over Halloween. Goodness was he stinky the day after. Red-velvet cupcake does *not* agree with my kitty's tummy.

"Daddy, what Master Mac was saying in the taxi sounds very serious. Anything I can do to help?"

Daddy pauses in the act of stuffing the cupcake in his mouth. He takes a more moderate bite, chews, and swallows, before he says, "Sweetheart, I don't want to burden you with this. A lot of it is very ugly."

If we were just partners instead of Daddy and little, I'd say something like "your burdens are my burdens." I must have said that to Ash a few thousand times. But it was a lie. My burdens in that relationship were my own.

I've given my burdens to Daddy and he's shouldered every one. That's what being a Daddy is for Logan. But that doesn't mean he has to weather the storms on his own.

I stretch my hand across the table and Daddy wraps his huge wolf paw around it. "Thank you for protecting me from the world's ugliness. I appreciate it. But a little takes care of her Daddy, too, and I can see you're going through it. How can I help?"

"I need to solidify support at the club. Could you reach out to some of the subbies? Twitch, Moon . . . I hate to ask but Pence, too? I need to know Bull, Sean, and Harry are with me on these votes. I got blindsided when Chess, Caddy, and Cris abstained on Mac's vote. I need to be a hundred percent sure."

"I already messaged Queen Twitch. We're meeting for lunch tomorrow. I'm sure Sean will support you but I'll contact Moon. Maybe Bren should contact Pence? I think he still holds a grudge about what happened over the summer."

Daddy nods. "I haven't always made the best choices in the heat of the moment. Or maybe they seemed right at the time and it's only with hindsight that I'm seeing how I've hurt my relationships at the club—"

I shake my head. "You've done some tough things but I think most of your friends at the club realize they were the *right* things. I heard Master Harold say Pence was out of control and needed correction. He agreed with the punishment. He took part in it. He can't blame you for it now, Daddy."

"I hope not but I need to make sure."

"Something you can be absolutely sure of is that the house submissives are behind you. Did you notice that almost all of them came to the Opening? Even Apple and Skye, who almost never come to Monday Madness or our other events, were there."

Daddy rubs his temple, smearing a few red-velvet crumbs into his sideburn. I control a giggle. I'll clean him up later. A cardinal rule of dealing with a wolfy Daddy? Do not come between him and his food.

"I hadn't noticed but you're right."

"I know facing the storm isn't easy, Daddy. I know you have lots of worries. But you're not alone. I'm right here, no matter what happens."

He squeezes my fingers. "I've never doubted that for a second, my little wonder."

When I wake in the morning, I'm alone in our big bed, which isn't unusual because Daddy likes to work out with Master Mac first thing and leaves me to have a lie-in. But he usually wakes me up for nookie before he goes, or at least a blow-job. That he didn't this morning niggles against my happiness as I contemplate Livvy coming back, lunch with Queen Twitch, and a mermaid afternoon.

I'm stretching and thinking about unburying myself from the lovely cocoon of warm blankets when the bedroom door opens and Daddy walks in, carrying a tray.

I sit up in the bed. "Morning, Daddy!"

"Morning, baby. How'd you sleep?"

"Excellent." Which is the truth. I haven't had any nightmares in weeks. Daddy's rigid adherence to my bedtime means I wake up every morning feeling rested and refreshed.

It occurs to me that I've responded as well to Daddy's schedule as Livvy's responded to Gracie's. Hmm. Well, maybe little humans just need consistency.

"Good to hear." He sits down on the edge of the bed and fiddles under the tray, opening the supports. When he has them unfolded, he sets the tray over my legs. The amazing smell of toasted bagels fills my nose. Daddy takes one of his mother's pretty dishcloths—I think the British call them tea-towels—off the top of the tray, revealing a breakfast spread underneath. There are three kinds of bagels, split open and piping hot. A bowl of cream cheese sits to one side, with a plate of smoked salmon. Breakfast tea steams on the other side, adding its spice to the air.

I clap my hands in delight. "Daddy! Ta so much! Did you go to Mr. Jan's deli so early to get bagels?"

"I did. He sent along homemade cream cheese for his favorite little customer."

I knit my fingers together to keep them from fluttering all over our breakfast. There's a garnish of ruby-red grapes with the bagels and I decide that's safest to start with since everything else looks hot. I twist off a grape and munch it while I decide between the poppy seed, onion and sesame, and whole grain bagels. After much deliberation and some stamping on that inner voice that barely ever whispers at me anymore, I decide on the poppy seed bagel. I point at it and let Daddy prepare it for me.

"Thank you so much for this, Daddy. It's a lovely way to wake up."

He smears on cream cheese like he's mortaring a brick wall. I bite my tongue to keep from saying that I only need a third of what he's slathering on my bagel. Daddy shows love through generosity. I never want him to think he needs to moderate showing me love.

When he finishes piling on enough smoked salmon to choke a grizzly bear, he offers me the bagel. I take it and try to figure out an approach vector to get it in my mouth, since the heaping bagel is nearly the size of my head.

"I thought you might like breakfast in bed. With Mac and Bren living here now we don't do it as often as we used to. I wanted you to know how much I appreciate you putting me first, little wonder. I love my girl."

"I love you too, Daddy." I mash the salmon down with my thumb and finally manage to get my teeth into it. I chew ten times, which is necessary with the fresh bagel, before I swallow. "Queen Twitch said no boys for lunch, so I was thinking we could meet at Konk? I'll take Livvy with me for fresh air."

Daddy nods as he makes his own bagel. "Sure. I hear we're going to the Aquarium this afternoon."

Honestly, how are Littles' Army plans supposed to stay secret when our chat leaks like a sieve?

"Sammi?" I ask.

"Probably. Jack was the one who put it in the caregiver chat."

"It was just a suggestion," I explain. "Sammi wanted a day in the Nursery without Bigs—"

"No," Daddy says immediately.

"Right? Can you imagine? The potential for destruction really can't be measured by man."

Daddy chuckles.

"I thought, instead, we could have a mermaid afternoon. That's gender-inclusive, of course. Mermen are welcome, too. We can go to the Aquarium. Livvy will love seeing all the fish. Then we can have a swim at Blunts followed by naps or quiet play in the Nursery."

"Emmy, baby, I can't think of a better way to spend the day. You don't have to include Livvy in all your plans, though. I'm sure we can find a sitter if you want."

I start to say I *am* Livvy's sitter but stop myself. Daddy clearly wants me to feel like her parent and, if I'm honest with myself, I feel that way more and more every day.

Instead, I say, "There will be times I want to do things just you and me or me and my little friends but today's not one of them. Today, I want to be mermaids and Livvy's the littlest mermaid. Wait until you see the swimsuits Bren got for us."

"Brenna bought you a swimsuit? What's wrong with the pink polka-dot one? I really like that one."

He likes that one because it's vintage, another find of Cynnie's, and ties in the front so my boobs are presented like eggs in an Easter basket. Daddy's eyes nearly popped out of his head when he saw me wear it for the first time.

"You'll like this one, too," I promise him, hoping seeing me and Livvy as mermaids distracts him from the lack of breast-presentation.

"Well, that sounds like a plan. I've got a quick job this morning, just a CCTV design, so I'll get that banged out while you're writing. If you're going to Konk for lunch, how 'bout I take Livvy for an hour and take her to see the Christmas tree in Rockefeller Center? We can meet up there and take the D to the Q train to Coney Island if you want to go to the big aquarium?"

I nod. I love the aquarium in New Jersey. It's very cozy and inter-active. But that might not be the best thing with Sammi. I can see him squeezing the life out of a starfish. Besides, Laurel's visiting and my dragon friend deserves the big aquarium with its tunnel of stingrays and sharks. Even though I'm a little scared of the sharks, I won't be if I'm with my flight.

"I'll make it an early lunch with Queen Twitch. Brunch if that's okay with them."

Daddy boops me on the nose. "Thank you for doing that, baby."

"It's not a hardship, Daddy. I love spending time with Queen Twitch. They've read everything I've read and fifty thousand other books besides. We can talk books for days."

"I'm glad you've found a friend there. I know Bull worries that Twitch's circle of friends is so small, they don't have people to lean on when things get rough. Thank you for making such an effort with the other submissives."

"I'm happy to, Daddy. You asked me to reach out to Master Ten, too. He didn't come last night. Do you want me to try again?"

Daddy shakes his head. "I appreciate the effort you've made. I think we've done enough there."

I'm not going to push because I don't know all the ins and outs of Daddy's political maneuvering but I've actually come to like Master Ten in the months since I first met him. He's a grizzly bear of a Dom. Growly and grumpy. But I suspect underneath he's fiercely loyal and expects that of anyone close to him. When they act in ways he doesn't expect, he feels betrayed. I understand betrayal. I still have the scars it leaves, even though Daddy's helped soften them a lot. I didn't expect to ever be anything but scared of Master Ten but I actually feel some sympathy for him.

"Can I invite him to the Aquarium?" I ask.

Daddy winces. "Why?"

"Because it's neutral ground. He didn't want to come to the party last night and I understand why but I'd still like to include him whenever we can. I think he's very lonely. Besides, Cappa and Fleur will come since they're pretty much unofficial Littles' Army members now and, although it is *always* a good thing for subbies to outnumber Doms, I don't want it to get too unbalanced."

"Particularly since Sammi's coming."

"Right? I have visions of him in the shark tank."

Daddy groans. "Do not tempt fate, little girl. Yes, you can invite him if you want to. Don't be hurt if he ignores you."

"I won't." I'm happy to keep shining my ray into Master Ten's life. It doesn't matter if he refuses to reciprocate. The sun doesn't care if you draw the black-out blinds; it keeps shining.

thirty

EMILY

MASTER TEN SENDS me a thumbs-up in response to my invitation to the Aquarium. I'm not sure if that means he's coming or he's just acknowledging the invitation but I'll take it.

Queen Twitch watches me put my phone away. We're waiting for our food in a corner of the restaurant, at a low table with armchairs, instead of a booth or table. When I first found Konk, I thought it was too trendy for me. But it's become my favorite café. No one blinks if I wear little clothes, or even fetish wear. The waitresses all know me now and greet me by name. They have a running joke about Daddy's cholesterol and steer him toward healthy menu choices. I love the setting: in a converted greenhouse. The roof is still cloudy glass and the restaurant is full of huge, potted plants. I like to pretend I'm off on a Victorian botany expedition to somewhere exotic like the Galapagos Islands but with smashed avocado toast and Tung Ting Oolong tea. I've even dressed for it today in a pinafore printed with antique maps over a high-necked, ruffled, green blouse with butterfly trim, and thick, green-and-white striped thigh-highs. I'm in my green mermaid phase.

Daddy added wire nipple clamps before I left the house because, sigh, Daddy. He promised to check them when I meet him at Rockefeller Plaza but didn't promise to take them off. Double-sigh. They keep my nipples hard and chafing against the fine cotton of the blouse. Good thing the pinafore is thick.

Queen Twitch looks as fabulous as ever, sprawled in the armchair across from me in a fitted paisley pants suit and deep purple shirt with an extravagant spill of ruffles down the front. They're wearing their crown atop silver-gray waves. You'd think that would look out of place at Konk but it doesn't. There are yummy mummies, college-aged kids wearing shorts which it is *definitely* not warm enough to do, a table of drag queens, a man with a beard redder than Niall's wearing a leather kilt and sporran, and holiday shoppers juggling their fifty million bags. You'd have to wear a full hazmat suit to truly look out of place at Konk and even then, I think everyone would just raise a mildly-curious brow.

Twitch sips from their sunset mimosa. "How are we going to unfuck this, darling?"

"Can you tell me what's going on with Georgie? I'm not blind. I could see the tension between you and Mistress Maude and then when Master Bull demanded Georgie pull down his bottoms so he could see if the terms of the loan were being observed . . . it was a lot, even from where I was standing. I could tell how angry your sir was."

"Incandescently," Twitch says before clamping perfect teeth on the recyclable straw of their drink. "Sir approached Elephant's Playground for a present for Kiki. Someone *deeply* submissive. Claudia recommended Georgie. We played together a dozen times. Georgie made Kiki so happy. Her own pet mousie. You have no idea what it's been like, with Kiki so sick. Sir and I would literally do anything to make her smile. Georgie made her laugh again. Em . . ."

Twitch trails off, looking at the ceiling, eyes shimmering. Before anything can mess up their perfect liner, they dab a finger at the corner of each eye and clear their throat. "Anyway. I guess Georgie met Maude coincidentally at the club. They played together several times. Georgie was honest with Sir about it and Sir said it was okay as long as it didn't affect our playtimes. Sir hadn't asked Georgie for exclusivity but I know he was considering it. The next thing we knew, Maude told Sir she was considering collaring Georgie and wanted Sir to give up any prior claim on him. Sir said no. He and Kiki were also considering collaring Georgie as Kiki's pet. Darling, from there it's just become a huge old mess. Maude and Sir can barely be in the same room without yelling at each other. I've been acting as a go-between and I hate it. I got them to agree to this *loan* business but it's been worse than negotiating the Treaty of Versailles. I've been trying to get Georgie to express a preference but all he'll say is that he loves all of us. He's *so* submissive."

I nod along to everything Queen Twitch says. I was there when Maude met Georgie. Georgie was helping me in the Blunts Library; Maude homed in on him like a hawk. Maybe love at first sight isn't a real thing but finding your perfect submissive at first sight? I'll buy that after seeing the way Maude and Georgie were drawn together. I understand that Bull, Kiki, and Twitch had a prior relationship with him—and Georgie probably would like to be owned in a kinky sense —but a prior relationship doesn't give Master Bull ownership of Georgie. And even though it's not fair and I shouldn't measure relationships this way, Kiki already has a master *and* a sub. Maude's alone.

"Was he okay after everything last night?" I ask.

Twitch nods. "Poor thing. He was *so* apologetic once he came around. He's never had a panic attack like that before. He said he thought he was comfortable in small spaces as a mouse. But being in that tunnel with a predator coming for him absolutely threw him, poor cherub. He must have apologized a thousand times to Maude, to me, to Sir. And it hasn't helped the situation at all. Now Sir's angry at Maude for putting Georgie in a situation where he panicked and Maude's furious at Sir for humiliating Georgie in the Stocks." Twitch throws up their hands. "*Such* a shitshow."

We both fall quiet as the waitress delivers our orders. Mulligatawny soup for me and vegan lasagna for Twitch. Once we're eating, I ask, "Is sharing him completely out of the question?"

"It's certainly not something Maude wants," Twitch says between elegant bites. "I gather she had a monogamous marriage before her husband died. Since then, it's been casual play with the house submissives. She never collared anyone but her husband. If Sir won't give up his claim, maybe Maude would accept some kind of sharing arrangement instead of losing Georgie completely but it's definitely her last choice."

"And you guys?" I ask.

Twitch sighs. "If I had a dollar for every time I've asked Sir to just back off and let Georgie go, I could buy my own tropical island, darling. But Kiki, oh, Emily, my Kiki. She talks about how much she loved having Georgie as a pet, how he kept her company when she felt low and how stroking his fur was the first *good* feeling she had after feeling nothing but nausea and dizziness for so long—" They break off and look up at the ceiling again. "I'm afraid Sir's going to do something *rash*."

I rub my breastbone, where a fierce ache has started. "I'm so sorry, Twitch."

They heave a dramatic sigh. "Me too, darling, me too. I wish I had half of old Sir Winston's negotiating power so I could find a way through this but nothing I've come up with has stopped those two from steaming toward a head-on collision like a pair of runaway trains."

There has to be a compromise. "Maybe I could speak to Maude?"

"I'm not sure what you could say that hasn't already been said but I'm not going to stop you. Anything's better than this terrible standoff."

I nod. "I will. I hate to ask this right now when everything's so horrible but bad things are happening at the club—"

Twitch waves a hand. "Don't hesitate. I've heard both too much and too little. Sir's been spending time with that smarmy Drew who's filling his ear with how Logan's ruining submissives." They throw their arms wide. "Do I look ruined to you?"

Grinning, I shake my head.

"Thank you. Here I am, entirely unruined, and instead of *actually* ruining me, Sir's doing group scenes with MacKenzie. *MacKenzie.* Nothing against a good orgy but I'm making Sir get tested before he sticks any bit of him in *any* bit of me."

I can't control a snigger.

"So, please explain to me why my Sir, who has up to this point made the occasional questionable decision about playing pick-up football games but rarely about his companions or the scenes he engages in, *why* is my Sir doing group scenes with that cabal of usurers?"

I slap my hand over my mouth to keep from giggling too loudly. "I'm sure they're just bankers."

"Whatever they are, they're unpleasant and unfashionable. White dress shirts and red power ties all around. At least have the balls to wear pink."

"Real men do," I agree.

"Your Daddy looks magnificent in pink. Sets off the dark hair and dark eyes and high cheekbones. You should make him wear it always." Twitch waves a hand airily. "*What* is going on behind the scenes?"

"Some of the members at Blunts have been treating the house submissives really badly," I explain.

Twitch sobers from their studied nonchalance: leaning forward and wrapping their hands around their knee. "I heard about Ten's inexcusable gaffe with DirtyGurl."

"That's the least of it, I think. Daddy doesn't want me to worry so he hasn't told me everything but there have been bad incidents with Shannie and Annabelle. Really bad. Leaving the club bad."

Twitch tuts. "And how are we going to fix this?"

I swallow hard. Daddy told me I could tell Twitch anything if I thought it would help. Twitch has always been amazing with me and

I trust them. "Daddy's going to try to get the members who have hurt the submissives kicked out of the club. If Chairman Chess resists, Daddy's going to move to replace him."

Twitch's perfect eyebrows shoot up. "Logan's going to take over the chair?"

I shake my head. "He's going to nominate Mistress Maude."

"Oh, dear God." Twitch sits back in their chair and takes a long sip of their drink.

"If Daddy calls a vote—"

Twitch waves their hand. "Any day before today, *any* day, I'd have said Maude has Sir's vote, without question. Today, Lord help us."

"Is this really going to be the end of their friendship?" I ask.

"Darling, I'd like to tell you that once we work out the Mousel Mess everything will go back to normal but I don't know. You know how these silly alpha men get about their women. I've seen your daddy do it around you. They all but beat their chests. Sir's quieter about it than other Doms but when it's about Kiki, well, he's just not rational."

"Can you talk to him about it? I'll talk to Maude and maybe we can bring them together. Common cause, right?"

Twitch nods firmly. "Common cause. I'll ask Sir to divorce his feelings about the Mousel Mess from his feelings about the club and focus on what's best for everyone. If all these terrible things are going on right under Chess' nose, then maybe it's time for a regime change."

"But it has to be done nicely. I like Chairman Chess."

"I do, too. And watching him come back to life as Tessa's owner gives *me* life. But maybe he took his eye off the ball for too long while he was grieving for Sara Ann." Twitch slaps their knee and points a finger at me. "You and I, dearling, you and I are going to be the instigators of change, the inciters of progress. Viva la revolución!"

I lift my teacup in a toast to change.

Everything is crazy and a little sad.

I still can't think of Blunts without Chairman Chess; every time I do, I want to cry. I know he's made mistakes and maybe, like Queen Twitch said, he took his eye off the ball while he was grieving for his wife. But Brenna's told me how good he was with her when she tried to resign: all the nice things he said about her and how he figured out a way for her to remain part of the Blunts family while being exclusive with Master Mac. He's done something similar for Austin after Dana collared him. I can't believe someone who cares that much about the house submissives could go so far wrong that he has to step down. I hope Daddy finds another way.

In the meanwhile, I'm a mermaid, with my merbaby, swimming through the seas under the watchful eye of the King of the Oceans (aka Daddy).

So, things aren't *too* awful.

Livvy *loves* the water. It's not a surprise after how much she likes her baths but discovering she can kick and splash with her arms as we swish her gently through the water, elicits peals of delighted giggles. She gets a surprise the first time she splashes herself but after one shocked wail, she's back to giggling.

Daddy and I pass Livvy back and forth as we stay in the shallows. Even though Daddy's healed and no longer in physical therapy, the doctors don't want him doing things that cause pressure changes in his brain, like swimming underwater or holding his breath. So he's happy to stay in the shallows and admire his mermaids.

We're worth admiring, if I do say so myself.

The swimsuits Brenna had made are so cute and so much fun. I love-love-love my pink polka-dot swimsuit but I don't think it's going to see much pool-time now that I'm a mermaid. Livvy's equally enraptured by her suit. She keeps kicking her legs up to try to snatch the filmy fins on the bottom. She hasn't figured out she needs to uncurl her fingers to grab them but I foresee a lot of re-attaching fins once she does.

Around us, there's a whole frolic of mermaids. I know a group of mermaids—merpeople, really—should be called a school or a pod. I've seen both online. But everyone's diving and splashing and twirling around in rubber rings, so "frolic" feels more appropriate. We have two water-dragons (Laurel and Yummy), a rubber duckie (Sammi), and a mer-bee (Cynnie) as well and they should be included in our group.

Definitely a frolic.

One of the water-dragons keeps stealing my merbaby but she makes up for her thievery by admiring my merbaby effusively and dishing the goss about Icky-Rick.

I honestly haven't thought much about Rick in the months since his horrible party with its horribler poisoned punch. For a few weeks, it looked like the poisoner, Rick's manager, was going to trial and Daddy would need to testify. But then she took a plea bargain. Daddy says she's likely to serve five or six years, which seems light for trying to poison people to me but I'm just glad she can't hurt anyone anymore. She was unhinged.

Daddy cut Rick out of our lives completely. Daisy's mentioned him once or twice when she's visited but I gather she's as done with him as Daddy. Although Rick threatened to involve Daddy in any lawsuits coming out of the party, that hasn't happened. I think Max had something to do with that, based on what I've heard him say to Daddy about not worrying about Rick ever again.

Still, Rick hit my Daddy. Not once but twice. *In the head*. While Daddy was recovering from already being hit *in the head* by the evil massage man. Daddy refused to press charges against Rick but any counterpunch karma would like to deliver would be richly deserved. When Laurel tells me that Rick's moved out of not just the City but the country, all the way to Mexico, to escape the backlash from the party, I can't help but feel a little schadenfreude. Lawsuits aside, what drove him away was that, while off his head on ketamine, he went crazy on two of the performers at the party and left one of them with permanent scars. She didn't sue but the group's Domme,

Harlow, blacklisted Rick in the community. Word has reached all the way to Laurel and Jiro's group in D.C.

Daddy wraps his arms around me and whispers in my ear, his lips pressed against my wet hair. "I see you gloating, little girl. Is that being the bigger person?"

"Probably not," I admit. "But it sure is satisfying. He hit you. Twice. *In the head.*"

"I remember. I don't think his fall from grace requires gloating, though."

I do but I keep that thought to myself. "Oookay, Daddy."

"You are a terror, little girl. Who knew someone so small and cute could be so vicious?"

"I'm the Pallas cat of littles, Daddy." I tell him, hugging his arms around my waist and kicking up my legs until he swishes me through the water like we've been swishing Livvy. I'll admit the baby's giggle is better than mine.

"What's a Pallas cat?" Daddy asks.

"The grumpiest cat in the world. They have these really round heads and small ears, like me. They keep their paws warm by putting them on their tails. So cute. They live on the steppes in China and Mongolia and Nepal and they're super vicious. I'll show you videos. I love them."

"I see. I'm not sure I approve of my little girl being a Pallas cat. I rather like the mermaid thing."

"Pallas cats swim." I think. Most cats can swim, right? "Their proper name is manul. I can be a mermaid manul."

Daddy chuckles. "Okay, baby girl. I do love your mermaid cozzie, if I haven't said so."

He has, several times but I'm happy to hear Brenna's gift is appreciated.

Speaking of my Big Sub Bestie, she's been showing off her breaststroke to a raft of appreciative littles: Sammi, Amy, Aggie, Cynnie, and Matty. I'm so proud of Bren. Master Theo is lazily steering the littles' raft. He didn't come with us to the Aquarium but he showed up PDQ when Amy arrived at the club. Hmm.

Master Theo's replaced Master Ten, who met us at the Aquarium. Ten grunted in response to Daddy's "hello" but when I asked him to hold my new penguin friend, Franklin—while I held Livvy up so she could see the stingrays—he tucked Franklin under one arm and lifted both me and Livvy so we had a super-view. That doesn't seem like he's holding a grudge. As soon as we got back to the club, he disappeared upstairs with Fleur and Cappa, which probably means we won't see the three of them again today. But I'm encouraged that he came to the Aquarium.

"I do, too," I say, dragging my thoughts back to where they should be: on Daddy. "It's got me thinking about another story for Olivia to follow up the first one. A mermaid story."

Daddy hugs me and swishes me. "Baby, your imagination just blows me away."

Mulling over ideas for Olivia's Undersea Adventure, I cuddle happily in Daddy's arms.

thirty-one

LOGAN

EMILY SUCCESSFULLY DISTRACTS me with her wonderfulness. Daddy's little mermaids. My heart is so fucking full.

Until I get to the Dom's changing room and find Bull waiting for me.

Unlike the last time we ran into each other in a changing room, he's dressed, which is something of a relief. I'm just wearing my swim shorts and after the moment's shock at seeing him sitting on one of the changing room's padded benches, I take off my shorts, grab a towel and my toiletry bag out of my locker, and walk my naked ass over to the sink to shave. He's seen me naked plenty of times. My nakedness isn't quite the weapon his is, and maybe looking vulnerable will help this conversation along.

"I got your message," he says, each word clipped. "I didn't like it. You've got no fucking room to judge me."

"You're right, I don't," I respond. "I regretted sending it a second after I pressed the button. I should have left it to you and your trio to sort out with Maude. My blood was up after seeing Emmy upset. I apologize."

"You're doing a lot of that lately," he retorts but his posture softens. "I should apologize, too. I know you're a good man, a good Dom, and a good friend. I've been letting innuendo twist my head around. You wouldn't do anything to destroy the club."

"Is that what people have been saying?"

I don't point fingers or name names. After Emily had brunch with Twitch and Ten showed up at the Aquarium, I have a damn good handle on who is a real threat to Blunts and our submissives.

"I'm ashamed for having listened to them," Bull says. He pauses as Theo comes into the changing room, followed by Jack, Bravo, and Faolan. They nod or glance meaningfully at me but head into the showers when I just nod back. "You'll leave what's going on with Georgie for me to resolve with Maude?"

"Absolutely." I've been in the middle of wrangles over subs before. There are no winners. Best to let the people involved sort it out unless the submissive asks for help.

"Thanks, Lo." Bull taps his fingers against his jeans. "Twitch mentioned you're worried about, um, politics. I'll always do what's best for the club."

"I'm struggling with what that is right now," I tell him. "I've got solid testimony from multiple house subs that we have two members who are putting them at risk. I want to remove them from the club immediately before they have a chance to do any further harm. I emailed Chess about it this morning." I check my phone to make sure I haven't missed a message. "As of right now, he hasn't responded. This is an emergency. I know he likes to 'sleep on things'—"

"The welfare of our subs isn't something we can sleep on. I get it. If you want me to help you force an emergency committee meeting, I will."

"Thanks, it may come to that."

"You gonna tell me who they are?" Bull asks, his tone slightly abrasive.

There's no mincing around this. "Drew and Emmett."

Bull drops his head to look at the floor. "Fuck."

"I can guess who was behind the 'innuendo.' It's smart, actually, waging a disinformation campaign before I go after them."

Bull lifts his head. "That's not gonna stop you?"

"No."

"You know the committee is split right now," Bull points out.

"I know."

"Lo, this is an ask. I'm not saying I don't believe you—"

"Is it me you don't believe, or is it them?"

Bull hangs his head again.

"Drew's views on dealing with submissives are controversial," Bull admits. "But I'm not sure they're wrong. We talk a lot about giving submissives what they need instead of what they want. That's what his alpha theory is, just taken to the next level."

I put my shaving supplies away. It's not the best shave I've ever given myself but in my defense, between our conversation and meeting Bull's eyes in the mirror, I'm a little fucking distracted. I'm lucky I don't have any serious nicks. Wrapping a towel around my waist, I go to sit on the bench with him.

"Tell me about this alpha theory," I say. "I haven't heard it."

"Drew says he can figure out what a submissive needs after a few scenes and going through a series of questions. Then he comes up with a plan to help the submissive reach and exceed their submission goals by giving them what they need instead of what they say they want. It's . . . it's not crazy."

No, it's not crazy. It's what I've done with every one of my subs, including Emily. As I struggle to find the difference between my approach and Drew's—because I won't share anything with someone who *hunts our subs in a fucking pack*—I latch on to that feeling of Daddyness.

"Does he do it out of a place of love or out of a place of manipulation to force the subs to give him what he wants?"

Bull's mouth hangs open after my question. He shuts it with a snap.

"It's fucking cold of you to question a brother Dom's motives after you've turned this club upside down so you can play with your submissive the way you want."

"If you'd sat with Shannie and Annabelle and seen how hurt and betrayed they feel by Drew's alpha theory in practice, you wouldn't say that."

Bull tips his head from side to side until his neck cracks. "I don't know what's going on with Annabelle. I don't know much about her past the fact that she's damn new. You, of all people, know that the club can be a shock at first to subs who have only submitted at play parties and shit like that. Blunts isn't a play party—"

"Agreed," I say.

"But I've heard about the thing with Shannie," Bull continues. "One of her submission goals was to submit to two Doms at the same time. Drew brought guests into that scene—which was an *open* scene—to help her get over the hurdle. Hart told him she's been struggling with it for months. Drew primed his guests and they did exactly what he asked of them. They distracted her enough to get her out of her head. They gave her what she needed. Hart says it was a successful scene."

"Shannie doesn't think so. She was so intimidated by their presence and chanting that she won't scene with anyone but Rob again. She doesn't feel anyone else can protect her. And if anyone's going to get her out of her head, it should be her Doms, not rando guests whose training and experience none of us have evaluated."

"Drew evaluated them," Bull objects. "They're all experienced Doms."

"They're not members. Drew left them in that room with Shannie—"

"And two Blunts Doms. They weren't unsupervised or anything like that."

"Shannie felt it devolved into a mob mentality. She was frightened."

"But it worked. Sometimes it's frightening to be pushed past a limit. You *know* that. I just—I hear what you're saying, Lo. I really do. I'm just not sure you're right."

"You won't vote to expel them, or even suspend them?"

Bull looks down at his feet again. "Not on what you've told me so far."

I rest my hand on his shoulder. "Thanks for being honest with me."

Bull sighs. "I hate this."

"Yeah, me, too."

"I've always considered you a friend. One of my best friends at the club. You were the third call I made after we got Kiki's diagnosis. How the fuck did we end up here?"

I squeeze his shoulder gently. "I'm sorry for causing strife within the club. I want us all to be friends. It's a gut punch hearing you question my motives. Please believe I'm trying to protect our submissives."

"I know you are." He snorts. "I've just connected the dots, you know. You've always been a Daddy Dom. You were just daddying our entire roster of house submissives. Now you're daddying one little *and* our entire roster of house submissives."

I hold my hands up. "You're probably right."

"We need you, Lo," Bull says. "Whatever the fuck happens, don't let anyone railroad you out of this club."

"Not a chance." Theo's voice breaks into our tête-à-tête.

I lift my head. Theo's leaning against the wall separating the changing area from the showers with a towel slung over his shoulder and everything else on display. He's gotten some new tattoos.

"Logan even thinks about resigning and I'll tie him to Chess' fucking chair," Theo continues. "There's no fucking parole for you, buddy. I've been reluctant to get involved in club management before but whatever you need, you have from me now that I've heard what's going on. Drew's been a Dom half as long as I have and hasn't ever been in a relationship with a submissive that lasted longer than five minutes. Bull, you've been married to your submissives for years.

You've walked through the fucking fire with them. Why are you letting someone with half your experience and a tenth of your wisdom dictate to you?"

"He's not dictating to me—" Bull protests.

"The fuck he isn't. I know shit with Kiki has been hard, man. You've got two fucking challenging submissives and I bet they make you question your dominance every day. God knows, Lynn did with me. And, yeah, I believe in giving our submissives what they need instead of what they want, *some-fucking-times*. But not when it terrorizes them. Not when it makes them run from us. Is that what this fucking alpha theory is at the end of the day? Because that's not okay. Yes, we can push them but it's to *help* them, not to fucking victimize them. I'm with Logan on this. Believe me, I haven't always seen eye-to-eye with our Master of Training. He's an asshole—"

"Thanks," I say dryly.

"You are," Bull says.

I lift my towel and flash both of them. "Eat me."

"But," Theo says, "he's right about this. Dominance is earned. We're not earning our submissives' trust if we're pushing them so hard they're leaving us in fucking droves. Has the turn-over in house submissives ever been this bad before? It hasn't in my memory."

Bull and I shake our heads.

"I can't think of a clearer sign that something's fucking wrong," Theo says, crossing his arms over his chest.

Bull rubs his hand over his face. "I hear what you're both saying."

"What has Drew said that was more compelling than what we're saying?" I ask.

I need to know before I hear it from the membership committee.

"His methodology is appealing," Bull says. "And I'll admit I've been putting it into practice with Twitch and things have gotten better."

"Have things gotten better because you're putting this alpha theory into practice or have they gotten better because Kiki's recovering and Twitch is leveling out now that he knows the other love of his life is going to be okay?" Theo asks. "Give yourselves some grace, Bull. You three have been through hell this year."

Bull hangs his head, nodding. "I'd like to say it's down to me but I'll admit I'm not sure. I love him more than I can fucking say but Twitch is endlessly manipulative. He could very well be leveling out because he wants me to think the things I'm doing are making a difference."

"Fuck, man." Theo rubs the back of his neck. "I don't envy you."

"Me, neither," I say, although I know that Emily could manipulate me as easily if she wanted to. Miranda certainly did. The difference is that my little wonder believes in me. Somehow, despite all my mistakes, I've earned her trust. "If you want an objective opinion, you know I'd be happy to scene with you anytime."

Bull pats my arm. "I know. Don't take this the wrong way. Twitch doesn't want to scene with Emily. It's not about her littleness or the age-play or anything like that. Twitch needs to be ruined in scenes and he doesn't want Emily to see him as anything less than fabulous."

"Ah." I nod. "I understand."

"I don't," Theo says. "Fuck, I'd use that against them. Softy. Another thing I don't understand? Why you don't use 'they' for Twitch. I've heard them ask other people to."

A sly smile breaks over Bull's face. "Part of our thing."

"Sure," says Theo. "It's just fucking confusing for the rest of us."

Bull shrugs. "Where did we end up in all of this? I got lost somewhere in the feels."

I chuckle. "Sorry, mate."

"No, it's good," Bull says. "Maybe I was getting my head turned around. Theo's right. The last few months have been a lot. I've been thrown severely off my fucking stride. Twitch has been acting out like a motherfucker, the way he does, and I've been so wrapped up in taking care of Kiki that I haven't been able to rein him in the way I should. I need to stop fronting to cover up the cracks in our relationship. I thought Georgie was going to fix everything but he's just a band aid. I need to fix our dynamic before I even consider bringing in someone else."

I reach out and squeeze his shoulder where it meets his thick neck. "That's a tough thing to realize and an even tougher thing to say."

Theo grunts. "Good talk. My balls are getting cold. Are we storming Chess' penthouse or what?"

I check my phone one last time. Nothing.

"Yeah, I guess I am."

"No, *we* are," Bull says, lifting his head and meeting my eyes.

"Thanks, mate. I will do this on my own but it means a lot not to have to."

thirty-two

LOGAN

WE DON'T, in the end, storm Chess' office but only because he sees us coming on the CCTV system *I installed* and opens the door for us.

Chess motions us into three, black-leather-upholstered guest chairs pulled up in front of his desk before he sits down in his huge wing-back chair. Tessa, in a full black leather puppy mask and mitts over her house submissive basque, kneels at his feet. He holds her leash loosely in his lap.

"Logan, you know I like to mull things over. Is this about something other than your emergency motion?"

"No," I admit. "But I don't think it can wait."

"I disagree," Chess says, tapping the handle of Tessa's leash against his thigh. "I think we need a cool approach to this. I've already said too much during an unguarded moment to Emmett. We all need to step back and think before we do anything unwise."

Tessa yips softly, lifting her paws to her chest. Chess reaches out and strokes the smooth top of her puppy mask.

"Yes, my sweet puppy, I told him if he ever made you uncomfortable again I'd unman him after I ripped his eyes out. It was unnecessary. I regret it now. I'm not charging into another confrontation with him like . . . well, a bull." Chess nods his dark head at Bull.

I bite the insides of my cheeks to keep from jumping in. Theo mentioned that Chess had a talk with Emmett after he and a guest scared Tessa. Theo did not mention anything about ripping out eyes.

Theo clears his throat. "That's quite a talk you had."

Chess rolls his eyes at Theo. "I said I regret it. I listened to everything you said to me the other day, Theo. I expressed my own concerns about Emmett and his guest. I don't see the need to call an emergency management committee meeting. I think there are ways to deal with this that don't involve a full-scale confrontation which might just allow certain factions within the club a podium at which to air their grievances."

Chess looks pointedly at me.

"You mean Ten and his cabal," I say.

"I mean everyone who is resistant to change. Logan, we voted Sante and Rachel out less than three months ago. Is this the reputation you want to build? Anyone who crosses you gets thrown out of the club? I don't relish a full-scale rebellion and that's exactly what we'll have if you're behind ousting two more members so soon."

I take a deep breath and settle myself. This is the moment when I could threaten to replace him with Maude. That's still my Plan B. But I understand what he's saying about coming in like the Grim Reaper. Maybe he has a better idea.

"What do you suggest?" I ask.

"That you let me sleep on it! Give me five damn minutes to come up with a solution that doesn't involve threatening bodily harm again. I'm as angry as you are, Logan," he says, tapping Tessa's leash on the glass top of his desk. "You haven't lived with shame for weeks because of the actions of a man you consider a brother toward a submissive you hold in the highest regard. You didn't see your own submissive's face, stiff with shock and fear, after those two mongrels abused her. I am *raging* inside. Don't you ever think I'm not. But I am a dominant of Blunts. I am in control of my emotions and actions. I won't let Emmett or Drew or their guests provoke another ill-considered response out of me. So let me mull it over and get back to you. Do me a little courtesy. Have I ever ignored you?"

"No," I admit.

"Why would I start with something this important?"

"I didn't know if you appreciated its importance," I say, feeling like a school-kid who has just been yelled at for failing to turn in his homework. In fact, I'm fairly sure that my third-year teacher at Heysham St. Peter's, Mr. Dillon, wore the same expression Chess is now wearing when I tried the "dog ate my homework" excuse.

Chess leans forward in his chair and stares me down. "I appreciate its importance."

Theo stands and digs his fingers into my shoulder. "That's all we came to say. Time to go."

"Theo, you're not even on the committee," Chess points out.

"I'm rethinking that," Theo says. "But it's a conversation for another day."

"Oh, please, let's have it today," Chess says. "Logan seems eager to bring all possible management committee business to a head in the same moment. Are you volunteering for a position? Master of Fur is still open."

Theo releases my shoulder only to dig his thumb into my ribs. "You owe me for this," he mutters at me. At normal volume, he says, "Yes, I'm volunteering."

"Excellent," Chess says. "Welcome to hell. I can't imagine anyone will object, given your standing in the club and how long the position's been open. I'll forward you our bylaws and management committee handbook, all two hundred pages of it, which you'll need to be familiar with before the emergency meeting. Happy reading."

"Fuck's sake," Theo mutters. To Chess, he says, "Great. I'll look forward to that."

"I'll copy you in on my response to Logan's emergency motion then, shall I? I'll consider it jointly submitted by the Master of

Training and the new Master of Fur. Congratulations on your collaboration, gentlemen."

Theo pushes me toward the door. "Sounds good."

Since I can read how Chess' mood has shifted just as well as Theo can, I grab Bull and drag him with me. Theo closes the office door behind us as I hear Chess say, "Up on my desk, my puppy. You need a little grooming."

The three of us, big, brave dominants, stand in the hallway looking at each other.

"He was about to blow a gasket, wasn't he?" I ask Theo.

"Yeah. I've only seen him do it twice but I don't need a repeat. He gets more and more caustic until he flays the skin off you. But if it's any consolation, his near melt-down's a good indication of how deeply he's feeling. What's the thing about his shame? The brother and the submissive he holds in the highest regard?"

I glance at Bull, who grimaces. All of the management committee have seen the CCTV footage of Ten's confrontation with Brenna in the hallway after she tried to resign from the club, although the committee's divided over what to do about it. There's no audio because when I first designed the system we all agreed that what we'd be hearing in the hallway were muffled screams from the dungeons and it wasn't desirable to have recordings of that. But after Chess saw the CCTV of the confrontation, he changed his mind. I upgraded all the CCTV in the club in September.

Despite the lack of audio, it's perfectly clear from the body language in the recording what's happening. Brenna's facing a camera when she uses her safe word and every Dom in this club knows what the word "red" looks like on a submissive's lips.

"Show him," Bull says.

I pull out my phone and load up the recording of the confrontation, which I have saved on my phone as well as in the club archives, just in case. I hand my phone to Theo who watches it in silence, his lips tightening.

"How long after this did those Neo-Nazi assholes attack her?" Theo asks.

"A few days."

Theo hands the phone back to me, shaking his head. "Is Ten on probation? There hasn't been a whisper about any punishment through the club, although I can see why you'd keep this within the committee since they weren't in scene."

"No," I respond.

Theo's eyes narrow. "Why not?"

"Because DirtyGurl doesn't want to pursue it and the committee is divided on how to deal with it if she ever does. As you've said, they weren't in scene. However, most of us believe a submissive's safe word must be honored no matter what the setting."

"I'm fucking pursuing it," Theo says.

"Talk to Maude first," Bull grunts.

"Why?" Theo asks.

"Because you're not the only one who wants to pursue it," I say. "Maude has strong views about Ten's stability and how it needs to be handled. She's maneuvered him into voluntarily going to therapy with that new girl, Krissy. But trust me, no one is ignoring it."

Theo's shoulders drop an inch. "Okay. Look, I work in a bureaucracy. I get that things have to be handled in a certain way and the wheels grind slow. But between this and what's going on with Emmett and Drew, it looks like the committee's lost sight of the duty we owe our subs to keep them safe and respect their limits. At least that's the way it looks to me as an outsider."

"That's the way it looks from the inside, too," I assure him.

"I know I'm going to regret joining the committee in about a hundred different ways but for now, I'm on side. Whatever you need. What do we do? What happens next?" Theo asks.

I glance at Chess's closed office door. "For now, we wait. We line up support. We talk to the house subs and make sure none of them have agreed to scenes with Emmett and Drew."

Theo nods. "I'll take A through M. You take the rest."

I clap him on the shoulder. In the wake of his assholism over Rick and Bren, I'd forgotten what it was like to have his support. Theo takes charge and gets shit done.

"Agreed. I'm going down to the Nursery to check on my little girl who should be napping now—"

Theo snorts. "We all know she isn't."

"Right. Give me a half-hour. If you want to do this together, we could meet up in the small conference room on the ground floor."

"Actually, I'll come with you. Amy said she was going to nap, too. I'm curious as to what that means with her. I think we should make the calls together. Better to be on the same page."

"Need me for this?" Bull asks.

"No, I think we're good—" I say, just happy we're in a good place again.

"Need, no," Theo interjects. "But you've been my friend and brother Dom for a quarter of my fucking life, Bull. I hate hearing that you have a reason to doubt Logan. If you don't need to be anywhere, stick with us this afternoon. Be our conscience."

Bull smiles. "I can do that. Lemme arrange a couple of things. I'll meet you in the small conference room in a half-hour." He jogs off toward the stairwell beside the lifts at the far end of the hallway.

"He's going to show us up by taking the stairs, isn't he?" Theo mutters to me.

"Yup."

"Asshole. I'm surrounded by assholes. I'm still taking the elevator. Come on."

Down three levels, Theo follows me into the Nursery. It's surprisingly quiet. Maybe not surprisingly, when I see Bravo, Warrin, and Faolan sitting in the storytime corner with Yummy, Aggie, and Matty on their laps. Bravo's reading from a book called "The Bumblebear," which I'm pretty sure Emmy got for Cynnie. Emmy herself isn't asleep—no surprise—but she is curled up in a sleeping bag on the floor beside Sammi. Olivia's on a mat between them with a few of her sensory toys scattered around. Unlike Emmy, my daughter's completely sparked out, spread like a little starfish.

Emily's gleaming eyes meet mine when I walk through the door. She doesn't close them and pretend to sleep because my baby girl doesn't lie to her daddy. She puts a gentle hand on Livvy's tummy and smiles at me.

I return her smile. I love seeing my two girls together.

"Ulp," says a soft voice from my right.

"Uh-huh, this doesn't look like napping," Theo says, peering over the edge of the "pirate ship" at where Amy and Hunter are sitting, putting together a Lego pirate ship that's a miniature of the ship they're sitting in.

"Lego," Amy whispers, as though that's an all-encompassing excuse.

"If you'd said you wanted to come up to the Nursery and play Lego after the swim, that would have been fine. But you told me you were coming up to nap."

Amy's pretty face screws into an expression that's one part remorse and three parts defiance. "Everyone else said they were coming up to nap, so I *thought* I might nap but then Hunt showed me where the Lego were—"

"Don't throw me under the bus, babe-girl," Hunter objects. "You asked me where the Lego were."

Amy shoots a filthy glare at the house submissive.

"You should have told me you were considering a nap *or* playing with Lego," Theo says firmly. "We could have discussed the importance of napping after the day you've had, walking all over the Aquarium and swimming, so you wouldn't be too tired to scene tonight. Since you avoided having that conversation with me, I'd like you to come to the Blue Harem room for fifteen minutes. I'm going to give you a warm bottom and an orgasm and see if that helps you nap."

Theo reaches over the rail of the pirate ship, offering his hand to

Amy. She stares at him with wide eyes, her rosy mouth hanging open, before she scrambles to her feet and takes his hand.

"Good girl," he praises her, before leading her out of the Nursery.

Chuckling, I make my way over to Emily. Beside her, Sammi is asleep, curled tightly around a huge purple teddy bear. When I sit down on the floor at her feet, Emily starts to sit up but I wave her back down. I find one of her feet through the sleeping bag, draw it into my lap, and start rubbing her little toes.

Emily collapses into a puddle. She pulls the top of the bag around her face and cuddles into it, the way she does with one of the throw blankets she keeps on our bed.

"Daddy," she whispers.

"Shh, baby. Daddy's helping you relax enough to have a nap. Everything's okay."

"Did you lay siege to Master Chess' office until he let you in?" she asks sleepily.

"We didn't need to. We had a talk. I'll wait to hear from him until tomorrow. You've done enough to help Daddy today, my little wonder. I'm very proud of you. Would you like to go out to dinner with me tonight? Just you, me, and Livvy. I saw a place I'd like to try when I was at Rockefeller Center. Steak and seafood. They have a private dining room that I'll get so you're not worried if Livvy starts to fuss."

"Oh, yes, please, Daddy."

"Good girl." I switch feet. Emily groans softly. "Let that thought carry you off to bowbies, little girl."

She closes her eyes. Her thumb sneaks into her mouth. Before Bravo even finishes the new book he's started reading, "Princess Jack and the Very Hungry Dragon," Emily's asleep. I sit and watch my girls for a minute.

This is everything I'd hoped for. This moment. My girls happy and peaceful in the place that's meant so much to me over the years. Surrounded by friends who understand my little's needs. Surrounded by love and acceptance.

How the fuck could anyone threaten this? How could I let anyone threaten this?

I lift my eyes from Emily and meet Bravo's. He's watching me even while he continues to read. When he takes in my expression, he hands the book to Faolan, shifts Yummy so she's leaning against Warrin, and rises.

I follow him out into the hallway.

"Mission?" he rumbles.

"Protect the submissives. Eliminate the Wolfpack."

"Want me to call in Henry?"

"Yes," I say.

"Names. Social security numbers would be helpful."

"I'll see what I can do," I say.

"So there's no confusion later, do you want them gone or gone-gone?"

How far am I willing to go? I know who Bravo and Henry are. Who Myles is, for that matter, if I call him in on this. I've never ordered a hit on anyone. I've never gone further than what I've been willing to do with my own two hands. I've killed in the service of my country. Was that a better reason, a higher cause, than the one I have right now?

"For now, gone. If I change my mind later and it's gone-gone, can you make it look like an accident?"

Bravo tips his head to the side. "Rather discuss that when it comes to it."

I understand his reticence.

"I'll get you the info today."

"Gimme an hour and I'll get Henry here and we can talk logistics. I'll have her bring a burner for you."

"Thank you. I know I'm not active service like you two are but I want in. I'd never ask anyone to do what I'm not willing to do myself."

"Noted," Bravo says. "Hen and me are a unit. We work with each

313

other a lot. I'm not sure if bringing in someone else would fuck that up but I won't cut you out."

"Deal. I'm going downstairs to make some calls. I want the house submissives on alert. Tell Emmy when she wakes up that I'm in the small conference room where we hold committee meetings. She'll know where to find me."

Bravo nods. "Don't second guess yourself, Logan. If it's gotten to the point where you feel the need to pull me in, you're doing the right thing. I know you haven't been a daddy for long but your instincts are solid. If they're screaming 'danger,' then there is fucking danger. You don't wait around for the danger to stick its head out of the foxhole. You hunt it the fuck down."

I take a deep breath and steady myself. He's right. I've been in combat. I know when it's time to go on the offensive. Now's the time.

"Thanks, mate."

He nods again and turns back into the Nursery.

I head downstairs, passing Austin at the reception desk. I stop and hold out my arms to him.

Frowning, he comes around the desk and gives me the hug I'm asking for. He may not need it. He may feel safe wearing Dana's collar. But I need it.

"I haven't apologized to you, Austin but I'm sorry I pulled back from the club. It won't happen again."

"You don't need to apologize to me, sir," he responds, patting my back. "And I know you're back to stay. I know you'll protect us and the club. You don't need to say anything to me or my Mistress. We're behind you a hundred percent."

"Thank you, Austin. I'll do everything I can to be deserving of your faith."

He pats me again. "Sir, you already are. Go get 'em."

I squeeze him before I release him.

thirty-three

EMILY

I'VE ALWAYS KNOWN my daddy is awesome but watching him mobilize support to protect the house submissives like a general commanding his troops makes him that *leetle bit* awesomer.

By the time I wake from my nap and give Livvy a feed, there's a crowd in the small conference room downstairs. Daddy, Masters Theo, Bull, Mac, and Javier, Daddies Bravo, Henry, Max, and even Laurel's Masutā. Faolan and Jack have stayed up in the Nursery to keep an eye on the subbies—well, mostly to keep an eye on Sammi— but they have ear-pieces in their ears and I think they can hear what's going on. When Faolan suggests going to the Stables to visit the fluffle and fainting mini-goat, I take Laurel's hand and peel off from the group as we troop downstairs.

"I think it's time for subbies to be involved, too," I say. "Will you be okay if there's some talk about things that have scared other subbies?"

"Yes." Laurel nods her proud, magenta crest without hesitation.

I squeeze her hand. She's the bravest person I know.

I lead her into the small conference room, which looks like the bridge of the Enterprise now. Max has brought some of his equipment and it's spread out on the conference table. There are three big screens and lots of laptops on the go. Daddy and Theo are huddled at one end of the table, working together on a laptop while Theo cradles a phone between his shoulder and ear.

I don't want to disturb Daddy, so I creep over to where Laurel's Dom sits at a laptop, typing with a frown on his face.

"Tatsu," Laurel says to get his attention.

Jiro nods and points at the floor next to his chair. Laurel kneels and I kneel beside her, which is somewhat awkward with Livvy in her harness on my chest but I manage.

"Petto. Emily," Jiro says after a minute. He turns in his chair to look at us.

"We'd like to help," Laurel offers.

Jiro nods. "Do you still have the number for that professional Domme, Harlow? I'd like to access her network as well."

"Yes, I do." Laurel gets out her phone, scrolls through it, and hands it to her Dom.

"Thank you." He takes her phone and makes a call. He doesn't say much other than identifying himself, letting Harlow know that a very troublesome situation has come to light at Blunts which affects the whole community, and asks her to call back. I gather the call's gone to voicemail.

He returns the phone to Laurel. "We're trying to identify all the members of this odious Wolfpack and the clubs and parties where they've been hunting submissives. We know of nine so far—"

I gulp. Daddy only mentioned Masters Drew and Emmett and a nasty guest named Hans. But nine! That's so much bigger than anything I'd understood.

"You type a great deal faster than I do," Jiro says to Laurel, holding up two fingers. Laurel and I giggle. "If you'll take my seat, I'll walk you through the searches I'm doing. Emily, I suspect your Daddy very much needs a hug by now."

"Yes, sir."

At Jiro's nod, Laurel and I rise to our feet. Laurel gives her Dom a long, tight hug. Jiro strokes her back and whispers something to her. I barely catch it but I think he says, "I couldn't prevent what happened to you, petto. I couldn't avenge you as much as I wanted to. But I can help stop this. I've given Logan my full support and my resources. I hope you agree."

"Yes, Tatsu," Laurel says. "I do."

I back away when he kisses her and steal over to Daddy's side.

"Baby doll," he says, rising out of his chair. "Is it dinner time?"

It is dinner time. A little past dinner time, if I'm honest. But this is more important than the faint growling of my tummy. I don't mind putting off surf and turf to another night.

"It is but that's not why I came to find you. I thought you might need a hug by now."

Daddy smiles and opens his arms. I unclip Livvy's harness so I can press against my Daddy. He takes her and cradles her in his left arm while he pulls me into a snuggly hug.

Daddy kisses the top of my head. "I always appreciate hugs from my baby girl. I believe you were promised a yummy dinner that you don't have to cook."

"I was," I agree, stretching up to kiss his jaw. "But I'm happy to take a rain-check if you're busy with this. It's more important."

Daddy slips his hand under my chin. "Nothing is more important than my little girl and Daddy always keeps his promises."

He kisses the tip of my nose before he releases my chin and pats the conference table. "Everyone, I think we need to take a break."

Theo tosses his phone to the table with a grunt. "I still can't reach Apple or Fleur."

"I've added them to the group chat," Mac says from across the table. "If they check it, they'll be able to see what's going on. I think a generic text that says to call you before they agree to any scenes is the best we can do without tipping our hand."

Theo scrubs his hand down his face and picks up his phone. "Yeah, okay."

"Dinner in the Trattoria," Master Javier says, not making it a question. "I'm happy to feed the troops for this excellent cause."

"I promised my girls dinner out," Daddy says. "But we'll be back in a few hours."

"No." Theo stands and pats Daddy's shoulder. "I think we call it a night. We've done a lot. Some of us have scenes planned. Some of us still have a sleep debt because of your *last* emergency. We all need a night to regroup and recuperate. We can check in first thing in the morning."

That quickly becomes the plan. Javier leads a group off to the Trattoria while Daddy and I retrieve our coats and Livvy's stroller and head for the train.

"Master Theo's such a daddy," I say as we whoosh across Manhattan on the train to Rockefeller Center.

"Such an asshole," Daddy responds but he's grinning.

"You like him. You're glad you're friends again. I can tell."

Daddy pecks me on the forehead. "We'll call him Cranky Daddy. That'll really wind him up."

I giggle. Yes, it will. And Master Theo deserves it.

"He's been a good friend today," Daddy admits. "He might not have been on the committee before but he plays club politics like a pro. I'm still not sure we have enough votes to get rid of Emmett and Drew. According to the club bylaws, I need seventy-five percent of the committee to remove a lifetime member, which Drew is. I can get Emmett punted with a simple majority. But for Drew, it could all hinge on the Three Cs."

I hate this for Daddy. I hate that he's losing faith in the leaders of his club. I remember when he first mentioned Blunts to me all those months ago. His eyes were shining darkly, in his wolfy way. He was smiling with his whole body. The club was something he loved, something he was proud of, even if there was some weirdness going on with his former submissive. Would he shine and smile today if he had to describe Blunts to a stranger?

"I believe in you," I remind him. "You'll fix this and things will get better. I believe that."

He shapes my face with his big, warm paw encased in a leather glove. "Thank you, sweetheart. I'm holding on to that like a life ring."

"Tell me about the restaurant," I say to distract him.

He grins. Since he won the fight with the insurance company and sold my house in Scotland, Daddy's delighted in giving us treats like this. It hurt him, not just his pride but his caregiver instincts, to be so restrictive when the evil debt-collector was threatening to take the house. I don't need lavish treats but it makes me happy to see Daddy's pleasure in giving them to me.

"They had the private room available," he says. "We have it for two hours. It looks out on the tree. I ordered the tasting menu, so we're going to have a little of everything. It doesn't matter if Livvy cries because we won't be disturbing anyone, so you can just relax and enjoy the meal and the view."

"And the Daddy."

He leans in to rub noses with me. "And the Daddy. Best thing about today?"

"This part. Although the foot rubs were most excellent. And the swishies."

Daddy squints in thought. "The swishies?"

"When you hugged me and swishied me in the pool. I don't like being thrown the way Jack was throwing Sammi because I don't like face-splashes but I love swishies."

He chuckles. "I see. I love giving you swishies. We'll make that a regular thing." He checks on Livvy, who is sleeping in her stroller. "She seems very sleepy."

"Probably the swimming. That was a lot of effort for her. She was kicking a ton. Could also be the rocking of the train."

"Ah, right. I'll incorporate lots of swimming into our schedules. Build her little baby muscles."

And conk her out but I understand what Daddy means.

"I was reading something in one of those baby books you bought about letting babies taste flavors. She can't have anything but milk for another few months, I know but the book said babies taste flavors when they're in utero and it's okay to put a mild flavor on your finger or on a paci and let her taste it. Do you think that's right?"

I nod, remembering that Gracie did that with Connor. "It helps develop their palate. Connor had days where he'd only eat one thing but in general, he wasn't a fussy eater. Gracie gave him tastes of everything she ate."

The Gracie-seal-of-approval reassures Daddy. She is my guru in all things baby-related. Daddy seems to have accepted her authority, too, now that he sees how well her schedule is working.

"We'll give her a taste of dinner tonight," Daddy says. "Since there will be lots to choose from."

He's not wrong. There's a ton to choose from at "Steak on the Rock." Black caviar in a tiny dish with silver spoons, oysters in a velvety green sauce, gingered tuna, steak tartare—which is easily my favorite as it melts on my tongue—meatballs, spicy octopus, delicate lamb chops in mint sauce, and the one Daddy gobbles down: maple-glazed bacon. Small bowls of lobster bisque and grilled asparagus arrive as sides. Or maybe just to break up the unrelenting parade of protein. Despite the carnivore overload, it's all delicious.

Livvy thinks so, too. When she wakes up with a huge stretch and a little coo, we give her tiny tastes of the tomatoey sauce for the meatballs, the mint sauce for the lamb, and the lobster bisque. She licks her lips after every taste and sticks her tongue out after the lobster bisque.

"You have such good taste, Livvy-bit," I tell her, as I dab my pinkie into the smear of soup left in the bottom of my bowl and touch it to her tongue.

Her grin is brighter than the lights on the tree outside.

The only thing I don't like about "Steak on the Rock" is a funny sense that we're being watched. The private room is on the second floor of the restaurant, with a wall of windows looking out over the square with its twinkling lights. People in the other buildings around the square can look in but I don't have any sense that they're watching us. The glass might be treated or something. Our nice waiter checks in twice but doesn't linger. I don't know why I have this hair-raising sense that someone has an unfriendly eye on us.

"Can we take an Uber home?" I ask as we wait for the waiter to bring dessert.

"Of course." Daddy wipes his mouth. "Are you tired?"

"A little. It's more that I feel like we're being watched."

Daddy straightens in the maroon-upholstered chair. "How long have you felt this way?"

I reach across the table and curl my fingers over Daddy's. "Hmm, maybe when we left Blunts but I'm still a little self-conscious in public when I call you Daddy, so it might just have been that on the train."

"I'm going to break the phone at the table rule for the sole purpose of putting Max on alert, baby doll."

I nod. Safety first.

Daddy pulls out his phone and sends Max a text before tucking the phone back in his jacket pocket.

"Thank you for always taking my concerns seriously, Daddy."

"Always, baby. Always."

Daddy's phone buzzes. He takes it out and reads the message, taps a quick response, and puts it away. "Mac's inbound. He should be here around the time we're ready to go, so there's no rush. I want you to relax and enjoy dessert."

"This has been wonderful, Daddy." I squeeze his fingers. "I love having all our friends around but sometimes it's nice to just be with you. And Livvy."

"I always want to make time for us, baby. And that can be just you and me if you don't want to spend time with Livvy. You've been wonderful with her but I appreciate you may want down time. This has to be taxing for you."

I shake my head, feeling my hair brush my shoulders through the thin fabric of my dress. "I love taking care of her. I'm a little more tired than usual but not too much. If you could add a nap for me now and then, I think that would take care of it."

"Okay, baby, I'll do that."

The door to our private dining room opens and the waiter brings the tasting flight of chocolate mousse, mini-cheesecakes, and three different types of cognac for Daddy. I don't get any creepy vibe from him. Daddy evidently doesn't either, although he gives the waiter an extra once-over before thanking him and asking for the bill.

As a special treat for being out together, Daddy gives me sips from each of the small glasses of cognac. I don't really like hard alcohol but the cognac is delicious. One's light and fruity, one's sharp and tingly, and one's smoky. I lick my lips like Livvy after each sip. Daddy, watching me, grins as he finishes off each glass of cognac.

By the time the waiter's come back and Daddy's paid for our meal—I don't look at the bill, this is a treat and I'm sure it was an extravagance but I trust Daddy to manage our money—Mac has messaged to say he's five minutes away. We pack up and head down to the street to wait for Master Mac.

There's a special magic to New York at Christmas-time. Everything's sparklier, rosier, merrier. People who would normally hurry past with their heads down meet your eyes and nod in acknowledgement. With the stores open late and playing Christmas tunes, there's always music in the air. I cuddle under Daddy's arm and soak in the atmosphere.

Until I meet a pair of bright blue eyes.

I straighten. She's standing across the street, wearing an oversized coat, a gray hoodie pulled up over her hair.

I move out from under Daddy's arm and turn Livvy's stroller so she's behind us, tucked against the restaurant's outer wall. I glare at Miranda.

Daddy follows my gaze. "Fuck."

Miranda ducks her head and crosses the street with a flow of pedestrians. As she approaches, Daddy shifts to stand in front of me.

"Stop there," Daddy says when Miranda reaches the sidewalk.

Miranda lifts her head and glares blue fire at Daddy. "Why? It's a public sidewalk. I can walk anywhere I want."

"Walk any closer to Emily and Livvy and we'll have a problem. You don't want to have a problem with me."

Miranda rolls her eyes. "If you touch me I'll scream, fall down, and develop bruises that will have you in handcuffs before you can blink. What would that bastard judge think of your fitness as a parent then?"

"Since I'm defending my daughter and fiancée from an unhinged stalker, I suspect the court would commend me. Turn around and walk away," Daddy's voice drops to a growl.

Behind me, Livvy starts to whimper, probably reacting to Logan's tone.

Miranda clutches her chest dramatically. "She's crying. She needs me. She needs her mother. How can you be so cruel as to keep my baby from me, James Logan?"

Her voice rises on Daddy's name. A few of the people milling around, waiting for the light to change, look our way.

Daddy shakes his head but I can see his shoulders tighten. He doesn't know how to deal with Miranda.

But I do. While Daddy's still shielding me, I take out my phone, start the voice recording, and slip it back in my pocket. Then I step up beside Daddy and slip my hand into his, pulling the stroller close behind me.

"Miranda." At her name, her eyes track to me. "Making a scene is not going to get you access to Olivia. Following us around New York is not going to get you access to Olivia. You're just alienating us and giving us evidence for a restraining order. What are you trying to gain?"

She sneers at me. "Don't talk to me, you dozy little mare. You had your chance. I told you to bring her to me. We could have worked things out, woman to woman. You ignored me, so I had to escalate."

I check her pockets. There's no bulge, no heavy hang to her coat. She could still have a weapon, though. She's a doctor, although Daddy said she hasn't treated patients in a long time. She could do a lot of damage with a scalpel and it wouldn't weigh down her pockets too much.

I shift the backpack of Livvy's diapers and Little Larrys off the stroller handle and into my free hand.

"This is escalating?" I ask. "Following us? Confronting us on a public street? This isn't going to get you anywhere." I step forward, holding the bag in front of me. "Why are you in New York, Miranda?"

"To be near my baby, of course." Her eyes redden. "There's nowhere else in the world for me."

"That's not true. You still have your house in England, by the river, isn't it?" I pause and when she nods in agreement, I continue, "You decorated it just the way you like, didn't you?"

"Olivia's never gotten to see her nursery," she says.

The first tear spills down her pale cheek. Her skin's mottled with red patches, like eczema. Stress? Or maybe she's not used to New York's dry cold?

"She's never going to, Miranda," I tell her. It's a little brutal but I want to snap her out of whatever crazy fantasy she's building in her head. "She's never going back to England with you. She'll never live with you. That will never be her nursery. But it's still your home. It's where you belong. Where your career is. Where your friends are—"

"Where her empty nursery is," Miranda spits.

"You can redecorate the nursery," I say firmly. "If you go home now, you could have it done for Christmas. You don't want to be here in New York for the holidays. I know how awful it is to be alone during the holidays. It's terrible for your mental health—"

"What do you care about my mental health, you bitch?" Miranda yells. Her hand, raw and red, plunges into her pocket.

I knew it. Behind me, Daddy shouts but I'm already bringing up the bag as Miranda lunges forward.

Everything slows down. I have time to focus on the glittering edge in her hand, to see her fingernails, chewed to the quick, pressed so hard against the handle of the small blade they're white. The impact on the bag staggers me back into Daddy. His hard arms close around me, catching me, keeping me from falling, the way he always does.

Miranda stumbles backwards, her hand flying to her mouth, tears running down her chapped cheeks. "Oh, God."

I'm a fierce, white, baby dragon and I'm not afraid of her.

I pull myself upright in Daddy's hold. "Knife!" I say, loudly enough to get the attention of everyone around us. People stop and turn to look at us.

"Motherfuck—!" Daddy's hands run down me frantically. "Baby?"

"I'm okay," I reassure him. Sharply, I say, "Miranda, go home. You just attacked me with a knife. Everyone here is a witness. I'm recording this. There's CCTV. If you don't want to spend Livvy's childhood in jail, go home."

She hunches over like she's going to puke, shaking her head. "I'm so sorry. Oh, God, I'm so sorry."

"Lo!" Master Mac shouts. I hear running footsteps but I don't take my eyes off Miranda.

"Miranda, I won't warn you again. Go home."

She straightens and looks at me, her eyes pleading. "Emily—"

"Don't you dare talk to her," Daddy snarls.

"It's okay," I say. "This is the last time she ever will. Go home, Miranda. Go home. This is done."

She nods, turns, and runs across the street, dodging traffic.

Daddy grabs my shoulders and turns me around. I hold the bag out to the side so the scalpel doesn't get caught between our bodies. Daddy looks down at me, his hand running down the front of my coat.

"Baby, where's the knife?"

I hold up the diaper bag.

Daddy chokes, then begins to laugh. "Livvy's diaper bag?"

I nod. "She may have hit a few Little Larrys, too."

"Baby." Daddy pulls me close and wraps me in a tight hug. "I'll buy you a million Little Larrys."

I reach behind him, grab the handle of Livvy's stroller, and move it back and forth so she stops whimpering. I couldn't hear her during my confrontation with Miranda. Tunnel hearing, I guess. But now I can hear her building up to a full fret. My psychic baby.

"I'm okay, Daddy," I promise him. "Can we go home now?"

He kisses me on the forehead and squeezes me before he lets me go. "Yes, my little wonder. Let's go home."

A hard arm comes around my back. I control a flinch. Miranda wouldn't touch me like that. It has to be Master Mac. I look up into his red face. He takes Livvy's diaper bag and glares at the scalpel handle sticking out of it like it's done him personal wrong.

"Don't touch it," Daddy warns. "It'll have Miranda's fingerprints on it."

Mac nods and holds the backpack horizontal so the handle sticks up out of it. A silver, accusatory finger. I imagine it chasing Miranda all the way back to England.

Mac leads us to an Uber where a very harassed-looking driver is trying to ignore the horns blaring behind him. We make quick work of climbing in, unclipping the stroller seat from its base, and clicking it into the seat belt. I settle on one side of the stroller seat and Daddy sits on the other, awkwardly stretching across so he can put his arm around my shoulders. I understand his need to have us both in his arms and lean in.

As the car pulls out in a fresh flurry of horns, I take a deep breath and let it out. It took a sword, a shield, and an attempted stabbing but the Mir-beast has finally been defeated.

thirty-four

EMILY

"DING, DONG, THE WITCH IS DEAD!" Bren yells, plucking Livvy from her bouncy chair and swinging her around. Livvy giggles madly.

I smother a giggle because Daddy doesn't like us calling the Mirbeast names but I share her sentiment. I pick up tongs to turn over the breakfast links I'm grilling. If I do a little "witch is dead" shuffle-dance, surely Daddy can't blame me for that.

Bren missed all the excitement. She's expressed to Master Mac, very loudly and in no uncertain terms, that she won't be left behind the next time he answers a distress call. I think it was all the curse words she used that got her the spanking I heard before she and Master Mac came down for breakfast. Her glowing pink cheeks and thighs don't seem to be dimming her enthusiasm this morning, though.

She holds Livvy against her chest as she bounces over. She smacks a kiss on my cheek and starts the coffee maker.

"C'mon, Emmy, you have to feel a little triumphant," she says.

I do. I also feel a little sad for Miranda. I can't imagine being that desperate. And she seemed genuinely horrified and contrite after that moment of madness when she tried to stab me. But she brought the scalpel along and people don't randomly carry scalpels—not even doctor-people—so she'd clearly thought about hurting me or Daddy before the confrontation. I don't feel so sorry for her that I stopped Daddy from calling Theo and lodging an official complaint. If Miranda can't come back to New York because of an outstanding warrant that would be too bad.

But what I mostly feel is proud. I handled Miranda. No one got hurt, except three Little Larrys and I think they might be salvageable with some careful stitching, and I didn't break any rules. Daddy's super-proud of me and I got all the Os last night after we put Livvy to bed. I'm proud of myself.

I'm a fierce, white, baby dragon. Hear me roar.

I tamp down my roar through breakfast because it turns into another strategy session when Jiro, Laurel, Bravo, Yummy, Maude, Javier, and Master Theo join us. I gather from the discussion that Master Chess has called the emergency meeting Daddy was pushing for. I don't have anything to add and they're talking serious stuff. I just listen and play with the world's cutest dragon-baby.

After breakfast, Master Theo takes a statement from me and I send him the recording from my phone. He takes the scalpel and puts it in an official-looking plastic bag that has "Evidence" printed in red across it. I see Daddy eying the bag and wonder what he's thinking until he murmurs that he's going to order a bunch of evidence bags so he can collect glitter as evidence of the Littles' Army's crimes. I object to that almost as loudly as Bren objected to Master Mac leaving her behind. Yummy joins in, berating Daddy for maligning the Littles' Army, until Daddy has to throw up his hands and apologize. I take my apology in kisses.

It's a very good apology.

True arrives after breakfast and we retreat to Daddy's office. I don't want to make the Avengers angry.

True watches two recorded classes and submits a quiz while I write. When I take a break to make tea for both of us, she takes off her headphones. "Is Fleur mad at me?" she asks.

"What?"

"She hasn't answered my texts in two days."

Something niggles in the back of my head. I pick up my phone. I don't have Fleur saved as a contact because I've never had a need to call her but she's in a bunch of chats with me, including the Littles' Army Plus chat where we organize outings. I flip through them and see that she hasn't looked at any of the recent messages.

I call Cappa.

"Hey, babe," he answers. His voice is ridiculously cheerful, particularly for someone who is not long off *five whole days* of orgasm-restriction. If something was bad wrong, he wouldn't sound so happy. My muscles relax a fraction.

"Is everything okay with Fleur?" I ask. "True says she's ignored her texts and I can't see that she's checked any of our chats."

"Mmm, hold on." I hear him tapping. "She hasn't answered me from yesterday, either."

I thought they lived together?

"Where are you, Cappa?" I ask.

"At Myles' apartment," he says, his tone sheepish.

That explains why he hasn't seen Fleur, although I suppose they could just be on very different schedules.

"Master Theo was trying to get in touch with her yesterday," I tell him, having placed that niggling feeling. "Is there any way you can check on her?"

"Yeah," Cappa says. "Don't worry about it. I'll track her down. She's probably in monster-mode, creating something new. She tends to turn off her phone. Tell True it's nothing personal and I'll make sure Fleur gets back to her. Is the kid doing okay?"

I glance at True, taking in the jeans and sweatshirt that fit, the glossy hair she's done in a Katniss Everdeen-type braid, the bright eyes. "She's good. Do you want to say hi?"

"Yeah, pass me over."

I hand True my phone and let them greet each other while I think. I don't want to make a big deal out of it if Fleur's just retreated into a creative space. And the last few days have been a lot. Everyone's on edge.

But I am a fierce, white, baby dragon. I have good instincts. I protect my dragon-friends.

I open the office door and walk into the kitchen. Daddy and several other people sitting at the table glance up.

"Fleur's missing," I tell them.

In the kerfuffle that follows, Daddy herds me back into the office.

"Sweetheart, this is your writing time. We'll find Fleur. You focus on meeting your deadlines."

I don't resist. I huggle him and kiss his chin. I know my Daddy will take care of it because that's what he does. I've done my part; I've roared. Now I need to retreat back into my cave and do the things I should be doing.

There are a lot of footsteps in the hallway as I get back to writing. True is still talking to Cappa, so I leave my phone with her. The stories in my head have always been at least as real as the life going on around me. It's not hard to refocus. But my back is tight and by the time I've reached my word-count for the day, the hard needle of a headache shoots up my neck every time I move. I leave my computer backing up everything I've written while I pad into the kitchen to make myself a cup of chamomile tea.

True follows me into the kitchen. She gives me my phone and I check my messages. Logan's gone to the club with Master Theo for the emergency meeting. Master Mac has Livvy and he's gone with Bren to her shop. Cynnie's asked me to go shopping with her later and there are Littles' Army rumblings about filling the pool at Blunts with rubber duckies but it looks like everyone's going to be out of the house for several hours.

Since it's just going to be me and True one-on-one for a few hours, I offer her a snack and take the opportunity to talk with her. Once we have our tortilla chips, hummus, salsa, and guacamole, I sit down across from her at the breakfast table and say, "A lot of my friends have shared their stories with you but I haven't. It's not because I didn't want to. It's because I wanted you to have a context for my story, since I'm not exactly the usual kind of submissive."

"You're a little, right?" True asks.

I nod.

"And you told me that's a state of mind, not a size or an age or anything," True says, dipping a chip.

"That's right. Littleness can mean a lot of different things, just like submission can be lots of different things."

"Can it ever!" True says, covering her mouth as she munches. "I had no idea how many different things it could be. Like, even watching scenes at Sacrum, I didn't have any idea. There's Brenna's kind of submission where she's always submissive to Master Mac and she's got really specific rules she follows and the punishments are hella scary. There's Justine's kind of submission where she submits to anyone who asks for scenes at the club but she doesn't have any rules outside of scenes and never gets punished. There's Cappa's kind of submission where he's submissive to more than one master but Logan gives him rules and then Mr. De Leon punishes him if he breaks them. There's so many different kinds of submission."

She hasn't even scratched the surface. "Daddy says there are as many different kinds of submission as there are submissives. I think that's a good thing. It lets everyone be themselves and find their own way."

"What's your way?" True asks.

I explain my relationship with Daddy, the rules I follow to keep me safe so I can be little all the time, and the difference between correction and punishment, which makes True's eyes go round.

"I wouldn't want to ever earn a punishment from Master Logan," True whispers.

I don't really want to, either.

"I love funishments from Daddy," I explain. "Those are spankings and paddlings and even floggings that Daddy gives me out of love, not to punish rule-breaking or prevent me from ever doing the bad thing again. Correction makes me feel bad because I know Daddy's disappointed with me but I appreciate that he's helping me follow the rules. Punishment is awful. A trillion percent, do not recommend."

True giggles.

"Worst punishment ever?" she asks.

I shake my head. I don't think True's a masochist and even if she is, I'm not going to scare an almost-sixteen-year-old with a description of my time on the wooden pony.

"I've only earned three real punishments. They were awful. 'Nough said. I know Cappa and some of the other subbies who have talked with you like to brat. I don't. I tease Daddy and play practical jokes on him but I don't resist his orders or break rules on purpose. I'm not comfortable with that. It's taken me a while to find a Dom who understands that I'd rather follow the rules than break them. It's important to understand your own needs as a submissive so you can communicate them clearly to your Dom or Doms."

True nods. "Everyone's said that. But I don't always want one thing. Like, I get that you don't want to break rules but what if I don't want to break rules one day but feel like breaking them another day?"

I grin at her.

"Tell your Dom and be prepared for a warm behind."

She giggles. "Is it bad that it sounds like fun?"

"No, not at all. Get rid of that good-bad switch inside your head. Have you played 'Assassin's Creed'? Everything is permitted. You just have to talk with your Dom about it first."

"Ooo, yeah, I have," True says. "Really, everything? Nothing I do is wrong?"

"Oh, no, lots of things you do *can* be wrong. Everything is permitted means that everything can be negotiated in kink. Do you want to play zombies and have your Dom pretend to eat you? That's permitted. Do you want play out a no-win situation, one where you're guaranteed to fail no matter what you do, so you earn a funishment? That's permitted. Do you want your Dom to yell at you until you get weepy because you need the catharsis of a good cry? That's permitted. It's all about communication. You just have to talk about it with your Dom."

Her eyes have grown round again at my descriptions of potential scenes. "Wow, I didn't think about all that. It could be so much fun!"

"It is," I agree. "It's the most fun I've ever had. The most freedom. The most happiness. Kink doesn't *solve* everything but it can *be* everything if you want it to be. You can live it all the time the way Brenna and I do. Or it can be something you do on weekends. It's up to you and your Dom to negotiate."

"I didn't think of it like that. There are so many rules that I thought it was all about following rules and getting punished for breaking rules."

"Want to know a secret?" I ask. "I barely ever think of the rules. They're there. I live within their confines." I reach over and tap the window overlooking the backyard beside me. "I don't think about them any more than I think about the glass in this window. The glass is there, doing its job, keeping out the cold, letting in the light. The glass becomes important when I bump into it, when it's dirty, or when it breaks. Then I think about the glass. The rest of the time? I don't need to. The rules are part of my life."

"Like gravity?" True asks.

"Like gravity," I agree. Daddy-gravity. I'll share that with him when he gets back. He'll get a kick out of being Daddy-gravity.

thirty-five

LOGAN

"BASED on the interviews I've submitted with Shannie and Annabelle and Chess' relation of Tessa's treatment, I move that Andrew Selman and Emmett Hornby be removed as members of the club and banned for life," I say. "That concludes the motion."

I sit down and look around the table.

We're short one member. Nico, our Master of Blood, wasn't able to get out of a family commitment to attend the emergency meeting. He's given his voting proxy to Karl, which makes me nervous, because Nico usually votes with me, Maude, and Javier, and I can't count on Karl's vote. But I have to have faith in my brother Doms. That's what this is all about.

It's hard to hold on to that faith when not everyone around the table will meet my eyes.

"We also have a motion from Master Logan for mandatory member re-training on guest security measures and to limit the number of guests per member at any time to two for a period of three months while the club reviews the security measures. This would exclude club events and members of the Elephant's Playground,"

Chess says, going down the printed agenda that's in front of everyone.

"Is the security retraining necessary if we eliminate these troublesome elements from the club, Logan?" Felix asks.

"Yes," says another voice before I have a chance to answer. It's Guy, Master of Wire, who handles the club's IT. "Frankly, I'd be more comfortable if there was mandatory security training every six months. Members are too lax about guests bringing their own equipment into the club. I've had to speak with people about guests having phones four times in the last two months. No guest should have a phone inside the club. It just needs to stop."

I nod at Guy, perfectly happy to let him make my point for me.

"Happy to amend the motion to a mandatory security training every six months," Chess says, making a note on his agenda. "Any other urgent business?"

When no one speaks, Chess nods. "Logan, Theo, please recuse yourselves. I've asked Drew to address the committee."

Fuck.

I tap my pen on my agenda. "Since when do we allow non-committee members to address the committee?" I ask.

"Since you railroaded Sante out of here," Franco responds. "Emmett's an annual member and I'm happy to vote without hearing from him. We refund him what's left of the year and that's that. No great harm done. But Drew's a lifetime member. Refunding his buy-in represents a financial loss to the club. We're depriving him of substantial privileges, including a spot on this committee that I know he's been working toward. He should have a chance to speak."

Maude reaches across and closes her fingers around my pen. I release it in disgust. Sante had few friends at the club but Franco was one of them. Clearly, he's harboring a grudge.

Theo cups his hand under my elbow and pulls me up as he rises from his chair. "Thank you, everyone. I realize this is a rough introduction but I'm looking forward to working with you all as Master of Fur."

There are nods all around the table. Maybe it will help that Theo's well-liked. He let me present most of the motion, since he didn't sit in on the interviews with Shannie and Annabelle but he offered support from our investigation yesterday, including that Emmett's been banned from The Pump House, a fetish club in Rochester, due to an alleged consent violation.

I walk out of the small conference room with him. Once the door closes behind me, I stop and rub the back of my neck to release the tension gathered there.

"Did we do enough?" I ask Theo.

"Time will tell. I hate to do this to you, buddy but I've got to get back to my desk. I've got a report to file for the district attorney and she'll string me up by my balls if it's five minutes late."

"No problem. I'll let you know what happens."

Theo pats me on the back. "Hang in there. We've got infinite opportunity to take these fucks down. This is just the first salvo."

"Right, mate. Talk to you soon."

He leaves me with another reassuring pat. There's nowhere to sit while I wait, so I retreat down the hallway to the room where we have the breakfast buffet on the weekends.

I nearly slam into Drew as he opens the door and strolls out.

"Ah, Logan." His smile is unbearably smarmy. "Good to see you."

"I wish I could say the same," I respond. "But hopefully this is the last time I'll have to see you."

His smile widens. "I wouldn't count on it."

I remember my little wonder, confronting Miranda and her fucking scalpel with a diaper bag. She was so calm. So completely confident in her position. I channel a fraction of that confidence and stare Drew down.

He nods, steps out of my way, and continues down the hall to the small conference room.

Fucker.

I sink into one of the folding chairs set around the tables where we eat on weekends. The room is cool and quiet. The hoods are pulled down on the buffet serving stations. The round tables lack their usual tablecloths. There's a faint smell of fried onions.

Rubbing the back of my neck, I take out my phone. One of the privileges of lifetime membership, I'm reminded, being able to have a phone in the club. I have a pile of messages that I prioritize quickly. Emmy wishing me luck and telling me she loves me. I send back an "ILY2." Max messaging about a new job upgrading the security systems at a small chain of private casinos upstate. I send him back a quick thumbs up. Mac saying that he's come for moral support and is waiting for me in the Trattoria with our angelic baby.

Grateful to leave this cheerless space, I hasten to the Trattoria. Mac's sitting at a table in the conservatory, looking out at the hay bale maze where we had our Doms v subs paintball war. God, that seems like a long time ago now. The angelic baby is in her car set on the table, alert but quiet, looking around with her hazy blue eyes.

I sink down next to Mac. "Thanks for coming."

"How's it going?"

I shake my head. "Chess punted me and Theo out while Drew addresses the committee. No one's ever been invited to address the committee on the subject of their membership before. Not in my memory. Franco said it was because I'd 'railroaded' Sante out of the club—"

Mac claps me on the shoulder. "Hindsight's twenty-twenty. You had no way of knowing then what you'd need to be doing now. Don't beat yourself up. Order something without caffeine and try to relax. You've done good here, son, whatever happens."

I nod and when the waitress circulates among the small number of tables that are occupied at this time on a cold winter's morning, I order Earl Grey tea. Emily would probably be happier if I ordered that curry-tasting crap but that's one taste bud too far today.

Mac rocks Livvy's carrier gently, making the line of toys dangling from the handle swing. Livvy bats at them with her little fists.

"You sure she's yours?" Mac asks.

I choke on my tea. "Are you serious?"

He grins. "I don't think she's yours. Look at her. She's just looking around, taking it all in. She's barely made a peep all morning. You were never this quiet. Not even during maneuvers on the damn sub. Well, I take that back. She's farted a couple of times. Maybe she is yours."

I punch his arm. "Asshole."

"Just trying to lighten the mood." Mac grins off into the distance. "She is a very easy baby, though. I think you and Emmy got lucky."

"I know we did. This schedule Emmy's got her on isn't hurting, either. I can't believe she's sleeping through the night already."

"Schedule's good, no question. But if she'd been born on her due date and there hadn't been any complications, she'd be coming up on eight weeks. Plenty of babies sleep through at eight weeks."

"Plenty don't," I say, with the authority of having read two whole baby books. "Thanks again for having my back yesterday."

"Anytime, son. You think that's the end of it?"

I nod. "Theo checked with the airlines. She bought a ticket for a flight back to London tomorrow. The warrant won't issue before her flight but Theo's going to make sure she gets it so she knows that if she tries to fly into the U.S., or at least New York, she'll be arrested."

"Powerful deterrent," Mac says.

"I don't think she'll risk it." I shrug. "But I wouldn't have ever thought she'd try to stab Emily, either, so I clearly don't understand her as well as I thought I did. I'm not going to relax any of my security measures."

"I wouldn't suggest that you do, although you can tell Maxie to back off about sticking a chip in my neck. That's not gonna happen."

I shake my head at him. I'll keep working on him. I'm chipped now. Emily's chipped. Bren's got one in a piercing she doesn't take out. He'll cave eventually.

The clack of heels approaching our table has Mac and me looking up. Maude walks toward us, her face expressionless.

That's bad. I stand and offer her my chair, grabbing another from an empty table and sitting across from her.

"Is the meeting over?" I ask.

She nods and sits down between us, crossing her legs and smoothing down her skirt. "There are times to push and times to retreat."

Fuck me.

"What the hell are you saying?" I ask.

"That you've lost the battle but not the war."

"You have to be fucking kidding me. I put two clear cases of Drew and his fucking wolfpack *stalking* our goddamn subs in front of the committee. No, I can't prove he was behind what happened to Cappa but Annabelle's statement was pretty damning. What the fuck did he say to the committee?"

Maude taps her fingernails on her knee. "He's clever. Maybe cleverer than I gave him credit for. He started by criticizing the changes you've been making. He suggested that they stemmed from your caregiving 'indulgences,' as he called them. He brought up your aversion to gang bangs and said you were creating a culture of intolerance toward hard sadism at the club—"

"Well, that is fucking rich," I burst out.

"I'm aware of the irony." Maude reaches out and covers my hand with hers. She locks our fingers together and takes a deep breath before she says, "He reminded us that we're dominants. That we are driven by the need to control. The house subs are driven by the need to give themselves over to that control. They don't always understand that about themselves and that's why they come to us, to help them discover those deep truths and explore their submissive nature.

"He reminded us that we are, in essence, hunters, and the subs are our prey. We wrap that in scenes and safe words but we will always have that need to control and subjugate and denying those needs is denying our own truths. He asked us to consider how we could hope to provide true dominance for our subs if we're lying to ourselves about what we are?"

I start to growl, "That is complete—"

"Hear me out," Maude says quietly. "He pointed out that although Shannie was frightened, she did, in fact, submit successfully to both Ty and Hart. The scene fulfilled one of her key submission goals. Drew reminded us that sometimes we have to use a sub's fear to get them where they don't just want but *need* to go. He called it a successful scene and there were a number of nods around the table, Logan."

"Then they're assholes. None of them sat there while we talked to Shannie. She doesn't think it was fucking successful."

Maude nods. "Unfortunately, Annabelle isn't as well known. She's too new. There were only a few committee members who had scened with her at all and almost none of the hard sadists. Drew expressed regret at her leaving the club and denied any knowledge of the threats made against her. He admitted being involved in the DVP scene but said it was negotiated in advance and she never used her safe word. He understood it might have pushed her physical limits but pointed out that she's given vaginal birth to two babies without mishap. Drew said he took that into consideration and wouldn't have attempted a DVP scene with most of the other house submissives. He came across as thoughtful and conscientious—"

"Then he's a goddamn sociopath because no one who thinks it's okay to *hunt* our house submissives has any shred of fucking conscience," I snap.

"We can't judge him on his morals, Logan, only his actions. That left the situation with Cappa which, as you know, didn't directly involve Drew—"

"The asshole who tore up Cappa so badly he needed sixteen stitches is part of Drew's fucking wolfpack," I growl.

Maude squeezes my fingers hard. "Direct your anger at a useful target. Caddy, Cris, and Chess said not one word against Drew or in your defense when he was accusing you and Mac of being too soft on the house subs because you're Daddy Doms—"

Maude breaks off at a sharp snort.

"I am not a Daddy Dom," Mac says, finally interjecting himself into the conversation. "In less than a month, I wrangled one of the toughest, sassiest subs here into twenty-four-seven submission. Something not a single other Dom here managed in five years. Not that I believe for a second that Logan's gone soft, or that a little softness in this situation isn't warranted. This is bullshit. That baby-faced prick is an abuser. Anyone with eyes can see it. If the committee doesn't see it, or isn't willing to do anything about it because they have a beef with Logan and me, then they don't deserve the house subs."

Maude's eyes flick from Mac to me and back to Mac. "What are you saying, Michael?"

"I'm saying that none of the house subs will be showing up for work until this club is a safe place for them. And that if they don't get full pay while they're off, I'll personally file hostile work environment claims for all of them against Drew and every member of the management committee who supports him."

Maude clears her throat. "Well."

"Navy taught me a thing or two about using what little the law provides," Mac says. "There are thirty-eight men and women here who are being put in an unsafe situation by their employers. Thirty-eight uniquely vulnerable men and women. And by God, Uncle Sam, and the great State of New York, I will protect them."

Having seen Mac get like this before over the men under his command and remembering what he said about letting him fight this battle, I sit back with a nod. "What he said."

"Michael, you're very new to all this—"

"Doesn't make me blind or stupid. No, I don't have the history with the people in that room that you and Logan have. But I have spoken with each and every one of the house subs over the last two weeks, which is something I'm betting none of the other committee members has done. More'n one of 'em's hurting. Many of 'em are scared. None of 'em will show up tomorrow if I send a message to the chat group every single one of them joined tellin' them it's not safe for them here." Mac chuckles. "Well, Briar Rose might. Have fun with her."

Maude looks faintly impressed.

"I suggest trying to catch the three Cs now, before any of them leave the building, and ask that they reconsider."

Mac nods and rises, scooping Livvy's car seat up by the handle. He holds Maude's chair for her like the gentleman he is and gestures for her to precede us out of the Trattoria.

"Even if this is the right decision, they won't like being strong-armed into it," Maude warns as we follow her into the hallway.

Mac shrugs. "I don't care what they like or don't like. They can kick me to the curb instead of Drew if they want. I'll still be taking the house subs with me and making sure they never submit again to someone who thinks hunting 'em without their consent is in any way acceptable."

I smile at my friend and mentor, who will always do the right thing, no matter the personal cost.

The Three Cs, Ten, Javier, and Franco are still in the small conference room when Maude knocks on the door and enters.

"Lady and gentlemen," she says as she holds the door open for us. "Michael has something to say that you need to hear."

Chess gestures to the seats around the table. Mac delivers his threat as coolly and smoothly as he did in the Trattoria.

Chess goes pale. Caddy's lips thin. Ten frowns thunderously.

"Logan, when you took back Master of Training—" Franco, the club's lawyer, begins.

Chess barks a laugh. "None of us thought you'd be staging a Subbie Rebellion." He starts clapping. "Well done."

Franco and Ten look at Chess like he's lost his mind. Caddy's black-hole gaze bores into me. Cris types something into his tablet.

"Mr. MacNally's right," Cris says quietly. "About the hostile work environment claims. That would be substantially more of a financial loss for the club than refunding Master Drew's membership fees."

"If proven," Franco says.

Cris tips his head in acknowledgment. "Punitive damages are a possibility under state and federal law. As the club's legal advisor, you'll need to tell us the likelihood of success of such claims but as the club's financial advisor, I can tell you that financially the decision is clear."

Franco pinches the bridge of his nose. "We can't let it even go to tribunal. As soon as the nature of the house subs employment becomes clear, it will be referred to law enforcement and the club will be shut down. I've warned the committee about this before."

"Yes, you have," I say. I wasn't going to play that ace in the hole unless I had to, though.

"Looks like you've gotten your way, Logan," Caddy says softly.

"What way is that?" I ask. "You encouraged me to promote age-play at the club and then you backstabbed me when I did it. You sat on your fucking hands while Drew and his fucking wolfpack terrorized our house subs—"

Maude reaches over and curls her hand around my forearm at the same time Caddy snaps, "You have no idea what I've done or haven't done, nor whether my actions have helped or harmed. What we do know is that only two wolfpack members at the club have been revealed—"

"Do you believe there're more?" Mac asks.

"I believe we'll never know now," Caddy says, her eyes boring into me. "Drew and Emmett will be expelled from the club but as they haven't been arrested, it's unlikely they'll face other justice. Logan's overt maneuvering means they know why they're being expelled. The rest of the wolfpack knows we know. Do you think they'll disband? Or that they'll just become more subtle? Abusers don't reform, they just find quieter victims."

"Theo's making a case against Emmett," I protest.

"But not against Drew," Caddy retorts. "I don't know if you've had a chance to speak with Emmett and Drew but five minutes of conversation would have made clear who is the beta and who is the alpha in their vile pack. Emmett's a follower. Drew threw him in our path and you took his damn bait, Logan—"

"Maybe if you'd ever fucking told me what was going on, I wouldn't have!" I flare.

"Did you take me into your confidence?" Caddy snaps. "I've been going on whispers just as much as you have. The only thing I know about Drew that you didn't is that he's related to me. Second cousin."

My gut knots. Javier mentioned that Caddy's uncle, the former chairman of Blunts, abused her. That piqued Emily's curiosity and she went digging through Blunts' archives and public records. What she found made my blood run cold. David was a pedophile and a rapist and his favorite victims were his own family members.

"On your uncle's side?" I ask, my voice choked.

Caddy nods.

"Was he—?" I can't complete the question.

"He was called as a witness but refused to testify against David," she responds, her voice cold and hollow. "As I said, I've only been going on whispers. Rumors. Dark glances. But I know that age-play is a trigger for Drew. I've overheard him bad-mouth it often enough. I've seen the looks he's given you and your little. I encouraged you to create the Nursery and promote age-play at the club as much to change the club's culture as to draw him out."

"Fuck's sake," I say. "If you'd said one word."

"What word?" Caddy asks. "You're the damn detective, Logan. I approached *you*. I encouraged you. I supported you behind the scenes. I made sure the Nursery was funded despite your ridiculous budget requests. A tree? You needed a goddamn tree in the middle of our club?"

"I really like the tree," Cris says. When Caddy swings her dark gaze at him, he holds up his hands. "What? I bet we're the only lifestyle club in the nation that has a tree in the middle of one of our dungeons. It's a selling point."

Caddy returns her fulminating glare to me. "This is on you. Drew won't stop and now we've missed our opportunity to stop him."

Her words settle deep in my chest.

"I won't give up," I say.

"Don't," she responds.

thirty-six

LOGAN

AFTER EVERYONE LEAVES, I sit with my head in my hands and parse through my fuck-up.

Did I fall for the fall-guy? Did I let the true villain of the piece get away? I can't accept that. No, I don't always "get my man." As I told Emily months ago, my clients often don't want the publicity and potential recriminations of an arrest. Often it's enough to stop the crime, get the money back, get an apology. Have I let the confines of my usual cases blind me when it mattered?

Slowly, I become aware that not everyone has left the room. Mac's sitting beside me, staring off into space, rocking Livvy's car seat on the conference table. That's not surprising.

What is surprising is that Ten is still sitting across from me.

Ten's expression is even more surprising. He's not red-faced and scowling. He's ashen.

"Fleur's missing," he says, when I meet his eyes.

"Cappa's on it," I reassure him.

Ten shakes his head, pulls his phone out of his pocket, and holds out the screen to me. I can't read the small type across the table.

"He's been back to her apartment. She's not there. There's no sign she's been home."

A cold finger runs up my spine. "Since when?"

He works his jaw for a moment before he says, "I mighta been the last one to see her. We did a scene after the party the other night, the Grand Opening, her, Cappa, and me. Cappa left afterwards for his shift in the nightclub. Fleur stayed with me until breakfast. I had a . . . thing. Once I was finished, I went to lunch in the Trattoria. She wasn't there and we hadn't planned anything, so I assumed she'd gone home."

"That was two days ago," I say, parsing through his timeline.

"Yeah."

"Fuck." I pull out my phone and call Theo.

He answers on the second ring. "Hey, I just heard. Good fucking job—"

"It isn't but I'll tell you why later. Fleur's missing. Cappa's been to their apartment. She's not there. Ten saw her at breakfast two days ago. That's the last time anyone's seen or heard from her."

"Fuck," Theo says.

"My sentiments exactly. Hospitals?"

"And morgues. Don't repeat that to anyone. Panic doesn't help," Theo says. "Do you know who her medical emergency contact is?"

"Cappa, I'd assume."

Theo grunts. "No point in you calling around. They won't tell you anything. Have Ten and Cappa file a missing person's report with my office. She's been gone long enough. I'll make sure a junior detective starts making calls as soon as the report's filed."

I lift my head and relate what Theo's said to Ten.

"You're with Ten?" Theo asks when I finish.

"Yes."

"Pass the phone over to him. I'll coach him through the report."

I hand my phone to Ten and while he listens intently to Theo, I turn to Mac.

"How badly have I fucked up?" I ask.

Mac chews on his lower lip for a moment. "You haven't. With the information we had, you did the right thing. You protected the house subs. That's your job, Lo."

"Caddy said—"

"I heard what Caddy said. That was a massive fucking guilt-trip. Based on what I've heard about her, I understand where it came from. She has my sympathies. But we have a justice system for a reason. You're not judge, jury, and executioner, Lo. You're a private investigator and you haven't even been hired by the damn club in this case. You exposed the bad guy. She's likely right that it won't stop the abuse but he won't be able to do it here. Take the win."

"Is it a win?" I ask. "What if there are Wolfpack members still at the club that we haven't exposed?"

"Then we'll find them and expose them," Mac says. "Caddy says Drew's the alpha of their pack. The rest of the pack will lay low without him. We'll keep an eye on the subs. If there's a whisper of a member stepping out of line, ignoring a safe word—" He throws Ten a hard glance; Ten lowers his eyes to the table. "Or breaching hard limits. We'll be all over them. I like Maude but she's not a warrior. Yeah, we have to win the war but that don't mean we can afford to lose battles. This was a battle we had to win. We won it."

His words soothe a little of the carnage in my chest. A sense of failure still weighs across my shoulders.

"C'mon. Time to go home," Mac says.

"But—"

"No, no buts. I've seen that expression before, Lo. You need to regroup. You need time with your little. Emily'll help you put this in perspective. We can pull Max into the search for Fleur." Mac nods at Ten, who seems to be wrapping up with Theo and is tapping on his own phone. "You've got better resources at home and Emmy's there. Time to go."

"Okay," I agree.

Ten says goodbye to Theo and slides my phone back across the table. He finishes typing on his phone and looks up. "I'm going to meet Cappa at Theo's station. Make the missing person report." He swallows. "Afterward, can I bring Cappa to your place? I know I'm not your favorite person right now but Fleur—"

I wave off our differences. "Of course you can."

"Thanks. Hopefully we'll be at yours by two. We'll bring lunch."

Mac snorts. "Emily will already have a five-star buffet laid out. Bring a pizza or something since Cappa eats like an alley cat but don't worry about feeding the masses."

Ten nods.

"If it gets lost in the shit," Ten says, his eyes flicking from me to Mac. "I'm sorry. I apologized to Brenna already but I'll say it to the two of you. I'm sorry. I've been talking to someone . . . she's helped me see that I let my fears get the best of me sometimes. I don't like change. It makes me feel like fuck. The changes you've been making . . . I've hated them. I let that translate into a hatred of you. But I know you're good Doms. Everything you've done with this Wolfpack fuckery, you've done the right thing—"

I know I shouldn't engage. He's apologized and that should be enough. But the sense of failure that's heavier than a hundred-pound barbell plate on my chest pushes out the words, "You voted for Drew."

Ten shakes his head. "I voted to kick out both Emmett and Drew. I've scened with Annabelle. She might be green but she's not a liar. You were short two votes on Drew. Three Cs abstained. Sure, I see what Caddy was tryin' to do and maybe she shared her fucking master plan with Chess and Cris but don't let her lay all of this fuckery at your door."

"If Drew walks away from this and does it somewhere else—"

Ten shakes his head. "This ain't over. Not by a long shot."

I take a deep breath and let it lift some of the weight off my chest. "Okay."

Ten nods at us before picking up his coat off the back of his chair and leaving.

"Honestly didn't think 'sorry' was in his vocabulary," Mac says after the door's closed behind Ten. He picks up Livvy's car seat but I hold my hand out for it. I need to feel one of my girls close.

"Yeah, I don't think I've heard it before, either," I admit.

Mac slaps me on the back. "Never let it be said this place is dull."

I grin at him. "Nope, it's never that."

Ten and Cappa don't come for lunch.

Cappa finds Fleur first, after utilizing the Blunts subbie network to call every hospital in the Tri-State area. I appreciate Theo trying to go through official channels and utilize his resources but he underestimates the ability of our submissives to get shit done. Cappa gives his personal information to the extended subbie network and with ten different men pretending to be him, they track down Fleur in less than two hours.

Manny offers to drive Ten and Cappa to Trinifas, a hospital outside Elizabeth, New Jersey, who have a Jane Doe matching Fleur's description. A tense hour later, information begins filtering back to the assembled crowd at my house, which swells through the day. A man who identified himself as Cappa but ran when hospital staff asked him for ID, left Fleur in the ER. She was taken directly into surgery. I walk Laurel and Emily out of the room when Ten, on speaker, begins describing her injuries.

Emily watches me with her big eyes, wet and red from the last few hours.

Jiro joins us in the kitchen, closing my office door behind him. He folds Laurel into his chest. "Enough, petto."

"I promise I'm okay, Tatsu," she says but she clings to him in a way I haven't seen before.

I beckon Emily to me. I need a hug even if she doesn't.

"When she wakes up, we should go, Daddy," Emily whispers as I wrap her in my arms.

"We will," I promise.

"She'll be okay," Emily says but I hear the quaver in her voice. "She's a dragon, too."

"I hope so, baby."

Maude's the next to emerge from my office. She has two spots of red high on her cheeks which match her eyes.

"I'm arranging to have her airlifted to Presbyterian," Maude tells me. "I don't trust Trinifas. It has one of the worst ratings in New Jersey. No wonder they hadn't even identified her yet."

I nod. "What can I do?"

"Hold down the fort." Maude glances at the dining table where True is sitting with Cynnie, playing a board game and watching Livvy while she naps. "Keep everyone here level. Georgie's coming over after work. I anticipate several more of the house submissives will arrive later as well. They'll need calm guidance as they process their emotions."

"Here rather than the club?" I ask.

She pats my shoulder. "If you haven't already figured it out, Logan, your house is a symbol of safety for practically every submissive I know. I'll be back once Fleur's settled at Presbyterian. Forgive his presumption but I believe Javier's just booked your business partner's transportation services for the next week. He should be here any minute to pick us up."

"Of course, it's fine," I agree. Max will rearrange any jobs Manny had lined up. I don't even have to ask.

"Create a rota while I'm gone if you have a moment," Maude says. "A Dom and at least one submissive at the hospital during visiting hours for the next five days. Four-hour shifts max. Austin probably still has the template we used when you were injured. He'll be here by dinner time."

"You had a rota for caring for me?" I never heard about this.

Maude pats my shoulder again. "Of course we did. We couldn't have that madness that descended when you first arrived home continue. It frightened Emily. I'll call when Fleur's settled. I'd prefer

Georgie stay here tonight rather than be alone if I don't get back at a reasonable hour. I apologize if that's an imposition."

"It's not an imposition." I already suspect we're going to have a subbie sleepover in front of the telly tonight. "If you need anything, just call."

"I will." She gives me a final pat, holds her arms out to Emily for a hug, then walks away.

I wrap my baby doll back into a hug and drop my face into the warm, sweetly-scented curls on her crown. "We're all lucky to have that woman in our lives," I murmur.

"I never got to talk with her about Georgie, Daddy," Emily whispers back.

"I think it's okay. Bull's realized he was using Georgie to plaster over the cracks in his trio. He's going to work on fixing things before he tries to add Georgie into the mix again. Maybe by then they'll have figured out an arrangement that suits everyone."

Emily snuggles, squeezing my ribs, which I discover are sore. Probably all the tension. "I'm glad. I don't want to come off as partial but I'm really rooting for Maude and Georgie. She's been alone for so long. She deserves all the happiness."

"We all do, baby," I say, a little breathlessly after another hard squeeze. "We all do."

I'm not wrong about the subbie sleepover.

Emily sets up her tent and a parade of subbies bring down armfuls of pillows and blankets. More people trickle in after their jobs end for the day and by the time Livvy's gone down for her "little sleep," there are over a dozen subbies camped out in the great room. Most of their Doms are also milling around, although Sammi is solo after Jack heads to Presbyterian, where he has surgical privileges. I give Emily a firm warning about Littles' Army shenanigans, since Yummy and

Amy are also here but the mood is so somber, it's probably unnecessary.

When Theo sends me a text saying he's on the way, I warn Max. He and Cynnie quickly decamp. Curiously, they take Amy with them.

After I see them out, I beckon Emily out of the subbie pile and draw her to the side.

"Something go wrong between Amy and Theo?" I ask.

Emmy bites her lip. "No."

I narrow my eyes at her. "Spill, little girl."

"Well, you know how Max used to do bad hacking things and now he does mostly good hacking things and only bad hacking things for a good cause?"

I'm not sure I'd characterize Max's online activities that way but I nod.

"So, he's like a morally gray hacker," Emmy continues.

"Sure," I say, not knowing where this is going.

"Amy's also a hacker, only she's a completely ethical hacker. Max calls her a 'white hat,' but I don't like to use that term because it correlates purity with color and that kind of language promotes racism . . . anyway, Amy's helping Max with the hacking and I don't think they want Master Theo to know."

I nod along but what I take away from this is that the Littles' Army has its own hacker.

"In any given situation, little girl, how many definitions would you say there are of 'good'?"

She gives me the owl-eye. "Is this a trick question?"

"No. I'd like to understand if there's a Daddy version of good, a little version of good, and a Littles' Army version of good."

Instant angry koala face. I knew it.

"Let me be clear, little girl. If the mommies and daddies find out that Amy has been hacking chats or whatever else in furtherance of Littles' Army plans, there will be hell to pay and I don't care if Amy doesn't currently have a caregiver. I will administer that punishment myself. This is a safety issue."

"So, when you say—" Emmy begins.

"No, this is not the time for qualifications. Are we clear? Amy doesn't do any type of hacking that would prevent the mommies and daddies from monitoring the Littles' Army plans and ensuring you're all safe."

Emily scrunches her face up further but slowly nods. "Okay, Daddy. That means we don't ever get to surprise you with anything, though."

"A situation that's extremely good for my blood-pressure, little monkey. Don't you want to put on a movie for everyone?" I nod at the big screen on the wall, currently dark.

"You don't think that's disrespectful?" Emmy asks, her tone hesitant. "I don't want it to seem like we're having a party when Fleur's so badly hurt."

Sweet baby. I kiss the tip of her nose. "No, it's not disrespectful, baby. I think it will help keep everyone's spirits up so we can give Fleur the support she's going to need. Put on something you think everyone will enjoy."

Emmy nods. "Goose movie."

I'm not sure what the goose movie is but I send her on her way with a pat on her panda-onesied bottom.

When Theo arrives, it's with the good news that the district attorney has agreed to issue warrants for five of the identified Wolf-pack members. The Doms cluster around the dining room table, listening to Theo elaborate, while I wake Livvy for a feed and her bath.

Taking care of my daughter calms and centers me the same way taking care of Emily does. It's the same set of core needs: to care and to protect. But there's no lingering shame. Emily's helped me unpick my caregiver needs from my sexual needs. Even topping Lucy and Cappa outside the club has helped separate the two. As I smile down at Livvy, and she coos and burbles back at me, I realize this is another gift Emily has given me. A future with my daughter without doubt, without fear that the feelings which tainted my adolescence might haunt my future.

I lean down and rub noses with Livvy as I dry her and put her in a fresh diaper and onesie. "Your mommy, the mommy of your heart who is the only mommy you'll ever know, is a wonder and we're going to spend our lives making sure she's the happiest little wife and mother there's ever been."

Livvy burbles in confirmation and grabs at my nose.

I carry Livvy downstairs for good nights. Checking on the subbies, I find several of them already dozing. Sammi's completely out, curved like a string bean in his green onesie between Bren and Lucy. I approve of the containment. Yummy's up on the couch under one of Emmy's fuzzy blue blankets. Austin's yawning as he watches a gaggle of geese run around after a girl on the TV screen. Emmy, Moon, Justine, and Laurel are painting each other's toenails. When Emmy sees me with the baby, she hops up and waddles to me on her heels, keeping her iridescent toes, trapped between bright pink foam spacers, elevated.

"Good night, Livvy-bit." Emmy takes the baby from me for a cuddle and a kiss before handing her back. "You're okay putting her down, Daddy?"

"I am, baby girl. And you have earned such a big reward."

"I have?"

"Mmm-hmm. I'll tell you why later. Relax with your friends."

Despite today's horrors, she smiles at me and returns to the subbie pile.

Livvy fusses when I take her upstairs and lay her down in her cot, probably stimulated by the attention. Even a week ago, I'd have panicked at hearing her little cries. But I've seen Emily deal with this. I give Livvy a pacifier, settle my hand on her tummy in case she's having trouble digesting her bottle, and sing to her.

Before I've finished Lennon's "Imagine," she's still and silent, sucking gently on the pacifier. I brush a kiss across her forehead and turn off everything but the adorable turtle night light as I leave my daughter to sleep.

thirty-seven

EMILY

I LOVE SUBBIE SLEEPOVERS, even if the reason for this one is awful. I love them even more when Daddy lets me fall asleep in the subbie pile but then carries me upstairs to our big bed. As good as sleepovers are, sleeping with Daddy is always better. He seems to understand that I'm too sad for Os and just cuddles me all night.

When I wake up in the morning, Daddy's still asleep beside me, even though it's well past the time he usually gets up. I think yesterday was a lot for him, too.

I ease my way out of bed and use the bathroom quickly because it will be in demand today with so many people in the house, even if Warrin, Bravo, and Sean took their subbies home last night and Jiro and Laurel went back to their hotel. A hotel that should become Miranda-free today. And, yes, I intend to call to make sure. Just because I don't plan to add to the woman's misery by pushing for her prosecution, doesn't mean I'm not going to ensure she leaves the country. The Mir-beast needs to go.

I check on Livvy, who is awake and kicking happily in her

sleeping sack but not crying. The floor around her crib is littered with Little Larrys, including one that she somehow managed to pull or kick off the bar of sensory toys over the crib.

"Has someone been caber tossing this morning, Livvy-bit? What a strong girl!"

I gather up the stuffed dinosaurs and baby. A quick change of diaper and onesie and she's ready for breakfast. According to her schedule, she's with Master Mac today but I don't know if Daddy will want to keep to the schedule with everything that's going on.

"We'll just be flexible today, won't we, baby?" I tell her as I take her downstairs. I hear footsteps and water running upstairs, so Mac or Bren or both are up. The great room is dark and quiet and someone's drawn the heavy curtain we rarely use between the living room area and the kitchen/dining room area. I duck through the curtain and find Mr. De Leon sitting at the dining table with a cup of coffee.

Daddy definitely did not give Mr. De Leon access to the house but it probably shouldn't surprise me that he's here.

"Good morning, Mr. De Leon."

"Good morning, Emily. I made some scrambled eggs and coffee. I hope you don't mind."

"No, sir, I don't mind." Daddy may but I don't. People who feed themselves without making a mess in my kitchen are my favorite kind of guest. I can't see so much as a dirty fork as I move around the island and take out packs of frozen breakfast links to defrost.

"I hear water running. Is your daddy up?"

I shake my head. "Yesterday was a tough day. He's having a lie-in."

Mr. De Leon turns his coffee cup around in his hands. "Yes, it was."

I saw him with Fleur at our Halloween-Eve-Eve party. They were cuddling during the ghost stories. Does he have feelings for her? Or is it just that he's been spending a lot of time with Cappa, and Cappa and Fleur are close?

Those aren't questions I'm going to ask today. They're not important in the face of what's happened.

"Have you seen Fleur?" I ask.

He shakes his head. "She's not conscious yet so they're only allowing her designated medical contact in. But Jack assisted with her surgery last night and I was able to talk to him when I got back into the country."

Was he out of the country? I thought Cappa was staying at his house?

"She had another surgery?" I ask hesitantly as I prepare Livvy's bottle.

Mr. De Leon nods. "The bone around her left eye was broken. The surgeon in New Jersey set it but the surgeon at Presbyterian was concerned about something called recession, so they did another surgery last night."

"Daddy didn't let me hear about her injuries yesterday. Are they very bad?"

Mr. De Leon tips his head from side to side but doesn't look up from his coffee cup. "I've seen worse."

I have a feeling he means on a battlefield. And that he's being cavalier because he doesn't want to upset me.

"Do they know when she'll wake up?" I ask.

"No. It could be a few days yet. They're letting her sleep as long as her body needs to."

I sit down across from him with Livvy and her feeding supplies. "Would you like to feed Livvy, Mr. De Leon?" I ask.

He glances up from his coffee cup, surprise written across his face. Mr. De Leon almost never looks straight at you, even when he talks to you. He has startling, gray eyes, like a Husky. Today, they're red-rimmed and bloodshot.

"Yes, I would, Emily. Thank you."

I push the feeding supplies across the table before walking around to give him the baby. He holds her correctly: at a 45-degree angle with the bottle horizontal, the milk just filling the nipple so she has to suck. I see he's remembered the British nurse's instructions.

"We're doing paced feedings," I explain to him. "She should be stopping to take a breath every three to five sucks. Less or more than that and we stop to give her a break."

Mr. De Leon nods. He holds the bottle like he'd hold a cup of tea, with his pinkie-finger extended. Livvy grabs his finger and stares up at him as she sucks.

"Hey, baby," he says. "Seriously doubt you remember me but it's good to see you again."

If she didn't remember him at all, she'd probably be fussing, although Livvy's very calm with strangers, possibly from spending the first month of her life in the hospital, being handled by lots of different nurses and doctors.

"Do you like babies, Mr. De Leon?" I ask.

He nods without looking away from the baby.

"Would you like some of your own some day?"

He chuckles. "Are you offering?"

"No, sir."

"Sorry, I know that was rude. I'm not used to people asking me personal questions. Yes, I would like a baby or two of my own someday but not until after my father dies. He's never getting his hands on my kids."

"Oh, I'm sorry."

"Nothing for you to be sorry for. How's your mum? I know she's in a home."

I prop my head on my hand and watch Livvy feed. "She's not doing so well. She has advanced dementia. She doesn't remember anyone. She has delusions. But the home she's in is very nice. They take good care of her."

"My mum was institutionalized for three years before she died," he says. "Sometimes, the best we can do for the people we love is let someone else take care of them."

"Is it the best we can do for them?" I ask. "Because some days it feels like a cop-out."

Mr. De Leon's eyes flash to mine. "You're a very good writer, Emily. I've read three of your books. Could you have cared for your mother and written your books, too?"

He's read my books? Stunned, I shake my head.

"I couldn't have done my job and cared for my mother, either. Just visiting her once a week left me a husk. The people who cared for my mother and are caring for yours have the skills and ability to do what we can't. So, yes, it is the best we can do for them."

I look down at the table and let his words sink in. They soothe a raw place in my heart that I wasn't even aware of.

"Thank you," I say quietly.

"You're welcome. If you'd ever like to talk about what's happening with your mum, I'm happy to listen. I understand what it's like to watch someone you love lose themselves by inches."

"I will. Sometimes I really struggle after I've visited her."

"You can call me anytime. Your daddy has my number."

"Thank you."

He sets the bottle down on the table, props Livvy up with a hand on her chest, and rubs her back. She lets out three, froggy burps and then coos.

Mr. De Leon chuckles before settling her back in the crook of his arm and offering her the bottle and his pinkie again.

"How are you liking being a mum?" he asks.

I could tell him I'm not Livvy's mum; I'm Daddy's best little babysitter. But I don't feel like a babysitter anymore. Livvy's as much my family as Daddy or Master Mac or my Big Sub Bestie.

"I love it," I tell him honestly.

"How's the balance of parenthood and littlehood?" he asks.

"Is 'littlehood' a thing?" I grin at him, which he must see in his peripheral vision, because he smiles down at Livvy. Littlehood is unquestionably a thing, I just like teasing him gently because he's new to the lifestyle. "It's good. Daddy's schedule keeps everything balanced. I'm more of a middle anyway. It hasn't been hard to wrap parenthood into my middleness."

Mr. De Leon nods without taking his eyes off the baby. "Do you think it would be more difficult to balance if you went younger and couldn't care for Livvy while you were being very little?"

"Probably," I admit. "But I also think I'd have trouble sustaining a very young mindset for long periods of time. I might just ask Daddy to build in a block of time every day for me to be very young while someone else looks after Livvy."

"That makes sense—" Mr. De Leon breaks off; his eyes slide toward the curtain. "Your daddy's up."

His hearing's really good. Now that he mentions it, I can hear the slap of Daddy's huge wolfy feet across the floor but I didn't notice it until he brought it to my attention. Daddy pushes through the curtain.

"Myles? Sorry, I didn't see your message until just now."

"That's because you were asleep when I sent it at four in the morning. Like a normal person." Mr. De Leon's mouth twitches. "You're allowed to sleep, Logan."

"Have you?"

Mr. De Leon's smile dies. "Not yet."

"How many days of 'not yet' is that?" Daddy asks.

"Two. I had trouble getting back on short notice. Had to do some hiking." His mouth twitches again. "And steal a motorcycle."

Daddy chuckles. "Baby, can I help with breakfast?"

The right answer is "no" because Bren and I have breakfast under control and anyone else in the kitchen just gets in our way. But Daddy's wearing his frowny line this morning even though he's only been up for five minutes: he hasn't even brushed his hair or shaved yet. I can tell he needs to feel useful.

"Yes, Daddy," I say, before rising from my chair and sinking down on my knees in front of him. I open my mouth.

Mr. De Leon swears softly. "I keep forgetting to ask for that."

Daddy cups my face in his big, warm palm. "The beauty of a relationship with your submissive is that you don't have to ask. Very good girl, Emily. Daddy's going to take a rain check until after breakfast. We'll take a shower together when Mac takes Livvy to daycare and then you can offer me your mouth. I love you very much, sweetheart."

"I love you too, Daddy."

He offers me his hand and I take it, letting him pull me to my feet. "What can Daddy do to help with breakfast?"

"Can you get out plates and silverware and stack them on the island, then get out the warming plate and big tray for the sausages? I'll put the sausages on the grill and then could you keep an eye on them and turn them every five minutes?"

"Yes, little girl, I can do all that."

I give him a kiss on the chin before trotting off into the kitchen.

Dana and Austin are next up, emerging quietly from the basement. Dana has a bad shoulder, Austin's told me, so sleeping on the floor, even on a pile of cushions and pillows and blankets and subbies, is out. Austin offers to help me in the kitchen while Dana takes a turn feeding Livvy. I get Austin mixing biscuits, which he can do on the other side of the island so there aren't too many butts in my kitchen, while I make gravy.

I hear Dana and Mr. De Leon talking quietly over the baby's sucking noises. They're using words like "drug withdrawal," "extensive therapy," "permanent scarring." I know they're talking about Fleur. Each word I catch makes my stomach whir horribly. I catch Austin's eye. He gives me a worried nod.

I've put the biscuits in and started scrambling eggs when I finally hear Master Mac and Bren come through the great room.

They're easy to hear because they're having a full-blown argument, even though they're trying to keep it quiet in deference to the five subbies still sleeping on the floor in front of the TV. But I know because Bren doesn't hiss like that unless she's pissed off. She also doesn't march into spaces with her arms crossed over her chest, even though she's just wearing a "Navy men know where to put their missiles" shirt that barely covers her thighs.

Mr. De Leon chuckles softly before he takes Livvy back from Dana and burps her.

As soon as Master Mac lets the curtain fall closed behind him, Bren whirls on him, planting her hands on her hips.

"I love you, Sir, and I say this with all due respect but you are fucking wrong."

It's Mac's turn to cross his arms over his chest. "Is that so, girl?"

"Yes. If you hadn't been born in the damn Renaissance you'd know that you can't keep a fifteen-year-old from finding out what she wants to know. Kids have unprecedented access to information now with nothing more than a phone. I'm betting True can program rings around you. Any parental control you set up, she's going to work around it. She's gotten a good look at kink now, and she's not going to let it go just because the authority figures in her life—most of whom she doesn't trust anyway—tell her to. Why are you forcing her to stumble her way into kink through what she finds on the internet?"

"Cause she's fifteen fucking years old. She should be in school, doing the things fifteen-year-olds do, mooning over rock stars and gossiping about who has a crush on who—"

"Oh my fucking Benevolence," Bren hisses, throwing her hands up. "Maybe that's what fifteen-year-olds did five hundred years ago when *you* were fifteen but that's not what they do now, Sir. She's already had sex. She's already watched scenes. She broke into a kink club because she identified it as a safe space. She's *actively seeking out submission* and you're denying it to her because of a number on a calendar."

"I'm denying it to her because it's the law, girl. Anyone who acts as her dominant right now is breaking the law."

"Only if they have sex with her! There are a thousand ways you or any other experienced Dom could top her that wouldn't break the law."

"Any *experienced* Dom is going to be a decade older than her."

"That's what this is about, isn't it? It's the same fucking thing over and over. It's the perception that an older man is preying on her, grooming her, when she's the one who is actively seeking out his dominance. You haven't done that to me, Sir, and you wouldn't do that to her. She needs rules. She needs guidance. She needs a safety net. Or she's going to find it on her own. She's going to get online with some goddamn predator who really does groom her. He's going to draw her into an unsafe space and break her. She's going to be preyed on just like—"

She breaks off, wild eyed and panting.

"Say it, little goddess," Mac growls. "Say it."

"Okay, just like I was! Is that what you want to hear? That I'm projecting my experiences onto True? I am. Because I know what it's like in the chat rooms and the clubs. I know what it means to get a fake ID and sneak in when you're far too young and inexperienced. I know what happens when you taunt someone who's a predator rather than a real dominant and they turn on you. I *know*, okay?" Tears roll down Bren's cheeks and she dashes them away angrily. "Please, Sir, please, can't we do better? Why does this have to happen over and over again? Can't we learn from our fucking mistakes?"

Mac holds out his arms and she rushes into them. He holds her against his chest while she cries. His big hand smooths her dreadlocks down her back.

"Yes, sweetheart," he soothes. "We can do better. We'll figure something out for True and you'll finally tell me what the hell happened to you before you found Blunts."

"It's ancient history," Bren mumbles into his collar, her voice broken.

"Clearly not if it has you tossing and turning all night and baiting your Dom first thing in the morning when you know he's not at his best before a cup of coffee." He rubs her back. "It's going to be okay."

She fists his sweatshirt and nods into his neck.

"Make me a cup of coffee and then come sit on my lap. I'm going to need you close for a bit."

"Yes, Sir."

With a final pat, Mac releases her. As she comes into the kitchen, wiping her eyes, Austin and I sandwich her in a hug. To my surprise, as soon as we release her, Daddy turns from the grill and folds her into a hug, too. Bren doesn't seek hugs, ever, and since Mac collared her, I've seen her sidestep hugs from other Doms. I guess Daddy's the exception. He's a good exception to pick; Daddy's hugs are the best.

We're just finishing breakfast when the doorbell goes. Daddy checks his phone before he gives me the nod to answer it. At least I know it's not Miranda.

A *crowd* of people are at the door. Master Theo, Mistress Maude, Daddy Bravo and Yummy, Charlotte and her gorgeous new master, Ian, Matty and Faolan, Saoirse and her daddy Sutter, and Master Ten. They file in quietly as I take coats and scarves. I get lots of hugs before people filter through into the great room. Finally, I'm just left with Master Ten as he removes his huge boots and sets them in a row with all the other footwear. Geez, I thought Daddy had big feet.

Master Ten turns to me. His eyes are even more red-rimmed and bloodshot than Mr. De Leon's.

He opens his arms to me.

What am I supposed to do? Master Ten and I are not on hugging terms. Or at least I didn't think we were. Maybe we are today.

I rush to him and wrap him in a big hug.

Daddy's hugs are still the best but Master Ten gives surprisingly good hugs. His chest is just the right balance of firm and giving. He squeezes me but not so hard it hurts. He doesn't crush my face into his pec but lets me find my own place to fit my cheek. He takes a lot of deep, broken breaths while he holds me. I think he might be crying. I don't lift my head or release him until his breathing's steady and his arms fall away.

I take his hand and lead him into the great room.

Only to find Daddy in a standoff with Saoirse's daddy, Sutter. Daddy's standing and despite the fact that he's barefoot, bare-chested, and still hasn't brushed his hair or shaved—or maybe because of it—he looks like a Titan. Daddy's crossed his arms over his chest and the position makes his shoulders, pecs, and biceps look even bigger. Like, Thor huge. Sutter's probably only an inch shorter than Daddy. Even though he's blond, there's something lithe, twisty, and mischievous about Sutter. Loki-ish.

"Why are you even here?" Daddy growls at Sutter.

"I invited him," Mr. De Leon says. He hasn't moved from the dining table. He has Livvy in his lap, propped against his chest. She's gripping both of his pinkies.

Daddy turns to shoot a death-glare at Mr. De Leon. You'd think Mr. De Leon wouldn't see it, because he's looking down at Livvy's wispy curls but I have a sense that Mr. De Leon sees everything.

He smiles at the top of Livvy's head.

Sutter shoots out a hand at Daddy and I catch my breath. Daddy does, too. But then he takes Sutter's hand and shakes it, probably a little too hard if the flexing of Sutter's back is anything to go by.

"I'd never let my personal vendetta get in the way of giving a submissive the support and protection she needs," Sutter tells Daddy. "Whatever my feelings about the club, I'm happy to put them aside until Fleur is on the road to recovery and whoever hurt her is neutralized."

Might just be the writer in me but the way he says "neutralized" sounds an awful lot like "eliminated."

Master Ten clears his throat and I realize I've stopped behind Sutter, ready to tackle him from behind if he's not nice to my daddy. I glance up at Master Ten. He glances at my free hand, which is balled in a fist. I tuck it against my tummy and blink up at him innocently. Should have worn my cat ears this morning. No one can suspect me of planning to jump on a Dom from behind and batter him about the head for being mean to Daddy when I'm wearing cat ears.

Master Ten chuckles and tugs me forward, around Sutter. Ten hands me to Daddy on the way into the kitchen to get himself a cup of coffee. He did visit quite a bit when Daddy was first home from being injured, so I guess he remembers where everything is but it's weird to see him make himself at home in our house when he's been so antagonistic to Daddy.

I guess we're all united in a common cause today.

thirty-eight

LOGAN

I CAN'T for the life of me understand why Myles would invite someone who wants to destroy Blunts to my fucking house, even in the midst of the crisis over Fleur.

"Because he's paying for it," Myles says, once we're seated in my office.

It's a reduced group: Myles, Theo, Bravo, Ten, Sutter, Mac, and me. Max is listening in on my earpiece. Maude and Javier rounded up half of the subbies and Doms and took them to the hospital. Fleur's still not awake but Cappa needs reinforcements. They're going until noon and then the "second shift" will go over. I've suggested to Maude and Javier that they bring Cappa back here at the end of the "second shift" but Javier just shook his head sadly.

I can't even check the app to see how Cappa's doing. He's not allowed his phone or monitoring band in the hospital room.

"Paying for what, exactly?" I ask, sipping a cup of tea Emily slipped into my hand as she herded us into my office. True arrived, Emmy set up her laptop and put Livvy in her rocking swing, and they got on with what they needed to be doing. My sweet little girl who follows her Daddy's rules, even when her Daddy's struggling to focus on anything other than the crisis at hand.

"For the moment, I'm paying for recon and surveillance," Sutter says. He's in one of the guest chairs in front of my desk. Theo's in the other one. Bravo's next to Mac on the couch. Myles and Ten are leaning against the two doors. "Depending on what the recon and surveillance dredges up, we'll see what else there is to pay for."

I look from Sutter's bright eyes to Myles'. Myles is looking at the floor, his hair falling around his face but I know he's aware of my gaze.

"Who's being surveilled?" I ask.

"The three members of the Wolfpack that Theo doesn't have enough on to arrest," Myles says without looking up.

How does he find out this shit? He's not a member of Blunts. He hasn't been involved in any of the management committee meetings. If I read his message right, he only got back into the country six hours ago. Bravo's the only person I've talked to about making the Wolfpack even "gone," but Myles is arranging fucking surveillance on them?

"Do you have my house wired?" I ask.

"Yes," Myles says easily. "And parts of the club now, too. You need to up the security in the staff areas. It was too easy for me to get upstairs once I got into the Spa for pool maintenance."

I grind my teeth.

Sutter lifts his coffee-cup at Myles. "No one ever notices the pool man."

Myles nods. "Logan, I'm never going to do anything with the information that would hurt the club, any of its members, or the house submissives. I'll agree to wipe all recordings after thirty days. But things are going on there that affect the people I care about. I need eyes and ears in there."

I could argue with him but I doubt there's any point. Myles is going to do whatever he wants to do.

"I thought it was four members of the Wolfpack," Sutter says, when everyone comes to the same conclusion about arguing with Myles.

"We can drop Jared Carr," Theo says, leaning an elbow on my desk. "He turned himself in last night after the grapevine ran red. I had a long talk with him off the record. He didn't know what he was getting into. Gave me some insight into how Drew approaches potential recruits. It's not directly relevant anymore but I've uploaded the recording of the interview into the cloud account Jiro set up. Drew was using the prestige of Blunts to prop up his alpha theory, so we may need to do some damage control in the local clubs where he was recruiting."

There are nods all around.

"Jared's not a problem," Theo continues. "The guy seems genuinely freaked out about all of it. He thought the Wolfpack was an inner circle within Blunts. That's what Drew and Emmett told him. They played on his desire to belong. He's been a guest at the club on and off over the past two months. He seemed more disturbed than turned on by a lot of what he's seen. He was part of the crowd during Shannie's scene. Drew primed them, telling them Shannie needed help to get out of her head during the scene. He was told what to say and when to say it. Jared's only mistake was not checking with Ty and Hart that what Drew told him was true but how many of us would interrupt a scene, particularly a scene we'd be told was difficult for the submissive, to question what we'd been told by another master? Ty approached Jared afterwards and criticized his behavior. Jared immediately apologized. I confirmed that with Ty. I think Jared's sincere. Drew invited him back to the club for the Nursery opening. Jared says he intended to confront Drew that night about what happened with Shannie but before he got a chance to, he witnessed the confrontation between Drew and you, Logan. When he heard the full extent of the claims against the Wolfpack, the guy was beside himself."

"He know where Drew is?" Ten grunts.

Theo shakes his head. "But I've uploaded all known addresses not just for him but also his family into the cloud."

"Drew's missing?" I ask. This is news to me.

Theo nods. "I had uniforms go around to all known Wolfpack members and give them a friendly scare. If they're going to lawyer-up, I want to know now. Emmett did but he's fucked. His lawyer's already talking with the district attorney about a plea if Emmett testifies against his fellow wolves. Uniforms staked out Drew's condo overnight. He didn't come home. No car in the parking space. Quick canvass of the neighbors—no one's seen him in days."

"He was at breakfast the morning after the Opening," Ten says.

Theo twists around in his chair to look at Ten. "Did you see him leave?"

Ten shakes his head. "I didn't notice. I only remember him being there because he stopped by the table to talk with Fleur and Zuki while I was in the buffet line. I think he scheduled a scene with Zuki."

"Fuck." Theo whips out his phone. "Pick up, pick up," he whispers as it rings. When a female voice answers, his face relaxes. "All okay?"

Whatever he hears reassures him.

"Did you have a scene scheduled with Drew this week?" Theo asks into the phone. "Good, good. No, if he or Emmett call you, don't answer. Call me."

Theo listens for a moment. "Yeah, that's fine. Did you hear Drew schedule a scene with Fleur at breakfast the other morning?" There's a pause while he listens. "Did she say anything else?"

He squeezes his eyes closed as he listens to her answer. "Thanks, Zuk. No, she's not awake yet. I'm sure you'll hear about it before I do, knowing the subbie network. Yeah, yeah, me, too. See you tomorrow, okay? If you need anything before then, call me."

After he says goodbye and hangs up, he rubs a hand over his face. "Zuki's safe. She canceled her scene with Drew as soon as Chess' email circulated saying that Drew and Emmett were no longer members. She wasn't a fan of the man. She heard Drew try to schedule a scene with Fleur outside the club. Fleur refused. She said she was off the clock and going home after breakfast because she had commissions to work on."

"He knew she'd be leaving the club," I point out.

Theo nods. "It's not proof but—"

"It's proof enough for me," Ten says. "Anything else? I'm going to start with known addresses."

Theo shakes his head. "I'll start an database search for his plate as a person of interest but until I have enough evidence for a warrant, my resources are limited."

Ten nods. "You can reach me on the burner. No other contact."

Theo sighs. "Don't do anything if you find him. Surveillance, right?"

Ten grunts.

"Ten, right?" Theo presses.

Ten grunts again, turns, and walks out. The front door slams a minute later.

We all look at each other. Except Myles, who seems fascinated by the pattern of my office rug.

"What's the price for a hit?" Sutter asks after the silence stretches.

Bravo starts shaking his head.

"That's not on the table," Myles says. "Detective D'Andrea has a badge. Logan and Mac have licenses. Bravo and Henry take government contracts. None of you are killing anyone."

It takes me a moment to hear what he's said. I narrow my eyes at him.

Myles lifts his head and meets my gaze for a moment. His eyes are more lupine than anything Drew's "Wolfpack" could have imagined.

They might fancy themselves hunters but there's a real hunter among us and it's not any of them.

"Did he just say what I think he said?" Max asks in my ear.

"Yes," I murmur. "We need to have a word with him."

"Uh-huh," Max agrees.

The meeting breaks up slowly. Mac collects Livvy and Bren and heads out to open his daycare. I offer Theo our bed since he looks like he's about to fall over but he says he'd rather sleep in his own bed. When he declines, Myles takes me up on the offer and trudges upstairs to sleep. Bravo asks if Yummy can stay the day with us before leaving to coordinate surveillance of the other two Wolfpack members with Henry.

Leaving me in my office staring at Sutter.

He leans back in his chair, crossing his long legs in front of him. He's wearing business clothes today: a tailored suit, crisp white button-down, and a red tie. He should be heading into a marketing meeting for probiotic yogurt or something, not sitting in my office asking the price of a contract on a man's life.

"You don't like me very much, do you?" he asks after enduring my scrutiny for a minute.

"We didn't exactly get off on the best foot, did we?" I respond. "I care about Blunts. For all its flaws, it's my second home. It's full of the people I love. My family. I feel a very personal sense of responsibility toward the house submissives. Threatening to disband my family and rob my friends of their employment and place of belonging doesn't sit well with me."

Sutter chuckles. "I could tell. I notice you did something about it, though. Faster than I expected."

"Did you know about the Wolfpack when you threatened me at the museum?"

"I threatened the club, not you. I'm all for dramatics but let's keep things in perspective. And no, I didn't know about this bullshit 'wolfpack,' as they call themselves but I knew that some of the Doms at Blunts had very unhealthy attitudes. If you'd asked me for a list— which I notice you didn't do—Drew and Emmett would have been on it."

"After you *threatened me*," I say emphatically. "I wouldn't have trusted you to tell me the truth about who you thought was a problem."

"Do you trust me now?"

"No but I'll take that list."

"Ten's on it," Sutter says, nodding at the door Ten exited out of.

I nod. "I'm aware of his issues. We're addressing them. Next."

"Karl Van Haas and the man who calls himself Shedo, although I believe his real name is Jun Hayakawa, on the committee. Among the general members, Cole Ward and Hart Garibaldi. They all made disparaging remarks about age-play and the people who practice it in Saoirse's hearing."

"I'm sorry they intimidated her," I say as I write down the names. Karl and Shedo are no surprise. They've been in Ten's corner all along. Hart's an unknown. He's a junior member, only at the club on weekends, and I don't think I've ever had a one-on-one conversation with him. He failed to protect Shannie from the Wolfpack, so he was already on my shitlist. Cole, on the other hand, I've scened with more than once, although all before I met Emily, and he was on my goddamn paintball team just a few days ago. If he had issues with age-play, he could have said something.

"Although Karl and Shedo are resistant to age-play, they're not bad Doms," I tell Sutter. "I think highly enough of Karl to trust him with the discipline of a submissive who is still exploring the depths of her masochism. I don't know Hart very well but I already have concerns about him that need to be addressed. Cole's a friend and I'll have a damn word with him."

Sutter nods. "Not everyone will accept age-play. *I* accept that. But there needs to be greater tolerance. Saoirse was just starting to let her little out and the attitude of the Blunts' Doms towards age-play set her back months. She was so repressed when she met me, that it took more than a week for her to introduce me to her stuffies. During that time, she stayed over at my place several times and I took her on a weekend to England. Can you imagine any little being without her stuffies for that long? Just because they made her too afraid to show me—*me*, her *daddy*—her littleness for fear of being judged."

Knowing how important Peter Aloha Bunny and her other stuffies are to Emily, no I can't. It makes my chest ache to know that my club brothers did that to Saoirse with their cruel, careless words.

"I can only apologize on behalf of Blunts and promise that there is change coming. It might not be as fast as you want but it is happening."

Sutter steeples his hands in front of him and taps his index fingers against his chin. "For all that we got off on the wrong foot, I believe you, Logan. And I was surprised at how quickly you started cleaning house. Surprised and impressed. So maybe we can agree to a stay of execution. Let's call it a probationary period."

As tempted as I am to use my pen like a dart and see if I can stick a bullseye right between his eyes, I ask calmly, "How long would this probationary period last?"

He spreads his hands. "Up to you. You're the catalyst of change."

"Two years," I respond, knowing that I'm trying it on.

He scoffs. "Six months."

"A year, that's the shortest it's reasonable to ask for an institutional, cultural change."

"I'll give you a year. I'll have some stipulations. Let's call them milestones. I'll email them to you."

The dart idea seems better and better. "You do that."

"Our littles are already friends, you know," Sutter says, his smile cracking wide.

That doesn't make us friends. I'll have to get past the whole threatening to dismantle my second family thing, first.

"I appreciate your help with Fleur," I say, a little grudgingly.

The smirk slides off his face. He sits forward, letting his hands dangle between his knees. "You're welcome. I'm sincere in my desire to help. Since Myles is involved, I can guess where things are going. I'm not ex-military the way you and he are but I've been hunting game since I was old enough to hold a rifle." He sits back and tips his head. "Hunting a wolf instead of a deer? I don't reckon it would be that different."

I've never hunted deer, or wolves but I suspect it is very different. It breaks something inside you, to kill another human being. It's a Rubicon you can't ever come back from. A wound that never heals. It's always there, you always know there's something you're capable of doing that other people aren't. Something deeply, deeply wrong, no matter how right the reasons.

I've seen a lot of those "two kinds of people in the world" memes but the true two kinds of people in the world are those who have murdered and those who haven't. I've come to terms with being among the former. I never want to encourage anyone to join that particular clique.

"How do you know Myles?" I ask instead of addressing the elephant in the room.

"I have a family problem, which is also a corporate problem since my business is a family business. Someone who knows someone recommended Myles to me as . . . well, a fixer. I need some corporate espionage done on the very down low. After interviewing Myles, I put him on retainer for a year. As we were talking, I realized we share certain *interests*. I mentioned I'd just joined Blunts. With a man like Myles, it's important to be scrupulously honest. A whiff of dishonesty and I'd never hear from him again. I told him about my intentions for the club—"

"Did you hire him to help you?" I interject.

If Myles accepted that assignment, I'll strangle him.

"No. Myles told me he wouldn't do anything to risk not being accepted in your circle of caregivers and littles. I understand and respect his boundary."

"Playgroup's great but it's not a substitute for Blunts," I say. "I'll accept your whole probation thing because I believe I can turn Blunts around but I'm warning you, I will fight you tooth and nail if you try to shut down my club."

"I believe you." Sutter's smirk slides back into place. "Nothing like a game against a worthy adversary, right?"

If he thinks he's my Moriarty, he can fucking well think again.

"Sure. Are we done?" I ask.

"Not quite. I'd like to formally hire you and your partners to investigate Andrew Selman and his wolfpack."

"Why? You've already got Myles on retainer."

"A number of reasons including client confidentiality. I have a feeling we're going to need it before we're done."

I can't argue with that. "I'll work up a cost estimate and email it to you. Ten doesn't work for us but if he's going to hare off tracking wolfpack members, I'd like to get his costs covered somehow."

"I don't need a cost estimate," Sutter responds with a wave. "I'll put you on retainer same as Myles. Thirty grand to start. If you antic-ipate going over that in a week, email me."

He slides his business card across my desk.

Sutter James, CEO

Whitley James Wineries

Winterwyne Entertainment Group

Who the hell is this kid? CEO at twenty-two? Throwing around thirty-thousand-dollar retainers? He's bullshitting; he has to be. If he's not, I need to get Max on him and make sure he's not fronting a drug cartel or something.

"Okay, I'll email you my terms of business. Any issues, call me."

Sutter nods. "That's fine." He stands and sticks out his hand. "I look forward to having my own P.I. on retainer." He chuckles. "My very own Daddy P.I. Talk soon, Logan."

After I shake his hand—reluctantly—he shoves his hands in his pockets and strolls out of my office.

thirty-nine

BABY DRAGON

IS it confirmation that the Mir-witch has left her hotel?

Is it that surprising hug from Master Ten?

Is it knowing that there are bad men out there who hunt and hurt submissives?

Is it the reminder of Daddy Sutter's threat to tear down Blunts?

Is it having my flight around me?

I'm not sure what it is but I am a fierce, white, baby dragon today.

After Mac takes Livvy off to daycare and Laurel arrives with her Dom, I drag Laurel upstairs. Together, we assemble a white dragon outfit. White thigh-highs, of course, because all outfits should start with thigh-highs. A white, patent leather mini-skirt that I honestly never thought I'd wear outside of Blunts. My sheer black shirt with thumb holes, because *thumb holes*.

"It's my obsidian skin," I explain to Laurel as I tug my shirt on. "Slings and arrows slide off it."

Laurel nods. "Very important for a white dragon."

I thought so, too.

We debate what to put over the shirt but eventually agree on a corset that I usually wear with my steam-punkier outfits like the ones I've been wearing to the Blunts Marketplace. It's white with black velvet stripes over the boning and black satin ribbons. Laurel helps me lace up. Cat ears on top, of course, because even though I'm a baby dragon today, baby dragons need cat ears. Well, this baby dragon needs cat ears.

I check my armor in the mirror. No holes in my breast like Smaug. My collar gleams at my throat. My engagement ring glitters on my finger.

"Ready for battle," I declare.

"Good. Let's destroy this wolfpack. Wolves don't stand a chance against dragons."

I agree but that's not who my battle is with today.

I've never been happier. Livvy was the addition to our family I didn't know we needed to make it feel complete. I can't imagine loving any man more than I love Daddy. And for the very first time in my life, I'm completely certain that the man I love, loves me the same way. We fell fast for each other but our love isn't fragile or fickle. It's weathered some serious storms; it's forever. After Ash, I didn't think I could believe in forever-love again but Daddy convinced me. He keeps convincing me every day. No matter what life throws our way, he won't stop loving me.

And I won't ever stop loving my Daddy.

But there's been a niggle in my happiness. I've tried to ignore it because I want to be the bigger person. But having her show up in my safe space last night when I didn't invite her and having her lean on Daddy for emotional support crossed a boundary.

I'm okay with him topping her with his app and their once-a-week scenes. I've watched enough of them to know that, for Daddy, it's purely service topping. He's helping Lucy explore her masochism safely.

Listening to the subbies tell their stories to True, telling her my own, I realized that I've been jealous not just of Lucy herself but also that she's getting something I wish I'd had. My first tops were good tops. They taught me a lot. But they weren't as wholly unselfish and caring as Daddy. It's an impossible standard, I know. There's a reason Daddy's Master of Training at one of the most prestigious lifestyle clubs in the country.

It's a jealousy I'm happy to set aside. Lucy deserves what so few of us get: a truly loving sadist. I'm happy for Daddy to continue giving her that.

I'm not happy for her to seek anything else from him, though. They don't have a relationship outside of the service topping. She's not allowed to look to him for emotional support. She has her own friends and family for that. Daddy might have been her friend before he withdrew from the club, and she could have been mine but when she asked him to top her outside of Blunts, she made herself not our friend. She moved our relationship onto a different plane. Maybe we can be friends in the future but I'm not okay with her now.

It's time she knows where the line is.

Once, this kind of situation would have sent me into a spiral. I'd have withdrawn into a book or one of my hobbies. I'd have let my insecurities convince me it wasn't worth the fight. Or I'd have let the niggle build until I exploded and provoked a confrontation. I always come out of confrontations humiliated, diminished, and indignant. I don't like them but I didn't understand how to manage myself to avoid them.

Not until Daddy.

As much as Daddy's made a safe space for me to live my best little life in, he's also made a safe space for me to express myself. He's taught me how to ask for what I want without shame, without confrontation. All I have to do is tell my Daddy what I need and he'll help me make it happen.

I don't stomp downstairs, because even fierce, white, baby dragons are respectful of their Daddy's staircases. Also, I think I heard Mr. De Leon come up for a nap in my little room while I was dressing, so I don't want to wake him. I go arm-in-arm with Laurel.

She mentions wanting to find a dragonish present from the flight for Fleur and I agree.

At the bottom of the stairs, I kiss Laurel on the cheek and tell her I'll meet her in the kitchen.

I turn into Daddy's office.

He's sitting at his desk, typing something on his computer. I kneel next to his desk and wait.

After a minute, he stops typing and I hear the whoosh of a sent email. I don't think Daddy knows how to turn off notification noises. My poor Luddite Daddy.

He turns in his chair and puts his bare feet on either side of my knees.

"That's a spectacular outfit, baby doll. I feel like it needs a jeweled pink butt plug, though."

Daddy and his thing for pink.

"May I be excused to get the plug, Daddy?" I ask.

"In a minute. Did you come to check on me or is there something you'd like to say?"

"Something I'd like to say."

"You have my full attention, little girl."

I fold my hands together in my lap and look up at him. "I'd like Lucy to leave. And I'd like to make it clear to her that I have no objection to your topping arrangement but I'd prefer that she doesn't come over outside of your scheduled scenes. The house is my safe space. I don't want her in it."

Daddy rubs his chin. "Okay, sweetheart. I hear you. This is absolutely your safe space and if there's anyone you don't want in it, I'm happy to exclude them. In fact, I'm happy to move my remaining scenes with Lucy to the club. Can I ask what brought this on?"

"I don't like that she came here seeking emotional support. I know what's going on with Fleur is upsetting for everyone. But she shouldn't be leaning on you for emotional support. That's not the relationship she asked for, nor the one you agreed to. I feel like this is pushing the boundaries in exactly the way I told you I was afraid of at the start. I've been understanding of her asking you to top her. I've been the bigger person even when I've felt the green-eyed monster nipping at me. I've obeyed your rules about being respectful to guests. But I'm not okay with her crossing this line."

Daddy smiles and holds out his arms. "Come here, little girl."

I climb up into his lap. He gives me a deep, sweet kiss, sinking his hand into my hair and holding me in that daddy way that tells me I'm safe and loved and appreciated.

"I am so proud of you, Emmy," he breathes against my forehead when he lets me up for air.

"Because I'm a fierce, white, baby dragon wearing cat ears?"

His chuckle buzzes against my skin. "Yes, that's exactly why. But also because I know how much courage it took for you to tell me this. You're my wonderful, brave little girl and I am so proud of you."

"You're not a little mad that I'm excluding Lucy from your house?" I ask.

"Not the tiniest bit. First of all, it's *our* house. You have just as much right as I do to say who can and can't be in *our* house. Second, I'm just so proud of you for recognizing that this crossed a boundary for you and telling me that I don't have any space in my heart to be mad. I ask a huge amount of you, Emmy. It's very important that you be able to say, 'this is enough, Daddy.' You say it so rarely, and I'm so pleased you have."

I squeeze his firm middle.

"Would you like me to go tell her?" Daddy asks.

"If I do it respectfully, can I?"

"Of course, sweetheart. Do you want backup?"

I consider it for a moment. "If I do it in the hallway with the office door open so you can hear me and make sure I'm saying the right things, would that be okay?"

He kisses my forehead. "It would but whatever you say will be the right thing, baby doll. This is your house, your safe space. There's nothing wrong about asking someone who is making you uncomfortable to leave it."

As resolute as only a baby dragon can be, I nod and climb off his lap. "With or without the butt plug?"

"Whatever will make you feel more comfortable, my sweet-heart," Daddy says, sliding his hand up my skirt to pat my bottom. "But please put it in afterwards if you decide to speak with Lucy without it."

I give him a cheeky salute, trot out of his office and upstairs to get the plug. The jeweled plugs don't hurt. They're not a trial to keep in. They're just a nice reminder of Daddy. I put in the plug, wash my hands, and shoo Sable away from the door of my little room. Some of the older doors in the house have antique handles that Sable can get a grip on with his naughty claws. If he catches them right, he can get the door open. I've watched him do it a few times, mostly to Daddy while he's in the bathroom. I haven't stopped my kitty those times because the results can be very funny. But I'm not sure how Mr. De Leon will react to having five pounds of cat land on his chest when he's trying to sleep. Or worse, ten claws embed themselves in his feet.

I click my fingers at Sable, which I hope won't wake Mr. De Leon but should persuade my kitty to follow me to the kitchen for a treat.

Meowing his head off, like he hasn't already had breakfast and a treat today plus a bug he found somewhere whose wing he left me to admire, Sable follows me down the stairs. He sounds like an air-raid siren. Poor Mr. De Leon. I grimace at my cat. I swear he smiles back at me. Maybe he doesn't like Mr. De Leon invading his space any more than I like Lucy invading mine.

I give Sable a treat to keep him occupied. Lucy's sitting at the dining table talking with True, Yummy, Sammi, Justine, Hunter, Laurel, and Jiro. While I'm thinking through what to say to Lucy, my phone buzzes with a text. It's Cynnie saying that she and Max are on the way over now that Theo's left. I send her back a million thumbs up and buzzy-bees.

I make myself a cup of chamomile tea and sip it, looking out at the blustery, gray day through the French doors. It's gotten cold since that day we played Doms v subs paint ball at Blunts. There's a little snow in the corners of the yard where it fell overnight and the watery sun hasn't melted it yet. There hasn't been a white Christmas in New York City in a long time. Certainly not while I've been an adult. I remember reading that the City had a white Christmas every six years on average, so we're overdue. But maybe with global warming that's a thing of the past. It would be nice to have one this year, although we won't be around to enjoy it for very long since we're flying to Vegas for the wedding right after what Daddy calls "Boxing Day": the day after Christmas. We're going to take in the opulence of the casinos, fly over the Grand Canyon in a helicopter, and go kayaking at this pretty place called Emerald Cave that Daddy said he's always wanted to see. Niall, Shaan, and Vashi are joining us for the week and everyone else who's coming to the wedding is filtering in before the ceremony on Sunday.

Like our collaring ceremony, there are a crazy number of people coming to what was an attempt to quietly elope. Daddy can't do anything quietly. I've overheard Master Javier and Mistress Maude plotting in the club's Library; something about Elvis. Between them and Master Niall who is coming as Irish Elvis and the penchant of our friends to role-play, I'm a little concerned the wedding might be attended by fifty Elvises of various ages and girths.

But one person I know isn't coming? The blonde sitting at my dining room table laughing at something True's said. She's not coming because I haven't invited her. Just like I haven't invited her into *our* house today.

Time to make sure she knows she's not welcome.

I put my empty teacup in the sink and walk quietly over to the table. I tap Lucy on the shoulder. When she looks up at me, I smile and ask if I can have a word with her. She looks startled but smiles back at me before she excuses herself.

One may smile, and smile, and be a villain.

I thought that about Miranda. Quite a bit actually and look how she turned out. I don't think Lucy is a villain. Just unhappy and looking for a way to carve out her own happiness. I understand that but I'm not going to let her carve her happiness out of Daddy.

As we pass through the great room, I nod at her bag which is sitting behind the couch with a dozen other bags. Most of the people who went to the hospital left their bags, so I assume they're returning tonight. I'm good with that. I like having a lot of friends around in times of crisis.

They just have to *be* friends.

"You might want your bag," I say.

"Oh, okay." She snags her bag with the straps over her forearm. It's a small bag. Maybe she didn't intend to stay a second night. She probably has to work tomorrow. I don't care. Another hour of having her in my house is too long.

I close the door to the great room behind her when she follows me into the hallway. She looks at me, her brow beetling, when I find her coat on the coat rack.

"Emily, is everything okay?" she asks.

"No, it's not," I say. "I'd like you to leave. I'm okay with you coming to the house to do scenes with Daddy but I'm not okay with you being here at other times."

Lucy blinks her blue eyes rapidly. Is it a blue-eyed, blonde thing that makes me feel particularly threatened? Hmm, probably not. Daddy's ex Rachel has caramel-brown hair and brown eyes. It's not even all of Daddy's former subs, because I get along well with his ex, Luisa.

"Emily, have I done something wrong? Have I offended you?"

It sounds mean in my head to say she has. But Daddy always encourages me to be honest. I try to say it kindly.

"I'm not offended," I say. "But I'm not okay with you seeking emotional support from Daddy."

"I-I'm not—" She sputters, then closes her mouth. She looks around, like she's seeking answers. When her eyes settle on me, they have tears in them. Her cheeks burn crimson. "I'm so sorry, Emily."

I nod. She's not a villain. She's a nice person at heart. Before she asked Daddy to top her, I felt close to her. Maybe when he stops topping her, we can be friends. But she's carrying a torch for Daddy and those feelings have driven her here, to seek solace from him, in my safe space. And that is not okay.

She holds out her arms. I could refuse her. Shove her coat into her waiting hands and push her out the door. But that's definitely not being the bigger person. I hug her quickly and give her an extra pat when I release her. She takes her coat and slides her feet into low boots. She lingers by the door and I can tell she wants me to say something to make it better. To excuse her actions and show she's forgiven.

She's not and I don't. I open the door for her and give her a smile as she leaves.

I close the door behind her and lean against it, drawing a deep breath in and letting it out slowly.

I am a fierce, white, baby dragon. Hear me roar.

Even if I roar quietly and with a smile.

Through the open door to Daddy's office, he calls, "Come here, my little wonder. I want a hug."

Grinning, I trot through and dive into my Daddy's embrace.

forty

LOGAN

I'VE ALWAYS THOUGHT of Max as an unassuming guy. In any group, he drops into the background. If he made any effort, he'd stand out. He's good-looking, scary-smart, and can find out anything about anyone in less time than it takes me to make a cup of tea. But he'd rather be wallpaper.

He's not unassuming today. He's angry. It crackles off him as he sets up at the dining table, unfolding keyboards and screens.

"You hacked Presbyterian, didn't you?" I ask.

"Yes," he says curtly.

"And?"

"And Theo's password was laughably easy to crack. Mother's maiden name and date of birth. Seriously? Someone should slap his IT department. I got into his investigation file. He barely has enough to hold the five he's brought in for questioning. The only one he's got enough to charge is Emmett. Unless someone rolls over, these assholes are going to walk. His file on Drew is three pages long. Background and bullshit. Nothing to hang the fucker with. He's too slippery."

388

I glance at our girls, who are in front of the television, watching a movie and playing Chutes and Ladders with True. They may be little but their ears are big. I appreciate that Max hasn't detailed Fleur's injuries in front of them.

"Okay." I acknowledge his anger with a pat on the shoulder. "What are we doing?"

"We're getting leverage. Two possibilities. That Hans asshole is in the middle of an ugly custody battle. If I can tie him to anything, we threaten to turn it over to his wife's divorce lawyer. She's a shark; if he's not careful, he'll never see his kids again. The other one is a long-shot. There are five years between Drew graduating from Mary Mann Academy and graduating from Cornell. He might have taken a gap year but that doesn't seem like his family's style. They're all fucking overachievers. I'm hoping he had an involuntary sabbatical during his time at Cornell. If there's an allegation of sexual assault that can't be substantiated, that's the way a lot of these colleges deal with the offender."

"Jack went to Cornell," I remember.

"I know. I'm hacking into their student records through his alumni email."

I shake my head. Max is fucking scary; I'm glad he's on my side.

I make a pot of coffee and let him work.

Myles doesn't emerge from Emily's little room until the onions Emily's frying for dinner waft upstairs. The shower goes on briefly. He stumbles downstairs looking like he still needs another eight hours of sleep.

Max clears enough of the table for Emily to serve dinner. The mood around the table's subdued. Max has spent most of the afternoon grunting in frustration. Twice, he texted phone numbers and a brief list of questions to me. I holed up in my office to do the interviews. I thought we were getting closer when the second call was to a woman named Mary Roberts who confirmed that she knew Drew at Cornell. As soon as I began asking about his year off, she hung up and blocked my number.

We don't have time for dead-ends.

After dinner, I sit at the end of the table among Max's electronics with Myles, Max, Mac, and Jiro. Max gives us a low-voiced update of what he's been able to find today, although it's not much more than he told me this morning.

"Drew's year off definitely wasn't voluntary," Max says, tapping a white stylus against his palm. "But the disciplinary file attached to his student records isn't digital. There's just a reference number. It's got to be to a paper file. Short of going to Cornell and getting that file, I don't know how much I'm going to be able to find out. We need a witness."

"What if we turn Mary Roberts over to Theo? See if he can get her to talk?" I suggest.

"Burns me unless you can figure out another credible way we found her," Max says.

"Drew and Jack are how many years apart?"

"Three. They overlapped at Cornell by a year."

"Friend of a friend?" I suggest. "Jack remembers something about Drew when he overhears us talking about him?"

"Plausible," Myles says, turning his coffee cup around in his hands. That's his third cup since he woke up. I don't think he intends to sleep tonight.

"I'll run it by Jack," I offer.

Myles nods. "I think it's time to discuss Plan B."

"What's Plan B?" I ask.

Myles lifts his head and looks straight at Jiro. "If you have moral concerns, now would be the time to leave."

Jiro holds Myles' gaze. "I don't think that will be necessary."

Myles watches Jiro for a moment, then nods. "Andrew Selman has substantial resources. A personal fortune in excess of three million and on his mother's side of the family, access to another fifteen or twenty million through immediate relatives. Not all of that is liquid, of course but it's certainly enough to get him out of the States and set up in a non-extradition country for an extended period. We're only going to get one chance at him. If Theo arrests him and he makes bail, he's gone."

Jiro, Max, Mac, and I nod.

"I have no definitive proof that Drew had anything to do with Fleur's injuries," Myles continues. "Fleur was given a cocktail of rohypnol and heroin. The likelihood she'll remember much about the attack is low, whenever she finally wakes up. The only things tying her attack to Drew are that he tried to get her to scene outside the club with him shortly before she disappeared; he knew she was leaving the safety of the club; and the combination of drugs she was given, which is very similar to what Cappa was dosed with. It's all circumstantial."

"It may be circumstantial but I think we all know he either did it himself or was involved," I say. "He's the alpha of this fucking Wolf-pack. Everything's been done at his instigation or on his order."

"I'm still trying to get the CCTV footage from the New Jersey hospital," Max tells us. "But if he's smart, and I think we can all agree he is, he won't have used his own car. He may have worn a disguise or gotten a lower-level wolfpack member to take her into the ER. I'm not sure we're going to get anything useable."

Myles turns his coffee cup around between his hands for a long moment. "Plan B involves not waiting for proof."

There's another round of nods.

My phone buzzes with an incoming text. I take it out and glance at it.

"Damn. Theo's on the way with Javier and Dana. Max, tell me what to pack up."

Max shakes his head. "Don't you touch my rig." He raises his voice. "Cynnie, baby? Help me pack double-time."

With the help of Cynnie and Emily—who is evidently allowed to touch Max's electronics even though I'm not—Max has everything but a very ordinary-looking laptop packed away by the time the door rings.

Theo looks even more in need of sleep than Myles. Javier's as pale as I've ever seen his usually swarthy self and Dana keeps making fists, then flexing her hands like she's fighting off the urge to hit someone.

I usher the Doms into my office.

"Fleur's not awake yet," Javier says when everyone's chosen a seat, or a place to lean, around the room. "But her doctors say her vitals are rising. She may wake tomorrow or the next day."

"Rota's ready," Dana offers from where she's leaning against my bookcase, still flexing her hands. "Austin and I will organize transportation to the hospital for each shift."

Javier nods. "Feel free to make liberal use of the limo."

"I will," Dana confirms.

"I've got five of the Wolfpack in lockup," Theo says. "I can hold them for maybe seventy-two hours if I stretch it out. Less if they get decent lawyers. Emmett's lawyer is dragging his heels, negotiating for a reduced sentence, before he'll let Emmett say anything. Jared Carr's cooperating but he was a low-level pack member, what they call an omega. He wasn't trusted with anything yet, so he can only testify about the recruitment process and what he saw at Blunts. I honestly think Drew was only interested in him because he's one of those tech millionaires. None of the other wolfpack members could afford membership at Blunts. The guy doesn't seem like he has the stomach for the Wolfpack's activities."

He falls silent, rubbing his eyes.

"Have you heard anything from Ten?" I ask gently.

Theo nods. "He's in Maine. I tracked Drew's plate to Boston. Ten thinks he took a train from Boston to Bangor. His family used to have a house on the river; he spent summers there in college. Knows the area."

"Has he spotted Drew?" I ask.

Theo shakes his head. "Best lead we have, though. If I can get enough for a warrant, I was going to send it along the wire to Bangor P.D."

I glance at Myles, remembering what he said about having one chance. He's watching me. He shakes his head.

I look back at Theo. "How much sleep have you had, mate?"

Theo waves his hand. "I'm in this for the duration."

Javier shifts in his chair to rest his hand on Theo's shoulder. "You're no good to her if your judgment is clouded by exhaustion."

"Some energy drinks and a dozen aspirin and I'll be fine," Theo grumbles.

I meet Javier's eyes. He nods. I can leave wrangling our guilt-ridden detective to him.

"I think we should call it a night," I say to everyone. "Theo, if you'd leave the burner you're using to communicate with Ten, I'll take point on communications tonight."

Theo's jaw sets. "I'm not going anywhere. I know what you're doing, Lo. You asked me to be more Dom and less cop dealing with True and I did."

"And I appreciate it. This is not the same. This is not putting down your badge for a couple of hours and then picking it up again. This is different."

Theo leans forward and knots his hands together on the edge of my desk. "They're my friends, too. Fleur, Cappa, Shannie. I've known them for years. I've scened with them. I've been *inside* all of them." Behind him, standing with his back to the door into the kitchen, Myles shifts. Theo continues without noticing, "None of them felt they could come to me. Do you know how awful that feels, Logan? I had a duty to protect them. A duty twice over and I *failed* them."

"I understand," I say. "I had a duty to protect them, too—"

"You went to bat for them. You took Cappa in immediately. You started escalating things at the club. I'm not deaf and you know what the club grapevine is like. I know you've been working on this for months. Against a lot of opposition. Maybe no one truly under-stood how bad it was but I've dealt with grooming and sexual assault cases for years and I should have seen what the hell was going on. Don't ask me to walk away now."

I look around the room and see the light of resolve in all the eyes looking back at me.

"You are my brothers and sisters and I will always be grateful for you," I say. "But this is where your involvement ends. All of you. It can't go any further."

"It damn well can," Theo growls.

"No, it can't. I need you to pick up your badge now and go back out there and defend the rest of the people who need your help, Theo. You're a good man and a good Dom. But you are not a killer. And neither I nor anyone else in this room has the right to ask you to become one."

Theo slants a hard glance at Myles. "I'm not leaving this to him."

"Because you don't think I'll get the job done," Myles says quietly, not lifting his gaze from the tips of his boots.

"It's not your responsibility," Theo snaps. "You're brand new to all of this. You barely know what being a Dom means. You're not a member of the club. You don't even know half of the house submissives."

"I'm not doing it out of responsibility," Myles responds, raising neither his eyes nor his voice. "I'm doing it out of love."

That silences everyone in the room.

Javier finally breaks the silence. He stands, walks over to Myles, and hands him a business card. "I won't ask you to incriminate yourself or do anything like that, mon frere. But I'd appreciate it if you text me when it's done. Just a thumbs up will do. I love Fleur and Cappa, too."

Myles nods and pockets the card.

As always, Javier gets the last word. Javier drags Theo out with him, after Theo slaps a small phone on the edge of my desk. Everyone shakes my hand as they leave. Max is last and instead of leaving once he's shaken my hand, he shuts the door behind Mac.

"Neither Logan nor I are leaving, Myles," Max says.

Myles lifts his head and pins us with that disconcerting, gray gaze. "No?"

"No," I say firmly.

Myles nods to himself. He walks over to the two of us and draws us into a tight circle, his arms curving over our shoulders.

"Who are we?" he asks.

Before I try to answer, Max says, "We're the sin-eaters. We're the ones who don't turn away. We're the ones who do the things that need doing."

What the fuck is this?

"We're the ones who stand and take the beating," Myles murmurs.

"We're the ones who get up afterwards and take it again," Max rejoins.

I have no idea what this exchange stems from but each word resonates in my bones.

"I don't want any misunderstandings later," Myles says, still looking at the two of us steadily. "This is murder. Premeditated murder."

Max and I nod without hesitation.

"We get caught, we go to jail for a very long time," Myles presses the point home again. "I have some contacts upstream but they won't be able to help us with this."

"I don't want to pull them in," I tell him. "No one else. This is between the three of us and Ten. We don't involve anyone else. We're not rescuing a mini-goat here. We're ending the threat to every submissive that Drew comes into contact with."

Myles nods. "I have a contact I'll need to involve on the back end. Max has met him. He's completely solid. I wouldn't involve him otherwise."

In this moment, under these surreal circumstances, I trust Myles without question. "That's fine," I agree.

"Pack for three days. I have weapons but if you prefer your own gun, bring it. We're taking my plane. Say goodbye to your girls. I'm going to call my driver. Twenty minutes until wheels up."

Max and I nod. That ends the discussion. Myles releases us. I go to find Emily and explain the unexplainable.

I take her up to our bedroom and sit on the edge of the bed with her in my lap. I rest my forehead against hers.

"I don't want you to know where I'm going. That way if you're asked, you can honestly say you don't know. I don't want to tell you what I'm doing. It would make you an accessory. Myles thinks we'll be gone for three days. I swear I'll come back to you, baby girl. There's nothing more important to me than coming home to you."

Her big eyes search my face. Is she looking for reassurance? Certainty? Whatever it is, she finds what she's looking for. The tension around her eyes eases. She cups my face in her hands.

"I won't ask you where you're going; I won't ask what you're doing. I know you're doing what needs to be done. I know you'll come back to me and you'll bring Max and Myles home safe. And Master Ten, too. Because that's who you are."

I hold her for half of my allotted twenty minutes, rocking her in my lap. "Mac will stay with you. He's going to be pissed off when he realizes where we've gone. Tell him I didn't trust anyone else to protect my girls."

Emily nods and holds me tightly. She's not clinging to me. She's not trembling. She's as resolute as I am. My baby doll.

When the time starts to worry me, she helps me pack in her quiet, efficient way. I make it downstairs with two minutes to spare. Opening my gun safe, I pull out my Glock and ammunition and take out two stacks of twenties. As I shove them in my bag, my fingertips brush something that doesn't feel like my clothes. I peer into the bag.

One of Emily's tiny stuffed dinosaurs is nestled between two pairs of jeans.

With a smile, I zip up my bag.

Mac's waiting in the hallway with Emmy and Bren. Livvy's on

Mac's shoulder. He pats her back and she rips out one of her froggy burps.

I glance at Emily and smile. She smiles back, although her eyes gleam with unshed tears. My brave little girl.

Mac eyes my bag narrowly. "Where the fuck d'you think you're going, son?"

I pat Livvy's back. "Emily will explain. I'll call every night no later than ten to say goodnight. I love you, Mac. You've been more of a father to me than my own dad. Keep our girls safe." I nod at Bren and Emily. "Keep our family safe."

Mac's jaw knots. "We're gonna have words about this when you get back."

I nod and grip his shoulder. Then I sweep up Emily in a final hug. As I'm releasing her, there's a knock on the door. When I check my phone, Myles stares back at me. I hadn't realized he'd left the house.

As I open the door, a firm hand lands on my shoulder and tugs me back. I turn. Brenna throws herself at me, hugging me fiercely. I smile over her shoulder at Mac and Emily as I hug her with my free arm.

"Come home safe, Daddy Lo," Brenna says, her voice rough.

I pat her back. "See you in a few days. I'd say be good but we both know that's not going to happen."

She cuffs me on the shoulder as she steps back, wiping her eyes. "Don't be an ass. I'm trying to emote here."

Chuckling, I leave with Myles. He leads me to a huge, black SUV that's idling at the curb. I put my bag in the boot and join Max in the back seat.

Max holds out a silvery bag. "Everything in here. Phone. Smart watch. Credit cards. Anything with a chip in it."

"Burner phone?"

Max shakes his head. "We'll coordinate burners in a minute."

I drop my electronics into the bag. I didn't bring my wallet, only the cash. Max tucks the bag away. He takes the burner for Ten, lines up four phones on his lap, and fiddles for a few moments. Then he hands me one of the phones.

"Five contacts in each phone. Ten is A. Myles is B. I'm C. You're D. Theo's burner is E—"

"How come Ten gets to be A?" I ask.

Max rolls his eyes at me. "Don't make other calls from that phone. We'll call home from another phone that I'll proxy through a cell tower in Milford, New Jersey. Three men matching our descriptions are going deer hunting in Stokes State Forest. They're each going to bag a white tail. Hope you like venison because Myles' deal with them is we take one carcass."

Max's grimace shows what he thinks about dealing with a deer carcass.

Myles chuckles from the front seat, where he's sitting next to the silent driver. "Venison for Thanksgiving. You'll eat it and you'll like it."

Fairly sure my baby doll already has a massive turkey in the downstairs freezer ready for Thanksgiving. Or maybe it's a goose. Whatever it is, it's ridiculously huge. Maybe she can do venison steaks as a side dish or something.

Max squeezes one eye shut and sticks out his tongue to illustrate what he thinks of that suggestion. "Anyway. The phone's not connected to the internet. You need to access an app or something, tell me and I'll figure out a way."

I nod. "I want to check on Emmy, Cappa, and Lucy while we're gone. Through your app."

"No problem," Max says. "You can do that from my phone which is pinging through Milford. On our way back, I'm going to get an injury which I'm going to have treated at the Lehigh Valley ER."

"What kind of injury?" I ask.

"Max is going to have a close encounter with a tree branch. Nasty slice and a big bruise. He might need a stitch or two. Happens when you're chasing after deer in the woods all the time," Myles answers.

I'll take his word for it.

"There's a private airfield ten minutes away from the hospital. Shouldn't take more than a few hours," Max says. "Happy so far?"

I nod. Max is fucking thorough.

"As for our *activities* during the next three days." Max pauses and shoots a meaningful glance at the driver, from which I take it that he thinks we need to watch what we say. I can't imagine Myles using a driver he didn't absolutely trust but I nod so Max knows I'll be careful. "We're flying to meet A. I'm going to text him now so he knows we're on our way. Probably be there by midnight. From now on we only use cash. We don't use names."

"Got it."

"Get some rest," Myles says. "Ninety-minute drive to my plane. It's going to be a long night."

I take his advice. I tuck the burner phone in my pocket, tip my head back on the head rest, and close my eyes.

Holding an image of Emily smiling up at me, her eyes soft and trusting, I let myself drift.

forty-one

LOGAN

BETWEEN MAX'S PLANNING AND MYLES'
execution, the op runs smoother than many I ran in the Navy. I can
only admire how meticulous and methodical the two of them are.
Their time in England, as much as Max bitched about it, made them
a team. They anticipate what the other is going to do; they finish
each other's sentences.

By the time we land in Bangor around one in the morning, Ten
still hasn't responded to Max's text. Max unrolls a couple of sleeping
bags and stretches out on the floor of the plane. Having napped
through an hour of the drive and nearly the whole of the flight, I'm
not sleepy. Myles paces around outside, probably wired from the two
hundred cups of coffee he's had.

When I see him unpacking an unusual-looking gun through the
open door of the plane, I climb out of my seat and join him.

He sets up a small target on the gray wall of the hanger, paces
back to me and moves the steel case back a few feet. "Ever used one
of these?" he asks me.

"Not sure I've ever seen one of these. What is it?"

He picks up the gun, which has a normal looking grip and then two very strange, long, skinny barrels. Beneath the two barrels is a tube that looks like a scope except it's on the bottom of the gun. No way to look through it.

"Dart gun," Myles tells me. "Hundred-foot range. Quiet and effective. Fires a thirteen-millimeter dart."

He shows me how to load the dart, which is a needle and syringe with a pink fluff on the end.

When he fires it, there's a puff of vapor. The dart sticks to the middle of the target; the pink fluff quivers. We both chuckle, watching it.

"What's in the syringe?"

"Your drug of choice. Ketamine."

"My—?" It takes me a moment to connect the dots to the drug that poisoned the punch at Rick's party. "Yeah."

"It's a veterinary dose. Used to take down horses. I don't expect him to survive it. You're clear on that, right?"

I nod.

"Okay, give it a try."

He hands me the strange gun. I take a minute to hold it and get used to the weight. I aim several times before trying to fire. The length of the barrel takes getting used to. Finally, I fire at the target.

I hit the second ring and watch the pink fluff quiver.

"Good enough," Myles say. "Go for center mass. Chest or back, anywhere is fine. Gun and dart are made to punch through animal skin. It'll penetrate clothes. If you hit on the first shot but the dart falls off, reload and hit him again. The objective here is to take him down quickly and quietly. I don't give a fuck how much of a dose he gets."

"Got it."

Myles packs the gun away, plucks the darts out of the bullseye and sticks them in a yellow sharps box in the gun's case.

"I've got two guns. C says you're a better shot than he is. You can carry one or you can just be my backup—"

"I'll carry one," I say. "I'm not asking you to do anything I wouldn't."

Myles nods. "Appreciate that. I decided the outcome of this as soon as I got my boy's text. If you'd told me I was on my own, I'd still be here. Experienced eyes and hands are always welcome but I don't want to stumble over you."

He won't.

"Whatever you need me to do, just tell me. I'm not proud. I know when I'm out of my league. This is your op. Tell me what to do."

Myles snaps the gun case shut and hands it to me. When I take it, he lays a hand on my shoulder.

"Not many people have seen me work," he says, meeting my eyes. "I won't pretend what I do is pretty but I try to keep it clean and clinical. I don't extract information. I don't torture. Elimination and disposal. That's what we're doing. C got used to following my lead in England. If you can do the same, once we find the target, this will be fast. I can't promise easy but I don't ever draw shite out. That's how ops go bad."

"Okay, I understand. I'll follow your lead. I won't get in your way."

"I appreciate the faith. You should try to get some rest. Tomorrow's likely to be a long day."

"Do you sleep during ops?" I ask.

He shakes his head. His gaze drifts down to the gun case. "Not much. I'm used to it. Don't worry about my focus."

I take him at his word. He's the expert and I saw how good he is at his job when he and Max had their adventure in England. With a nod, I take the gun case back into the plane, stow it with my bag, and climb into the nest of sleeping bags Max has made on the floor. Neither of us are used to sleeping alone anymore and I figure if my morning rocket ends up pressing into him, or his into me, Max won't punch me.

When I wake, groggy from the broken sleep, stiff and disoriented, Max and Myles are close to the front of the plane, huddled over a phone, speaking quietly.

I crawl over and prop myself against one of the seats, rubbing my bad leg.

"D is awake," Myles says into the phone.

Ten's voice responds. "Welcome to the party, D."

"Good morning, A. What'd I miss?"

"Target acquired," Ten says. "I've given B and C the coordinates. Small complication in that the target's not alone. I'm hopeful the girls will leave soon, though. I think they're the kind of company you pay by the hour."

"Other than the paid companions, anyone in the house?" Myles asks.

"Not that I've seen but there's a visible security system," Ten responds.

"Disable or lure out?" Myles asks, lifting his eyes to Max.

"I'll evaluate it on site. If it's linked to the local police, disabling it might set off an alarm. If it's hard-wired, luring him out's the better option."

Myles nods. "Car's just pulling up. We'll give the delivery boy ten minutes to clear off. We're twenty minutes away. See you in thirty."

Ten grunts. "What're you planning to do when you get here?"

"First we're going to evaluate the physical security and decide on the approach. Once we have the target isolated, we're going to tag him and bag him."

"We're not taking him back to the fucking, uh, *authority* where we came from," Ten growls.

"No, we're not," Myles agrees. "We're the garbage men."

There's a short silence while Ten processes what Myles has said.

"Yeah, okay," Ten says. "I'm on board with that. Bring lunch when you come. There's nothing around here. Fucking suburbs."

With chuckles that sound strained to my ears, we sign off.

"Stay low and out of sight of the cabin windows," Myles tells me.

"A couple of prospects are dropping off a car since I don't want a rental car paper trail. I don't care if the prospects see my plane number since we drove to Jersey but I don't want them seeing our faces."

I nod and slide down to sit near them on the carpeted floor. I spread my legs and ease into some of the stretches Hendry taught me.

"While you've been sleeping, I've set up a backup evac plan," Myles tells me as Max slides down on the floor in front of me, spreads his legs, and offers me his hands for a deep stretch. I let him pull me forward slowly and groan as the tension in my back and hips releases.

"I'm listening," I assure Myles between groans.

"If we get separated, I've set up a rendezvous point away from the air strip. There's cash, food, and water there. GPS has been sent to your burner. If any of us go for more than two hours without contact from any of the others, we stop what we're doing and head to the rendezvous point. If that means leaving the target behind, even after he's down, that's what we do. Clear?"

I nod. "Clear."

"We wait at the rendezvous point for six hours. Once any one of us arrives at the rendezvous point, the GPS in our burners will trigger a count-down that's sent to all of the burners so everyone can see how long we've got to rendezvous. If you cannot reach the rendezvous point before the end of the countdown, go to ground. If you're injured, seek medical help. If you're not, best bet is to hitch-hike back to New York. We're clear to be back in New York in seventy-six hours. The hunting license will have expired and that's enough time for C's injury to be treated."

"Okay," I say, panting a little as Max and I turn around until we're back-to-back, lock elbows and start twisting side-to-side. Tension releases down my bad leg in a series of pops.

"I've primed my guy on the back end," Myles continues. "We're calling him F. He knows we're coming in for disposal. He's been paid.

We hand off the target in a body bag. F won't open it. F's club has the controlling interest in a crematorium. The target will be run through the crematorium's oven and ash grinder and the ashes buried in the crematorium's rose garden."

Max grunts. "That the same club who have a cozy bunker somewhere in Ohio?"

"One and the same," Myles confirms.

I gather this is the same motorcycle club that provided a safe room for Max when he hacked two animal research labs to expose the weakness in WEDGE, a defense-department security program. I don't ask for names. Max was clear when he told me, Mac, and Manny about it that the bikers were cool and professional but also armed and unflinching when they saw Max's teacher-turned-nemesis in a gimp hood and zip-ties. They do the jobs they're paid to do; they're not people you mess with.

"Since you're the only one of us who can fly," I say. "If this goes south, you're out of the equation, and one of us needs to drive the, uh, target to the club, how do we find them?"

"I have an idea for that," Myles responds. "But I need to see what car they bring."

I don't understand why the plan would depend on the car but I trust Myles so I nod.

We go silent as the thrumming of a car motor and the crunching of tires on gravel sound through the plane's cabin. I continue to stretch, wanting to be as limber as possible before we meet Ten. I've been on plenty of stake-outs. Stiffness and greasy food are the order of the day.

Myles starts a timer running on his phone. Before it reaches three minutes, a message flashes up on all our burners.

F: Car delivered. Prospects heading back to base.

Myles acknowledges the text.

"Grab whatever you need for the day. Wheels up in five," Myles tells us.

I slept in my clothes, as did Max. I take a minute in the plane's tiny bathroom so I'm not stinking out the team, grab my go-bag and the gun case, and meet Myles at the bottom of the plane ramp.

He takes my bag and the gun case and stores them in the large, midnight blue SUV that's parked at the mouth of the hangar. He hands me a plain black hoodie. I shrug out of my jumper and put the hoodie over the long-sleeved Henley I'm wearing for warmth.

The hoodie's noticeably heavier than a normal sweatshirt.

"Body armor?" I ask.

Myles, who is wearing his own black hoodie, nods. "Move around and get a sense of the weight so it doesn't throw off your aim."

I do as he says. It's like wearing a wool coat and nothing like wearing Kevlar.

"What is this?" I ask as I windmill my arms. "Much too light to be steel mesh."

"Spider-silk? Space-age polymer? Fuck if I know," Myles responds as he slides behind the wheel and fiddles with the dashboard. "It'll stop most blades and low-caliber bullets. That's all I care about."

Seeing the sense in that, I nod.

"We get into a firefight, pull the hood over your head," Myles says. "Same material."

"Do you anticipate a firefight?" I ask.

Myles shakes his head. "Never say never. Until we're able to do some recon, I've got no idea what Selman has or what he's capable of. But run most predators to ground, and they'll turn and fight. I'm not assuming anything because he's decided to run. This may be a safe house he established a long time ago full of guns, ammo, and cash. I'm not assuming fuck all."

I take a deep breath. Over the smell of oil and a tang of disinfectant, there's the smell of Maine: pine trees and the brine of the ocean. "I spent two summers at sports camp here when I was in high school," I tell Myles. "Have you spent any time in Maine?"

Myles shakes his head. "I've passed through a few times."

"People in Maine are a different breed. Resilient. Secretive. Anti-authoritarian. You can count on most of them to mind their own business. But if Drew's known here and we're outsiders, that won't go well for us."

Myles finishes whatever he's doing and sits back. He pulls his hair back into a ponytail and fastens it with a black tie from around his wrist before putting on a pair of sunglasses. "I'll keep that in mind," he says. "I've programmed the club's GPS location into the car's sound system. It's the first playlist. Be sure to delete it if you end up having to drive the car to meet up with them, although they'll probably torch it just to be safe."

"Okay," I agree. "You're thorough."

"Did you think I wouldn't be?"

"No. I saw how well you took care of C."

"I've been doing this a long time," Myles says. "That I'm not dead or in jail should tell you all you need to know."

I grunt in acknowledgement. "Any thoughts about retirement?" I ask.

"Lots," he admits. "But the people who still call me are persistent bastards. Hard to tell them no. I understand one of them called you."

Remembering the call from the deep-voiced gentleman on the D.C. number, I nod. "Persuasive guy."

Myles chuckles. "I can imagine what he threatened you with."

"Smell the audit."

"Uh-huh. *He* hits mandatory retirement age in two years. He's grooming a successor; he's already tried to rope me into jobs for her and some of his other *friends* but they don't have the direct connection to me that he has. He can guilt trip me into taking jobs. They don't have that kind of leverage. Thing is—" Myles takes a deep breath and blows it out slowly. "Once I'm no longer on the payroll, so to speak, I won't have any more excuses to wriggle out of my family responsibilities. I figure you've investigated me, so you know what those are."

"Yeah," I admit. "No love lost between you and your old man?"

"No. Fucking monster," Myles responds. "C better not be taking a dump. What the fuck is taking him so long?"

I chuckle. With Max's ever-perfect timing, he pokes his head out of the plane's open door and gives Myles the finger. "I'm cleaning up your messy fucking internet signature, dickhead."

"Thirty seconds and I'm leaving you behind," Myles snipes back.

I know banter is their love-language but this feels a little more loaded. The nerves of the op working on both of them maybe.

Despite the finger, Max is out of the plane and in the car in just under thirty seconds. He directs Myles to a mom-and-pop store just off the secondary road we take out of Bangor. They have paper bags of sandwiches and snacks ready for us. I pay cash and we're back on the road in less than two minutes.

"I picked that place because I couldn't find any sign they had a CCTV system," Max tells me once we're back in the car. "Did you see any cameras?"

I shake my head but Sacrum was wired to the eyeteeth without me seeing any cameras, either.

"On the way back, if we have time, I want to stop and sweep that place for signals," Max tells Myles.

"Relax keyboard warrior," Myles responds as he steers the big car with one hand gripping the wheel and bites into a breakfast burrito. "I'll make time."

Max grumbles but settles into his own food.

forty-two

BATMAN DADDY

WE MEET Ten on a bend of the Penobscot River outside the city limits. Turning past another small store, bizarrely proclaiming it's full line of "western wear," since we're nearly as far east as you can go and still be in the States, we roll down a quiet street and pull up next to a green pick-up truck.

Ten climbs out of the truck and into the front passenger seat next to Myles.

"House is at the end of the cul-de-sac," Ten tells us, tipping his head further down the street. "Two cars still outside. No signs of movement yet."

"I like the street," Myles says, still munching on his burrito. "Only one way out. What's past the house?"

"River," Ten responds. "There's a dock but the boat's up for the winter."

"Still, we don't want to chase him through the water."

"Nope," Ten agrees. "It's fucking cold."

There's more snow on the ground here than in New York, icy and compacted, and it looks like it's here to stay. Myles has the heat on in the SUV and I'm warm in the armored hoodie but I'm glad I brought my parka.

Max offers Ten the paper bag of food. He takes out a sandwich, picks out the pickles, and eats.

"Fleur wake up yet?" Ten asks after he's eaten half the sandwich and washed it down with a bottle of water.

"No," Max answers him. "But her doctors think it will be today or tomorrow."

Ten grunts and sips more water. "Maude's got her good care. I don't know how she's going to afford the co-pay but Presbyterian's one of the best."

"No names," Myles says quietly. With the sunglasses on, I can't tell where he's looking but I think he's watching the street. "It's taken care of. All she needs to do is get better."

"High-handed," Ten grumbles.

Myles shrugs. "Whatever it takes."

There's a long silence that Ten finally breaks. "I want to be involved."

"I only have two tranq guns. Are you a better shot than D?"

"D?" Ten twists around and looks at me, resting his arm across the back of his seat. "Oh, right. Dunnow, we've never been to the range together. Your head injury affect your aim?"

"No."

"I outshot you the last time we played pool," Ten points out.

"Not at all the same," I respond.

"Yeah, okay. Probably better that you have the gun." Ten flexes his big hands. A fine tremor runs through them. "I'm outta my routine. Meds don't work as well when I'm off my schedule."

I nod.

Ten turns back around and says to Myles, "That's not what I meant. I wanna be involved in her recovery."

Myles dips his head without turning his face away from the street. "Even if it involves a lot of caregiving?"

Ten grunts. "Yes."

"Okay," Myles says. "We can't sit here for too long without one of the neighbors noticing the strange car. C, you're with me. We're going to take a walk and scope out the house's security. D, you and A drive around a little. Stay off the interstate if you can. Less chance of the plate getting picked up."

"Ready," Max confirms, pulling on a coat and slinging a bag across his chest.

I take the wheel since Ten is still eating. Driving up along the river, we pass signs for a country club, which is probably the draw for the houses nearby, along with the river. Maine's beautiful in a severe way: all stark contrasts with the white ground, barren trees, and pale blue sky.

Ten doesn't say anything as I drive around. It's not a strained silence but it's not overly comfortable, either. By the time I'm headed back down Route 2 toward the house, Ten's leaning against the window, eyes closed, mouth slightly open.

He probably hasn't had much more sleep than Myles.

Max is waiting at the store advertising "western wear," pretending to window-shop. When he climbs in, he directs me back toward Bangor.

"Myles wants surveillance from the other side of the river. Cross over at the first bridge you come to."

"Right. What's he doing?"

"Possibly breaking and entering," Max says. "I've learned not to ask those sorts of questions. They only irritate him. The house's security system is hard-wired. We can't risk trying to disable it. The lack of connection might alert whatever security company it's connected to. Hacking it and storming the house is definitely a plan of last resort."

"Okay," I say. "Maybe if he hires other paid company that's the way in?"

"Could be simpler than that," Max says. "There were take-out containers in the recycling. A lot of them. I don't think he's cooking for himself."

"Haven't seen any delivery drivers," Ten says, although his eyes are still closed.

"He's bored already," I surmise. "He's getting take-out, hiring girls to keep him company. Was there any sign of a problem with the girls?"

"No but he's been burning something. Big oil drum in the back yard with fresh ash in it."

I swear softly, wondering what evidence has gone up in flames. But maybe it doesn't matter. This isn't going to end in a prosecution. Still, there are other Wolfpack members I want to put away.

I drive up the far side of the river and help Max take the surveillance videos Myles wants. When we return, Myles meets us two streets away. He climbs into the back.

"What's the plan?" I ask Myles.

"There were a lot of take-out containers in the bin. I'm hoping he leaves the house to get dinner. I say we do it tonight. Sunset is at four. I want to do this in the dark if we can. Nice wrap-around porch. We tranq him as soon as he locks the front door. Anyone opposed?"

I shake my head and see Ten do the same out of the corner of my eye.

"That's the plan. D, you're on the north side of the porch. I'll take the south. A, you're driving the car. C, you're back up."

We all agree. Myles slips back out of the car to take the first two-hour shift watching the house. I drive around some more so Ten and Max can nap without someone calling us in as vagrants. Ten takes the next shift; the tremor in his hands is markedly worse when he returns and I'm glad we're not counting on his aim. I take the third shift, by which time the girls have left in one of the cars. Ten reports they don't look any worse for wear when we hand-off, so that's one less thing to worry about.

Twilight comes early this far north and darkness follows quickly, cold and bitter. There are a few streetlights carving small, yellow circles in the blackness but it's fucking dark out here, far away from the cities. Once the street is blanketed in blackness, Myles pulls us all back to the SUV and Ten's truck and gives the go-ahead to move them close to the house. There aren't any lights on in the house closest to Drew's, which is a typical New England salt box while Drew's house looks like a mutated barn. Drew's place has sprouted a two-story addition at the back. A wrap-around porch has been slapped incongruously around the front and sides.

The car grows cold but Myles says it's too conspicuous to leave the motor running. The exhaust will plume in the night air. I'm grateful for my parka and a sleeping bag that Max breaks out to spread across our legs. He's on a tablet, the screen black with white code running across it, barely illuminating his chin. Otherwise, there are no lights and barely any sound other than the wind rattling the bare-branched trees.

"Signal out," Max whispers. "I think he's making a phone call."

"Positions, gentlemen," Myles says. "D, we're going to get cold fast. Find a spot out of the wind if you can. If you feel your fingers start to get numb, come back to the car no matter what. A missed shot is worse than no shot tonight. We don't want to spook him."

"Got it," I confirm.

Max hands me the gun and dart pack. Myles and I ease out of the car and cross the icy ground as quietly as possible. As we come up to the house, I crouch down. The lights are on at the back, spilling long, yellow rectangles across the snow. There's a great spot between two bushes growing against the porch. I'll be invisible between them and out of the wind. But pushing between their branches might be noisy.

Myles breaks away from me and begins to cross the front yard. As he's passing the car in the driveway, the house's front lights come on.

I duck down behind the bushes. It could be motion-activated, although I didn't think Myles was close enough to the house to trip something like that. Lifting my head to see through the branches, I load a dart and aim at the front door.

Myles crouches in the shadow of the car. He's visible to me but the car should hide him from anyone coming out of the door. He'll have to shoot over the car's boot, though. It's good cover but not a great shot.

Footsteps rattle the decorative glass in the front door. Drew opens the door a moment later, his blond hair blazing under the porch lights. He's wearing dark trousers, a sweater, a wool blazer, and leather driving gloves but no coat. I bet he's one of those psychos who runs around in shorts in February.

I wait for him to step out, taking the smallest, shortest breaths I can through my nose so my breath doesn't give me away. He pulls the door closed behind him and angles his body to fit the key into the door lock. I wait until I hear the tumblers click before I fire.

My dart hits an inch to the left of his lapel, pink puff quivering against the green of his sweater. A second dart snicks into his upper arm.

He takes a ragged breath, his hand rising to pull my dart out of his chest. He meets my eyes through the screen of branches as I load another dart. That's right, fucker. You're not escaping justice.

He staggers back a step. Pawing ineffectually at his chest, he slumps against the door-frame, his eyelids flickering.

Myles slithers up the front steps like a shadow and catches Drew before he hits the ground. I follow him, stowing my gun in my parka pocket. I pull the keys out of the door and tuck them into Drew's blazer before drawing his arm over my shoulder. Myles takes the other side. We carry the limp weight off the porch and onto the driveway as Ten brings the SUV up behind Drew's car.

Max meets us at the car's boot and helps hold open the body bag as we maneuver Drew into it. Myles zips up the bag and closes the boot.

In less than two minutes, we're out of the cul-de-sac, heading back to the airfield. Ten follows us in his truck.

After a quick stop at the place where we picked up food so that Max can do something nefarious, we arrive back at the airfield. We part ways at Myles' plane. Ten assures us that he's okay to drive back to New York on his own but says he's going to visit a friend in Boston for a few days first as cover. He leaves as we're loading the body bag into the plane's luggage compartment.

After a short pre-flight, we lift into the clear night.

"Pink ring around the moon," Max says, looking out a window. "It's going to snow."

Snow'll cover any tracks.

"How long do you think it'll be before anyone looks for him?" I wonder aloud, not really directing the question at anyone.

"Doesn't matter," Myles answers from the cockpit a few feet away. "Cause no one's ever going to find him."

That ends the discussion. Once we're at altitude and Myles tells us we can move around, we distribute the rest of the food from the paper bag and eat silently. Max sits next to me and offers me a strange phone with a black antenna sticking out of it. I check the time and see with relief that I'm not late calling my baby doll. I keep it short and just confirm that everything's fine and I'll see her soon. I can hear the tears in her voice as she tells me she loves me but she speaks clearly when she asks if Livvy can sleep with her tonight. I've read about co-sleeping with kids and generally view it with dread but agree just for tonight so Emmy's not alone in our bed. Max leans in to joke that he and I slept together last night, which gets a small giggle out of Emily before I say goodbye.

I hand the phone back to Max so he can call Cynnie.

We land just after midnight, flying low over winter-seared fields to an airstrip that's barely more than a cross in the darkness, lit by faint green lights. We taxi to a hangar with a black "C" painted on the high, white wall. A black SUV with tinted windows idles next to the hangar, the exhaust pluming exactly the way we couldn't let ours do in Maine.

Myles tells us to wait on the plane. He lowers the stairs, leaving the door open, and greets two men who emerge from the SUV. They're both bearded. One wears sunglasses even though the airfield is barely lit this late at night.

The two men help Myles move the body bag into the boot of their

SUV. After quick hand-shakes, the SUV drives off and Myles climbs back aboard the plane.

"We can sleep here or in New Jersey," he says.

"Are you going to actually sleep?" I ask.

"Probably not until we're in New Jersey."

"New Jersey," Max says firmly. "I'll tell you knock-knock jokes to keep you awake and you can fart at me."

"Fuck off," Myles responds but his tone is affectionate.

Max joins Myles in the cockpit. I listen to the low murmur of their voices as we climb back into the night sky, although I don't hear any knock-knock jokes. I tip my head back against the seat and let their voices wash over me as I drift.

A few bumps as we land wake me but not for long. Max pulls me out of my chair and onto his sleeping bag pile. I'm nearly asleep again when Myles settles into the messy pile behind Max.

"Stay away from my ass," Max mutters at him.

"Your arse is safe from me," Myles retorts. "Might make use of that smart mouth in the morning, though."

"Only if you want tooth-marks on your dick," Max responds.

Myles chuckles. "Stop thinking about my dick."

Myles grunts and I surmise Max has elbowed him. I roll away from the two idiots as they wrestle, pull a sleeping bag over me, and give myself over to my exhaustion.

We stay in New Jersey for a day to establish our alibi. Myles sleeps heavily. Max sets up his array of electronics, pinging and proxying and doing whatever he does to keep us safe. I'm able to check his app. Lucy's fine but Cappa's graphs are still flat, which tells me he hasn't left Fleur's bedside. I text Javier and Maude from a phone Max assures me is okay to use. They both respond to say they're with him and are making sure he gets rest breaks and regular meals. Despite Fleur's vitals continuing to rise, she still hasn't woken.

As Myles sleeps into the afternoon, Max sets up a call with Cynnie and reads to her from a book on his phone. Since I've missed Storytime for two days, I get Max to conference Emmy in and listen to her and Livvy giggle together as Max reads.

The giggling wakes Myles. After he eats the last sandwich from the bag and rubs his face blearily for a while, he asks, "Ready to go home?"

"No encounter with a tree branch?" Max asks. "I'm still willing to take one for the team."

"I think we're good. No reason to think anyone saw us or reported the cars. Has F confirmed disposal?"

Max nods, handing Myles a phone. Myles thumbs through the messages. "Car in Maine's been disposed of, too. No issues. I don't know about you, gentlemen but I'm ready to go home."

Max and I nod.

After a short flight to the private airport upstate where Myles keeps his plane, we pack everything into his waiting SUV. The three of us sit in the back with the privacy screen up between us and the driver. As we roll back toward the City, Myles says quietly, "I want your permission."

"For what?" I ask.

"To be a daddy. I know I have a lot to learn. I know you doubt me. Just don't poison anyone at the playgroup or Blunts against me. Particularly not Fleur and Cappa."

"Neither of them are little," I point out.

"I'm not convinced of that," he responds. "Not after watching them with the other littles before . . . what happened. I won't push. I won't do anything to undermine their recovery. But when they're ready for a caregiver, I want it to be me."

I don't have to think about it too hard. Not after the past two days. "You have my permission. You'll need a mentor. Maybe more than one. I know Bravo would be happy to mentor you."

"I appreciate that but I want you to mentor me."

That surprises me. "Why?"

"Because your dart hit first."

I don't have any response other than: "Okay."

"Bravo can be backup," Myles says. "I know you have a lot going on."

I do. But this is something I'll make time for.

The City's bright lights and constant sounds welcome me back as we cross the bridge into Manhattan. I've got nothing against the quiet places of the world but they're not home. Not like this City is.

When we arrive at my townhouse, there's a crowd waiting at the door. Cynnie rushes down the stairs into Max's arms. Emily and Bren stand in the doorway with Mac peering over their shoulders. Emily has Livvy in her arms and a smile as brilliant as Christmas morning on her face.

Before I head up the stairs to them, I pull Myles into a hug. He stiffens for a second before patting my back.

"If you have any nightmares, call me," I say to him and Max, remembering how Max suffered for months after the deaths we caused and witnessed in the service.

Max smiles at me over the head of the woman held tightly in his arms. "I'll sleep well tonight. If *you* have any nightmares, call me."

I nod at him but there's no darkness in my mind. I've done what I needed to do. I've protected those who couldn't protect themselves.

I look up at the people waiting at the entrance to my home. I think I'll sleep well tonight, too.

James Logan
&
Emily Martin

REQUEST THE PLEASURE OF YOUR COMPANY
AT THE CELEBRATION OF THEIR MARRIAGE
ON THE

4th of January

AT NOON IN THE
LITTLE CHAPEL OF LOVE
LAS VEGAS, NEVADA

Reception to follow

DADDY
&
ME

Are getting married!
You coming?

4TH OF JANUARY

at noon in the

little chapel of love

las vegas, nevada

epilogue

EMILY

DADDY'S always beautiful to me.

He's all long lines: jaw and throat, the straight set of his shoulders, the curving planes of his chest and abs, the sweep of thigh and calf, his ridiculously big feet.

His toes curl as I watch him.

He stretches and slides an arm behind his head, his skin golden against the white pillows despite it being deep mid-winter.

"I can feel your eyes on me, little girl," he says. His low, gruff tone makes my tummy curl tighter than his toes.

He may be able to feel my eyes on him but he can't *see* me. In contrast to all his long, rugged lines, a frilly, hot pink mask covers his eyes. Rhinestones spell out "baby doll" across the mask.

Daddy absolutely refused to spend the night before our wedding apart. Yes, he agreed when I argued, it's traditional. But life's too short not to spend every night in each other's arms.

I couldn't really argue with that. But I did insist that he didn't see the bride the day of our wedding until I walk down the aisle.

Thus, my blindfold.

"I really like you in pink, Daddy," I say, as I tease my fingertip up and down his instep and watch his toes curl again. "Queen Twitch says it's your color."

"Batman wears black," Daddy responds.

"*Batman Daddy* could wear pink," I suggest.

He grumbles but he's smiling. I think he'll wear pink more often for me.

"Just because you got me to wear this blindfold, don't think you're in charge, little girl. Stop trying to tickle me. Get up here and sit on my face."

I giggle wildly. Although I enjoyed blindfolding him while he was still asleep, I don't ever want to be in charge. Not with my Daddy. I may be a dragon but I'm a *baby* dragon.

I feel like a queen dragon when I climb up the bed to straddle my Daddy's shoulders. I grip the padded headboard and lower myself slowly. Daddy's hot hands land on my thighs and slide up to cradle my bottom. He guides me down onto his waiting mouth. I lean forward, bracing my intricately-hennaed forearms against the headboard.

For a moment, he just breathes on me. The heat, the anticipation, draw a moan out of me. With him blindfolded, this is a rare chance for me to close my eyes, since he usually demands that I look at him during sex.

If it were anyone but my Daddy, I would. I'd close my eyes, shut out our suite at the Excalibur overlooking the turrets of the castle, and focus on whatever fantasy I'm building in my brain.

But Daddy's my fantasy. And I obey his rules, even when he can't see that I'm doing it.

I watch his brow furrow as the tip of his tongue traces through my pussy. His forehead relaxes as he pulls me down more snugly over his face, my knees rubbing along the sheets as he urges my legs wider. He licks a long stripe up to my clit and hums against that most sensitive flesh.

I grip the headboard and squeal softly as he overwhelms me in sensation.

I should know better than to think Daddy's going to be satisfied with one orgasm this morning. He licks and nips and hums and even roots with the tip of his nose until I writhe and pant and shake through two. He ignores my protests that I'm too sensitive and tongue-fucks me until I'm needy and mewling again. Then he topples me off his face and into his lap.

Before I have a chance to do more than sprawl across the rumpled covers, he lifts my hips, lines himself up, and sinks home.

I whimper and reach for his shoulders.

"No, little girl. Hands behind your back. Daddy's going to fuck you across the bed. You don't get to hold on. Give yourself to me."

"Yes, Daddy." I tuck my hands behind my back, even though lying on them while impaled on Daddy's wolfy cock and spread across his thighs puts a lot of strain on my shoulders. But Daddy wants me to give myself to him, so I do, relaxing into his hold and letting him push me forward and back across the silky bedding as he thrusts. I watch pleasure light his face, spreading in a ruddy flush down his bristly neck. I'm sure I have beard burn across my inner thighs but I can't feel it in this moment as all the sensation in my body narrows down to the nerves wrapped around him. Daddy grunts as he thrusts, hot and wolfy, a term I refuse to give up despite the nasty Wolfpack. Daddy was my wolfy Daddy first. They don't get to ruin anything.

We won't let them.

Daddy doesn't let me fall off the bed but he does push me to the edge, until my head's hanging back and spinning wildly. He leans over me, mouthing at my breasts, smearing my own wetness across my skin.

"Give me one more, my little wonder, my little wife," he growls.

"Please, Daddy?"

"Yes, Emmy. Give it to me."

He latches on to my nipple and gives it a tug with his teeth. The sharp pinch sends me over, my body slip-slip-slipping out of my control as I shake against him. He holds me tightly, right on the edge but never letting me fall, as he pounds his own pleasure into me. Finally, he stills, dropping his face between my breasts as we both gasp for air. I float and spin pleasantly through the afterglow.

"Happy wedding day, baby," he rumbles.

"Happy wedding day, Daddy," I say, my voice dreamy. "Can I touch you now?"

He chuckles breathlessly. "Yes, my baby."

I bring my aching, tingling arms out from behind my back and thread the fingers of one hand through his soft hair. I stroke the sweaty skin of his spine with the fingertips of my other hand. "Thank you for my many Os. Ta very much."

"It was absolutely my pleasure, little girl."

"Can I ask you something?"

"Mmm? What's on your mind this morning when I don't want you thinking about anything but the wonderful day we're going to have?"

I swallow. I should probably just take my orgasms and be super-happy about them. But I've been wondering about something the whole time we've been in Vegas.

"Please don't take this wrong, because I really-really-really love my Os but I expected you to deny me for a few days before our wedding like you did before our collaring ceremony. I'm not complaining! I'm just wondering why you didn't?"

"Do you have any thoughts on why I might not have?" Daddy asks, sounding extremely pleased with himself. Was he waiting for me to ask?

"Because you know it's not my favorite thing?"

"Yes. That was half of the reason. Anything else?"

"I'm not sure but maybe because you want this to be different from our collaring ceremony?"

He kisses me, a little sloppily because of the blindfold, on the tip of my nose. "You know I like orgasm denial and I will ask you to agree to it from time to time because it fills my soul. Don't think you're getting out of it forever. But I'm well aware it's not your favorite thing. And, although you're getting much better about incorporating it as part of your submission, I'm also well aware that it makes you a tiny bit resentful. This is your wedding week, my sweetheart. You've been so relaxed leading up to it. You've approached the ceremony joyously, exactly as I want you to. The last thing I want you to feel is resentful. So this—" He shifts his hips, pushing a little deeper into me even though he's no longer fully hard. "Is still an O Zone. Which might be among your cutest terms. Does that make sense?"

I nod vigorously. "Thank you for all my Os. Love you the most today, Daddy."

"Hmm, I'm not sure that's possible." He pulls me back up onto the bed and rolls us onto our sides. I slide my right leg over his hip and hook him to me with my calf. He's taught me to cherish these moments of peaceful intimacy as much as the wilder ones. Even if these moments are a little messy.

"It is, though," I say. "Because today I become your forever-little, and everyone knows forever-littles love their Daddies the most."

"I haven't heard that," he says. He traces my face with his fingertips, a little clumsily. The tip of his index finger slips into my nostril as his other fingers trace my lower lip. "I think this might be more Littles' Army propaganda."

I grin and suck two of his fingers into my mouth. There have been serious Littles' Army shenanigans this week. A glitter bombing over the Grand Canyon. A water balloon battle on the Stratosphere's Big Shot. A day-long hide-and-seek game through the casinos which I *won*, thank you very much, although I was neck and neck with Matty and Sammi's team until the end and they *might* have let the bride win. Still.

We've also been extremely well behaved this week. We didn't want to get kicked out of the Lost City escape room, or the tactile game arcade at Luxor, or during high tea in the Bellagio's exquisite

Conservatory for my bachelorette party. Being on our best behavior has been a strain, especially for Sammi but it's been worth it to catch our Doms off-guard when we have executed our best-laid plans.

Actually, hearing Master Javier's scream when four of us hit him with water balloons as that crazy ride shot him a thousand feet in the air over the Vegas strip was worth it all on its own. That's a sound that will resonate forever in my best memories. I thought I was one-hundred-percent masochist until that moment but I think I might have discovered my one-percent sadist just then.

"I can feel you grinning, sweetheart," Daddy says. His fingertip wiggles in my nose.

I nip his fingers when I realize that fingertip is there on purpose. Chuckling, Daddy slides his hand down my throat to rest on my collar.

"I was thinking of Master Javier's scream on that crazy ride on top of the Stratosphere," I tell him.

Daddy's chuckle blooms into a laugh. "That was brilliant, baby doll. I've never seen him look so surprised."

I have. During a scary moment in the escape room, Matty ran to him and jumped up into his arms. She wrapped her arms around his neck and kissed him. He looked just as surprised as he did on top of the Stratosphere. Then he sank his hand into her wild curls and held her still for a very long, very thorough kiss.

I'm not sure what's going on there but Faolan and Javier are best friends and have been forever. Matty mentioned they've shared submissives before. Matty hasn't let me in on her plans, so I don't know if Matty's pushing for it, or if this is something she and Faolan cooked up together but I think Matty's angling for two daddies.

I just hope she doesn't fall victim to Master Javier's "one year and done" rule, which is widely rumored at the club.

"What time is it, little girl?" Daddy asks. "I hate not being able to see anything."

"Frustrating, isn't it?" I ask him with more than a little glee, since he blindfolds me all the time. "It's five minutes to seven."

Daddy grunts and slips out of me, rolling onto his back. "I know it's a little earlier than planned but I'm ready to get up and start the day. It's a big day."

"Is it?" I ask innocently.

He pinches my hip. "You know it is."

"Hmm, because we're meeting some friends at noon?"

Daddy rolls over and squashes me into the mattress. "Because today I'm making you my wife." He kisses me and tickles me at the same time until I squeal.

When he's finished torturing my ribs, he rolls off me and fumbles his way to the bathroom with his arms outstretched. I don't offer to guide him because Tickling Daddies are an evil which must be deterred. He closes the door behind him and the shower goes on.

I roll over, pulling the bedding around me until I'm a burrito baby. I wriggle my arms out, rest my chin on my folded arms, and look out at the turrets of Excalibur's castle. In rooms all around the hotel, our friends will be getting ready. I've helped Laurel, Cynnie, Vashi, Aggie, Sammi, and Yummy with their outfits, because they're my bridal party. And I know what Master Niall is wearing, even if he's crazy. But everyone else has been very secretive about what they're wearing to the wedding.

To be fair, that might be because of me. I originally wanted a Teddy Bear's Picnic wedding, similar to my collaring ceremony, only probably with less bunnies since a fluffle is hard to find here in Vegas. That's what I put on the wedding invitations. But after becoming a fierce, white, baby dragon and finding my flight, I changed my mind. When guests RSVPed, I emailed them to let them know they were free to dress any way they wanted. We're getting married by Elvis, so I expect some wild outfits.

But everyone's been "keeping mum" about what they're wearing, to use a Daddyism. Even Daddy's been super-secretive, squirreling away in his office on video-calls with Niall. Cynnie, who usually can't keep a secret for more than a millisecond, suddenly became Fort Knox after going on two shopping trips with Daddy. I'd be put-out but she really is the Queen Bee of thrifting, so whatever she helps him put together will be awesome.

On that thought, I smile at the view and worm my way out of my burrito.

I put on one of the fluffy hotel robes and amble into the other room of the suite. I picked the Excalibur because, *castle* but also because it's one of the older hotels on the strip and so the rooms aren't as expensive for our guests. That also meant Daddy said it wouldn't be too extravagant for us to upgrade to a suite.

Livvy's crib and sensory mat were in the second room of the suite until yesterday. Mac and Bren demanded "Livvy time" and whisked her away for the night, which was really nice of them, since it let Daddy bang me over practically every surface in both rooms last night. He's so wolfy.

Bren's been trying to convince me to leave Livvy with them and go on a honeymoon, just me and Daddy. But I don't want to. I've loved having her with us this week. Besides, Daddy's talking about finishing the Mexican cruise that was so horribly interrupted by the evil massage man. Niall, Shaan, and Vashi said they'd join us. There's a lovely sense of closure to that, so I'm holding out for a belated honeymoon in Mexico at the end of February when New York is dreary and I'm ready for some sun.

Besides, I'd like to eat more of that lobster ceviche. I'll think of Miranda with every bite. And not gloat. Because that wouldn't be a bigger person thing to do.

But fierce, white, baby dragons need a tiny bit of a gloat now and then when they've *won* and protected their Daddy-dragon and baby-dragon from the Mir-witch. Dragons can be gloaty.

I pick up a couple of Livvy's sensory toys and a slightly sticky Little Larry. She can't possibly be teething yet but you wouldn't know it from how well-gummed all her toys are. I tuck the sensory toys away in the toy bag and leave the Little Larry to wash when Daddy's out of the bathroom.

As I'm hydrating, and logging it into Daddy's app with only a small eye-roll, there's a knock on the door.

I'm not expecting anyone yet. My bridesmaids are coming at nine for hair and makeup. If there was a problem with Livvy, Bren would have texted.

I open the door and find five mostly naked men.

"Good morning," I say warily. I'm not opposed to mostly naked men at the door but I'm confident this was not on Daddy's schedule for today. They're also looking extremely furtive.

"Is Lo up?" Max asks in a whisper.

"He's in the shower. What are you up to?"

"Stealth mission," Daddy Warrin says, tightening his towel around his waist.

"Really. Would Daddy approve of this stealth mission?"

Master Niall, who is also wearing a towel, although his is around his neck, chuckles. "Nah." He waves a hotel key card. "But we got special access to the pool."

The outdoor pool is closed for the winter, although we've been swimming at Mandalay Bay, which was really nice. Although it's January, the temperature got up to seventy the second day we were here and the swim was refreshing. It's supposed to be cooler today, though, and since the sun's only just come up, the pool won't be refreshing. It will be like an ice bath.

"Are you planning on dumping Daddy in?" I ask.

"Something like that," Max admits.

"We're gettin' in with 'im," Niall protests.

I step back from the door and let them in. It's their funeral.

They Daddy-nap him out of the bathroom. There's a scuffle and a little yelling and, when they emerge, Daddy Jack has a very red ring around his eye. They've got Daddy in black boxers, so at least they won't get kicked out of the hotel. Daddy's blindfolded, ball-gagged, handcuffed, and being led by Jiro and Max.

"Don't worry, Emmy. We'll return him after we've had a little fun with him," Max says to me.

I'm not worried. I know these men well enough to know they wouldn't do anything to spoil my day, especially not after the lost collar escapade. They may not like what Daddy does to them in retaliation, though.

I grin at Max. "I'll consider this a hall pass for any Littles' Army shenanigans." I raise my phone and snap a picture of them before sending it to the littles' chat.

Max grimaces. "Traitor."

"I'm extremely loyal," I protest. "Just not to your cause."

Chuckling, Max leads Daddy and his band of Merry Men out of our suite.

Daddy returns an hour later, blindfolded, and being led by Niall. No ball-gag; no handcuffs. Niall's wet. Daddy isn't. I don't see a lot of bruises but I suspect that some of the five who walked out of here with Daddy have them.

I've checked in with Bren—who says everything is fine and Livvy's on schedule—and ordered room service while Daddy's been roughhousing with his groomsmen. The décor at Excalibur might be a little dated but there's nothing fusty about the food. I'm happily munching on fruit salad as I let Daddy and Niall back in.

"Mmm." Daddy immediately sweeps me up into his arms. "I smell watermelon."

I touch the other half of the piece I was eating to his lips. He sucks it into his mouth and chews contentedly.

"Did you throw them all into the pool?" I ask.

"Aye, he did," Niall grumbles, throwing himself into one of the chairs in the small dining corner and helping himself to some of my fruit salad. I give him what Daddy calls my "angry koala" face. Niall chuckles.

"While still handcuffed," Daddy says after he swallows. "Wankers."

"It was the best compromise I could come up with," Niall says around a mouthful of fruit. "You kept vetoing the strippers."

Daddy shakes his head. "Doms don't need strippers. You idiots got me drunk two nights ago. That's enough bachelor-shit for me." He grins hugely. "I'm ready to be a married man."

Niall snorts. "Lots to be said for it, t'be fair."

I lead Daddy over to the table, help him sit, and cuddle up in his lap. "I got breakfast sausages, bacon, pancakes, scrambled eggs, and fruit salad. What would you like me to feed you?"

Daddy stretches back in the chair, holding me snugly to his chest. "You're going to feed me?"

"I am, unless you'd rather I go in the other room so you can take off your blindfold and have breakfast with your second-best man."

Master Niall growls.

The role of Daddy's best man has been hotly disputed between Master Niall and Max. Niall claims he's Daddy's "brudder from another mudder" while Max says he's known Daddy longer and has his bank account and credit card numbers. Daddy told them to fight it out, preferably during the joust that's held every night at the hotel. It's been great teasing material all week.

"Yeh can have Emmy feed you any day for the rest of your life," Niall grumbles.

"I know," Daddy says smugly. "I might make it a new ritual. Blindfolded Breakfasts. But you know what the great man said, 'Live each day, as if it were your last.' I want every minute with you, Emmy. Feed me, baby."

Grinning at Master Niall, I lean forward and spear a bite of eggs and sausage.

"I'd best be off anyway," Master Niall says, stealing another piece of melon before wiping his mouth and hands. "Gotta get dressed and be at the airstrip by ten. Limos leave here for the drop zone at eleven. Don't let Max make you late, one-upping shiteheel."

Daddy laughs before he takes the bite of breakfast and chews. "See you there."

"You will if yeh look up," Niall says. "Drop him off across the hall when you're ready to have this sad sap outta yer hair, Emmy. Shaan's ready to make him presentable."

I make a last-ditch effort. "What will Shaan be wearing, Master Niall?"

He makes a zipping motion across his mouth before bounding up out of the chair and smacking a kiss on my cheek. Then he grabs Daddy's face and smacks a kiss on Daddy's lips.

Daddy sputters. "Red, red, you wanker."

Laughing uproariously, Master Niall strolls out of our suite.

I wipe Daddy's mouth with one of the nice napkins that came with breakfast before I offer him a bite of scrambled eggs and pancakes. After he chews, he says, "Not bad but nowhere as good as yours, sweetheart."

I wriggle at the praise. "Food here is good, though. So much to choose from."

We've been utterly spoiled for choice in the cuisine-department since coming to Vegas. We've had sushi, comfort food at a very upscale diner, Italian, surf and turf, and gorged ourselves at a totally ridiculous buffet that had over five hundred different foods. I've never been so stuffed.

Even Master Javier's had to admit that the food in Las Vegas is very good, although he looked only slightly less agitated than when we water-balloon-bombed him as he said it.

"Have you had a good week, baby?" Daddy asks as I feed him.

"Uh-huh. Have you?"

"It's been wonderful. More than anything I'd hoped for. I haven't been to Vegas before except for work. We'll come back, just you, me, and Livvy, don't you think?"

I giggle. No, I don't. "Daddy, if you haven't figured it out by now, your friends are never going to let us vacation alone. And you don't want them to. You love having them around."

Daddy's hands circle my waist and squeeze. "I'd protest but you're right. You know me too well, little girl. You got one thing wrong, though. They're *our* friends. These people are here for you just as much as me."

Given how tightly our circle of friends has gathered around us in the past month, with Niall, Shaan, and Vashi finding a house in Queens, Jiro and Laurel taking an insanely luxe co-op in Gramercy Park that's almost wall-to-wall windows, and Daisy buying a summer house on Fire Island just down the beach from Master Nico's, I can't argue with him. I see my friends, little and Big, every day. Even as I lose my last real family to the shadows of dementia, I've gained the biggest, most loving family I could imagine.

And with four exceptions, they're all here in Vegas to celebrate our wedding.

Daddy grumbles as I lead him to Niall's suite to change into his wedding clothes. He's had me in his lap for the last half-hour, first bouncing my way to a mutual O even more delicious than the fruit salad, then cuddling in the afterglow. He suggests we just show up in towels at the Little Chapel and spend the rest of the morning fucking until the limos arrive. While his suggestion has a lot of appeal, it would really disappoint my bridesmaids, who have bets going on whether Daddy faints when he sees me in my wedding gown.

I trade Daddy for Vashi and take the clothes bag she's had with my gown in it, since I know Daddy's sneaky ways. If it had been hanging in our closet all week, he'd have gotten a look at it somehow.

Hand-in-hand, Vashi and I return to the suite while she tells me about winning a thousand dollars in the casino last night. She was playing poker. Master Niall says she has the best poker face of anyone he's ever played.

But she can't beat me at Hearts.

Vashi checks the amazing henna she's done on my hands and forearms while we wait for the rest of my attendants. I can't really call them bridesmaids because one of them's a boy. It's kind of a silly tradition anyway and I almost did away with it until I heard about the crazy competition going on between Master Niall and Max for the title of Daddy's best man. Then I decided we needed a full bridal party to defuse their competition before someone got hurt. Probably Max, since Master Niall's very muscley. Although Max was scheming to get Master Niall locked up for twenty-to-life for a crime he didn't commit, according to Cynnie.

Men.

Anyway. While we wait, I try to get what Shaan's wearing to the ceremony out of Vashi but she's just as tight-lipped as her master. Niall's right, she does have a good poker face. She barely smiles when I make outrageous suggestions: one half of a Yellow Submarine, Baby Shark, a Minion. She just pats my hands and tells me the henna's set perfectly.

I finally get my baby back when Bren arrives with the other attendants at nine. Livvy burbles her new sound at me, "ah-goo," and laughs when I kiss her fingers and toes. Bren and Vashi get to work on my hair, creating a complicated mass of braids to hold up my tiara and veil. Everyone else sits for Daisy as she does their hair and makeup. I offered to bring in a pro but Daisy demanded "the honor" in exchange for being part of the bridal party. I don't know why she ever thought she wouldn't be. Maybe she thought I'd only want subbies. But as soon as she RSVPed, I knew what I wanted her to do. I can't walk down the aisle without my Best Mommy Domme.

Daisy's just finishing Sammi's makeup, in extravagant emeralds and marine blues to go with his outfit, when there's a last knock on the door. Laurel answers and gives True a big hug as she enters with her foster-mother. We've had to pull some major strings to get her here, since her case-worker was against her traveling out of state, even for a wedding. But after I asked True to be my flower girl, Maude promised she'd make it happen and she did.

True sits for Daisy, who does more green and blue makeup but adds splashes of pink. I watch this avidly for hints. Bren planned the flower girls' outfits and won't tell me what they are.

It's a little worrisome how good my friends are at keeping secrets.

Daisy does my makeup last, keeping it mostly natural except for pink, white, and gold wings around my eyes. While Daisy puts on her suit, Aggie and Vashi help me into my dress, which is definitely a three-person job with the corset, tutu, train, cape, and veil. The corset, train, and cape are heavy with metal and beading but I've practiced in them several times and by the time we're ready to go, I'm managing them on my own.

Bren, True, and my baby have disappeared when we come out of the bedroom. I stamp my white, platform Mary Jane. "What are they wearing?"

Everyone laughs. Laurel pats me on the shoulder. "There have to be some surprises, even for the bride."

I roll my eyes. She giggles and takes my hand as we troop downstairs to the limos.

Daddy's limo has already left and our limo has tinted windows so Daddy won't see me. The limo driver grins when he sees us in our outfits and seems in really good spirits as we roll toward the drop zone. He plays "I've Got The Magic In Me" by B.o.B. and "I Gotta Feeling" by the Black Eyed Peas and we all sing along. Sammi and Daisy harmonize like they're professional singers.

When we get to the drop zone, a sandy lot near the "Welcome to Fabulous Las Vegas" sign, there are three other limos, two SUVs, and a red Cadillac waiting. I try to peer into the other cars but the windows are all tinted like ours. I know one is Daddy's and the groomsmen's. Bren, True, and Livvy might be in the third limo but who is in the other one?

When I ask, my attendants trade secretive smiles but no one answers me.

"I hate you all," I huff.

Cynnie kisses me on the cheek. "But we lurve you, Emmy."

I roll my eyes at her.

The driver opens the moon roof and I forget all about my pique as a silver plane circles in the bright blue sky overhead. One after another, eleven bodies dressed in brilliant white spill out of the plane. Even at the distance, I can see they all have slick, black quiffs, except one.

I squeal and point at Irish Elvis. Vashi squeals with me.

The Elvi circle in the air and join hands. They drop together in a huge circle for several terrifying minutes, although they look serene. Finally, they separate. Their chutes pull them higher with a jerk. We clap and whistle as they float down. When they land and remove their chutes, they surround my limo.

One of them blows a note on a pitch pipe, and then all of them break into "The Wonder of You." They have lovely voices. Not as good as The King but that's an impossible standard to measure up to. I can pick out Master Niall's voice among them: a deep baritone. His accent makes me grin.

Tears threaten when I hear them change the lyrics to "that's the wonder, the wonder of little you."

Daisy leans across the footwell and dabs at the corners of my eyes. "We're going to put the waterproof claims of the mascara and liner to the test today, aren't we?"

I nod helplessly. Daddy got them to change the lyrics for me. I blink through a crystal veil.

After an extra chorus, the Elvi blow kisses at me before they load up in the Cadillac and the SUVs. In a mismatched cavalcade, we roll out to the chapel. The driver puts on "Can't Help Falling In Love" and I sing with my attendants, smiling through my tears.

We're the last car to pull up at the chapel, which I sense is by design. The Elvi are waiting to escort us in. They're witnesses—not that we don't already have dozens of witnesses—but it was part of Master Niall's deal with them. They surround my limo, preventing me from seeing what's going on in the parking lot, while they sing "Blue Hawaii" and "Can't Help Falling In Love." By the time they open the limo door and help me out, the parking lot's full of cars but empty of people.

I glare at Cynnie and Vashi, who just giggle.

The Elvi clearly deal with a lot of brides. They help me get my train straight and one of them carries it for me so it doesn't snag on the lot's asphalt. Master Niall beams at me, his smile brighter than the rhinestones on his white outfit, as he holds his arm out for Vashi. In a double-phalanx like they're guarding the President, the Elvi escort me inside and into a small room with round tables and chairs.

It's hard to sit in my tutu without showing the whole world the color of my panties (pale blue, although not borrowed) but I have to because my knees are knocking together so hard. It's not that I'm scared. How could I be scared of marrying my forever-Daddy? It's just all the emotion of the moment. I don't think I've been this crazy emotional since before my first period. There's nothing to be scared of but I'm shaking all over. I want this. I've thought about it for months. I've planned it down to the small details. Is it that I don't want it to be over too soon? Is that why my hands are shaking so hard that I have to set the small bouquet of white and gold paper flowers I crafted with the Littles' Army on the table to avoid dropping it?

Vashi kneels next to me, using one hand to tuck the skirt of her gorgeous pink and red sari under her legs and the other to flip back the flare of her cape so it's not caught under her butt. She takes my hands in hers.

"It's okay to be nervous," she says, squeezing my fingers. "I was most nervous on my wedding day."

"I don't have anything to be nervous about," I wail. "I'm just so emotional."

My attendants cluster around me, patting me and saying "aww." Several of them are teary, too.

The officiant, a very portly Elvis, comes in to speak to me and get me to sign something. I have no idea what I say to him but it seems to be the right thing because he bustles away smiling.

"Is Daddy definitely here?" I ask Vashi, even though I know it's a ridiculous question.

"Do you want Master to check?" she responds, humoring me.

I nod. "It's stupid."

Niall sweeps down to kiss me on the cheek, his bright red quiff quivering. "Nothing's stupid on your wedding day. Shaan and I were old hands at the wedding thing by the time we married Vashi and I still sent our best man to check on her about a hundred times."

I laugh tearily.

"Did he really?" I ask when he leaves.

Vashi nods. "Men are so silly. Where was I going to go? Shaan had my plane ticket."

Everyone laughs.

Master Niall returns after less than a minute. "There's a bloke down the hall who resembles your daddy, except he's a wee bit green around the gills. Think he might be waiting for you. Ready for your surprise?"

I nod.

Niall opens the door. Brenna and True walk in. Bren has a white wicker basket over her arm. True's carrying Livvy. All three of them are dressed in long gowns, flesh-toned at the top with beaded sea-shells cupped over their breasts. Their skirts are layers of blue and green. Livvy kicks her feet in a froth of ocean gauze.

Mermaids. They're mermaids.

The tears run. I can't help it.

Bren smiles at me as her own tears start.

I rush to her. "You can't cry. You're a mermaid. Mermaid tears are precious."

She hugs me, careful of my scaled cape. "You're precious. Get out there. Logan's going to faint before he even sees you and I can't let Sir win a hundred dollars."

"I'm ready," I tell her, even though I'm not. I have no idea if I can make it down the aisle. Maybe it's good we have a lot of attendants. They can carry me.

Bren turns, showing the jewel-toned mermaid and baby among the tattoos on her upper back, and walks out into the corridor, beckoning True after her. Master Mac steps in around her, giving her a quick kiss and a smack on the ass as they pass each other. He's

439

wearing a morning suit in dove gray, his tie and cummerbund rippling with blue and green to match the mermaids. He takes off his top hat and bows to me. "Come on, sweetheart."

I nod since I can't manage one word.

We line up. Sammi first, then Aggie, then Yummy, then Laurel, then Cynnie and Vashi, arm-in-arm since their Doms are co-best-men.

Daisy helps arrange my veil over my face, careful not to snag it on my tiara. I know a veil is super-traditional and patriarchal but I didn't wear a veil when I married Ash and I want this wedding to be as unlike that one as possible.

Daisy offers me her arm. She's wearing a suit similar to Mac's, only hers has a leather mini-skirt that shows off her long legs, and a pink tie and cummerbund. Her outrageously high, velvet platforms are the same hot pink. I love her movie-star sense of style.

On my other side, Mac offers me his arm. Daisy scoops my bouquet off the table and passes it to me. I realize she's wrapped a white linen hankie around the bottom of the bouquet.

I sniffle at her gratefully.

Between my Best Mommy Domme and the Mac Granddaddy, I walk out into the hallway. Bren and True stand on either side of the closed door to the chapel itself. I can hear the faint strains of "Ode to Joy." Daddy's choice. Because of all the joy I bring to his life, he said.

I blink through fresh tears.

With a wink at me, Bren opens the door. True and Livvy walk through first, Livvy burbling and kicking. Bren follows them, handing out tiny bouquets of white paper roses right and left into the audience as she goes. My eyes follow her motion. At first, I think the Elvi are taking up the back rows. Then my eyes catch on an imperiously gray-quiffed Elvis. Mistress Maude grins at me.

Elvi. A whole sea of Elvi in brilliant white jumpsuits with flashing rhinestones. Short, tall, Mistress Dana whip-slim, Master Harold barrel-chested in his open white shirt. Queen Twitch's crown matches the jumpsuit's rhinestones. Elvi everywhere. They've *all* come as Elvis.

I begin giggling.

Sammi follows Brenna, holding his arms out so his aquamarine cape, attached at his wrists, flares open behind him.

Spreading into wings.

My flight proceeds down the aisle, flaring their wings: blue-green, purple, orange, emerald, yellow, and red.

I try to be a fierce, white, baby dragon as Daisy and Mac propel me forward but really I'm a sobbing baby dragon. Everyone stands as I walk down the aisle, which I'm not prepared for. A lot of them wave and smile at me. I try to smile back even as I blubber.

As Cynnie and Vashi move to the left at the end of the aisle, I finally see the people waiting for me. A bald Elvis. A red-haired Elvis. A nerd Elvis wearing a shirt that says, "Are You Lonesome Tonight?" over the IP address for a well-known porn site. An Elvis wearing a black, red, and gold jumpsuit instead of the white jumpsuits that fill the audience. An Elvis that's powder-blue head to toe. A dreadlocked Elvis. A GI Elvis at the end.

I smile tearily at all of them.

GI Elvis salutes and the Elvi part neatly.

My Dark Knight steps forward through the Elvi gap.

My heart thumps so hard in my chest it bruises my ribs.

Daddy's wearing black leather. I've seen him in black leather before, of course but this is seriously hot black leather: boots, leather pants that show off his sculpted thighs, a waistcoat that buttons up to his chin. He's not wearing a shirt under the waistcoat and his muscled, bare arms show under the edges of a cape with a high collar that frames his face. The leather of the cape and waistcoat are tooled into scales. In one hand he carries a golden leash.

Dragon-Tamer Daddy.

Daisy and Mac stop in front of him. Mac takes my bouquet as Daisy folds my veil back. They pat me before they move away to join the other attendants.

Daddy's dark eyes slide down me, taking in my tiara with its tiny, pink-jeweled horns, my winged cape covered in golden-edged scales and decorated with iridescent white sequins, the matching bustier and train, the white tutu edged with pink ribbon that falls mid-thigh, revealing my old pink and white stripey thigh-highs held up with a borrowed garter.

With Daddy's hot, wolfy gaze on me, my knees give out. I drop onto them.

Daddy takes a step forward and clicks the hook of the leash through my collar. "Mine."

"Yours, Daddy," I whisper.

He holds out his hand. I take it and try to stand but I'm shaking all over. He draws me into his arms. "Hug me, little girl. Hug your Daddy and know that everything's okay. I love you so much. Nothing will make me prouder than making you my little wife."

I swallow the huge lump of tears in my throat. "I love you, too, and I want to be your wife, I'm just super-emotional."

He kisses my forehead gently. "Me, too, sweetheart. My knees are knocking together so hard they're going to cause an earthquake."

I giggle. "Not as hard as mine."

"Twice as hard as yours. C'mon, baby. I got a ring with your name on it. You want it?"

I have one for him, too. "So much, Daddy."

"I think Bald Elvis wants a word."

Giggling, I let him lead me two steps forward. He keeps hold of my hand. His palm is a little sweaty.

I turn, expecting to see the portly officiant.

Master Javier smiles at me.

"Bald Elvis?" I ask, grinning.

He winks at me. "Welcome, friends. We're gathered here today to celebrate the union of this Daddy with his little . . ."

I hiccup and the tears start again.

"Logan and Emily, have you come here to give yourselves freely in marriage?" Master Javier asks.

"I do," I whisper.

There are soft chuckles around me.

Daddy squeezes my hand. "We have," he says.

"Repeat after me, Daddy Logan. I, James Logan, take you, Emily Martin, to be my lawfully wedded wife. To command and to hold, to love and to cherish, for better, for worse, for richer, for poorer, in sickness and in health, from this day forward. You are mine. You live in my heart and soul forever."

Daddy repeats each word, his voice breaking when he says "mine."

"Repeat after me, Emmy," Master Javier says. "I, Emily Martin, take you, James Logan, to be my lawfully wedded husband. To obey and to hold, to love and to cherish, for better, for worse, for richer, for poorer, in sickness and in health, from this day forward. I am yours. You live in my heart and soul forever."

I whisper each word raggedly.

"Please exchange rings as a symbol of your infinite and unending love, faith, and loyalty to each other."

Bren pulls a red velvet box out of her basket. Mac fishes its mate out of his jacket pocket. I asked for simple rings to go with the slight ostentation of my pink diamond engagement ring.

Daddy's idea of simple isn't really the same as mine.

They're gold, his thicker than mine. A gemstone band runs through the middle of each ring. Daddy's band is dark opal, flashing with deep blues and greens. My band is pink opal. I didn't even know pink opal was a thing until Daddy showed it to me on the internet before we commissioned the rings. When we picked up the rings and I saw how mine looked against my diamond, I cried for an hour.

Pretty sure I'm going to cry for longer today. I can't stop the tears. They drip off my chin. Daddy gently wipes them away, then licks my body's salt off his fingers. "Happy tears?" he whispers.

"The happiest," I promise him.

"Do I get a ring?" he asks.

I nod but I can't remember a word of the ceremony we wrote. "Help me, please?"

"Of course, sweetheart. 'Daddy, with this ring, I thee wed'."

Once he starts me off, I remember the rest. I take his ring from Brenna and say, "Daddy, with this ring, I thee wed. I offer my heart and soul to you, for you to keep safe alongside your heart and soul, because they are joined forever. Wherever you go, please take me with you. Wherever I go, I'll know you're with me. As long as we both shall live."

I slide the band onto his offered finger and stare at it there. It doesn't feel real. Or maybe it's too real. Surreal. Good surreal but surreal.

"You with me, baby?" Daddy whispers.

I nod, not wanting to ruin the moment.

Daddy picks up my ring out of the box Mac is holding. He takes my left hand and gently slides off my engagement ring.

"Emmy, my baby doll, with this ring, I thee wed. I accept responsibility for your heart and soul. I will do everything in my power to keep them safe, alongside my heart and soul, because they are joined forever. Wherever I go, you are with me. Wherever you go, I am with you. As long as we both shall live."

He slides my wedding band and engagement ring back onto my finger.

Everything snaps into place. We're married. I'm Daddy's little wife and Daddy's . . . Daddy's my Daddy.

That thought settles me more than my mantra ever did. Daddy's my Daddy. He always has been. He always will be. I beam up at him.

He smiles back at me. "There you are, wife."

"Hi, Daddy. Is it time for the kiss yet?"

There are chuckles all around us.

"I think Bald Elvis has to say something first," Daddy responds.

Master Javier clears his throat. "By the power vested in me by the State of Nevada, I am delighted to pronounce you husband and wife. Please kiss the bride before I do."

Laughing, Daddy sweeps me up into his arms. I wind my arms around his neck as he lifts me off my feet. He rubs noses with me as we look into each other's eyes. "First kiss of the rest of our lives together, baby."

"Lay it on me, Daddy."

His laughter buzzes against my teeth as he seals our mouths together. He runs his tongue along the ridge of my teeth before lapping against my tongue. Breaking the kiss, he smiles into my eyes again before taking another, even deeper kiss.

Daddy lowers me onto my heels. He takes my left hand, twines our fingers together, raises our linked hands, and presses a kiss to my knuckle just above our rings. Then he lifts our joined hands into the air.

Everyone cheers and from the back of the room, the skydiving Elvi launch into "All Shook Up."

With the Elvi singing our recessional, Daddy leads me back down the aisle. I wave like a crazy lady at everyone, much too happy to wave like a queen.

Daddy's little wife.

Our reception's at A Golden Affair. I hadn't heard of it until I realized we were going to have an absurd number of guests at our "elopement" in Vegas and began researching venues. As soon as I saw the pictures: all pale wood, high ceilings, white drapes, and soft lighting, with huge windows looking out in the sere, folded landscape of Red Rocks National Park, I knew it was what we wanted. There's a dance floor, a dining area separated by a low wall, the buffet screening the kitchen, and two bars at either end of the open-plan building.

Daddy commandeered arranging the music, which means we'll be dancing to Eighties tunes. Master Javier claimed the catering was his wedding gift to us. Knowing what Master Javier's like when he's thwarted, I gave way and just asked for some nice herbal teas to be available along with everything else. Of course, that was before Master Javier somehow became qualified as an officiant in Nevada and took over the ceremony. I should have known he was up to something when I saw him lurking in the Blunts' library all autumn. He pretended it was his new favorite place for scenes and made Cappa serve as his footrest for hours on end while he read. I should have known, though. Master Javier really isn't as devious as he thinks he is.

My only sadness is that Cappa's not here to see the outcome of all those back-breaking hours.

The venue's as serene and beautiful as I imagined. They've strung fairy lights along the edges of the tables and along the exposed beams in the ceiling. Runners of the palest pink, rich with gold embroidery, drape the ten tables: Niall, Shaan, and Vashi's contribution. White pillar candles flicker on each table, adding to the warm, sunset glow off the desert beyond the huge windows. The centerpieces are white and gold paper flower bouquets, grouped around a Little Larry.

We've all been back to the Excalibur to change. True's stayed at the hotel with Livvy, who she's babysitting tonight, under the supervision of her foster-mother. Although the venue is vanilla, Master Javier reassured me he'd hired kink-friendly servers and everyone could wear what they liked. The skydiving Elvi have been intrigued enough to stick around for the reception. It's a free meal and an open bar which probably does a lot to assuage any prudery; more than that, I get the sense that those who cater to tourists in Vegas have pretty much seen it all. The Elvi's white jumpsuits mix with Yummy's dragon onesie, Georgie's fursuit, Cynnie's adorable round bee outfit, and leather in every color. They don't seem shocked. Everyone mingles, talking and laughing together.

I expect fussy French food; it's Master Javier after all. But he surprises me by serving a feast to delight any little. Lobster Mac and cheese balls. Tiny hamburger sliders with a quinoa alternative that has me clapping my hands when I see them. Pizza rolls. Regular and sweet potato fries arranged in boxes like crayons. Triangular pastry puffs that conceal quiche Lorraine, curried chicken, or egg and cress within their fluffy folds. The caterer has included some western dishes like marinated cactus salad and burnt ends. There's a healthy cornucopia of fruits and vegetables. But there's also folded ice cream and sorbet in several flavors, drizzled in fruit coulis or chocolate. At the very end of the buffet, there's a giant, ice-sculpture clamshell full of shucked oysters so fresh they still smell like the sea. Oysters in the desert. That's so Master Javier.

I eat a little of everything, even an oyster.

I'm honestly too stuffed to consider another bite by the time they bring out the wedding "cake." Five different people offered to make our wedding cake but I turned them all down. I really didn't want a wedding cake. The ones I've had have always been dry and nothing could top the *Beauty and the Beast* cake Sammi and Jack made for our collaring ceremony anyway.

Then Martyn, from the inn where we had our collaring ceremony, RSVPed. When he offered, I changed my mind about the cake. I begged him not to be as extravagant as he was for my *Alice in Wonderland* tea party because I wanted him and his little, Piper, to have fun while they were here. He just laughed.

The caterers bring out a round, three-tiered stand. On each level, there are cupcakes. Big cupcakes. Mini cupcakes. Cupcakes frosted with a rainbow of colors. Cupcakes topped with macarons. Cupcakes piled with fluffy meringue. Cupcakes dipped in chocolate ganache.

I throw my arms around Martyn and Piper before I find the smallest, lemon meringue cupcake I can and add it to my groaning stomach.

Daddy's still licking ganache off his lips when he leads me out for our first dance. He's still in his Dragon-Taming Daddy leathers, although he's shed the cloak and changed his boots for black shoes he can dance in. His bare arms and shoulders look huge against the black leather. Yum-yum, Daddy.

He pulls me to him, planting one of his wolfy paws on my

bottom, squeezing through the silky fabric of my skirt. When Cynnie and I were planning outfits, I told her she had free rein over my dress for the reception. The only thing I wanted was to be able to wear thigh-highs because they drive Daddy so crazy.

Cynnie delivered.

The two-piece outfit is white, silk, and makes me feel even more delicious than Martyn's cupcakes. The top wraps my shoulders and crosses over my breasts, tying in a huge bow in the small of my back, with ribbons trailing to my knees. There's a tiny strip of skin exposed across my belly, just enough to give Daddy a flash of my brand. The skirt falls to mid-thigh in the front and to my knees in the back, for best visibility of my sheer white thigh-highs, printed with little pink bows. The skirt has the softest poof; the overlay of white gauze embroidered with butterflies and tiny pink pearls along the hem swirls around me as Daddy spins us to Berlin's "Take My Breath Away." I've replaced my dragon tiara with fluffy white cat ears. Cynnie added a layer of veil that brushes my shoulders, giving me the best shivers.

Is it possible to feel adorable and elegant at the same time? Because I do.

I know what Daddy and I must look like, him looming over me all in black, me pressed up against him, small and white. It's a true image because Daddy always has been and always will be my ruthless protector.

But it's also an illusion. Because a little takes care of her Daddy, too. In finding my forever-Daddy, the Daddy worthy of my love and care, I've discovered my inner dragon. She sleeps most of the time, guarding her treasure. But when she rises . . .

Hear me roar.

We dance as darkness falls outside the windows to Cyndi Lauper, The Bangles, Lionel Richie, Peter Gabriel, Journey, and Madonna. As the stars glitter over the desert, we dance to Thompson Twins, Spandau Ballet, Bryan Adams, Tears for Fears, and Roberta Flack. All of Daddy's favorites. We dance until the ache of an overfull stomach is replaced by an ache lower in my belly from being held so close to Daddy's hard body as we move together.

I could wait. I haven't talked to everyone. A few people just arrived yesterday and I want to catch up with them, too. Even though we told everyone absolutely no presents, there's a table of them by the door and we haven't opened any yet.

But there will be time for those things. If I don't catch up with people here, I can in New York, because now that Daddy's made Blunts safe again and so many from our playgroup have joined, we're there practically every day. And if we don't open our wedding presents today, someone will bring them to the hotel and we'll open them tomorrow, probably at the big brunch Maude's hosting tomorrow at a place called The Hash Hut, which is not a hut at all but does have cool Polynesian theming.

There's never enough time with my Daddy.

I slide my hands around his neck and tickle the fine hairs there with my fingertips. His groomsmen dragged him off for a Turkish bath and barber the morning after they got him drunk. He was still hungover when he got back but he had a sharp haircut.

"So, Daddy, I've been thinking," I begin.

He looks down at me, his eyes hooded and happy. "What have you been thinking about, my little wife."

I go up on my toes to whisper in his ear, "Since we're all married now and everything, maybe we could go back to the hotel and get started on making a brother or sister for Livvy?"

I had my appointment before we left New York. My gynecologist said it might be a month or two before the contraceptive effect of the implant wore off but I'm perfectly happy to keep trying in the meanwhile.

Daddy stops dead in the middle of the dance floor. "What?"

"I had my implant removed before we left New York." I had to hide the inside of my arm from Daddy for the first few days we were in Vegas until the little incision healed so I didn't spoil the surprise.

"So, we could get started on our 'sibling for Livvy' project right away."

Daddy's eyes go impossibly hot and dark.

"Breeding kink unlocked," he growls, before he tosses me over his shoulder and strides out of our reception. "Enjoy yourselves everyone! I have a little wife to impregnate. See you tomorrow."

The laughter of our friends, high and low, sweet and deviant, follows us out the door.

The End

glossary of slang and unusual terms

Bastard: (British) rarely used in the literal sense but rather as a generic term for a man, often affectionately.

Bottom: (BDSM) in an older, stricter sense, the person who is penetrated during a kinky scene or activity but this term has evolved to be synonymous with submissive and is used primarily when there's no power exchange between partners.

BDSM: an acronym for bondage and discipline (BD), Dominance and submission (DS), and sadism and masochism (SM); covers a huge range of activities, not all of them sexual.

Cozzie: (British) bathing suit.

Daddy Dom: (BDSM) a Dominant who is a caregiver to his or her partner.

Dominant: (BDSM) the person who holds and exercises control over another in a kinky activity, usually within the context of a power exchange; abbreviated Dom; the female version is Domme; synonymous with *top*.

Funishments: (BDSM) a scene or kinky activity that would, under other circumstances, be punitive for the submissive but in context is playful and enjoyable.

Gordon Bennett: (British) an exclamation; used instead of "good God" or other oath.

Gourd: (British) head.

High Protocol: (BDSM) a formal set of behavioral rules for a submissive, enforced by a Dominant; always restrictive and frequently punitive.

Little: (BDSM) a submissive who enters into a scene or relationship with a caregiver partner; some littles enjoy child-like activities and frames of mind.

Masochist: (BDSM) a person who derives sexual pleasure or emotional gratification from receiving pain and/or humiliation. Not synonymous with submissive or bottom, although some submissives and bottoms are also masochists.

Master: (BDSM) the person who holds and exercises control over another in a kinky activity, within the context of a power exchange.

Nillas: (slang) Vanilla wafers; slang for people who are not in the BDSM lifestyle.

PDQ: (slang) abbreviation of pretty darn quick.

Sadist: (BDSM) a person who derives sexual pleasure or emotional gratification from inflicting pain and/or humiliation on another. Not synonymous with Dom or Top, although some Doms and Tops are also sadists.

Safe word: (BDSM) a word or phrase used by a participant in a kinky scene to alert other participant(s) that the person is having a problem and needs the activity to stop, at least momentarily.

Scene: (BDSM) a kinky activity, usually with a distinct beginning and end, as opposed to the *lifestyle*, in which kinky activity may take place at any time or even all the time; *the scene* usually refers to the BDSM community.

Slave: (BDSM) the person who surrenders control to another in a kinky activity, within the context of a power exchange.

Submissive: (BDSM) the person who surrenders control to another in a kinky activity, usually within the context of a power exchange; abbreviated sub; synonymous with *bottom*.

Subspace: (BDSM) a state of altered consciousness induced in a bottom or submissive by kinky play.

Switch: (BDSM) a person who both tops and bottoms.

Ta: (British) thank you (usually used by children).

Top: (BDSM) in an older, stricter sense, the person who penetrates another during a kinky scene but this term has evolved to be synonymous with Dominant and is used primarily when there's no power exchange between partners.

Topspace: a state of altered consciousness induced in a top or Dominant by kinky play.

coming soon

It takes a woman who makes monsters to love one.

Fleur

I wake, screaming, thrashing against the imaginary hands holding me down, tearing me up.

"Sh, sh, baby. Shh."

Warm hands catch at me. Try to hold me.

I shove them off, throw myself out of the bed, and run to the bathroom.

I make it to the toilet before I throw up. This time.

The warm hands that tried to soothe me gather my hair and hold it back while I heave. There's not much to come up. I don't have any appetite. But the two glasses of wine I had after dinner are burning vinegar the second time around. My sinuses stream while I straighten up and flush.

Cappa hands me a wad of toilet paper. I take it from him with a grateful nod and pull my hair out of his hand so I can move to the sink.

"Sorry, Cap," I say as I wipe my nose and mouth. "Go back to bed. You've got work tomorrow."

"They'll understand if I'm late. Tell me about it, baby."

I shake my head. Cappa has enough nightmares of his own. He doesn't need mine taking up real estate in his head, too.

"I don't remember anything. Just a terrible feeling," I lie. "I'm okay. I'm going to take a bath to calm down. Go back to sleep."

Because he's my friend instead of my Dom, he smooths his hand over my hair, kisses me on the cheek, and leaves me to my bath.

I sit in it until the water is as cold as the tears on my cheeks.

Despite my broken sleep, I'm up before Cappa. He's working at the club today and he's right, they will understand when he's late. My customers won't. So I'm up early to demold today's orders and shoot some promo for social media. I often don't show my face in my videos, so no one will question my red eyes and ratty hair.

After I post the videos and before I start packing orders, I thumb over to a message string.

I had the nightmare again.

Preorder the next Daddy P.I. mystery, Midnight Fleur's Monsters, here: https://books2read.com/midnightfleur

Read the free prequel to Midnight Fleur's Monsters here: https://dl.bookfunnel.com/nlplonbm99

about the author

Looking for delicious, alpha heroes who would burn down the world for the women they love? You've come to the right place. I write couples who would do anything for each other and characters you want for your best friends.

Constitutionally incapable of settling into a genre, I bounce in and out of contemporary mystery, space opera, and paranormal romance, all with a decidedly kinky twist. Connect with me on Facebook, Twitter, Instagram, TikTok, and Goodreads for previews, giveaways, and book talk.

Bring cake.

Want a really deep dive into my worlds? Join me on Patreon!

If you've enjoyed *Daddy P.I. 3.0*, please consider leaving a review on your platform of choice. Reviews mean everything to independent authors!

Looking for a truly *magical* romance? Discover the world of Bevington College for Magickal Instruction.

Start here with Teddy's Boys:

Teddy's Boys

Magic Academy, MMFM RH, Paranormal Series

Three boys.

Two murders.

One terrible choice.

Twelve years ago, my mother climbed into a limo with a fae stranger and left without looking back. Seven years ago, my magic came in, marking me as an Earth-witch, the Element most feared by other mages. One month ago, my father exiled me to college in another country.

I may be a stranger in a strange land, but no one will keep me down.

Charlie, Gabe, and Darwin.

Three boys who are more than my match.

My best friend. My new love. My worst enemy.

Are they also killers?

When a fellow student is murdered, the finger of suspicion points at my boys.

Can I prove their innocence?

Or will I be their next victim?

Meet the Bad Boys of Bevington ...

Teddy's Boys is the first book of the Bevington College trilogy. The trilogy is complete. *Teddy's Boys* contains darker themes and elements of power exchange and is intended for mature readers only. Available widely: https://books2read.com/teddysboys

Neon Blue

M/F, Paranormal Romance Series.

Demons.

Can't live with 'em.

Can't kill 'em.

My name is Tsara Elizabeth Faa, and I have a demon problem.

My ex-best friend summoned an incubus and left me to deal with him. Now he's after my soul.

Thing is, the more time I spend with him, the more I want to give it to him.

Read *Neon Blue* here: **https://books2read.com/u/mZZ292**

Neon Blue is a contemporary mystery romance set a few years before the *Bevington College* series. Characters cross over between the series. *Neon Blue* is intended for mature readers only.

Capricorn

M/F Paranormal Standalone

The end is nigh? Not on my watch.

Evan Lords is a Capricorn, but that's meant nothing to him for nearly forty years. Less than nothing during the seven years he's spent in prison for a murder he didn't commit.

Now, the Helm of the Sea Goat has called Evan's name and the Capricorns have arranged his release so their promised leader can save them from mysterious force Hell-bent on destroying their sacred charge: wild magic.

But his freedom isn't the only thing Evan lost seven years ago. He also left behind his love, his Little. With the fate of the world's magic hanging in the balance, can Evan save the Capricorn Guild, and will it cost him the woman he loves?

Read *Capricorn* here: https://books2read.com/capricornmoz

Capricorn is a spin-off, stand-alone mystery set seven years after the end of the *Teddy's Boys* trilogy. *Capricorn* is intended for mature readers only.

Snowburn

M/F , Scifi Romance.

Unleash the monster. Save the girl.

Hale Hauser is a Company killer. Perfectly engineered, highly trained, superbly effective. But when ordered to assassinate his own kind, Hale rebels, and the Company buries him in a hole so deep that no one has ever escaped.

After escaping, Hale hides on Kuseros, a backwater Colony on the Deep Frontier. He begins a new life as Sandringham Snow, pilot and smuggler. Hired by Kez, a local runner, to retrieve a box of black-market glands, Hale follows her through the maze of strange loyalties and twisted customs of Kuseros' underground gangs. In payment, he takes the one thing only a woman can give him, and discovers the one thing his new life is missing.

But Kez has a secret, which will threaten them both. To protect her, Hale must unleash the monster. Can he control the killer inside long enough to discover the truth before it destroys them? Or will he lose everything just as he's found it?

Read *Snowburn* here: **https://books2read.com/u/m2Z9ko**.

www.ingramcontent.com/pod-product-compliance
Lightning Source LLC
Chambersburg PA
CBHW050913030726
47503CB00007BB/2280